How to Marry a Rockstar

....

Arabella Quinn

Copyright © 2023 by Arabella Quinn

All rights reserved.

No part of this publication may be reproduced, distributed, or transmitted in any form or by any means, including photocopying, recording, or other electronic or mechanical methods, without the prior written permission of the publisher, except as permitted by U.S. copyright law.

If you purchased a copy of this eBook, thank you. Also, thank you for not sharing your copy of this book. This purchase allows you one legal copy for your own personal computer or device. You do not have the rights to resell, distribute, print, or transfer this book, in whole or in part, in any format, via methods either currently known or yet to be invented, or upload to a file sharing peer-to-peer program. It may not be re-sold or given away to other people. Such action is illegal and in violation of the U.S. Copyright Law. If you would like to share this book with another person, please purchase an additional copy for each recipient. If you're reading this book and did not purchase it, or it was not purchased for your use only, then please purchase your own copy. Thank you for respecting the hard work of this author.

The story, all names, characters, and incidents portrayed in this production are fictitious. No identification with actual persons (living or deceased), places, buildings, and products is intended or should be inferred.

Dedication

In loving memory of my dear mother,
The one who championed my writing journey,
These books stand as a testament to your never-ending belief in me.
As my biggest fan, your encouragement was unwavering throughout
the years I spent writing this book series. Though you're not here to
see the culmination of my efforts, I know you are watching over me,
cheering me on from a place where love transcends all boundaries.
Your absence is deeply felt, but I carry your love and support within
me, inspiring me and giving me the courage to chase my dreams.
You are forever in my heart.

Contents

Chapter 1	1
Chapter 2	10
Chapter 3	21
Chapter 4	27
Chapter 5	38
Chapter 6	50
Chapter 7	69
Chapter 8	78
Chapter 9	84
Chapter 10	98
Chapter 11	109
Chapter 12	121
Chapter 13	137
Chapter 14	145

Chapter 15	156
Chapter 16	164
Chapter 17	176
Chapter 18	188
Chapter 19	200
Chapter 20	207
Chapter 21	217
Chapter 22	223
Chapter 23	234
Chapter 24	241
Chapter 25	249
Chapter 26	256
Chapter 27	265
Chapter 28	274
Chapter 29	281
Chapter 30	290
Chapter 31	299
Chapter 32	304
Chapter 33	310
Chapter 34	318
Chapter 35	326
Chapter 36	334
Epilogue	349
Rock Me series	360

Arabella Quinn Newsletter	364
Other Novels by Arabella Quinn	365
Also By Arabella Quinn	368
About the Author	370
Excerpt	371

Chapter 1

Bash

"Mᴏʀᴇ! Mᴏʀᴇ! Mᴏʀᴇ!" ʜᴇ chanted.

I glanced sideways at the little tyrant standing on his chair at the table in our eat-in kitchen. "Manners, Kody."

He giggled. "Please."

"I'll get you some more, but please sit down. No standing on the chair."

I missed the ugly plastic booster seat he used to sit in. At least then he was buckled in and couldn't escape, but cleaning that thing was a giant pain in the ass. At three-and-a-half years old, Kody's baby days were long behind him. Now, he was a master at getting into mischief, making enormous messes in record time, refusing to take naps, and changing his food preferences on the daily.

I pulled the second slice of bread from the toaster, slathered it with peanut butter, and then added a few banana slices on top of it.

When I turned back around, Kody was sitting on top of the kitchen table, his big toe pushing a mushy banana slice around his plate.

I grumbled under my breath. "Kody, I said, sit down."

He grinned. "I am, Dad."

"I meant on your chair, you little stinker. We don't sit on the table."

I placed his new slice of toast on the table and then scooped him up into my arms. I hugged his wiggling body for a few seconds and then deposited him back into his chair.

Before he could take a bite of his toast, his eyes lit up, and he shrieked, "Jojo!"

Josie came into the kitchen and rumpled his hair. "Good morning, kiddo. I told you I was going to be here in the morning."

Kody nodded happily and then went to work stuffing the toast into his mouth.

Josie's eyes swung over to me. "The question is: what are you doing here? I wasn't expecting you home so early."

Ha! Neither was I.

Josie had come over to babysit last night because I'd had a date with a woman I'd met a few weeks ago. Usually, Kaylie and Sid took Kody overnight when I needed them to, but Kaylie was very pregnant with twins and due any day, so I'd enlisted Josie's help.

She lowered her voice and looked around. "She's not here, is she?"

"No!" I replied, a little too defensively. "I came home last night. You were already sleeping."

"So, did the date go well?"

I pinched the bridge of my nose. "Not as well as I'd hoped it would."

If I thought Josie would let it go at that, I was sadly mistaken. "It was date number three, though. Did you take the bald-headed gnome for a stroll in the misty forest?"

"Huh?" It was too early in the morning to understand what Josie was going on about. Whatever it was, it was probably a dig at my expense.

Josie wiggled her eyebrows up and down. "You know, the four-legged foxtrot."

Kody spoke up from the table. "More, please." He was busy licking his fingers clean.

I glanced at his empty plate. "Jeez, Kody. How much toast can you eat?"

Josie bustled over to the kitchen counter where a large Tupperware container was sitting. "I made your favorite, Kody — banana-chocolate chip muffins. Do you want one?"

He nodded his head vigorously.

Josie pulled a muffin out of the container and peeled off its baking paper before she plunked it down on the plate in front of him.

He chirped out a thanks and then began demolishing it.

She turned to me with hands on her hips. "So, did you attack the pink fortress?"

I grimaced. I had a vague feeling I knew what she was getting at, but I didn't want to discuss it. Especially not with her.

My hand tunneled through my hair in frustration. "What in God's name are you talking about, woman? Just say what you mean."

She tilted her head in Kody's direction. "I was trying to spare little ears. But I take it from that grumpy response that there was no hanky panky involved. You struck out, huh?"

"I didn't strike out," I grumbled. "She didn't live up to expectations."

"Oh!" she drew out the word sarcastically. "So, you did play hide the salami, but she didn't meet the standards of the master delicatessen owner?"

Christ. Josie knew how to needle me like no other. I felt a headache coming on.

Kody crammed the last bit of muffin into his mouth and then began climbing down from the chair. Before he escaped, Josie wrangled him over to the sink to wipe his face and wash his hands. As soon as she set him free, he scampered off to find some toys in the other room.

Josie turned to me, waiting for an explanation. She was like a junkyard dog with a bone.

"We had a nice dinner and then I came home. End of story."

"Nothing happened?" She didn't sound convinced. "I thought the entire purpose of me staying overnight to watch Kody was so that you could make the beast with two backs?"

"Let's just call it sex! Or fucking. Your choice. And it didn't happen last night. Are you satisfied?"

"Jeesh," — she threw up her hands — "don't take it out on me!"

"Sorry. I just had high hopes the night would end differently."

I met Addison at a party about a month ago. She zeroed in on me right away. She was full of energy and really sexy, so it'd boosted my ego a bit since I was in a serious dry spell as far as women went.

My entire lifestyle changed virtually overnight when I found out I was a father. Since then, sure, I'd had sex with groupies while I was on tour, but they'd all been fast, soulless transactions only meant to slake my thirst. I hadn't spent more than an hour with any of them. I always felt the need to get back to Kody as soon as a show was over, so sex was quick and dirty.

Off-tour, my sex life was non-existent. When Sid and I used to live together, we were partying every night. Now Sid was married to my little sister, and they were expecting twins. My other bandmates were no better. Ryder had a wife and an eight-month-old baby. Knox was talking about getting married to Summer. Hell, even Ghost was in a serious relationship, even if it was with two other people. Hanging out with all of them was still fun, but it was completely different from the old days.

In a way, I felt like I was getting left behind. I'd started thinking that maybe it was time that I settled down, too. I was 32 years old and had a kid. Maybe it wasn't completely fulfilling to stick my dick in any willing hot chick. Maybe it was time to date around and find the woman that I wanted to spend my life with. I'd watched my bandmates fall in love with incredible women and damn if I didn't feel a bit of jealousy. I wanted that, but I wasn't sure how to get it.

So, after hanging out with a bunch of couples for too long after our last tour, I jumped at the chance to go to a party. I'd become friends with Davis, a guy in an upcoming band that I'd met on tour last year. He was as wild as I used to be.

He was in town between tours, so he invited me out a few times. I met Addison one of those nights when I was out with his crew. She and I ended up fucking that night in the coat room.

I was intrigued by her. She was flirty and sexy, making me feel special. The sex was quick, but it had been hot, so I got her number.

I thought about her a lot, so after a few days, I gave her a call. She was going out with friends, so she invited me to meet her at a club. That second meeting, she gave me a quick and dirty blowjob in a car full of drunk people.

Maybe that should have been my warning. I didn't really give a shit who saw her give me a blowjob, but why didn't she? They were her friends. If I was being honest with myself, it made me slightly uncomfortable. I tried to brush it off. She was younger than me, around 25 years old, and she still partied hard. It's not like I wasn't like that when I was 25.

The next time we met, she was out with her friends again. She was hammered by the time I got there. I left after I made sure she got home safely, despite her slurring pleas for me to fuck her.

That led me to last night. I had asked her out to dinner so that I could get to know her better. On a real date. Just her and me.

Dinner was great. She was sweet. She asked about my music, my friends, and my experiences with my band, Ghost Parker. I even told her about Kody. She seemed really interested in everything I had to say.

I found out more about her. She told me about growing up in southern California and about her large family. She and her friends hung around the underground rock scene in L.A. — that's how she knew Davis and his band. Addison was younger, so she did talk a lot about partying and had thought little about her future, but that was okay.

She knew that I'd booked a hotel room so that we could spend the night together. I wanted to take my time and explore every inch of her. I had a feeling she was used to taking everything fast, and I wanted to show her that slow and thorough could be amazing.

While we were sipping wine, gazing at each other across the candle-lit table, I had the brief thought that I should have invited her to my home for our date. I could have impressed her with my fancy house and my cooking skills. I could have woken up with her in my bed, given her an orgasm or two, and then impressed her with a fancy breakfast.

My mother had always said to my sister growing up that a man who cooked was a man that you should marry. Out of necessity, I'd learned a lot about cooking over the last couple of years. It didn't make sense to hire someone to cook for me when I was on the road with the band so much. It had been easier to figure it out on my own.

Taking her out to dinner had been great. Getting to know each other without either of our friends around had been fun. I'd stepped way back from the spotlight the past few years and now hardly anyone ever recognized me out in public. After witnessing all the shit my bandmates had to go through, I was grateful.

I was excited to get Addison back to my hotel room. She went to the restroom while I was settling the bill. As soon as she got back to the table, I knew something was off with her.

Josie broke into my thoughts about the date. "What happened? You two didn't have a good time together?"

I slumped into the chair at the kitchen table. "Dinner was great. We were getting along fine. I thought we really had a connection. Then she went to the ladies' room."

"And?" she prompted.

"When she got back to the table, she was suddenly talking up a storm. Jumping from one subject to the next. When she wiped her nose with the back of her hand, I fucking knew. My insides froze." I closed my eyes, trying to blot out the memory. "When I looked closely, I saw that her eyes were bloodshot. Her pupils dilated. And there were traces of white powder under her nostril."

Josie sniffed her disapproval. "Cocaine?"

"And to think I almost brought her around Kody!" I moaned with frustration. "I can't believe how fucking stupid I am."

"Don't beat yourself up about it." Josie placed her hand on my shoulder. "You did everything exactly right. When you have a son to think about, it's true, you can't bring home women willy-nilly. You've got to vet them first, which is exactly what you did."

"But we were getting along so well. I really liked her. She made me feel good." I moaned and put my face in my hands. The dumb shit coming out of my mouth was just giving Josie great ammunition to use against me. I was sure she was memorizing every dumb word to throw back in my face someday.

"There's plenty of fish in the sea."

I looked up. "Kody's getting older. He's going to start noticing the kind of women I have in my life. I can't just keep hooking up with fast, easy women. Who I bring into his life is important."

"So, what you're saying is that you're looking for a girlfriend and not a fuck buddy?"

While I was talking, Josie refilled my coffee mug and fixed a coffee for herself. Then she put some of her muffins on a plate and brought it all back to the table.

"Something like that." I made a face, just for the fact that Josie just said fuck buddy. "I need to get to know a woman a little better before I fuck her. Vet her, like you said. Take her out with my friends and see if they get along. If she passes the test, then maybe we can take Kody places together and I can see if Kody likes her."

She pulled up a chair across the table from me and sat down. "Whoa. You're getting ahead of yourself. First, you have to just start dating."

"That's the problem. I don't know how to date."

She slid a muffin over to me. "What are you looking for in a woman?"

I eyed the muffin like it was poison. I had an irrational hatred of raisins and Josie knew that. She was forever trying to sneak raisins into my food. Kody loved them — the little traitor — and never warned me. I eyed the chocolate chips with suspicion before I took a bite.

I thought about what I wanted in a woman while I chewed on the delicious muffin. "She has to like kids. She has to enjoy the music scene and everything that comes with it. And, of course, she has to like sex. A lot of sex."

"Kids, music, and sex," Josie summarized. "Does she have to look like a model?"

"No," I answered right away. "But I have some standards. She can't be hideous. I don't want to have to fuck her with a bag over her head."

"Very funny."

I smiled. "I'm not as hung up on looks as I used to be. Personality is more important than appearance." I really couldn't believe the shit coming out of my mouth today.

I took a sip of my coffee and frowned. It was black; there was no flavored creamer or sugar added to it; yet, it had a weird taste to it. A sweetness that tasted off.

Josie smiled. "I think I know someone who meets those criteria. I'll set you up. Even if it isn't a love match, it could give you some good dating practice."

"I don't know, Josie. I don't think set-ups are my thing. I rather find women to date by myself."

"And how's that working out for you so far?"

I refused to answer, but she had a point. I took another gulp of coffee, immediately tasting the off-putting flavor. As I swallowed, something small and lumpy knocked around inside my mouth. I gagged.

It was a fucking raisin.

I sprang to my feet and rushed to the sink. My stomach heaved; I was about to throw up. I spit the foul black demon out of my mouth and began retching while my eyes watered. Later, I found out that the entire cup of coffee was loaded with them. Fuck, it was nasty.

When I could finally speak again, I looked over my shoulder at her with disgust and just the tiniest bit of admiration. "You better watch your back, woman. This means war."

Her smile was cunning. "You know, Kaylie offered to pay me triple what you pay. You're going to miss me when those twins are born."

Chapter 2

Lacey

I STEPPED INTO THE swanky reception area of the doctor's office in Beverly Hills. I'd waited close to six months for this appointment and it couldn't have come at a better time.

Walking across the white marble floor, I approached the reception desk to check in, right on time.

The lovely receptionist, with her incredibly flawless skin and blindingly white teeth, smiled up at me. "I'm sorry. The doctor is running late today. A few complications arose with a procedure this morning, so he's behind. The wait will be at least another 45 minutes. Would it be more convenient for you to reschedule?"

No, it wouldn't be more convenient to reschedule. At all. It had taken me forever to get a consultation with this world-renowned doctor. I wasn't going anywhere.

I'd been waiting long enough. The clock was ticking. Figuratively

— I looked down at my Blancpain diamond watch with the mother-of-pearl dial and ostrich leather strap — and quite literally.

"No, I'll wait."

She nodded serenely. "Can I get you anything to drink? Coffee? Perrier?"

"No, I'm fine."

Her head tilted slightly. "Please have a seat and we'll get to you as soon as we can."

The waiting room wasn't utilitarian, like an ordinary doctor's office. Everything was done in shades of white, including the walls, curtains, furniture, and floor, but it didn't feel sterile. It was elegant. The furniture was plush and inviting – small tufted sofas with throw pillows — instead of the vinyl-covered chairs that you'd normally see. Elegant lamps lit the room and expensive artwork broke up the white walls. Soothing music was gently playing in the background and the scent of lavender was diffused into the air.

The entire effect should have been calming, but I was a bundle of nerves.

I sat down on one of the small sofas and crossed my legs. There was one other person in the room, presumably another patient who was waiting to be seen. A quick scan of her ivory suit, obscenely expensive handbag, shoes, and jewelry told me that she was quite wealthy. She was probably thinking the same exact thing about me as she looked me over. She smiled faintly and then returned her attention to her phone.

As I sat on the couch and waited, I wondered what people would think if they could see me now. What would my father think? Or my 81 employees? What would the posse of kickass girls — the one that shrunk every year as they got married off — the posse that worshipped me as their 'queen b' think? Or how about the many men whose hearts I'd crushed under my lethal stilettos over the years?

Would they feel sorry for me? Think I was pathetic? Or would they be impressed with what an empowered woman I was? Probably a mixture of all of that. I wasn't even sure what I thought of myself, but I wasn't going to dwell on any insecurities I was harboring. I was a tough bitch — an expert at pushing away any unwanted emotion.

The white door across the room opened, and a nurse poked her head into the room and addressed my silent companion. "Mrs. Davis? We're almost finished up in here. We'll be ready for you in about ten minutes."

The lady in the white Chanel suit raised her hand in acknowledgment. It trembled faintly as she placed it back on her lap.

I averted my eyes, but it was too late. She had caught me watching.

"I'm here to see if my embryo transfer was successful." Her face remained neutral, but her voice wobbled slightly.

"Oh." I was startled that she'd shared that with me. "Good luck to you."

She placed her long fingers at the base of her throat as if trying to ease the tension there. "This is our second attempt. The first one failed. We just got married, and we're trying to have a baby. I'll be 44 in a month."

I folded my hands on my lap, not quite knowing what to say. "I hope it works out."

She nodded. "It's a real bitch going through this. Don't wait."

I pressed my lips together but didn't say anything.

My 34th birthday was coming up. It had crept up on me silently until suddenly, the realization slammed me in the face.

I'd spent my twenties proving to the world that I'd earned my position in my father's company through merit, not nepotism. I'd climbed the corporate ladder until I was running the A&R department. Even though I was called a savant at finding and signing talent, it came down to more than natural ability and instinct. I'd worked my ass off.

I was known as a barracuda in the industry and I wore my success and confidence like a shield around my heart. Thoughts of babies or families never crossed my mind. I used men sexually and needed nothing else from them. I sowed my wild oats and had no regrets.

In my early thirties, I began noticing people around me pairing off. Getting married. Starting families. I felt nothing but a smug satisfaction that I was better than them. Stronger. I'd been promoted to Executive Vice President of Castle Music. I was at the top of the food chain. Revered and feared by most of the company. Women hated me because I took what I wanted. Men hated me because they wanted to be like me. Did. not. care.

I'm not sure when I started questioning everything. Maybe it was after I'd spent another lonely night after I'd kicked a man out of my bed. Maybe it was after one of the many dalliances I'd had with the members of the rock bands I worked with. After I'd tangled with a few members of Ghost Parker, a noticeable disquiet started seeping in. I'd felt a pang of rejection. It was foreign and ugly. I didn't like it. That was the first hairline crack in the armor.

In a frenzy to bury these insecurities, I started seeing a 22-year-old, hot-as-fuck, bad-boy rocker. He was covered in tats and attitude, with a body to match. His infatuation with me was like a balm to my bruised ego. He couldn't stop coming back for more and he kept me extremely satisfied.

Until I walked in on him fucking a girl. A young, dumb girl. Someone who'd so far achieved nothing in life except existing. The girl squeaked like a mouse when she saw me. Without missing a thrust, he asked me if I wanted to join in. God, I felt every one of my 30+ years at that moment.

I wasn't devastated or mad, more like letdown. My ego checked hard. I was surprised to realize that I felt this possessive towards him. I couldn't blame him too much. He had no concept that I might actually feel any emotion. It was twisted, but I never showed any vulnerabilities to a man. He fucked her simply because he could; we'd never talked about being exclusive. There was nothing real between us. I ended up signing his band to Castle and then making sure never to cross paths with him again.

That was a moment of revelation. An epiphany. I didn't love him, but something that we had was important to me and it wasn't sex. I went through what I classified as a minor heartbreak.

On the other side of that moment, I became more human. Right about that time was when I helped Kaylie through some rough times. I'd never had a friend before, but now she was my best friend who'd co-founded an amazing charity, Cyber Angels, with me. She'd gone through a lot, but now she was married to a man I had a brief hot fling with long ago.

After my epiphany with the hot rocker, I decided to settle down. As I did with everything else in my life, I methodically approached my new relationship goals. I was looking for commitment.

I found the guy who checked off all my boxes: successful, attractive, charismatic, assertive, social, driven, mature, and not involved in the music industry. Theo was all of those things, and he wasn't threatened by my success. I'd never been swept away by romance before, and it was exhilarating. He was always telling me how gorgeous I was and how lucky he was to find me. He even called me 'beautiful' as a nickname, and it made my heart melt each time he said it. And the cherry on top — he was extremely skilled in bed. I was smitten. I really thought he could be the one.

Until we went sailing on a yacht with his work buddies, who he was trying to impress. I thought there would be some other women there, but it ended up being me and him with three other guys.

He'd asked me to wear a particular bathing suit that was his favorite. The suit was almost obscene with how little skin it covered. I protested. That suit wasn't something I usually paraded around in. Somehow, he managed to convince me. He told me I had a rocking body, and he wanted to show me off. All the other girls would look hot, so I couldn't show up wearing some frumpy get-up.

I reluctantly went along with it, but then felt uncomfortable when there were only guys on the boat and they were all ogling me like a piece of meat. I'd never been shy about my body, but something about the whole thing felt off.

The entire afternoon, Theo was plying me with drinks. I almost suspected that he was trying to get me drunk. He was so insistent that I'd started dumping them overboard when no one was watching.

I closed my eyes and the horrible day came back to me with a clarity that was painful.

♫♫♪♪♪

Theo joined me on the deck of the yacht. He handed me a new drink. I felt dizzy. The yacht was anchored, but it still swayed slightly in the waves. I hoped it was the boat moving and not all the alcohol I'd consumed. I'd been secretly tossing most of it since Theo was bent on everyone having a good time and wouldn't take no for an answer.

The boat pitched — or was that me? — and Theo grabbed my waist as I awkwardly stumbled to keep my balance. He pulled me closer and then slid his hand into my bikini bottom.

My fingers curled around his wrist to stop him. "No, Theo. We're not alone."

"No one's here right now." He began nibbling on my ear and I could smell the alcohol on his breath.

"But they could be here at any moment."

His hand slid up my back and before I knew what was happening, he yanked on the string that was the only thing keeping the two tiny triangles of fabric over my breasts. "You've got me so horny, beautiful, I can't help it."

I scrambled to cover my tits with my hands and he laughed.

He gently tried to pull my hands away. "You've got a gorgeous body. Show it off for me. Let everyone see what is mine."

I gasped. This didn't seem like him. "No. I don't want to."

"Don't be a prude." His hand tangled in my hair and he pulled my head up to look at him. "I want to fuck you good. Let them watch. They'll be standing back there with their dicks in their hands while I've got you. I'll fuck the shit out of you. It'll be so good, beautiful."

I pushed against his chest, but he didn't even seem to notice. His other hand had encircled my waist and pulled me tight against his erection. He pulled my bikini bottom halfway down my thighs and then lightly smacked my ass with a growl. Lust was blazing in his eyes.

I tried to reason with him. "Theo, you're drunk..."

He licked his lips. "I'll lick your pussy while they watch. Tell me that doesn't turn you on. I bet you're soaked right now just thinking about it."

The idea was turning me on, but somehow his presentation was turning me off. He just wanted to show me off? "No, Theo. What if someone took a video?"

He growled. "I bet we look so hot together. Fuck, Lacey. You can't prance around in that bikini all day and not expect me to get horny."

Theo spun me around in his arms and I realized that one of his friends was standing not even ten feet away from us, watching while he drank his beer. Theo's forearm was resting under my breasts, pinning my back to his chest. His other hand pinched one of my nipples, before snaking down my stomach and then sliding between my legs. His fingers began stroking me, circling my clit teasingly before penetrating my pussy over and over again. In and out.

He was groaning in my ear. "You're so fucking wet. You like this, baby." It was a statement, not a question.

I couldn't pull my eyes away from the guy watching us and I wondered briefly if he was going to join in, but I wasn't sure if I wanted him to.

I fought the orgasm that I felt building, but Theo knew exactly how to touch me. It didn't take long before my head was tossed back against Theo's shoulder and I was coming. I clamped my mouth shut, not making a single peep.

"Fuck, beautiful, I've got to get inside of you."

He yanked my bikini bottom all the way down my legs, then spun me around so that I was facing the railing. By that time, I noticed that the other two guys had joined the first to watch the show.

Theo placed my hands on the warm metal railing. "Hold on tight, beautiful."

I stared at the bouncing waves while he pulled his shorts down. He kicked my legs further apart, thrust his dick into me from behind, and then began fucking me like a pornstar. This time, I didn't orgasm. It felt like forever but probably was only a few minutes when he finally pulled out and shot his load on my lower back and ass with a caveman-like grunt.

I spent the rest of the time on the yacht below deck. Several times, Theo tried to get me to join the men, who were up on the deck drinking, hanging out, and laughing like nothing happened. I told him I was tired and he let me be.

♫♪♩♪♪

That was the beginning of the end for Theo and I. When I confronted him about it later, he claimed that what we did wasn't so bad, just a little kinky.

That was true. It wasn't even close to the kinkiest thing I'd ever done. My heart wanted so badly to give Theo the benefit of the doubt. We were both drunk. And I'd hoped that he was going to be the one for me. I was starting to think about marriage and babies.

But I couldn't stop that niggling of suspicion. I was suspicious of his motives. After remembering what Kaylie went through, I started worrying that there might be hidden cameras in his bedroom. I just didn't trust him anymore. I wondered if he was cheating on me during all his business trips.

I dumped him about a month after that sailing trip on the yacht. He didn't put up too much of a fight, so I obviously did the right thing. Fuck him and fuck men. Why did it have to be this hard?

Kaylie helped me through that heartbreak. Did I mention that I'd had a threesome with Kaylie's husband and her brother back in my wilder days? That was all firmly in the past. She and Sidney were meant to be together. They were soulmates. And I was lucky to be the maid of honor at their wedding.

During that awful breakup with Theo was when Kaylie told me she was pregnant with twins. That's when the biological clock really began to tick. It was ticking with an urgency. Somehow, time had crept up on me. I was 34 years old. I needed a plan. Hopefully, the doctor could give me some options.

The lady in the white suit glanced over at me and then smiled

HOW TO MARRY A ROCKSTAR

faintly. She was nervous.

I held back for a second, then it all just came sliding out. "I'm thinking of getting my eggs frozen. Or maybe just skipping over that part and getting pregnant using a sperm donor."

She arched an eyebrow. "How old are you?"

"Almost 35."

She nodded. "Get pregnant as soon as you can."

I don't know why I kept talking. "I'd prefer for my baby to have a father in the picture. But all the men I know are weak assholes. If I wait for prince charming to come around..." I shrugged.

The room was silent for a minute or two.

"I don't love my husband. He doesn't even have the faintest clue how to satisfy me in bed. He's just the sperm donor in my case."

It seemed like an awfully harsh thing for her to say about her husband. "I, uh, I don't know what to say. That's..." My voice trailed off.

"Sad? Nah. I chose my husband specifically for his ability to be a good father. I get all the sexual satisfaction I need elsewhere."

"Oh." I didn't know her situation, so I wasn't about to get all judgy on her.

"My therapist told me that sometimes very strong women have trouble giving up control in bed." She cocked her head as if in thought. "Let me ask you, have you ever been in love?"

I thought for a long moment. "No, not really."

She nodded sagely. "I recognize myself in you." She paused for a few seconds and then pressed on. "Did you work to earn your money, or did you inherit it?"

I raised my eyebrows at her boldness but then answered. "Both."

"Ahhh. Even worse than I suspected."

What did how I came about money have to do with anything?

She dug into her purse and then pulled out what looked like a business card. "I had to learn how to be more submissive in the bedroom before I could really feel free. Of course, it takes an experienced, dominant man — or woman, if that's your thing — to safely take the reins to allow that complete surrender. It's changed my whole life. Giving up that control is freeing. It's the greatest feeling in the world. Absolute nirvana."

"You're talking about a BDSM relationship? Dom/sub type of thing?"

Honestly, I couldn't ever imagine submitting myself fully to someone else. It wasn't just laughable to me; I almost found the thought repulsive. I just wasn't made that way.

Some of my thoughts must have shown on my face, because she smirked knowingly.

Just then, the door across the room opened again. "Mrs. Davis, we're ready for you."

The woman stood up. She handed me the card from her purse. "My advice is to choose the sperm donor."

I looked down at the card in my hand. One word was written in red script on the black business card: Scarlett. There was a phone number underneath it. The rest of the card was empty, including the back. I wasn't even sure what Scarlett was. I'd probably toss the thing as soon as I could.

The woman walked across the room and, just before disappearing behind the door, she turned back to me and winked. "And don't throw away the card." The door shut behind her and she was gone.

Chapter 3

Bash

Date #1

I SHOULD HAVE PULLED the plug on date #1 right away. As soon as I opened the door, I noticed Maryellen wasn't the type of girl I would have normally chosen to go out with.

She might have been attractive if she'd put a bit of effort into it. She was wearing a faded blue T-shirt covered with short, white animal hairs and a pair of jeans that had weird stretched-out, drooping knees. It was a hot sunny day; how the hell was she wearing denim without overheating? The most distracting thing about her was the way her brunette hair was cut and styled. Her bangs were super short and stubby – a look even really edgy girls could rarely pull off. They looked like Kaylie's bangs had that time she'd taken a pair of scissors to them when she was six.

Altogether, her features weren't ugly, but when she smiled, her painfully crooked row of bottom teeth stood out. When I introduced myself, she held out a hand for me to shake. It was awkward.

Not sure what to do, I invited her inside. Unfortunately, that choice to be a nice guy instead of ending it on the spot led to an awkward get-together of pure agony. Fuck. It was brutal.

She stepped inside my house. "Wow, you're so not what I expected!" She seemed excited. "Josie told my grannie that you play drums in a band? That's neat."

I was about to answer when her phone rang. She held up a finger for me to wait and then she turned her back to me before she lifted the phone to her face. "All clear, Nugget. Thanks."

She giggled and then turned back around to face me. "So, yeah, I used to play the trombone for years. I was in the marching band in high school. My mom wouldn't let me go to band camp with the cool kids, because ... well, you know. But I went to a lot of competitions. Even some overnights!"

"Huh." I was at a loss for words.

She kept babbling. "Yeah, I was thinking about bringing over my trombone. Maybe you'd want to jam together? I mean, I was thinking about doing it, but I really wasn't. Besides, my trombone playing is probably really rusty, so ..."

Rusty trombone? Was she trying to make sexual innuendos? I wasn't sure, but my dick was busy trying to burrow into my body in hiding. I was definitely not attracted to her.

How did I ditch her without being a complete asshole? She was looking at me expectantly. I panicked. "Would you like a drink? Water, beer, wine?"

"Oh!" Her eyes widened. "I don't drink alcohol. Well, maybe one drink would be okay. Social lubrication, and all that. But, I'm driving. So, water would be good."

Did she just look at my junk when she said lubrication? Or was I just freaking out? "Water. Okay. One moment."

I bolted out of the room toward the kitchen, hoping she wouldn't follow me. I grabbed a cold bottle of water from the refrigerator and then took a few deep breaths.

So, it was obvious this wasn't a love match, but I didn't need to be a dick to her. I would be a gentleman.

But I was going to kill Josie for this.

When I went back into the living room, Maryellen was holding a framed photograph of Kody that usually sat on the side table.

Her face was scrunched up with confusion. "Is this your brother?"

Brother? "No, that's Kody, my son."

Her eyes widened. "You have a kid?"

"Yeah."

She looked around the room. "Are you married?"

She seemed to be shocked, so I kept my answer simple. "No."

"Does his mother have custody?" She peeked over at me. "You see him every other weekend or something?"

My lips pressed together. "I have full custody. You don't like kids?"

She let out a high-pitched squeak. "Meep. I'm just not used to them. It seems like a lot of responsibility to take care of them. I've got a Pomeranian and taking care of Sookie is overwhelming at times."

She put the picture of Kody down and then swiped her phone a few times before pointing the screen at me. "That's my Sookie."

It was a picture of a white ball of fluff. A tiny dog sitting on a couch. "Cute," I mumbled.

"Let me guess, you're a cat person? Dogs are so much cooler! Do you want to see Sookie's Insta page? She's got a ton of followers. I don't do social media — my therapist told me to give it up, too much anxiety — but I help Sookie out with her page." She gave me a wink and then added, "If you follow her, she'll follow you back. Sookie_Pom."

I took a step back. "I don't really do social media either."

Her eyes widened with surprise. "You don't! Wow, we really are compatible. Do you love animals? I thought we could go to the zoo for our date. I mean, who doesn't love animals?"

Fuck. I wasn't about to spend all day at the zoo with this crazy girl just to be a nice guy. I had my limits. "Honestly, I'm not really a zoo person. I had a bad experience there once."

"Oh shit!" She nodded. "I saw a male gorilla humping a female gorilla right behind the glass when I was a kid. He was huge. I mean, crazy big. And it happened like five feet away from me. It was really traumatizing. And that would be so awkward if that happened on a date."

My hand tunneled through my hair. I was starting to sweat. "Maryellen, I couldn't help but notice that you didn't seem comfortable that I had a son."

She couldn't meet my eye. "It was quite the surprise. Josie didn't mention that to my grannie."

"He's a big part of my life. Actually, he's the biggest part of my life." I kept my tone nice and even. "So, I'm not sure that we are all that compatible."

Her hand flew to her forehead. "I'm really sorry! I hope you aren't too upset. I just … it's not you, it's me. You seem so great. I just…"

I started leading her to the door. "It's okay. Thanks for being honest with me."

Just as she got to the front door, she stopped. "I have this friend, Nugget. She really loves kids. I could give you her number?"

"No, that's okay." I bit my lip. "I think I'm going to take a little break from dating."

She nodded. "I understand."

I pressed my phone to my ear as I listened to it ring and ring.

"Pick up," I muttered.

Finally, Josie answered, "Did you get lucky?"

"Cancel the date you set up for Saturday," I growled into the phone. "I'm not spending another minute of my time with some whack job you set me up with."

She gasped. "Maryellen is not a whack job."

"Fuck, Josie. You did that on purpose, didn't you?" I accused.

"You said you weren't looking for a model! Maryellen may not be that gorgeous, but she's got nice titties. Perky!"

I paced around the room, trying to let off steam without yelling. "I wouldn't know if she had nice tits; I couldn't see past all the dog hair on her chest."

"Oh yeah, she loves that dog. Dresses him up in pink tutus and stuff. What's his name? Nookie?"

I let out a huff of breath. "She was telling me all about her glory days in marching band–"

"See, she likes the music scene. You said that was important to you."

I ignored her and continued my rant. "And she wouldn't shut up about her dog's Instagram page. And watching gorillas mate at the zoo."

"Aha! She likes sex. That was important to you. I mean, she named her dog Nookie, so that tells you something."

My teeth were clenched so hard, I was surprised they didn't crack. "I'm not into gorilla porn. Christ, Josie, you set me up with a complete nutter!"

"So far, you two sound perfectly compatible. The both of you share a love of music and it sounds like sex might be kinky with her. What's the problem?"

I took a calming breath. "Well, she absolutely freaked out when she found out I had a son."

Josie paused for a moment. "Huh. I didn't know that about Maryellen. That's too bad. "

"Yeah. Too bad." I sounded like a petulant dick, but I no longer cared. "So, please, for the love of God, cancel the thing you set up for Saturday. I'm done with dating."

"No can do. Angelique already has your address, and she made dinner reservations. It's too late to cancel."

I had to put my foot down. "Look, I refuse to go out with another girl you set me up with. I don't trust your judgment."

She wasn't backing down an inch. "I happen to know Angelique loves kids. She's beautiful and 'hot to trot', as you kids would say."

"No one says that. Not even old people."

She ignored me. "So, Angelique loves kids. She loves sex. That meets two of your criteria. And I bet she loves the music scene, too. She's got piercings. Two that are visible. Maybe you might be able to find some others? Some hidden ones?"

"She's got piercings," my tone dripped with sarcasm, "so that means she into the music scene?"

"Exactly!" she agreed. "That means she checks all of your boxes. And she's way sexier than Maryellen. Trust me."

I grunted. That wasn't saying all that much.

"C'mon, Bash. Just go to dinner with her. How bad could it be?"

Chapter 4

Bash

Date #2:

I'd been texting with Angelique for days. She seemed cool, and she'd been a little flirty with her messages, but we hadn't exchanged photos, so I was still a bit nervous. Josie said she was hot, but ... I didn't put too much stock in that.

The plan was that she'd pick me up because the restaurant she made reservations at was closer to my place. When the doorbell rang, I was so fucking nervous. I was half expecting a hideous hag to greet me when I opened the door.

I was pleasantly surprised and very relieved at the same time. She was attractive and age-appropriate. Thank God. She had dark hair cut in an edgy bob, a stud on the side of her nose, and a lip piercing. She was dressed in a white blouse with a flouncy, short skirt, and combat boots.

Angelique let out a nervous little laugh. "I was worried, but Josie really undersold you. She said you were a little out of shape, but not too hideous looking. Frankly, I was worried you'd be fat and sweaty, but you're hot. Is this your house?"

I waved her inside. "Yeah. This is home."

She looked around. "Wow, it's really nice. You're not a complete deadbeat loser. When Josie said you played the drums in some band, I had my doubts, but you must do nicely for yourself."

I smiled. "Yeah. I do okay."

"I love musicians!" There was a sparkle in her eye. "I love the creativity and the energy surrounding them. I'd love to hear you play sometime. A drummer! That's badass!"

My cock was waking up, responding to the praise. "I have to admit, I was a bit worried about who Josie was setting me up with, too."

She chuckled. "How do you know Josie?"

"She's my nanny."

She scrunched up her face and groaned. "You have a nanny? Shit."

A burst of laughter escaped. She was so cute. "I meant my son's nanny."

Her eyes widened. "You have a son?"

My gut tightened with anxiety. "Yeah. He's three years old. Do you like kids?"

She didn't hesitate; she was emphatic. "I love kids!"

I gestured to the picture of Kody on the table. "That's my son. Kody."

She walked over to get a better look. "He's so cute."

I'd followed her, so when she spun around, we were only a few feet apart.

She bit her bottom lip. "The last time Josie set me up, this guy in a three-piece suit showed up at my door." She made a disgusted face. "He brought me flowers. I mean, why bother — they'll just die, anyway."

I made a mental note never to buy her flowers. Jesus, dating was complicated.

"And, then—" she was chewing on her lip now. "I saw something. It was…" She trembled slightly. "… just bad. Kind of traumatic."

She stepped closer to me and rested her hands on my chest. I placed my hands on her elbows, not sure how to comfort her. "What did you see?"

She shook her head and then pressed her whole body up against me. Her arms circled around my neck and then she smiled at me with perfectly straight teeth.

She felt amazing pressed up against me. I slipped my hands down her body until they were cupping her ass cheeks over her skirt and pulled her tighter against me. I was sure she could feel my hard cock trapped between our bodies. Hopefully, I wasn't scaring her off by being too forward.

"Can I see your dick?"

I was stunned. I guess I wasn't being too forward then. "Like, right now?"

"Yeah," she whispered.

I squeezed the globes of her ass. "You want me to take it out?"

She nodded.

I was hard as a rock now. "Okay, sweetheart. I'll show you my dick."

Well, this was promising. I'd only met her for five minutes and already my dick was throbbing. I unzipped my pants.

She dropped to her knees, dragging my pants and boxer briefs down with her. She certainly wasn't shy.

Her mouth was inches from my dick while she inspected it with wonder.

"It's beautiful." I could feel her warm breath as she said it. "It's a great size. And you've got two balls! Thank God!"

It was the weirdest fucking thing a girl on her knees had ever said to me, but it was making my cock pulse with need.

"You have the perfect dick." Her words were coming out all breathy. "It's making my mouth water."

Fuck. "You want a taste of it, sweetheart?"

She glanced at the smartwatch on her wrist. "By my estimate, we've only got about four more minutes, but that should do the trick."

Four more minutes for what? I had no clue what she was talking about, but I didn't care because she was licking her lips and unbuttoning her shirt.

"I really like my nipples played with while I suck cock. It gets me off. Pinch and squeeze them, both of them, but not too hard."

Okay. She knew what she wanted and wasn't afraid to ask for it. This was a bit fast and unexpected, but it was exactly what I wanted right now. Damn, this girl was perfect.

She opened her shirt and then pulled her bra cups down under her tits. She didn't have huge tits, but they looked gorgeous raised up as if in offering, especially propped up by her bra. It was a beautiful sight. My dick certainly appreciated it. I was seeping and Angelique hadn't even touched me yet.

I tweaked both her nipples gently at the same time, and she let out a hum of appreciation as she slid her hand into the waistband of her skirt.

"You're going to touch yourself, sweetheart?"

She nodded.

"Then, I want to watch. Pull your skirt up so I can see."

HOW TO MARRY A ROCKSTAR

"Yessss," she hissed. She pulled up her skirt, and she wasn't wearing anything under it. She spread her knees wide on the floor so I could get a good look. Then she slid her finger over her sex. Her flesh was glistening and pink. I could smell her arousal.

Fuck, this date was turning out better and better.

First, she checked her watch and then slid her lips over my cock. She felt like heaven. She was fairly skilled, taking me deep, working with my rhythm as I thrust into her mouth. Since my hands were busy playing with both of her nipples, I couldn't anchor her to get any hard thrusts in. Even though my thrusts were shallow, her cheeks were caving in as she hoovered me hard. Watching her touch herself was the icing on the cake because this girl was not shy. She was fucking herself with her fingers and moaning around my cock. It was hot, and I was already imagining all the things I wanted to do to her.

Suddenly, she stopped bobbing on my cock and brought her wrist up to her face to check her watch. She stopped for a moment to read a text. I patiently waited, even though it felt like torture, softly running my thumbs over her taut nipples.

She pulled her mouth off my cock. "Sorry, time's up. If you want to cum, you've got about one more minute. So hurry up."

One more minute? What the hell?

She sucked my cock back into her mouth and started bobbing on it frantically. I took one of my hands off her stiff nipple and wound my fingers through her hair, so I could guide her head back and forth on my cock as I thrust hard into her mouth.

She was fucking me deep with her mouth and she had no trouble taking it all. She reached up and started fondling my balls. That should do it. Another few thrusts. She pressed a finger against my asshole and two thrusts later, I spurt down her throat.

She milked me for everything I had, pulled off, licked her lips, and then asked where the bathroom was. While she was gone, I got myself together. I was feeling loose-limbed and fantastic.

She came back, kissed me on the lips, and then her lips trailed across my jaw toward my ear. She whispered, "I didn't cum, so you owe me one, lover-boy."

I grinned at her. "Give me a few minutes and I'll have you screaming, sweetheart."

She patted my chest. "I'll hold you to it. We've got to go now."

I remembered she wasn't wearing any panties, so my hand slid down to her ass as we exited my house. Living out in the suburbs, there was no one around to see my hand as it slipped under her skirt and grabbed a firm ass cheek. I half expected her to playfully bat my hand away, but she didn't.

There was a minivan in my driveway and it took me a few seconds to realize it must be hers. It wasn't the type of car I expected her to have.

Then, as we approached, I realized there were kids in the car. Lots of kids.

I was puzzled and a little uneasy as I got into the passenger seat. The kids, all clearly under the age of ten, were either yelling or crying.

When Angelique got behind the wheel, the oldest one, a boy about seven years old, yelled, "Mom, that took way too long. I'm so hungry!"

She turned around in her seat to address them. "Everyone settle down. I'm sorry it took so long. I had to finish something important, but we're ready to go now. Kids, this is Bash. He'll be having dinner with us tonight."

Oh my God. What was happening?

"These are all your kids?"

I turned around to study them. There were four of them. I couldn't get a good look at one of them because they were in a car seat facing backward. A toddler boy, younger than Kody, was buckled into another car seat. Two older kids were in the back row, sitting in booster seats.

She started the car and began backing out of my driveway before I had the chance to escape. "Yep. These are my babies. Charlie and Harper are my little ones. Amelia and Will are the ones in the back."

Will shouted from the back, "Mom, I'm really hungry!"

Angelique pulled out onto the road and then glanced in her rear-view mirror at her son. "Good thing you're hungry, because we're going to Pop'em Possum for dinner."

My ears almost started bleeding with the high-pitched shriek of glee they all let out.

Pop'em Possum was a local restaurant franchise geared toward kids that was known for its giant opossum mascot, greasy microwaved pizza that tasted like cardboard, and arcade games. I'd never been there, but the local billboards and TV commercials made it look horrifying.

I gripped the armrest. "I thought you had reservations somewhere?"

She looked over at me and smiled reassuringly. "I have a friend who works there. I get a good discount and can get the kids some tokens. It keeps them busy and out of my hair. They love it."

It was loud in the car. The kids were constantly yelling. As soon as we got out of my neighborhood, I realized that Angelique was a terrible driver. She was cutting people off, not braking soon enough, and flipping off people who beeped at her. It was twenty minutes of a white-knuckled car ride from hell.

It took a considerable amount of wrangling to get the kids all checked in with hand stamps and wrist bands and then to get them seated. All six of us were crammed into a booth together. Will spilled his soda all over the table while we were waiting for the food, so there were wads of wet napkins all over the place.

Angelique's kids were busy coloring on the paper tablecloth and fighting. Complete pandemonium was going on all around us: kids running and screaming everywhere, horrible carnival music blaring, and a nightmare-fuel, giant opossum wandering around to freak out the kids who were already hopped up on junk food.

I skipped the "pizza" and only nibbled at the soggy french fries. The kids slammed down their food in record time. When we were about done eating, a greasy-haired guy who looked as high as a kite came over with a bucket of tokens for the kids. After a collective squeal of delight, all but the littlest one ran off to play arcade games.

"Thanks, Karl." She knew him by name. And I was pretty sure she was giving him some kind of weird eye signal.

It was ridiculously hard to communicate since it was so damn loud. There was a strange blue light pulsing in the background, which was making me feel queasy. Or maybe that was the fries? Either way, I was convinced I was in the 7th circle of hell.

Angelique was busy on her phone. I was wondering how I could escape. Before I could come up with a plan, she stood up.

"Would you keep an eye on Harper for a minute? I have to use the bathroom."

"Sure." I looked warily at Harper, but she seemed to be fairly content picking at the food left on her plate. As soon as she realized her mom was gone, she let out a giant wail.

I tried to soothe her, but after no success, I knew I had no choice. I unbuckled her from the seat and lifted her up. She looked me over, but then thankfully stopped crying.

For at least five minutes, I held Harper in my arms, trying to keep her calm. When she got fidgety, I walked over to the arcade area to check on the other kids. When I found Will, I asked him to point out the other two, because I couldn't pick them out in the swarm of kids. They were all wearing their wristbands, and they couldn't get out of the place without the matching wristband of the parent. It was a pretty secure setup.

Our table was still empty when I returned. Where the hell was Angelique? Was everything okay? Maybe the horrible food was not sitting well in her stomach?

Then I had a terrifying thought. My gut twisted. What if she abandoned her kids? Left them here with me and took off — just like Kody's mom had abandoned him. It was a crazy thought. I tried to shake it off, but where the hell was she?

I couldn't keep still. I was antsy. I headed to the bathrooms. Girls and their moms were coming and going from the ladies' room. It was too crowded to go in there and look for Angelique, so I asked a young mom to check if she was okay.

She came back a few minutes later and told me there was no Angelique in the bathroom. I was starting to panic.

Out of desperation, I checked the men's room. I was a bit uneasy about bringing Harper in there, but I was too worried for it to stop me.

I poked my head inside the door. A row of urinals, most of them the shorter urinals for little dudes, lined the wall. Each of them was decorated with a hissing opossum face as a target to pee on. I thought the bathroom was empty and was about to leave until I heard a rustling of movement behind one of the stall doors.

It only took me a few seconds of listening carefully and seeing the arrangement of feet under the stall door to realize that someone was having sex in the stall and I had a pretty good idea who it was.

"Angelique" — my angry shout startled Harper, so I modulated my voice to a gritty snarl — "Get the fuck out here right now."

I waited outside the restroom door for her to come out, hoping like hell she'd get out before I had to stop any kids from going in there while she was having sex. I was no angel, but having sex in a restroom at a kid's restaurant crossed a line.

The greasy-haired employee came out first. He walked by without a care in the world. A minute later, Angelique strolled out. Silently, I handed Harper off to her.

She looked at my clenched jaw and laughed. "What? You wanted to be exclusive or something?"

I bit back my response.

She snorted. "I don't do monogamous. I'm polyamorous."

♪♫♪♪♫

I waited about 30 minutes for my car to pull up after I booked it on the ride-sharing app on my phone. When I got settled in the car, I called Josie, needing to let off a little steam.

I started right in when she answered. "I'm done dating. Never set me up again. I don't care who it is; I won't go out with them."

"Huh! I wasn't too surprised about the 36-year-old virgin dog lover; she may not have been the perfect match. But Angelique? She's perfect! She likes kids, she likes sex and I'm sure she could handle your rock star lifestyle. She meets all your criteria of what you wanted in a woman."

I blew out a frustrated breath and growled into the phone. "She's a polyamorous 27-year-old that already has four kids."

"You are too picky!" She tsked. "And what's wrong with being polyamorous?"

"She was having sex with some other guy on our date!" I couldn't keep the heat out of my voice.

"Don't be such a bigot."

"Josie, you drive me crazy."

She laughed.

"I think I want to remain single forever."

Chapter 5

Lacey

If this turned out to be a giant scam, I was going to hunt them down and rain fire down on every single one of them. For all I knew, the impeccably dressed woman with the sob story in the fertility clinic was a cold, cunning con artist. Maybe she skulked around in places like the clinic where she could target rich women who were in vulnerable positions so she could hand out her cards and reel them in.

If I'd been that vulnerable woman who got played, these fraudsters were going to regret it till their dying day. At least I had an address of where to start my rage-filled campaign of destruction if it was needed, as this was the second time I'd been to this nondescript building that was supposedly an underground sex dungeon. The last time, I'd forked over an assload of money, only to sit in a conference room filling out paperwork for a couple of hours.

I'd signed a contract stating that I was paying for a subscription to a matchmaking service, purchasing the 'Scarlett' app which required monthly fees to use, and signing up for training courses. It explicitly stated that there would be 'no exchange of sexual acts for money'. I really hoped that the woman at the fertility clinic hadn't been fooling me. If this was just a super expensive matchmaking service, then I'd be pissed. I wanted that nirvana she'd been going on about, and I wasn't going to get that through training modules.

After the contract and a confidentiality agreement were signed, I was asked to fill out my kink profile questionnaire which would be used to match me with the right kink 'coach'. The questionnaire was incredibly personal and ridiculously detailed. In the wrong hands, it could be dangerous. When that was completed, I was required to watch several videos with low production value and unique titles like Intro to Kink and Safe, Sane, and Consensual, or I wouldn't be able to meet my 'kink coach' match.

The first time I'd come, before all the boring stuff, I'd been insanely excited. An anxious trepidation churned through my stomach. My barely there panties were wet even before I walked in the door. I'd gone out of my way to glam up my appearance. I was wearing a favorite dress that fitted my curves perfectly and paired it with the highest heels I knew how to walk in. Underneath, I wore obscenely expensive lingerie that would make a whore blush. My hair and makeup were glamorous enough for clubbing and I sprayed my favorite designer scent on all my pulse points, including the one between my legs. And, of course, I was freshly waxed.

I'd left that appointment frustrated as hell after spending most of the day there, thinking about sex. Ever since I'd walked out of the supposedly exclusive club, I'd half expected to be blackmailed with that damn intimate questionnaire I'd filled out. Even though they promised anonymity to their clients, I knew it could never be 100%

guaranteed.

Today, I dressed to fit my cynical mood. I was wearing weekend loungewear with flip-flops, and my hair was pulled up in a messy bun. Makeup was almost nonexistent and my undergarments were as ugly as they were comfortable. I owned period undies that were sexier.

I was greeted by the same woman again, the only person I'd met at the club so far. She took my phone for safekeeping until I left, as she had explained was club policy.

She smiled. "Our algorithms have processed your questionnaire and have selected the perfect partner for you to begin your journey of exploration with. I'll take you to the blue room where you can relax and get to know your coach. Unless you'd prefer to review the safety information again first?"

"God, no." I spit out. I'd had about all the training I could endure on safe words and communication. Guidelines were important, but I didn't need to be told the same things over and over again. I was ready to get on with it.

We passed through a door that led toward the back of the house. "This part of the house is a private residence. Whatever takes place after you meet your kink coach today or at any future date is not part of your agreement with us. You may leave at any time you wish, but please don't forget to retrieve your phone before you go. Do you understand that your activities are no longer under the auspices of Scarlett?"

"Yes." I worked with lawyers all the time. Of course, I understood Cover Your Ass when I heard it.

I followed her down a small hall and then we stopped at a door that was painted blue. My heart fluttered as I wondered if this was going to be the blue room of pain, but when the lady opened the door, it turned out to be an ordinary room with a few couches and chairs to sit on.

She turned to me before she left. "Would you like anything to drink while you wait?"

"No thanks."

I wasn't wearing a watch today, so I had no clue how long I waited, but it was too long. There were no magazines or other reading material lying around and without a phone to keep me busy, I was bored. I only had my thoughts to keep me company. I'd never been kept waiting this long by anyone in my life before. Time was money. I was seriously contemplating leaving when the door opened.

The guy who walked in was interesting. Tall and well-built enough to be physically intimidating, but he had a laid-back vibe going on with his casual clothes and longish hair that was tied back. He was an unusual mixture of athlete and hippy.

He had a slight smile on his face while his eyes gave me a long and lingering once-over, but for some reason, his friendly perusal made me bristle.

"Are you my match?" I raised an eyebrow.

He crossed his arms over his chest. "Did I give you permission to talk?"

Oh, so that's how this was going to go. The question was, did I like that? And if not, what was I going to do about it? "I didn't realize I needed permission."

He pinned me with a stare, not speaking for what felt like an uncomfortable amount of time. "I read through your entire questionnaire, Baby Girl. I've become very familiar with all your desires, your previous experiences, and your hard limits. Did you lie or exaggerate on any of your answers?"

Baby Girl? Um, I wasn't a fan of that. "No."

He nodded and dropped his arms to his sides, standing in a more relaxed position. "You indicated you haven't used a safe word before.

Are you comfortable using the traffic light system? Green, Yellow, Red?"

"Yes, that's fine."

"Only use 'green' if I specifically check in with you and everything is fine. Use yellow at any time if you are close to the edge. I'll either adjust what I'm doing or stop to talk it through with you, depending on what I see. Red means stop. And everything will stop. Never be afraid to tell me, Baby Girl."

"Uh, yellow."

His eyes narrowed. "Speak."

"I don't want to be called Baby Girl. It doesn't ... do anything for me." I had to force myself not to scrunch up my nose in disgust.

"Hmmm. It does something for me. As soon as I saw you, I knew you were my baby girl. And you want to please your Daddy Dom, right?" He had a knowing smirk on his face. He had to know this rubbed me the wrong way. It sounded stupid. Not sexy.

I breathed evenly. "I'm not into calling you Daddy. How about Sir?"

"No. Only one person calls me Sir."

Was he not going to back down on this? If I had to call him Daddy all the time, it would kill the mood. "I don't have any daddy issues. In fact, I have a great relationship with my dad. A healthy relationship. Calling you Daddy just seems weird."

"I went over your questionnaire very carefully, Baby Girl. I am extremely in tune with your needs and desires. For instance, I've never come across a score lower than yours for submission through service." He chuckled. "So, Baby Girl, I wouldn't ask you to clean toilets or mop floors for me. It wouldn't please you to do it for me, so it wouldn't please me. So, having you call me Master and calling you my Slave wouldn't be a great fit. It's not going to be our dynamic."

"There's no freaking way I would do chores like that for you." I spit out the words like they were acid.

"I know." His eyes were twinkling at my disgusted outburst.

I forced myself to calm down. "So, how is calling you Daddy a good fit?"

"Good question, Baby Girl. Take off your shirt and I'll tell you."

Okay. Now he had my interest, but my eyes flicked to the open door behind him. Someone might walk by, but that thought only sent a ripple of anticipation through me. I pulled off my T-shirt and tossed it on the couch next to me. I was wearing a plain white bra. Nothing fancy, but I'd been aware since a teenager that I'd been blessed with really nice breasts. Unfortunately, he didn't even peek at them, which was oddly disappointing.

"Your answers indicate you're looking to be dominated in the bedroom as geared more toward a romantic or sensual experience, where you could surrender completely to a partner you trusted and loved. You want to relinquish control without becoming a slave. Does that sound right, Baby Girl?"

I bit my lip. "That sounds nice, but I don't want it to be all lovey-dovey and gentle. I want other stuff, too."

"Good girls get all sorts of rewards. And, if I need to, I will punish you when you misbehave, Baby Girl, but it will always be for your own good. Daddy will take good care of you. You're already pleasing me. Take off your pants."

It sounded good, in theory, but hearing 'Daddy' still made me cringe internally. I slipped off my flip-flops and loose-fitting yoga pants until I was standing before him in white cotton panties and a white bra.

He finally looked at my body. "We can revisit it another time, Baby Girl. But I bet when I'm rewarding you for being a good girl by licking your pussy, you'll be happy to scream out to Daddy."

"Yes, Daddy." A smile of amusement traced across my lips. What he just said made me hot, and he did seem to be pretty in tune with what I was thinking. If he was going to lick my pussy anytime soon, I'd call him Daddy if that's what it took.

He stepped close to me, resting his hand gently on my cheek and rubbing his thumb across my bottom lip. A shiver ran down my spine.

Then he lowered his hand and stepped back. I missed his closeness. "Tell me if this sounds right," he ticked things off on his fingers as he listed them, "you have a healthy interest in all types of bondage, you'd like to explore light impact play like spanking or hair pulling, you currently enjoy a variety of sexual activity, mild sensation play, a slight curiosity with humiliation, an interest in roleplaying mainly when it has to do with bondage and exploring exhibitionism and voyeurism and zero interest in torture, service acts or fetishes."

He got all that from the questionnaire? "I guess that all sounds about right."

He frowned. "Who am I, Baby Girl?"

"Daddy."

His lips twitched. "That's right. That's how you address me. Take off your bra."

I knew he was exerting his dominance, which was a bit like playing mind games with me. Maybe I wasn't a natural submissive because I really wanted to exert my own will, but I wanted to know where this was all going. I wanted the experience, so I'd play along. I unsnapped my bra and pulled it off my shoulders. I didn't have twenty-year-old breasts anymore. They were heavy, and they sagged a bit without a bra on, but I knew they still looked fabulous. I tossed the bra aside and met his eyes.

"I know what your hard limits are, and I won't ever go there unless you change your mind down the road and get curious. Then we'll talk it over, but for now, while we're still building trust, I'm going to take it slow with you. And you have your safe words. Do you trust me enough to play, Baby Girl?"

"Yes, Daddy." I still didn't like calling him that, but at least I wasn't thinking about my own father when I said it anymore. Thank God!

He smiled when I called him Daddy and damn, I didn't want to feel the spurt of happiness that I'd pleased him. The shit going on in my mind was complicated. I realized that I was going to be the biggest obstacle to my own desires. If I wanted this to work, I had to stop faking everything and give in. It wasn't my inclination, so it wouldn't be easy. I'd have to fight myself every step of the way.

"Do you have any questions for me?" he asked.

"Yes, how long do these ... appointments last?" I'd been wondering all day.

"Sometimes people call it a 'scene', but that's a bit limiting for what you and I'll be doing here. Anytime you're here with me, we'll call it playtime. We might do specific scenes during our playtime. All the safety rules you were taught will apply during the entire playtime." He shifted on his feet and then continued, "And playtime has no time limit. It could be short, maybe only 15 minutes if you're being really bratty or it could last all day and night. It's up to me to decide."

"But what if I have something for work? An urgent meeting? Or a doctor's appointment?" I couldn't just drop everything for days on end without knowing how long it might last! Could I? Would I want to?

"If you didn't clear your schedule in advance, you'd miss your meeting or whatever it was. Any other questions?"

"Do I just call the number when I want, uh, playtime?"

"No, I schedule playtime through the Scarlett app that's on your phone. You'll get a notification. I give 48-hour notice."

Shit, that was so not going to work. "What if I'm busy? I travel a lot for work."

His arms folded across his chest again. "I expect you to come, Baby Girl. I can be reasonable if the circumstance is extreme, but if you think fitting me into your schedule will be a problem, I'm not the Dom for you."

"No!" I said it a little too breathlessly. "I was just curious."

His eyebrow lifted as if he didn't quite believe me. "Any other questions?"

I had so many. "How many other clients do you have?"

"Several, but when I'm with you, I'm focused entirely on you."

"Are they all women?"

"No."

I could tell he didn't want to talk about this, but I was curious and he was answering, so I continued. "Are they all submissives?"

"Yes, but each dynamic is different. I don't switch — I'll always be a Dominant, but I'm a different type of dominant for all my subs."

"Is it like playing a role? Acting?" I wanted to know more, but maybe I was needling him a bit, too.

He sighed. It was subtle, but I noticed. "You're new to this, so I don't expect you to understand, but it's not acting or playing a part. When you're in a relationship like this, you can be exactly who you are with no judgments. There's no need to act a certain way. There's a beautiful give and take based on trust and love. It's a power exchange that goes way beyond sexual gratification."

"So you love all your subs?"

He didn't hesitate. "Yes."

"What if you match with someone who is uncooperative? Or physically repulsive looking?"

His hands crossed against his chest again. I was beginning to see that as a sign of his disappointment. "Uncooperativeness usually indicates a sub trying to get attention. If there are differences that just can't be worked out, I'll terminate the relationship. They can try a different Dom. And physical appearance doesn't factor into how I feel about people. A human's worth has nothing to do with how they look. I just ask my subs to maintain a certain standard of cleanliness."

How enlightened to be above it all. Maybe it was just the superficial bitch in me, but I wasn't sure I believed everything he was spewing.

"So, you love me?" I challenged as innocently as I could.

"Yes, I feel the beginning of a loving relationship, Baby Girl."

The next question was forming on my lips when he cut me off. "Enough questions for now. Take off your panties."

Well, okay. He didn't have a never-ending well of patience, after all.

He held out his hand as I slipped off my white bikini briefs. I slid them down my legs, stepped out of them, and then placed them in his outstretched hand.

He tucked them into the waistband of his pants. "These are mine now."

Before I could decide if my panties were some kind of trophy he took from all his submissives or if he'd sell them on the internet tonight, he stepped right in front of me and placed his hands on my shoulders. When I kept staring at his chest, he tilted my chin up until I was staring into his eyes.

"What was the best sexual experience you ever had, Baby Girl?"

I thought for a moment. I'm not sure if it was my best, but it popped into my mind first. "It was a threesome."

"What made it the best?"

My nipples were pebbling. "Having two men focusing all their energy on me and my needs. Making me cum, over and over again."

He never broke eye contact. It was unnerving. "And your worst sexual experience?"

That one was fresh in my mind. "I was forced to put on a show for other men."

"You don't like being watched?" he asked.

I swallowed. "No, I did. It turned me on."

His thumbs were gently rubbing circles on my shoulders. "What didn't you like about it, then?"

"I didn't trust him."

The pause of silence seemed to last a lifetime. Then he leaned in and kissed my forehead. "Good girl."

I was feeling a little vulnerable sharing my secrets with him, but I knew that was all a part of the experience.

He stepped back again. "Daddy bought you some gifts. Do you want to see them?"

I nodded.

In a few strides, he crossed the small room until he came to a white-painted side table next to the gray couch. He slid open the small drawer on the top and pulled out some black objects from it.

He came back to stand in front of me. "Hands out."

I watched as he strapped a neoprene wristband snuggly around each of my wrists. Each wristband had a metal D-ring attached to it, which he somehow fastened together once my hands were behind my back.

I'd been handcuffed, and I loved it. It made me feel naughty.

Daddy circled around to the front of me again to inspect his work. The position of my arms was making my breasts jut out toward him like an offering. This time he was looking, and it made me even wetter.

I realized he was still holding something else in his hands when he stepped toward me and began fastening a leather collar around my neck. He fiddled with it for quite a bit of time, making sure it fit properly before clicking a leash made of chain to the metal ring.

A spurt of concern shot through me. Oh, hell no! I was not going to crawl around on the floor. Was I? No. I'd put my foot down at that. It was too degrading. Did I mark that down as a hard limit? I couldn't remember.

He waited while I was trying to process everything. It was on the tip of my tongue to blurt out 'yellow', but I didn't. I held off. For now.

He put pressure on the leash. A gentle tug, not hard enough to move me, but hard enough to pull me out of my spiraling thoughts. "You've got something to say?"

I held my tongue.

He led me out of the room into the hallway. At least I was walking.

I was buck naked, being led around on a leash like a dog. It was degrading.

Naughty.

I could feel the wetness between my thighs.

Chapter 6

Lacey

I TUGGED ON MY cuffs, wondering how tough they'd be to escape. Even though they were comfortable, they didn't have any give at all. The cuffs would be impossible to work loose on my own without a lot of time, especially with them behind my back.

I didn't know where 'Daddy' was leading me or who was going to be there, wherever there was. What if he paraded me in front of a bunch of people? I'd always had an exhibitionist streak, and I was sure that my questionnaire answers reflected that, but was I ready for it?

The unknown was ratcheting up a mixture of anxiety and anticipation in me. I had given him control. I'd let him handcuff me, so now I was completely helpless. Physically, I still could fight back somewhat, but he would easily overpower me.

Did I trust him? Not really. I didn't even know him. Gah, this was one of my stupider escapades. I'd done some stupid things in my life and taken chances when I shouldn't have, but this had the potential to be the most consequential and dangerous.

He opened another door in the hallway. A set of stairs led downwards. A sliver of pure fear snaked down my spine. Was he taking me to the basement dungeon, never to be seen or heard from again?

He stopped and looked at me. "I won't push you past your limits. Do you trust me, Baby Girl?"

"Not really."

His eyes tightened subtly. "Explain."

He wanted the truth; he was going to get it. "You're kind of giving off Ted Bundy vibes right now."

His eyes widened with surprise, and then he laughed. "It's normal to be nervous at first. I'm taking you to the playroom. There are several sections down there, but we'll just stick to the basics. I want playtime to be fun today. I want to play with your body and see what you'll give me. Nothing hardcore. Good?"

"Okay." I swallowed, feeling the collar press against my throat. "Is there anyone down there?"

"This is a private dungeon, but there's always a dungeon monitor down there if someone is playing. I don't do first-time sessions when it's crowded." He paused for a moment. "But I believe there's another sub down there cleaning. She'll probably sneak glances from a distance, but she'd stay out of the way and wouldn't speak at all. She's not my sub, but I can ask her to give us privacy if you want?"

"No, that's okay."

He cocked an eyebrow. "Anything else, Baby Girl?"

"No, I'm ready."

He tugged on my collar and led me down the stairs. The smell of heavy incense became more and more prominent with each step into the lower level. I stopped at the bottom and looked around. To my left was a series of small rooms. The only room that I could see the interior of looked like a doctor's office. I hoped it was for medical play and not an actual doctor's room to treat real injuries. Across from the staircase was a business office filled with bookcases and filing cabinets. I was pulled forward by the collar, but not before I glimpsed the large and open space to the right of the stairs. It was definitely a sex dungeon.

Before I could check it out, we stopped in front of the office door. A fierce-looking man was sitting behind a metal desk. He was covered with tattoos, even his bald head was inked. He had a full beard of black hair and dark, glinting eyes.

"Bruiser, this is my newbie. I'm going to dirty her up a bit."

The dungeon master's name was Bruiser? That didn't sound very PC at all. The guy in charge of safety was named Bruiser?

He pulled down on my chain. "Kneel."

This was the bullshit that I hated. I hesitated a moment, but then with another tug of the leash, I got down on my knees. The floor was hard — some type of vinyl that was made to look like natural stone.

I lifted my head to shoot a hard glare at Bruiser. I wasn't about to keep my head bowed like some meek submissive.

"Would you like to inspect my baby girl? See how sweet she is?"

Bruiser didn't blink. Not a single muscle of his twitched. His countenance oozed sheer intimidation.

Over the years, I'd perfected the cold and ruthless bitch look, but I didn't think it'd work on a man like this. I poured every internal negative thought into a look of loathing directed at him. There was no way I'd let this beast touch me. I'd bite his hand first. I'd scream my safe word.

Staring hard at him, I dared him to touch me.

I held my breath as I waited for him to answer. Fuck, this was turning me on and I didn't like it. Was this some form of humiliation that Daddy had mentioned I wanted? Was it exhibitionism? Having this man's hands on me while Daddy watched...

My arousal was noticeable. My nipples had hardened. I was sure both men could smell the wetness gathering between my legs.

Daddy chuckled. "Up." He pulled on my chain and I awkwardly stood. He glanced at Bruiser with a faint smile on his lips. "I'll let you know when we're finished."

He pulled me away from the room and I felt relief. Right? Or was that disappointment? Had Daddy just been bluffing about sharing me like that? And when did I start calling him Daddy in my head? Was I so weak as to give in to all of this so easily?

Giving up control was going to be difficult for me. I was still fighting every single little thing that happened internally. I didn't want to enjoy the thought of Bruiser doing anything to my body, but I sure as hell did. What I needed to do was to stop over-analyzing everything. I thrived on always controlling the outcome, but here I'd given up that control. If I could get out of my own head, I just might enjoy it. I might find that nirvana that the lady had intrigued me with.

We entered the large portion of the dungeon that hosted a plethora of kinky furniture and implements. My eyes darted around the room, spying the variety of whips, cuffs, and chains that decorated the gray walls. Padded benches that looked like mutated gym equipment were scattered among a medieval pillory, a steel cage, and even a St. Andrew's cross that took up significant floor space. I spotted a sex swing suspended in one corner and what looked like a handmade wooden gallows of some sort. What was that used for? Damn, I didn't even want to know! I counted at least five black pleather couches and a scattering of bondage chairs and spanking benches.

Daddy led me over to a small nook against the wall that was marked off by what looked like black gymnastic mats on the floor. A section of the wall was padded with the same mats, but wrist and ankle restraints were embedded into these. Daddy turned on a floor lamp that lit up our section of the gloomy room.

He tugged on the leash, pulling me closer to him. He had an amused smirk on his face when he spoke. "You're mad at me, Baby Girl?"

I guess he noticed the fire shooting out of my eyes when I was staring at Bruiser. "No."

"What are you thinking right now? I want the truth."

He wanted the truth? Fine. "I'm thinking that this would be a lot more fun if you were the one in the collar and I was pulling you around by the leash."

He cupped my cheek with his palm. "That would be like every other day for you, wouldn't it? You lead men around by the balls?" He stroked my cheek with his thumb. "And I think you're enjoying everything I'm doing to you so far. Except, you're disappointed Bruiser didn't take me up on my offer."

I made a noise, somewhere between a grunt of annoyance and a growl.

"Spread your legs."

I slid my legs open a bit more. I hadn't broken eye contact with him the entire time, so I didn't even know what he was doing until his finger had already penetrated me. The surprise of it pulled a gasp out of me that I really hadn't wanted to give him.

"I'd say you're enjoying this just fine. You're drenched."

It was undeniable, so I didn't even try. He pulled his finger out and held it up between our faces. It was glistening with my juices.

"Who gets a taste? You or me?"

Was this a trick question? "You."

He brought his finger to my lips. "Open."

This was undeniably hot. I opened my mouth and waited. "Lick my finger clean."

I pulled my lips around his finger and began sucking. I was getting wetter.

His other hand reached up and squeezed my nipple. "I said lick it, not suck, you greedy slut."

Damn. I hated this. I really did. But, I loved it too. I pulled my mouth off his finger so I could lick it. It wasn't quite as hot for me to lick his finger, but him ordering me around and feeling as if I had no choice but to obey was strangely freeing in a way.

After an excruciatingly long minute, he finally pulled his finger away. "Turn around."

When my back was to him, I felt him working on my cuffs. Within seconds, my hands were no longer cuffed together.

"Lay down on the mat on your back. Head toward the wall."

I shrugged my shoulders to loosen them and then did as he ordered. Anticipation rocketed through me.

"What is your safe word?"

"Red."

"Use it if you need to."

He began hooking each of my wrists into a hook at the bottom of the wall behind me until my arms were spread out and over my head. Just the sound of the metal clicking as it locked me into place had me thrumming with anticipation.

"You don't have any injuries that you didn't mention on your questionnaire, do you?"

I shook my head.

"Spread your legs."

I was spread-eagled on the mat, my hands bound to the wall.

"You look beautiful, Baby Girl. Make sure you keep those legs wide open or I'm going to tie them down."

Was that a threat or a promise? I didn't even know anymore. I was panting with need. This was sexy as fuck. I was so turned on.

Closing my eyes, I tried to get my body's reaction under control. Why was I affected so much? Sexually, I'd never been a shy girl. I was never afraid to take what I wanted. I'd even been to a few sex clubs in my life, but those clubs hadn't done all that much for me.

When some of my friends had gone, I'd gone along mainly out of curiosity. I enjoyed watching some activities, and I even participated in some kinky sexploits, but only with some of the friends I went with.

It had been more of a lark, not a serious interest. I thought about the reasons I'd never enjoyed those sex clubs more and it mostly had to do with my slight fear of germs — even the hand sanitizer mounted on every spare foot of wall space and the people discreetly cleaning couldn't erase the ickiness I'd felt in those clubs.

And I hadn't been excited about the people who attended those clubs. They tended to be a bit older and more average looking than I'd expected. It was like a cross-section of people you'd see at the grocery store on any given day. I was looking for someone more attractive. I guess I wasn't as enlightened as Daddy was. In my fantasy, looks mattered.

Bruiser was not someone I'd ever be attracted to, but looks-wise he stirred something in me. Daddy was an attractive man. I definitely didn't mind him dominating me. But would it have killed him to wear a pair of hot leather pants? Maybe take off his shirt so I could see the defined chest I was sure was hiding under there. Maybe I could see his pecs or his tight abs flex as he moved. I wondered if he had any hair on his chest or if he was smooth. Or that yummy treasure trail that ran down the V...

Daddy was tapping on my arm. My eyes flew open.

"Did I lose you there? Answer me," he demanded.

"No."

He knelt down next to me and I saw that he had a cardboard file box in his hands. He set it down next to my head. "This is your toy box. I got you some items that I think you'll enjoy. They are yours to keep. Take them home with you after each session, keep them clean, and bring them all back for playtime."

"Okay."

He crossed his arms over his chest. "The correct response is either 'Yes, Daddy' or 'No, Daddy'. When you orgasm, you say 'Thank you, Daddy'. Got it?"

"Yes, Daddy." I gave myself a mental gold star for not rolling my eyes.

He dug around in the box. "When you're obedient, you get rewards."

"Yes, Daddy."

He glanced over at me, probably to check if I was being sarcastic. I was being all sorts of naughty in my head, but perfectly obedient on the outside.

"Brat," he muttered. He found what he was looking for and then pulled it out of the box. It was a butt plug. Not a huge one, thank goodness.

"Feet together and up in the air."

I did as he asked. My head lulled to the side so I could watch him as he began smearing some lube on my tight hole. His thumb circled it over and over, sometimes gently pressing into it. The next time he pressed into it, I tried to lift my hips and force his finger in, but he slapped my ass cheek instead and continued.

The slow tease was torture. Finally, his finger penetrated me, but it was so shallow. Then he pulled out and went back to massaging me. This repeated over and over until I was aching to be filled. My pussy was throbbing and begging for its own attention.

When my legs began shaking from staying up so long and I wasn't sure I could take it anymore, he finally slid the plug into me.

"Beautiful." He studied my ass for a few seconds and then landed another slap on my other ass cheek this time. His slap had me clenching around the butt plug.

"Legs down and wide apart."

He pulled a small flogger out of the box, and a shiver of anxiety ran down my spine. "How are you doing?"

"Green, Daddy."

He dragged the soft lashes of the flogger over my skin, painting up and down my thighs, skimming across my belly and chest, and running between my legs and upwards over my mound. The sensations raised goosebumps on my skin. It was erotic, but I couldn't fully enjoy it because I didn't know what was coming next.

I was just beginning to relax when he started flicking his wrist rhythmically so that the flogger dusted against my thighs over and over. The sensation wasn't the stinging pain I'd expected. It was a dull thwack that eventually turned into a warmth that spread with each stroke.

He moved to my belly and repeated his actions. The first contact made me flinch, but then I relaxed into the odd sensation. He obviously wasn't using anywhere near full strength, and I wondered if these hits would get harder.

My skin was feeling pleasantly warm, and I was letting down my guard. It was a mistake because suddenly the flogger flicked across my left nipple with a distinct snap.

"Fuck." My wrists pulled against the cuffs and my legs jerked closed. It had stung, but I'd felt a jolt of pleasure right between my legs.

"Open your legs." He'd gone back to slapping my belly in a figure-8 motion with the flogger.

I slid my legs open.

"Do you need to use your safe word?"

"No, Daddy."

The lashes of the flogger whipped across my right nipple. This time, my hips were thrusting up into the air. Fuck, that stung but felt amazing at the same time.

He stopped and put the flogger down. He ran his hands gently over my pinked-up skin and it felt amazing — alive and tingly. "I'm going to give you an orgasm for being such a good girl."

Oh, fuck, yes.

My eyes closed, and I took a few deep breaths. I didn't expect what happened next. I guess I was looking for something more personal in nature, but suddenly I heard a soft buzz, seconds before Daddy held a wand vibrator against my clit and turned up the vibrations to a high speed.

Sure, I'd used vibrators on myself plenty of times, but I'd always been the one in control of them. I'd used them during sex only on occasion because I preferred the man I was having sex with to do that job himself. Since I was already pretty worked up from being restrained and flogged, the stimulus my clit couldn't escape from was incredibly intense, almost to the point of pain.

It didn't take long for me to feel the orgasm coming. It didn't build up leisurely; it powered through me like an F5 tornado, destroying everything in its path.

I was wiggling and bucking to escape the sheer intensity of my climax and my legs were trying to slam closed even though Daddy was holding them down.

"No! Stop, no more!" I was begging for mercy.

He lifted the wand from my clit and pressed it against my right nipple, which had my inner muscles clenching just as violently. "Are you using your safe word?"

Was I? I was trying to think. I wiggled my hips, trying to get relief, but didn't answer.

He switched the vibrator to my other nipple and began stroking between my legs with his other hand. He was rubbing and firmly patting my pussy. It felt so good.

"Baby Girl, are you using your safe word? Tell me."

Fuck. I needed to cum again. My pussy was throbbing, and it needed relief. "No, Daddy."

As soon as I said it, he put the vibrator back on my clit and didn't let up.

This time, he moved the wand around a bit, pressing between my folds and hitting every secret spot. I tried to hold it back, but it wasn't long before he ripped another orgasm from me. I had no choice but to give it to him.

He pulled the wand off me. "You cum so fast, Baby Girl."

I wasn't sure if that was a compliment or an insult. The last time I'd had sex was with Theo, so it'd been a while, plus, I'd never had much trouble having an orgasm before. I silently thanked God when he turned off the vibrator and took a moment to try to control my insane panting, wondering what the hell was coming next. Then I remembered I was supposed to thank him. "Thank you, Daddy."

I think that pleased him because he petted my hair and rubbed my cheek tenderly. Then he leaned over and began releasing my cuffs from the wall anchors.

Were we done? I didn't want to be. In fact, with him leaning over me, I had the strongest urge to pull him down and kiss him. I wanted him to rest his body weight on top of me, kiss me senseless, and then fuck me slowly. Even after I'd just had two shattering orgasms, I was incredibly horny for him.

When my wrists were free, he pulled back from me. "On your hands and knees. Ass in the air for Daddy."

Oh, I guess we weren't done. Was he going to plow into me doggy-style? Not as romantic as I hoped for, but that would work.

I did as he ordered, trying to strike an alluring pose with my back arched gracefully and my ass upturned in the air. Instead of feeling his dick probing me, I felt the sharp, stinging slap of his hand against my ass cheek. Son of a bitch!

After about the third slap — who could keep track — the painful sting started to turn into a spreading warmth with each subsequent thwack, which in turn activated something like a deep longing in my pussy.

When he switched to spanking me with a paddle, the sting was gone and a dull thump landed on my bottom. The sensation switched over to almost pure pleasure, so I embraced it. My arms collapsed to the ground, but I made sure my ass was still ready to be spanked. I didn't want it to stop yet. I was so focused on the tight need suffusing my pussy that I didn't realize Daddy was talking to me until he ran his hand down my back.

I hadn't heard what he asked. Did he ask if I wanted to stop? No! Or did he ask me if I wanted more? Yes, please. So, I did what I did in high-powered meetings or cocktail parties when I was distracted. I would disregard the question I'd missed and just tell him what I wanted.

"Thank you, sir. May I have another?"

Oh shit! Did I just say that? Neither of us spoke or moved for an uncomfortably long pause. I didn't mean to quote Animal House to him; it just slipped out. I wasn't exactly in my right mind at this moment. Was he pissed? Did he think I was mocking him? Because I wasn't. I just wanted more. I needed more.

Finally, he moved away from me, and I took a breath. He began rummaging through the toy box again. I didn't dare look over my shoulder to see what he was pulling out.

He walked over and knelt by my head. He stroked my jaw and then commanded, "Open."

Sucking his cock was to be my punishment, and it gave me a little thrill. I was good at it. I'd do my best to work him up—

He slid something into my mouth. "Put the ring behind your teeth."

Fuck. He was gagging me. He pulled the strap around my head and secured it. My mouth was forced to remain in an open position around the silicone ring.

He opened his hand up, and resting in his palm were four marbles. "Put these in your right hand. You drop these if you need to use your safe word. Do you understand?"

I nodded.

"On your back, hands by the wall." His voice was curt and rough as if he was disappointed in me.

I didn't move a muscle while he clipped my wrist cuffs back into the wall hook. I slid my legs apart and waited.

He stood up and looked down at me as if deep in thought. I closed my eyes and waited.

His warm hands were on my breasts. Massaging. It felt good. Then, he was playing with my nipples, pinching them, tugging at them.

"These are adjustable nipple clamps. I'm not going to tighten them that much. Drop the marbles if you need to."

I took another deep breath. Fuck, I wasn't sure if I'd like nipple clamps. I'd never used them before because I always thought my nipples were really sensitive. Why didn't I mark them as a hard limit on the questionnaire?

I didn't have too much time to think about it because Daddy was already squeezing my right nipple into a clamp. There was no doubt that it made my nipple sore, but I also felt an answering excitement between my legs.

He made quick work of clamping both nipples and then tightening the first one slightly. Before I could even ponder the ache deep in my pussy, he had the wand vibrator on my clit again.

Fuck, I wanted to be filled. I was throbbing for it. It was almost torture to be so stimulated and to be denied this whole time. I felt empty.

The wand moved to the butt plug, sending vibrations deep inside me. I was starting to wiggle again, but Daddy was keeping a firm grasp on my legs. The wand moved from my plug up to the clamp on my right nipple. My hips thrust forward. Then it moved to my left nipple while Daddy's other hand was massaging my pussy.

I moaned with need, with frustration, feeling some drool slip down my cheek. Daddy gave my pussy a small tap with his hand.

A shot of pleasure ricocheted through me. I moaned again.

The vibrator moved back to my butt plug and then I felt a sharper slap against my pussy. My eyes flew open. It was not his hand. He tapped me three times quickly on the pussy with a crop that was shaped like a miniature fly swatter.

The vibrator centered on my clit again. Then my nipples. A hand rubbed my pussy. Tap, tap, tap of the crop on my pussy. My eyes rolled back in my head and I groaned, a drawn-out and desperate sound.

This time, I could feel my orgasm building. If he touched just the tip of his finger inside me, I was sure I'd explode. Instead, he stuck his finger inside my mouth.

The minute he strapped that gag on me, I'd really felt fully out of control. Speaking had been my last line of defense. But now I was restrained. Gagged. Naked. And his finger was working inside my mouth, pressing against my tongue, pushing back too far for comfort and remaining there. I tried to turn my head, but that only triggered my gag reflex. When I stopped gagging, he slid his finger right to the back of my mouth again. There was no escape from it.

At this point, my eyes were watering, and I was a drool factory. The vibrator was rolling over my nipples again. And then, tap, tap, tap on my pussy with the crop.

I was starting to drift.

Vibrator on my butt plug. The finger moving in my mouth. Vibrator on my clit. Fingers massaging my clit.

Nipple clamps being released. Oh, my God. The sensation was explosive.

Tap, tap, tap on my pussy.

The orgasm was indescribable. I saw stars. detonated. And, apparently, dropped all the marbles because everything stopped even though my body was still writhing and moaning in ecstasy.

He leaned over me to unhook my cuffs and then slid my wrists out of them for me since I wasn't quite capable yet. Then he undid my gag and wiped the drool from my face.

"Good girl."

My response was almost automatic. "Thank you, Daddy."

He was looking deep into my eyes, probably trying to assess my condition, but I was feeling the stirrings of other things. "Will you kiss me, Daddy?"

"You take what I give you, Baby Girl." And then he was picking me up off the ground and carrying me across the room.

We ended up in a small bedroom. He placed me on the bed and I really didn't have much energy to do anything, let alone check out my surroundings. He handed me an open water bottle that he'd gotten from somewhere in the corner of the room and ordered me to drink.

I took a few sips as he stripped off his shirt. I only had a few seconds to catalog what he looked like shirtless before he climbed onto the bed and slid in behind me, pulling me close to his body and spooning me.

My body was visibly shaking now. He pulled a light sheet over us and began running his hands gently over my skin.

"Talk to me, Baby Girl. Tell me exactly what's on your mind."

I closed my eyes and tried to relax. "Oh, so now you want to hear me talk?"

He chuckled. "Yes. It's important for me to know how you felt about everything. Tell me. What did you like? What did you not like?"

"Um, let's see. I loved all of it, but I hated all of it, too."

His hands were rubbing my shoulders, and it felt comforting. "I could tell, but I need you to be more specific."

I didn't want to talk. Instead, I wanted to enjoy having his hands on me. I wanted to enjoy being close to him. "Is this the aftercare bullshit? Where you have to analyze every last little thing? Because I don't want to."

His hand stopped moving for a second and then continued. "It isn't bullshit. It's very important, and it's actually one of my favorite parts. I feel so close to my subs after a great scene."

"Do you feel close to me?" I asked.

His fingertips trailed across my belly. "Yes. You shared a piece of yourself with me. I had a lot of fun and I want to do more. I want to show you more. Do you feel closer to me?"

"I'm not sure." Yeah, I did, but my protective defenses were up.

"Ouch."

I rushed into an explanation, even though I doubted he really could feel hurt. "My natural instinct is to go against everything you tell me."

"I know, Baby Girl. That's why, when you don't — when you give in — it makes me so proud. You're doing it for me and for yourself. For our relationship to grow."

The experience had been amazing, but I didn't necessarily feel like my soul was freed. I bit my lip. "I came here because this lady I met told me about a crazy state of mind she got from doing this. She called it nirvana. I don't think I felt it today."

He turned my head so that we were looking at each other eye to eye. "Subspace? Baby Girl, you're not going to get there until you truly submit. Not pretend to submit. There's a huge difference. You're not there yet, and that's okay. It's going to take a lot more trust to be built up. Then, I can take you there. We're going to take it nice and slow. You did great today."

"Okay." He was bringing out some feelings in me. I was more afraid of this side of the man than the dominating one. He was tender and snuggly. I really wanted to kiss him, but I was afraid of being rejected once again.

He rubbed my lip with his thumb. "We have plenty of time to get you to nirvana."

"Did you feel nirvana?" Why was the dumbest stuff popping out of my mouth?

"It felt really good, Baby Girl."

I couldn't hide my skepticism. "Please, I didn't even touch you."

"I have a request for you to do something right now that would make me feel really good. Maybe even nirvana." He had a devilish smile on his face.

"What's that?" I couldn't help but smile.

"I want you to warm my cock."

What now? Not what I was expecting. Was his cock cold? Did he want me to rub it briskly? Why not just ask for a hand job? So many questions...

"I want my cock inside you, Baby Girl."

"You want to have sex?"

"No, I want to relax with my cock inside you. Will you let me?"

"Um, okay." Wasn't that called sex?

"Don't move." He got up off the bed and of course, I moved. I wanted to see him. He pulled off his pants, and I finally got to see his whole body. It was magnificent. He was toned and muscled. I noticed a nipple piercing I hadn't before and a few tattoos on his chest. His cock looked pretty average size-wise. But, then, when he squeezed some lube from his hand onto his cock and pumped it a few times, it got bigger.

He slid back into the bed behind me, using his fingers to apply some lube to my pussy. I'd been silently begging to be penetrated for the entire play session, so now that his finger had casually entered me, my pussy flared back to life.

He adjusted my leg and then slid his cock into me from behind. I bit back a moan. It felt like heaven.

Then he curled up behind me, lightly running his fingers through my hair. And, did ... nothing. He didn't move. He didn't thrust into me, despite the fact that I was like a live wire, ready to be tripped.

The need was growing in me with every passing second. My ass pressed backward. No response. My hips wiggled.

"Shh. Just relax, Baby Girl." His warm breath near my ear caused a shiver to run down my spine.

My inner muscles clenched. That got a grunt, so I did it again. His arms tightened around me. I pushed my ass back against him.

"Stop wiggling." He locked his legs around mine, laying half on top of me. I tried to break free of his grasp, but he was strong. He'd essentially locked me into position.

"Just relax."

I bit back an angry retort. So, he wasn't going to fuck me? He was actually just going to lay there with his dick inside me? And do nothing?

I was pissed. This was so unsatisfying. The opposite of relaxing. I tried to move again, but he easily contained me. I felt like I was a wrestler caught in a hold and pinned into submission. Instead of tapping out, eventually, I just gave up. I had no energy left to fight it. I was done. Slowly his muscles began to relax too, but he still stayed wrapped tightly around me.

Once I got past the sexual aspect, our position was strangely intimate and relaxing. Almost cozy. My mind began drifting. I thought about our session together and the intense feelings it brought out.

When I'd been in the midst of it all, I hadn't been able to fully let go. I'd still been analyzing everything that was happening — what he did well, what things he could do that I'd like better, and even how it compared to other experiences. And, I'd always been wondering if my acquiescence had meant that I'd submitted fully to him.

I knew I hadn't let go of my full control and maybe I could do that with more trust. Over time, like Daddy had said. I really felt like I'd turned over my body to him, but not my mind or spirit. What would it be like if I submitted it all? Was that the key to finding my nirvana?

I was drifting into a peaceful, blissful space. I felt safe and protected.

Chapter 7

Bash

As soon as I hit the stage, the massive crowd roared to life. They had been screaming and stomping for us to come back out for an encore for the past ten minutes. We usually didn't keep them waiting that long, but we all needed to recharge so we could give it our all for the last two songs.

I climbed up the riser and sat behind my drum kit, then kept my left foot light on the hi-hat pedal while I crashed my drumstick against the cymbals. The insanity level of the crowd climbed higher. There was always that bit of doubt when a band left the stage that the show was truly over, but that one explosive sound was all the confirmation they needed that there was more to come.

The other guys began entering the stage and the shrieking in the stadium grew deafening. Sid crossed the stage first, followed closely by Ryder. As usual, they stood in front of me and to my right. Sid wasn't as expressive when he played bass, but he and Ryder usually found a groove together and played off each other well. Ghost positioned himself front and center and Knox moved into place, stage left. Knox was more of a showman and moved around the stage, but he wouldn't go far for the next two songs. A lot of pyrotechnics were about to go off.

Another roar from the crowd rolled over the stage when a spotlight suddenly illuminated Ghost. He began speaking to the crowd, amping them up, but I wasn't really listening to what he was saying.

I was trying to absorb the moment. With only the single spotlight lighting the stage, I could see out into the writhing audience. We were at MetLife Stadium in New Jersey, in front of the largest audience we'd ever played for – at least as the headline act. Years ago, we'd been one of many bands at a festival in Europe where the crowds had been monstrously huge, but tonight, all these people were here to see us.

We were in the middle of a mini-tour, almost all stadium shows, but all the venues were where only top-selling bands could perform. We'd just played in Boston and then at Madison Square Garden, and soon we'd be off to Philly and Baltimore before I could go home for a short break.

We were at the peak of our careers. Sure, it was possible we could hang around for years to come selling out stadiums, but that kind of magic only happened with a handful of mega-bands. Most likely, by next year, we'd be riding the downward slope of that bell curve of our band's popularity.

Even with the most talented and stable bands in the world, change was inevitable. Band members got older, and being on the road got harder when away from loved ones. We'd already made modifications to our tours to reflect our changing needs, and our record label was bending over backward to keep us happy exactly because we were at the peak. The changes all started with me having Kody and trying to prioritize him without giving up my passion for music and performing, but now, in one way or the other, my bandmates were all in the same boat. I wasn't the only one with a kid now, which was great because our tour schedule wasn't as brutal. Change happened. Who knew what the future would bring? Maybe I wouldn't be in the band anymore after this tour?

I chuckled to myself. Here we were at the very top and I was already mourning the loss of it. Was I depressed about it? Scared? Resigned? Or was I oddly okay with it? Performing in front of a crowd like this was the greatest high in the world, but here I was looking out at the massive, cheering crowd and thinking about Kody.

I missed him. I didn't like being away from him for so long, but he seemed fine with my parents. Even though my parents recently moved to California to be closer to their grandchildren, I asked them to move into my house while I was on tour so that Kody would suffer the least disruption to his schedule.

Kody had preschool classes three days a week, and he also had his swim lessons and the kiddie gymnastic classes where he tumbled on mats like a crazed nut for an hour. He was too old to drag around on a tour without getting bored and antsy. I'd had a video call with him right after our sound check, where he excitedly told me all about the trampoline they'd just been allowed to try at the gym. Two more shows after tonight and then I could go back and see him for a few days.

Ghost stopped talking to the crowd and looked back at me. That was my cue. I beat my sticks to count the band off and then I was immersed in drumming while we played an older Ghost Parker song that was a big hit with our fans.

I was tired, but it was my job to keep a consistent beat and set the overall energy level, so I dug deep. Feeding off the energy of the crowd,

I added some rolls and fills to break up any monotony.

The giant screen behind me that was projecting images to the crowd was casting a mix of lights and shadows all over my drum kit. Strobe lights and a giant puff of smoke that was released from above the stage added to the choreographed chaos. Sometimes I missed the simplicity of playing in a small venue without all the bells and whistles. I liked seeing individual faces in the audience, not just a mass of thrashing humanity.

The song was coming to an end. I transitioned with a six-stroke roll, moved from the toms to the snares, punctuating my strokes, then slammed down on the crash cymbals to signal the ending.

Instantaneously, I cued our last song, as I didn't want the buildup of energy to wane even a fraction. As soon as Knox played the opening riff, the crowd went crazy. They knew we weren't going to leave without playing it. We've played it in the encore for every show, sometimes first but usually as the last song of the night.

There was no question that *Okay Babe* was our most popular song by huge magnitudes. Except for Sid, we all grumbled about having to play it — Ghost grumbling the most — even though we owed so damn much to that song. We all got writing credits on it, even though Sidney did most of the work. Just that one song alone had made me enough money that I could retire at the age of 31 and never work again, but what the hell would I do if I didn't have the band?

I shook off my distraction and focused on the song, accenting certain beats to help lock in and shape the energy around the song, making sure not to overshadow Ghost's vocals. When the crowd began to sing along with the lyrics, Ghost held out his microphone to encourage them. Sid always chimed in on the chorus for this song, and with Ryder's voice added to his in front of the shared mic, they sounded pretty good.

HOW TO MARRY A ROCKSTAR

I blocked out the words and focused on the pulse and rhythm of the song. The other guys complained about it because it was a catchy and upbeat pop song that didn't fit our harder style. I hated it because it was about my sister, Kaylie, and anyone who followed the band knew that, too. When Sid and Kay got married, that cat was out of the bag.

The sexual innuendo in the lyrics was unmistakable. I still cringed every time I heard it and even had to endure a few people in the media asking me how it felt to sing those lyrics about my sister.

Sidney had been my best friend for more than a decade and now he was my brother, too. Sid and Kaylie were happily married and had brand new baby boys, my twin nephews, so I should be over being squeamish about it, but hearing those words still pissed me off. Fucking Sidney. Someday I'd get him back.

Ghost was doing a back-and-forth with the crowd, but the five columns of sparks that blasted up behind me reminded me to move the show along. I had about two minutes to be at the end of the song if I wanted to have the final note coincide with the spark column going dark.

A shallow pool of white smoke had been pumped across the stage, creating a surreal cloud-like effect that was lit from underneath. Beams and streaks of light from the lasers caught in the swaths of smoke that hung in the air above the stage. To round off the pyrotechnics, waterfall sparks and a few starbursts were exploding from the trusses.

Ghost finished singing, and I began my wind down, keeping a careful eye on the cold spark machines. I closed the song with a frenzied crescendo of drumming, adding in a few stick tricks to make it look sick before the final note crashed through the stadium.

I tossed my drumsticks out to the screaming mob and headed off stage while Ghost was calling out thanks to the crowd and saying our goodnights. Drenched in sweat, I verified that it was too late to call

Kody and say goodnight, even with the time difference between here and California, before I hit the shower.

I took my time, so it was at least 30 minutes later when I made my appearance in the already packed room. I grabbed a bite of food from the catering table and then looked around.

We'd done some press and hosted a meet and greet with fans before the show, so now the only VIPs in attendance were bigwigs that our label, BVR, wanted us to meet, and Donovan seemed to be managing that. Now the room was slowly filling with excited girls, probably over half of whom I'd given out backstage passes to since the other guys weren't really handing them out as much anymore.

I was the only single guy left in my band and since Sid rarely stayed out late anymore, I'd invited my friend, Noah, a guitarist in a younger band we'd played with before to come to our shows and hang out while we were in New York City.

I spotted Noah with his tongue down some girl's throat. His hand was slipping up her ridiculously short dress, exposing her ass to everyone. I thought it would be fun partying with Noah, but the last few nights had worn me out. He was only four years younger than me, but when you had responsibilities like I did — a kid and a house — the difference was enormous. I couldn't keep up with his drinking, the partying, and the non-stop women. Plus, I was throwing all my energy into performing while he didn't have to. Last night, I'd left him at 4 o'clock in the morning, pretending I was about to go have freaky sex, just so I could call it a night. Before Kody, I would have called myself a pussy for doing that.

I almost didn't want to go out at all tonight. I'd rather go back to the hotel and get some sleep. Hoping I'd get a second wind, I grabbed a beer and then sat down in the back of the room, away from the bar. I just needed to decompress, trying to come down from the adrenaline

HOW TO MARRY A ROCKSTAR

high of the show.

Within minutes, a blonde girl in a tight tank top and mini-skirt sat on my lap. I grabbed her hips and then repositioned her more comfortably against me. She said something and then repeated whatever it was when I didn't respond.

"Just give me a minute, honey."

She giggled but thankfully remained quiet.

I'd almost finished my beer when Sid walked over with a new one and sat down on the couch beside me. He handed me the beer. "Fucking awesome show tonight."

I grunted in agreement. I gave the blonde my empty bottle and then took a sip of the new one. "You going out tonight?"

He rubbed his chest. "Nah, I'm going to head back to the hotel and call Kaylie before she goes to sleep."

"How are Brady and Emerson doing?"

"Fuck, I miss them, man." He ran a hand through his hair. "Did you know that Kaylie's staying at your house with the twins?"

"No." I shrugged. "What for?"

He took a swig of his beer. "Even though she has the nanny to help with the boys, she was struggling a bit. And feeling lonely. So, she brought the twins and the nanny to stay with your parents, at your house, until we get back. Lacey is staying out there for a few days, too. They're having a girl party or some shit. Playing with the kids and swimming and doing pedicure stuff — that's all I know."

The girl in my lap started wiggling around and pretending she wasn't trying to press her ass into my cock.

"Lacey's there? I didn't think she'd be into hanging around so many babies."

I was surprised Lacey was at my house, even though she was Kaylie's best friend. They struck up a friendship after Kaylie had been assaulted and became the target of revenge porn by her ex-boyfriend. Lacey had helped Kay through it all, and they'd become very close. I often wondered if that was weird for Sid since he'd had sex with Lacey, even if it was well before he'd gotten together with Kaylie. But even though we were like brothers and shared everything in the past including women, Lacey was the one thing I could never stomach asking him about.

Sid shrugged. "Kaylie says she's great with them."

The girl on my lap started sliding off me. Poor thing. She was probably getting bored.

She slid down to the floor between my legs.

Oh, she was going to suck my cock.

My cock was already semi-hard from all her wiggling on my lap, but once she pulled it free from my pants, she wasted no time getting it rock hard.

I looked around the room while she started bobbing on my cock and noticed all the young girls, showing plenty of skin, queuing up to be the next one in line. They were practically salivating at the opportunity.

I sighed. "Fuck, when did all the girls start looking so young?"

Sid crossed his leg over his knee. "You know CC checks their IDs. They're all at least drinking age."

"Or they have fake IDs." I pointed over to a skinny brunette who looked no more than 14 years old. "That girl can't be 21."

And now that I'd pointed, I'd caught the brunette's attention. She was watching the blowjob with wide eyes. Fuck. This kind of shit never bothered me before, but this didn't feel right.

Maybe being a dad changed me, or maybe I was just getting older. These girls just seemed so young, and they were offering themselves up so casually. It bothered me, especially since I was the one that invited a lot of them into this debauched scene.

"Fuck." I pulled on the girl's hair until her mouth popped off my dick. "Thanks, honey. We're done here."

Sid chuckled at the confused look on her face. I ignored her and began to tuck my hard dick back into my pants; it was no easy feat.

She looked over at Sid and smiled. "Your turn?"

His eyebrows rose. "No thanks. I'm good."

"Fuck." I repeated when she flounced off.

My cock was not happy. I might be more discriminating with my choice of women, but I still had needs. I didn't turn into a monk just because I was a dad.

Sid gave me the side-eye as I shifted in my seat, trying to get comfortable despite the steel rod in my pants. "Christ, they're circling. The crew's still working on load-out. There's not enough available cock in here."

I looked up. He was right. Why did I give out so many backstage passes? I spotted Noah being worked over on a couch in the middle of the room by at least two girls. Maybe three, but I couldn't quite see because I was suddenly blocked by a woman with jet-black hair, wearing a black leather bustier. She was heading my way with a few girls on her tail.

She licked her lips. I felt like a fresh piece of meat that had just been dangled into a tank filled with barracuda.

"Fuck," I muttered again.

Sid patted me on the arm and then stood. "I'll leave you to it."

Chapter 8

Lacey

This was the twelfth time I was entering this building over the course of four months. Usually, I passed through this door brimming with heady anticipation, but this time I entered with a sense of dread. I handed over my phone to Mistress Xenna and made my way to the Blue room to await my Daddy Dom.

Just thinking about him had my stomach twisted in knots. He'd come to mean so much to me. Too much. Not only had he given me a thorough education in kink, but he unveiled aspects of myself that I'd only barely glimpsed before.

The sexual pleasures he'd given me were plentiful: too many orgasms to count and the resultant cocktail of feel-good hormones I'd never experienced before. The mental release was even better. Playtime was an escape from life and all its demands and responsibilities. Stress melted away. It was an incredibly addictive emotional high.

The first time Daddy Dom led me down the stairs to the dungeon, I hadn't trusted him. I fought against giving up my will every step of the way. But he was a perceptive, experienced, and patient instructor. The things we'd done together absolutely required that trust. He meticulously earned it.

When we first started out, I had been giddy with these new possibilities and I wanted to try it all. I felt like I had this great big, wonderful secret and I wanted to experience it to its fullest extent, but Daddy Dom introduced me to new things at such a glacial speed, I'd been frustrated. I thought he was holding me back, but I now realized he was protecting me. That was the first building block of trust that was established.

The frenzy of the honeymoon period eventually wore off. Then I got to know my individual kinks even better. Daddy was a master at teasing out the things I didn't even know I loved. He was able to satisfy a need I burned for and then offered the intimacy that I craved in aftercare.

Between the cuddling and talking, the petting and care, I felt loved. He was very skilled at it. The first time I'd met him, he'd told me that he loved all his subs and I didn't quite believe him. But now, I'd experienced his love.

Our relationship had grown even further. I trusted him. I knew that he would never physically hurt me and he'd do his best to give me everything I wanted. He wasn't playing any mind games as I'd first believed. He loved me. And I loved him — maybe not in the traditional sense, but in the same way that he loved me. Like he loved all his subs.

From the moment he'd read my questionnaire, he'd sussed out that I wanted a more sensual experience and he tried to provide that. It was strange because I always questioned whether he was acting a certain way to give me what I needed. Was that his authentic self? Those tiny doubts were a stumbling block in our relationship and ate away at me like acid.

Several times, in aftercare, I had such an incredible and overwhelming urge to kiss him. He was always so sweet and tender, making me feel cherished. As desperately as I wanted him to, he never kissed me. Not once. And, after that first day, I'd never asked him to again.

As close as we'd become, we'd never had sex — at least not by my definition of it. All my orgasms were pulled from me with toys or by extreme stimulation from kink play, never by his fingers, tongue, or cock. And I'd never seen him cum. Even when I sucked his cock on his command, he never let me finish. He never put his mouth on me in a sexual way and he never put his dick inside of me except to warm his cock.

It made me think that he saved that kind of love for someone else. It was a real wake-up call.

Maybe I was too selfish, but I wanted more. I craved more. I wanted to find a life partner, not someone who satisfied me within these four walls, but someone I could share my hopes and dreams with. There was so much to do in the world; I wanted to go to the movies with him — go to dinner or parties with friends, hit the beach, go on vacations overseas or to concerts in crazy clubs, watch Netflix and chill, or visit my cousin's house. I wanted to share my entire life with someone.

During aftercare, I was sometimes chatty. I'd shared some private details about my life, my job, my friends, and my family with him, but he never reciprocated. He listened intently, almost like a therapist would, but offered nothing of himself. In reality, I knew next to nothing about him. Did he have another job outside of being a Dom? Did he have other relationships besides those with his submissives? Was he married? Did he have kids? I had no clue. I didn't even know his name.

So, I'd come to trust him implicitly with my physical well-being, but I couldn't fully invest in an emotional relationship with him. I was still probably overthinking everything. The hamster wheel in my brain was always spinning. The only time it ever stopped was during playtime and sometimes aftercare. As soon as I left the building with the secret sex dungeon, the wheel started up again.

Even as a tiny seed of doubt was growing within, outside of our sessions, I started to think about Daddy constantly. Obsessing about him was slowly overtaking my days. He was becoming more important than work, friends, and my own needs, goals, and desires outside of the bedroom. I craved his affection. I craved his praise. When we were together, I'd do anything to please him. At this point, I was flexible putty in his hands.

It wasn't how I thought this would all work out, and it frightened me. For my own sanity, I needed to leave. I was getting in way too deep emotionally, and I knew I had to cut loose before I got hurt.

I refused to lose sight of myself. I wanted to be the center of someone's universe. Someone who loved me and only me. I wanted someone to share my life with, get married, and create a beautiful family together. I wanted that so much more than I wanted handcuffs and spankings.

My mind was spinning. I was so deep in thought that I didn't hear the door open.

"Why are you still dressed?"

I turned around, and I felt the first pang of my determination crumbling. "I wanted to talk."

He crossed his arms over his chest. "About?"

He wasn't pleased, and that automatically had my heart thumping with agitation. I didn't like to displease him. "After the last few sessions, I didn't feel that good about everything. About us."

He frowned. "We talked about that, Baby Girl. I explained it to you. That's sub-drop."

Hearing him call me, Baby Girl gouged out a piece of my heart. I knew he cared for me in his own way, but it wasn't enough. That was why this was going to be so hard. No part of me wanted to walk away, but I'd determined it was necessary. My self-preservation was instinctual and real truths had to be faced.

"I'm talking about something else. Not sub-drop. I'm talking about long-term emotions. You've been an amazing teacher, but I've realized that I need something different. Something more."

"I'll give you the moon, Baby Girl. Just tell me what it is you want." He looked so earnest when he said it; it tore another crack in my heart.

"Being loved is not enough. I need 100% from a partner. I need to own it all. Every fiber of their being. Every thought. Every breath. I need it 24/7 and I won't share with anyone." I felt my eyes brimming with tears as watched his face.

His chest heaved with a sigh. I didn't think he understood me completely. Even if I could have articulated it perfectly, he wasn't made the same way. He might not have understood what I was feeling, but he absorbed everything I said and knew we were over.

Resignation dawned in his eyes. "You can contact me anytime through the app. I'll always be here for you, Baby Girl. Sometimes, daddies have to let their baby girls go."

Fuck, this felt like a real breakup. It hurt. Deep. Tears spilled from my eyes and then he was wrapping me in his comforting arms.

He didn't fight for me; I hadn't expected him to. It only confirmed I was making the right decision. If he had dropped it all for me, I would have stayed with him, but that was never going to happen. He was just losing a client while my whole world felt like it was imploding. That wasn't entirely fair, but I wasn't feeling very magnanimous at the moment.

It felt like I'd been knocked down and dragged through not only mud, but through shards of glass, then impaled on a cactus, and put through a meat grinder. But I'd get back up again. It was smart of me to end it now before I got in any deeper.

I'd be back to square one — which was nowhere — on the relationship front, but who cared? I wasn't one to sit around and wait for life to happen to me; I took what I wanted. This BDSM experiment had sidetracked me so that I never pursued the fertility avenue.

Having a baby wasn't a simple decision, but one that I should think about now that I wasn't distracted by my Daddy Dom. My biological clock was still ticking away; I wasn't getting any younger. All of this love and need I had could be put into a baby. I could do it by myself. If my career had to take a backseat — hell, if I had to give it up — so be it.

I pulled out of Daddy's arms. "Thank you for understanding."

His arms dropped to his sides, and he smiled sadly. "You're still chasing nirvana?"

"I guess I am."

He studied me for a long moment, caressing me with his eyes. "I release you."

Huh? I thought I was releasing him.

I tilted my head playfully. "I release you." Giving him a wink, I walked out the door.

I heard him chuckle as I headed for the exit.

Chapter 9

Bash

THERE'S A PROPER WAY to drink absinthe. Most connoisseurs diluted it by dripping cold water over a sugar cube directly into the distilled spirit using specialty spoons and glasses. Drinking it straight was discouraged because it was brutally strong, tasted like fire with a dash of herbs, and the high alcohol content could fuck you up quickly.

Last year, for Sid's 30th birthday, I'd gotten him fancy absinthe glasses, a set of slotted absinthe spoons, and an absinthe fountain in brushed steel to add some sophistication to our annual birthday ritual. It really did taste a hell of a lot better when it was prepared right.

The tradition started the day Sid turned 20. Our old band, Downward Spiral, was playing a gig that night, and none of us had a lot of extra money to spend on going out to celebrate. Somehow Curtis had a mostly full bottle of absinthe and we ended up passing it around that night until it was empty. It turned into an epic night of drunken hilarity and pandemonium, at least the parts we could remember.

Since that night 11 years ago, Sid and I never missed toasting his birthday with a shot of absinthe and I wasn't about to break tradition tonight. I had a flask tucked into my inside jacket pocket with enough absinthe in it to fell an elephant.

A small group of us were in Vegas to celebrate Sid's birthday. The girls arrived on Thursday to make it a long weekend. They'd done the girl stuff: spas, shopping, pool cabanas, shows on the strip, and whatever else they got up to. Most of the guys got in yesterday, but I didn't get here until this morning. I didn't want to leave Kody for too long.

The band only had two guys from Vector Security with us because we decided we wouldn't leave the hotel. Ghost had been getting some attention in the hotel, but when Greyson Durant got here, it was ten times worse. Luckily, the security at The Venetian was able to work with our guys to keep us from being constantly disturbed.

My bandmates — Ghost, Knox, Ryder, and Sid — along with our manager, Donovan, and Greyson met up in a swanky cocktail bar while we waited for the girls to primp for the evening and join us.

We could hear them before we could see them as they'd been sucking down cocktails all day long. Ryder's wife, Talia, led the pack with her old roommate from Ohio, Ellie, by her side. My sister followed with her friend, Lacey, on one side, and Summer, Knox's girl, on the other. I could tell that Kaylie was already tipsy. She'd always been a lightweight, but between her pregnancy and caring for two baby boys, she hadn't been out partying in a long time. I thought about telling her to slow down a bit, but that was Sid's job now. Remi, the third person in the Remi-Ghost-Grey triad, followed behind the pack of girls along with Summer's friend who lived here in Las Vegas.

We moved our loud party of 14 from the cocktail bar to the restaurant and a couple of hours later headed to the nightclub where we had bottle service at a premium private table set on a raised dais that was cordoned off with velvet ropes and just off the dance floor. The place was packed, and I was grateful we didn't have to get our drinks from one of the three bars. We'd already collected plenty of champagne bottles, two bottles of different flavored vodka, a bottle of tequila, and a bottle of Johnny Walker Black — and that was just what I could see on my side of the table.

We were there for over an hour before I had a chance to talk to Sid. Kaylie was on the dance floor with some of the girls, including Lacey, who was watching over her, per Sid's request. I knew Kay wouldn't last much longer, so I plunked down in the seat next to Sid.

Leaning close so he could hear me, I shouted, "I've got something for you in my pocket."

Whoa, that didn't sound right, but I'd put away a decent number of drinks myself already.

Sid growled. "I've seen your dick, and I'm not interested."

I frowned at his dumb joke. "I'm talking about the Green Fairy."

"Is that what you're calling your dick nowadays?"

"Go fuck yourself." My words were harsh, but they lacked any bite. He knew I was kidding.

I pulled out the flask, keeping it low and under the table. Even though we'd already dropped thousands of dollars here, I didn't want to get us kicked out of the damn club for sneaking in my own liquor. "It's not your birthday without it, brother."

"Fuck." Sid grimaced. "Kaylie's wasted. I can't drink anymore. I've got to take care of her."

"One shot. You have to or else it's seven years of bad luck."

"That's bullshit." Sid grinned. "But, I gotta do it. We doing a straight shot like the old days?"

I felt my pockets, pretending to look for something. "Yep. Forgot to bring the fountain."

We both drained the last bit of alcohol from our glasses. Sid lowered his empty glass under the table. "Give me a light pour."

"Pussy." I unscrewed the cap from the flask and then poured a shot into both of our glasses before returning the flask back to my jacket.

We clinked our glasses together. "To another year. Happy birthday. Cheers, brother."

He glanced out at the dance floor. "I'm a lucky bastard."

"Yeah, you are." I tossed the drink back and swallowed in one gulp. For a split second, I tasted the strong anise flavor and was tricked into thinking that the shot wasn't as bad as I remembered. Very quickly, the burn started. I suppressed a cough, and it felt like fire was shooting out of my nostrils. Then the burn traveled all the way down my throat and into my stomach. It took close to a minute before I could talk again.

Sid shook his head. "Fuck, that went down harsh."

I was much looser after that shot. I even went out to dance with the girls, dirty dancing a bit with Ellie, even though Donovan had been sniffing around her all night.

It was about an hour later when Sid dragged Kaylie back to their room. With the birthday boy gone, it wasn't long after when Summer's friend left, and then Summer and Knox quickly disappeared.

I made myself another drink and then sat back to relax a bit. The DJ was spinning non-stop electronic dance music made with stacking drum samples and drum machines. I'd been counting beats in my head all night and it was getting repetitive and frustrating. It was like an annoying earworm that wasn't just in my head, so there was no way to ditch it. It wouldn't go away until it felt like the synthetic beats were actually burrowing under my skin.

I was faintly surprised when Ghost got up from his seat and came around the table to sit next to me. I'd do anything for the guy — he was my brother — but we didn't talk much. So yeah, I noticed when he went out of his way to talk to me.

"How's it going, Bash?"

I threw back the rest of my drink. "I know you like this music, but it's starting to fuck with my head."

Ghost laughed. He actually laughed. I was stunned for a moment. Getting together with Remi and Grey had changed him. He was way happier. Thank God that didn't mess up his performance ability because he was still a rock god on stage. Somehow, I'd taken on the grumpy role in the band when I'd always been such a laid-back partier.

He turned toward me. "How's everything going with you?"

I gave him a quick rundown of my life and about Kody. Somehow, I started talking about my worries about balancing Kody with drumming for and touring with Ghost Parker. The alcohol was flowing through my veins and he was actually listening to me, so unguarded shit was coming out.

"Let's set up a band meeting with Donovan when we get back. As a band, we've grown and we all have different needs now, but we can make this all work for us the way we need to. We've got tons of fucking leverage now; we just have to apply it." He slapped my shoulder. "We'll figure it out, man. We're not going to lose you, Bash."

I nodded. It felt good to hear him say that. So fucking good.

"How are you doing?" I gave him a sly smile. "How's the never-ending threesome working out?"

"Good."

I shot a look across the table at Grey. Remi was by his side, but she was talking with Lacey. Grey was watching us. "How about outside of the bedroom? It's got to be tricky."

"You sound jealous. You should try it."

"Nah." I shook my head.

His finger tapped the edge of his glass. "Do you miss your sandwich moves with Sid?"

Sid and I used to come at a woman from both sides, usually quite drunkenly when we were interested in some three-way action. Somewhere along the line, our bandmates started calling it the sandwich move.

"Fuck, no. He's with Kay now. I can't even think about sex and Sid in the same sentence anymore." I thought about what I just said and then amended —"Not that we ever crossed swords. There was always a female between us."

Fuck, my tongue was loose. Hopefully, I hadn't offended him. "Not that there'd be anything wrong with that. If that was your thing."

He took a long drink, watching me like he was deciding what to say. "My relationship isn't just about sex. There are deeper feelings. Between all of us. It's just an added bonus that the sex is great."

I wasn't quite sure how that all worked, and I wasn't even sure I wanted to know. "You seem happy."

"I am, in a way I never thought possible. The past was really weighing me down, but I've let that shit go."

Having your dirty laundry aired to the entire world was freeing, I guess. I'm not sure I could overcome all that he did.

"You trust them both?"

"Yeah." He glanced over at Grey and Remi. "Now, the only fights I have are with Grey. We constantly rumble for dominance, but I always win."

"What?" I was skeptical. "Grey is big and fit. Are you sure you always win? Or is he just letting you win?"

He laughed again. Hearing the sound and seeing him look so peaceful and content was like taking a shot of pure joy.

"Is he watching us now?"

Ghost's back was to Grey, but I just had to turn slightly and I could see him. "Yes."

"I can feel him watching. He doesn't like me talking to you." Ghost put his hand in my hair and ruffled it.

Startled, I asked, "The fuck you doing? Trying to get the shit kicked out of me?"

He chuckled. "Just riling him up a bit. It'll make for one fucking good night."

"Jesus," I muttered. "Are you looking for a foursome?"

Ghost pushed that aside. "I'm not into sharing what's mine."

I shook my head in disbelief. "It's all too complicated. Even one woman is too much for me. I'm the last holdout. I'm never going to get tied down."

"Right. That's why you're sitting here all alone. Why aren't you on the prowl?"

"The night is still young." I glanced nervously at Grey again. If looks could kill, I'd be dead already.

Ghost smirked. "If you lean over and whisper in my ear, he'll lose his shit."

"Don't fuck with me, man." I couldn't help but laugh at the absurdity of it all.

He grabbed my shoulder and squeezed. "We're gonna head out. I've got to get these two out of here before Grey bursts his aorta."

"Yeah, everyone is leaving. Bunch of pussies."

Some time while we were talking, Ryder and Talia disappeared.

Ghost looked around. "Lacey's still here."

I gave a noncommittal hum in answer.

"What's wrong with her? She's hot as fuck. You've had sex with her before."

"So has everyone else." Even to myself, I sounded petulant.

"Not me."

I was surprised. "I thought you did. We all did."

"Nope." He said the word emphatically. "I tried one time. Just for curiosity's sake, but she turned me down."

"You're kidding?" I grunted in disbelief. "I didn't think you ever got turned down."

He rubbed his chin in thought. "I'm not sure I ever have. But she did."

"Huh," I said quietly.

"And I know Knox never had sex with her."

"Why are we discussing this?"

He ignored me. "Just because you and Sid fucked her doesn't mean we all have."

God, that brought back some uneasy memories. My eyes slid to Lacey. Of course, I'd noticed how hot Lacey looked tonight. She always looked hot. All the girls were pretty damn gorgeous, but Lacey wasn't with any of my bandmates, so I could check her out without feeling guilty.

I'd been attracted to her the first moment I'd ever seen her, but she was the ultimate party girl. It took me years to find out how smart she was and that she had a high-powered career. I'd never asked. I always believed that image she put out there — party girl looking for a good time.

It bothered me that it was Sidney that had lured her into our threesome. I'd had sex with her — an incredibly fucking sexy night — but she wouldn't have given me the time of day without Sidney. There was something between them. A weird dynamic that always pissed me off. Even though Sidney was married to my sister now, and I knew he didn't even look twice at Lacey anymore; it still pissed me off.

The bitterness came out in my tone. "She liked Sid."

Ghost stood up to leave, so I stood up with him. He gave me one of those manly half-hug, half-backslapping goodbyes. It felt good to get the friendly vibes from Ghost, even if he was probably doing it to make Grey jealous. Any attention Ghost doled out gave you the same feeling a great hit from a bong did — the warm fuzzies.

I said goodbye to Remi, giving her a kiss on the cheek, which earned me a bone-crushing handshake and a bruising 'tap' on the shoulder in the way of goodbye from Grey.

Donovan and Ellie were grinding on the dancefloor, doing more making out than dancing. I sat down next to Lacey, who was the only one remaining at our table. "Looks like we're the last ones left."

She sat back. "How's Kody doing?"

"Great."

She pursed her lips. "You don't have to hang out here with me. You probably have better things to do."

Was she trying to get rid of me? Probably. I had a Kody-free night. If I were smart, I'd find a willing chick, and I'd enjoy some improper Vegas activities, instead of forcing my company on Lacey.

She tapped her finger against her glass. "I haven't talked to you in a long time."

Had we ever really talked? "You haven't been out in a long time. At least not with Ghost Parker."

"I've been keeping it pretty low-key lately. I broke up with my boyfriend, Theo, a few months ago. Yes, I tried the whole boyfriend thing. It didn't stick very well." She laughed it off, but she seemed sad.

Fuck. I did not want to see her sad. "I tried the whole dating thing, too. Josie set me up on blind dates with some girls. It was horrible."

Her eyes widened with surprise. "Josie? The granny nanny?"

"Yeah." I laughed. "It went about as well as you'd imagine it would go."

"Were they ... uh, older women that she set you up with?"

"One was a 40-year-old virgin, ape-sex voyeur. The other was a 26-year-old mother of four, who had sex in the bathroom stall of Pop 'Em Possum with an employee for a free bucket of tokens while I held her baby."

Jesus, her sweet peal of laughter had my dick twitching.

"No way!" She pushed out between laughs. "She cuckolded you? On the first date?"

I grumbled a bit. "She didn't cuckold me."

She was gasping for air. "You watched her have sex with another man on your date! While you were holding her baby! That's being super-cuckolded. Holy shit, Sebastian!"

I shot her a look of surprise. Nobody called me Sebastian; not even my mother anymore. Only when Kaylie was mad at me did she occasionally call me that.

Lacey abruptly stopped laughing and couldn't meet my eye. It must've slipped out, and she felt embarrassed. She called me Sebastian. Huh. And I liked it. What the fuck?

I liked Lacey. I mean, I always lusted after her and wanted to hook up with her, but I didn't actually like her. Did I? Not with all that Sid crap. Was that jealousy? Fuck, you're losing it, man.

I began searching through the empty bottles littering the table, desperately looking for some alcohol. "There's no way we went through all that alcohol." Our dedicated server had disappeared long ago and hadn't come back to check on us in a while.

"What about that stash in your pocket?"

I gave her a cocky smirk. "You've been watching me, Lacey?" The smile slipped as I realized she'd probably been watching Sid.

"All night long, Archer." She cocked a perfectly manicured eyebrow. "What are you hiding in there?"

I was disappointed that she'd dropped calling me Sebastian, but her tone was teasing. Was she flirting with me? "Absinthe. It's a tradition for Sid's birthday."

"Absinthe? Let's do a shot."

I stopped rummaging through the empty bottles and looked at her. "It's really potent and you've already been drinking. It'll knock you on your ass."

Her chin jutted up. "You think I can't handle it?"

Fuck. My head was already spinning from too much alcohol, and being so close to Lacey was always disconcerting. I, a confident guy, always acted so supremely uncool around her. And now I was having all these strange thoughts about her. "Fine. We'll do one shot. But tell me your room number now, so I'll know it when I have to drag your ass back there later."

"Good try, Romeo." She made pointy circles at me with her finger. "Now pour us some absinthe."

Shit. Did I just sound like I was trying to get into her room? See, so uncool.

I pulled out the flask and then discreetly filled two glasses for us. I didn't sputter so much when I did the shot this time. Maybe I was already too drunk. Maybe I just enjoyed Lacey's over-the-top reaction to the shot too much to focus on myself. She sputtered and coughed and then fanned herself as she wiped tears from her eyes.

My head was definitely spinning now. The room started to close in around me. Between the flashing lights and the repetitive beat that I was continuously counting in my head, I couldn't think straight.

I grabbed her hand and stood. "Let's go someplace quieter."

She stood, and I took that as agreement. I pulled her out of the club and then kept walking with our hands interlocked.

"Do you want to go check out the Strip?"

She stopped us and lifted up her foot, pointing to her high-heeled shoe. "Does it look like I want to go walking anywhere? My feet are killing me."

"Jesus, Lacey, those shoes are worth it. They make your legs look sexy as fuck. Along with the rest of you." Apparently, there wasn't a filter on my words anymore.

She stared at me for a few seconds. "Let's go back to the cocktail bar. It won't be as crowded or loud."

I adjusted my stride to match her pace and walked, keeping hold of her hand until we got to the bar. We ordered some drinks that we didn't need and then sat next to each other on a banquet seat in a dark corner of the room.

We talked. And talked.

She told me about some upcoming bands she was looking into signing for her company. We talked about touring in general and she gave me some suggestions on what Ghost Parker should do as a band as next steps. She was so smart on the business end of things.

I admitted that I wasn't totally sure about my future with Ghost Parker. She reminded me that the band loved me and that they were all starting families now and that having Kody didn't mean I had to give up my passion for music.

Then I told her about my idea to start a boutique record label. I hadn't even confided that to Sid yet. My idea was to produce a solo album for Ghost so he could create the music he wanted to make without the corporate handcuffs. I wanted to move away from purely making money to creating stuff.

The wheels were turning in her head. The music business was her wheelhouse, so I was listening to everything she said. The problem was that I was kind of mesmerized by her beauty. And I'd put her feet on my lap, took off her sexy shoes, and was massaging her feet. And my fingers kept climbing up the silky smooth skin of her calf. I couldn't help it.

We did another shot of absinthe. I don't know who suggested it, but it was a dumb idea. But I'd do anything to keep her with me longer.

That's why I wanted to bite off my tongue when some jealous bitterness slipped out. "Is it weird for you that you had sex with your best friend's husband?"

She froze for a second. "Is it weird that you had sex with your sister's husband?"

"Fuck!" I slumped down a few inches in the seat. "I never had sex with Sid. I just had sex while he was there. Big difference."

She pulled her legs off my lap. "If I recall, you were there too, so now you're going to judge me?" She was pissed, and I didn't blame her. Fuck, I was an asshole.

"I'm talking about after. You had sex with him again." Without me, I'd almost accused.

"That was way before he was with Kaylie. And if she's okay with everything, what the hell do you care?"

"I don't care about Kaylie. Truthfully, Lacey, I was jealous! That you chose him instead of me."

My words hung in the air between us.

She looked stunned. "What are you saying?"

"I don't know. Just forget it. I'm drunk."

I pulled out the flask and added a splash of absinthe to our glasses. We quickly threw back the contents.

She wiped her mouth and then leaned forward. "I didn't think you wanted to be chosen."

We stared at each other. Fuck, my head was spinning.

Lacey peered at her empty glass. "This stuff is like truth serum."

I slid closer to her. "You're very beautiful. And intelligent."

She giggled. "You're slurring your words."

My hand rested on her thigh. "You've been slurring your words for the past hour."

Her head tilted. "I have a question for you. A very, very important question. You have to tell me the truth."

"Okay."

"First, more truth serum." She picked up the flask and then poured out the remaining liquid into our glasses and onto the table, too.

I could tell she was really drunk, so I chose the glass with the bigger pour. I was seeing double at this point, but I was still a gentleman.

"C'mere, beautiful." I patted my lap. "And ask me this important question."

Chapter 10

Lacey

I was pretty sure I'd been awake for a couple of minutes, but my brain was only just sluggishly starting to work. I knew two things for sure. Something was vibrating my right ass cheek every few minutes, and that's what had woken me up. And secondly, I was in bad shape.

When I tried to place in my mind where exactly I was, my mind came up blank. I tried to work it out. In a bed, but not at home. On a cruise? A small boat? Because the bed was swaying and I felt seasick. Had I been drugged and kidnapped by a pirate? One who was using a vibrator on my ass this very second?

I forced my eyes to open. Ouch, that hurt. Not a boat, but a hotel room. And, yes, it was spinning. I closed my eyes to regroup. Things were slowly coming back to me.

Las Vegas. Girl's weekend. Sid's birthday.

Okay, that explained why I felt so awful. A quick assessment of my condition led me to the conclusion that on my worst-hangover-of-all-time scales, this one was near the tippy top. My stomach rolled with nausea. A sharp stab of pain behind my eye added to my throbbing headache. Damn. Maybe even straight up the worst hangover of all time.

My ass buzzed again. What the hell was that? I couldn't move yet, so I just ignored it. But I was naked. And sometimes that meant...

Fuck!

I rolled over slowly, not wanting to puke and afraid to discover the source of the warmth I felt behind me.

I was in bed with Bash. Sebastian Archer. Kaylie's brother. I guess it wasn't all that surprising. Almost all the men in our Vegas group were already coupled up, and I'd already had sex with him years before. It wasn't that big of a deal. Right?

Did we have sex last night? I tried hard to remember. It sucked if we did because I couldn't remember it and he was hella skilled in bed. I remembered that 'night of the threesome' fondly, often with a vibrator between my legs.

He appeared to be naked, but I wasn't totally sure because the lower half of his body was covered with sheets. Despite feeling like I'd been run over by a dump truck, my eyes raked over him. His arms and upper body were freaking phenomenal. Even though I usually preferred a man with a bit of chest hair, his smooth chest was exquisite. I wanted to run my hands along the smooth skin, exploring his broad shoulders and well-defined pecs. His taut, muscular arms were just as mouth-watering, from his bulging biceps to his corded forearms. My eyes trailed lower, over his chiseled abs and down the distinctive V-shaped torso that disappeared under the sheets.

Years of drumming had honed his body into masculine perfection.

Unfortunately, I didn't have x-ray vision, but from what I remembered, everything below the sheets matched the top, including his cock.

All that sexy goodness was topped with a handsome face with short, dark hair that always looked perfectly messy. Flawless features like his angular cheekbones and granite jaw were only overshadowed by his criminally pretty eyes. They were a green color so stunning that it made my stomach tumble with nerves when he laid them on me. Just to highlight those breathtaking eyes, he had the thickest lashes I'd ever seen on a guy. It almost looked like he was wearing guyliner, they were so damn thick. Those eyes would surely make him the prettiest boy in the world if his other very angular and sharp features didn't balance it all out. I'd witnessed girls mooning over this man's looks for years.

He opened those pretty eyes, and I gasped. Fuck, he was almost too handsome to look at directly.

"Lacey." The rough and gravelly way he said my name had my lady parts clenching.

My head decided to remind me it was in agony by shooting a dagger of pain behind my right eye. I groaned. "I think I'm still drunk. The room's spinning."

"Aw, fuck." Sebastian rubbed his face. "Yep. I feel like shit, too."

I felt vibrations again, but this time nearer to my secret spot since I'd just rolled over. He must have heard the buzz of vibration because he made a face. Instead of ignoring it again, I reached down between my legs and pulled out ... a cell phone.

Sebastian looked puzzled. "That's my phone."

I flipped it over and groaned. "Sid's calling. And he's been calling a lot."

He took the phone from me and declined the call. "Shit, it's 1:30."

My stomach lurched. "Ugh. I missed the brunch. We both missed brunch. Oh, God."

"My head hurts—"

I didn't let him finish. "Oh, my God! What was your phone doing down there? Did we take pictures? Or video? Give me that!"

I tried to grab for it, but he fended me off. If I didn't currently feel like I'd been trampled by a herd of buffalo, I would have put more effort into it.

I watched in muted horror as he opened the camera app and clicked through the recent photos. Yes, there were photos of us. Not naked photos, thank the Lord. But kind of disturbing?

I inched closer to him so I could see them on the screen. It wasn't lost on me that my bare breasts were rubbing up against his arm and my naked body was only inches from his.

He scrolled back to the first photo we'd taken of ourselves last night. It was a harmless selfie with our faces squished together. We were both laughing, obviously very drunk.

"I don't remember that," I admitted.

"Me neither. It looks like it's from that cocktail bar. We went back there after the club."

The next photo was of him smiling into the camera while I was kissing him on the cheek. He was holding one of my legs up, which was bent and raised in front of him. It was like a sexy, pin-up pose. We didn't usually have that friendly, joking dynamic between us, but we'd been drunk. There was no need to feel embarrassed. Right?

"That's fucking sexy."

His words shot straight to my girly parts. How could I be turned on and feel like I was about to die of a hangover at the same time? "Looks like we were having fun."

He flipped to the next photo. The background was dark, but it looked like we were in a car, and I was sprawled out all over him in a highly unflattering position. My short dress rode up my thighs so high that my ass was exposed. Neither of us was smiling in this picture; we looked like we were ten seconds from full-on fucking.

"That looks hot, Lace."

I enlarged the photo to look more closely at the background. "Were we in a limo? Did we go out last night?"

"I don't remember, but I wish I did."

The next picture was of him carrying me piggyback style.

"I hope no one was behind us. My ass was probably hanging out."

His chest rumbled with laughter and then he flipped to the next one. Someone else had taken this shot from a few feet back. Sebastian's hands were cupping my cheeks, and he was kissing me so tenderly. My stomach twisted. This photo was perhaps the most embarrassing so far. There was so much emotion behind it; it looked so real — like we were a real couple.

He must have felt something similar because he quickly flipped to the next one instead of lingering on it as he had with the others.

In this one, we were kissing again, but this time, his hands were resting on my waist and my arms were wrapped around his neck.

The next four photos were all variations of us making out. I guess we gave the mysterious photographer a good show. In the last one, we weren't kissing, but we were wrapped up in each other's arms, just staring into each other's eyes. This one was so painfully romantic, I had to look away.

I needed to break the odd tension that I could feel building between us. "At least we didn't make a sex tape."

The phone began vibrating again. It was Sid. As soon as he declined the call, a text from him popped up. It looked like he'd been blowing Sebastian's phone up all morning.

"I can't believe we went out somewhere."

He tossed his phone onto the nightstand and then turned those devastating eyes on me. "Maybe we just rode around the Strip in a limo. I remember you saying your feet hurt, so you didn't want to walk."

Suddenly, there was a pounding at the door. I squeaked and then slid further under the covers.

"Shit, that's got to be Sid. He's not going to go away."

"Oh my God," I panicked. "Don't tell him I'm here." I pulled at the sheet and rolled off the bed simultaneously. It was a bad idea. My stomach revolted, and I almost vomited. As fast as my body allowed, I waddled into the bathroom on horribly shaky legs and shut the door. The movement caused the jackhammer in my head to speed up.

I assumed Sebastian answered the door when the pounding stopped. I leaned against the door, swallowing down a rush of bile, and listened.

"You couldn't answer your damn phone?" That was Sid's bellowing.

Sebastian's answer was too muffled to hear. As I stood hunched over, I realized that my bladder was about to explode. The conversation was getting louder; it sounded like Sid was moving closer to the bathroom door. I winced as I picked out a few words here and there: 'fucking some chick', 'missed brunch', and 'panties on the lamp'.

My head was beating out of my skull and I desperately had to pee, so I couldn't care anymore about their conversation. I limped toward the toilet, holding my gurgling stomach, and realized Sid was talking right on the other side of the bathroom door. If I peed, he would hear.

"What the hell is this?" Sid was asking.

I turned on the water faucet, but it was one of those low-flow water savers that made virtually no noise.

"Who cares? They're just some flowers. I probably stole them off a table somewhere. Now that you know I'm alive, would you just—"

I turned on the shower. Finally, enough noise to cover the sound of peeing.

When I was done relieving my aching bladder, I drank water from the sink faucet by cupping water in my palm. Nothing good was happening in my mouth.

I splashed some water on my face, wincing when I caught sight of my sorry reflection in the mirror — pale skin, raccoon eyes, smeared mascara, and ratty hair. Lovely.

I walked over to the shower and turned off the water. The water in my stomach that I'd just slurped down started to roil and bubble. Oh fuck ... I was going to—

Yes, I hurled. Until my stomach was empty. I flushed the toilet, but then I threw up again. It felt like my stomach was being wrung out. Violently.

I was dry heaving for a few minutes when a knock sounded on the door.

"Lacey, are you okay? Sid is gone."

I stood on weak legs and shuffled over to the sink. "Give me a second." I rinsed out my mouth and then splashed some water on my face. Somewhere along the way, I'd dropped the bedsheet. I looked around and saw it curled around the base of the toilet, so I grabbed one of the big fluffy bath towels and wrapped it around my body.

Sebastian was leaning up against the doorframe, wearing only a pair of black boxer briefs, when I opened the door. "Are you okay?"

"No." I moaned. "Not at all. Do you know where my clothes are?"

He walked over to a lamp and pulled a tiny piece of black fabric off them. "Well, Sid spotted your panties over here on the lampshade. He stepped on your dress, which is on the floor by the door. I don't think he recognized it. There's a shoe on the chair over there, but I don't know where the other one is."

I looked around the room for my bra while Sebastian gathered up my clothes. I noticed the flowers Sid was asking about. It was a pretty bouquet of white roses and hydrangea. "Where did you get those flowers?"

He shrugged. "I don't know. We probably swiped them off a table."

That's what he'd told Sidney, too, but the stems of the flowers were wrapped in satin ribbon. That pinged a tiny warning bell, but my head felt like it weighed two tons and my legs didn't feel like they could hold me up much longer.

He came back to where I was slumped up against the wall with my clothes, minus one shoe and my bra.

I slithered back into the bathroom to dress but realized quite quickly that my dress was torn almost in half. I slipped on my panties, which were so skimpy they covered almost nothing, and then wrapped the towel back around myself.

When I poked my head out of the bathroom, Sebastian was wearing a T-shirt and gym shorts. "My dress is torn to shreds. Can I borrow something to wear? A T-shirt maybe?"

"Sure." He walked over to his small suitcase and started rummaging through it. "I didn't pack that much stuff. I've got an extra T-shirt. No sweatpants, though. You want these shorts I'm wearing?"

I couldn't stand upright anymore. I gingerly made my way over to the bed and collapsed on top of it. "The T-shirt would be great."

He sat down on the bed next to me and handed me the T-shirt. "I'm sorry about your dress. Do you think I, you know, ripped it?"

I grunted. "What do you think?"

He ran his hand through his hair. "Damn, Lacey. We drank all that absinthe. After we'd been drinking all night. I was so drunk. Honestly, I don't think I had the ability to perform last night. Do you, uh, feel anything?"

I sat up and the room spun violently. "Like if we had sex?"

"Can you tell?"

"Well, if we had sex, it must have been very gentle because I don't feel a damn thing." I rolled my eyes, and that was a mistake. It hurt.

He grinned. "Yeah, you would have felt it for sure if we did anything. We must have just passed out."

"We managed to get naked…"

His eyes flicked over my body, but then he caught himself. "What's the last thing you remember?"

"Doing a shot at the nightclub." I thought for a moment. "No, wait. We went somewhere. Back to the cocktail bar? We talked for a while. It's so fuzzy."

"Yeah." He nodded. "We talked for a long time. We had some more shots. We finished the absinthe. You were calling it truth serum. Then I started seeing double. That's about all I remember."

I pulled the T-shirt over my head and then pulled the bath towel out from underneath. The T-shirt was large, but my boobs filled it out pretty nicely. I laid back down on the bed again, not caring that the T-shirt rode up my legs.

"Can I take a picture of you now? You're so sexy and I can't enjoy it right now because my fucking head hurts so bad. I need a picture so I can look at it later and appreciate it."

His voice sounded like raw sex. And it pissed me off. I sat up and scowled.

"Really?" I packed a heaping of disgust and irritation into that one word.

"I'm sorry, that was … fuck, are you crying?"

Yes, water was leaking out of my eyes. I swiped at the errant drops, feeling foolish. "I don't know why I'm crying; I'm just feeling so sick."

"I'm sorry, Lacey." He leaned over and hugged me, holding me in his arms.

And it felt so right. Comforting. Too good. I pulled away. "I know you were just joking, but this whole thing is so fucked up, Sebastian."

He froze. "You called me that last night. I remember."

"Ugh. I don't know why." Frowning, I shook my head. "I think of you as Sebastian in my head. Kaylie calls you that sometimes, and it just stuck in my head. I'm sorry."

"No, it's okay. I kind of like it." He was rubbing soothing circles on my back. "So, you think about me a lot, huh?"

"What? No! I'm just confused right now. With Sid barging in here. And we both missed brunch. I don't even know why I give a shit about that..."

"It's going to be okay."

I continued spewing out my train of thought. "I got blackout drunk. I've never done that before. Maybe a few details get blurry now and then, but nothing like this."

"I know it's a bit unsettling. I don't remember how we got back here, either. But I probably just brought you back here. I don't think we did anything but get naked. I don't see a condom lying around..." His voice trailed off.

God, could we have had sex and not even remember it?

He stood up, grabbed his pants off the ground, and dug through the pocket until he found his wallet. He opened it up and smiled.

"Condom is still in here. I don't think ... What's this?"

One side of his lip turned down. His eyes darted to mine and then he pulled a folded-up piece of paper out of his wallet. It looked like he unfolded it in slow motion, but maybe that was just my alcohol-poisoned mind.

I didn't imagine his sharp intake of breath. "Oh fuck."

"What is it?" I grabbed his arm and pulled it closer to me so I could see it.

It was a receipt for $102 and some transaction fees for the Las Vegas Marriage License Bureau. It was dated last night at 1:36 a.m.

Holy fuck! "Did we…"

"No. Just because I have this … No. It doesn't mean we actually got…" He couldn't even say the word out loud.

Jesus. I felt nauseous again. "But, we got the license—"

"We must have been just fucking around."

I wrapped my arms around my stomach. "The pictures. We were in a limo."

He laughed nervously. "Yeah, it doesn't mean anything."

Sebastian was in complete denial, but all I could think about was that bouquet of flowers with the ribbon-wrapped stems. It was a wedding bouquet.

We'd gotten married last night.

Chapter 11

Bash

LACEY LOOKED LIKE SHE was about to keel over. I found some pain relief meds in my toiletry bag and shook out a few pills into my hand. Then I grabbed a cold bottle of water from the mini fridge and gave them to her.

"Here, take this. Sip slowly."

She swallowed the pills down with shaky hands and then hugged them around her stomach.

I felt awful. I shouldn't have let her do those damn shots. My head was pounding and my stomach was queasy, but I'd survive. Lacey, I wasn't too sure. She looked like death warmed over. "Why don't you lay down and rest?"

She whimpered. "I've got a flight. And I have to check out of my room. I'm already late."

"There's no way you're going to make it. I have this room for another night. You can stay here. Get a new flight tomorrow."

I could tell how badly she felt because she didn't even try to argue. "My personal assistant. Her card is in a slot in my phone case. Tell her to cancel my flight and get me a new one for tomorrow."

"Yeah. No problem. Give me your room number and keycard and I'll get your stuff and bring it here for you."

She rubbed at her eye. "You're a lifesaver."

I wasn't about to take any credit when I felt responsible for making her get so drunk in the first place. "Do you have anything hidden in your room? Or in the safe?"

She began crawling across the bed and then slipped under the comforter. "No, I didn't bring anything valuable. Room 118, 32nd floor. Keycard in my phone."

"Alright, I'll take care of it. You just try to get some rest."

"Thank you, Sebastian." She buried her head in the pillow and moaned.

It took me a few minutes to find Lacey's phone. It was under a chair near the door. I found her assistant's card and her hotel keycard. I placed her phone on the nightstand and then stepped out into the hallway so I wouldn't disturb her. It would be best if she could sleep off her hangover.

I spoke with her assistant, who assured me she'd text Lacey with the new flight details, and then returned to the room. Lacey was lightly snoring. I tiptoed into the bathroom, took some medicine for my headache, brushed my teeth, and then showered.

Ten minutes later, I grabbed my wallet and then went in search of some food. I finally found a casual dining restaurant that didn't look crowded. It was between meals, so I was able to choose a booth in the back corner away from the other diners.

I ordered an eclectic mix of foods that I knew were good for soothing my stomach post-alcohol abuse: eggs with toast, a banana, and a hamburger. Then I spent the next ten minutes on a video call with Kody. His cheerful enthusiasm about everything brightened my afternoon.

I said goodbye to Kody when my food came and then I gobbled it up quickly, happy that my stomach wasn't in full revolt with the addition of food. Before I left, I procured a few items for Lacey, some soup crackers and a banana.

I had a few hours before I had to get to the airport. Packing up would only take a few minutes, and I wanted to make sure Lacey ate something before I left. I wanted to make sure she was okay. And I had to grab her stuff out of her room.

Before I headed back up to the rooms, I walked around until I found a store that sold drinks. I bought a can of ginger ale and a sports drink and added it to the bag with Lacey's food. I'd left her with the water bottle, but I doubted that she was drinking any of it. Before I left, I'd get her to rehydrate, too.

I stepped onto an elevator and rode it up to the 32nd floor. I located her room and entered it with no problem. The room was tidy, compared to the state of my own. Her bed was made and nothing looked out of place. I'd grab her luggage, do a quick check to make sure I didn't leave anything behind, and be out of there in a few minutes.

I found her suitcase inside the closet where a bunch of clothes were hanging up. Okay, I'd have to fold those and fit them into the suitcase. They'd probably get all wrinkly and shit, but it'd have to do. I rolled the suitcase across the room and placed it on the bed. It was light. Good, she was a light packer. I unzipped the case and...

it was empty.

She had no clothes in there? Did she bring just the few items from the closet? That couldn't be right. Then I realized and strode over to the dresser. I lived out of suitcases; I couldn't remember the last time I'd ever unpacked anything. I slid open the top drawer.

It was overflowing with lingerie and skimpy undergarments. Oh fuck. I slammed the drawer shut. I couldn't paw around in Lacey's underwear. It would be pervy.

I backed away from the drawer and then sat on the bed next to the empty suitcase. It all hit me at once. Lacey. The pictures. Waking up with her in bed with me. The receipt.

I pulled the piece of paper out of my wallet and unfolded it. I read it and reread it a few times, making sure I wasn't mistaken. Las Vegas Marriage License Bureau. I paid the fee with my credit card. Last night at 1:36 a.m.

There was no doubt that we applied for a marriage license. But why? As a joke? Or was there something more behind it?

We could have gotten married last night. Actually married. Lacey could be my wife.

I'd done a lot of fucked up things in my life. I had a baby and didn't even know who his mother was. Now, I'd gotten married? I waited for the sheer panic to set in. Sitting back, I waited some more. I wasn't panicked, even though somehow I'd managed to stumble through life and obtain a kid and wife by accident. The kid turned out to be the best thing that ever happened to me. And Lacey?

I always had some unresolved feelings for her after our three-way with Sid. I brushed it off as a weird, competitive thing with Sid. Maybe there was some jealousy involved.

But I couldn't deny that I did like Lacey. I was attracted to her; what was there not to like? At first, I thought she was just a party girl, but I'd seen so much more over the years. She was a high-powered shark at her job and garnered the respect of the entire music industry. When Kaylie most needed help, she'd been a compassionate friend, and now they were best friends. She'd co-founded a charity, launching it with her own money and working tirelessly to help others in need. And she was a sex goddess. There was no disputing that.

I lusted after her, but I genuinely liked her as a person. I didn't want this mistake to get between us. What if she never wanted to see me again? I didn't want to lose her as a friend. Fuck, I was so confused about it all.

Grabbing my phone, I opened up the pictures we took last night. I scrolled through them, studying each one after the other. Yeah, her dress had ridden up and shown off her gorgeous ass in one of the photos, but I passed by that one quickly. It was the other photos that had my gut clenching. There was something about the way I was looking at her. I was drunk out of my mind, but I looked happy. I looked like I was in love.

Feeling uncomfortable looking at them, I quickly closed the app and stood up to finish packing up her stuff. I had a plane to catch.

Fitting all the clothes that were in the three drawers into her suitcase was going to be a problem. Did she go shopping while she was here? How could they have all fit in there? Plus, there were the clothes hanging in the closet and three pairs of shoes and two pairs of flip-flops.

After 15 minutes of folding, refolding, and trying to stuff everything into the suitcase, I decided that I'd have to stuff some of the outfits and a pair of glittery high heels into my own suitcase. I packed as much as I could and then threw the drawerful of lingerie on top without looking at any of it.

I was proud of my accomplishment until I poked my head into the bathroom. Fuck, there were toiletries everywhere! I found her toiletry bag in the vanity beneath the sink and it was way too small for the explosion of makeup and lotions. What the hell? How was this possible?

I didn't have the patience. I put all the makeup-looking stuff, the tiny brushes, and personal care items into the bag until it was full. Pilfering an empty garbage bag from one of the trash cans, I filled it with the rest of the bigger bottles of goop, her curling wands, and multiple hair brushes. Christ, then there was a bag that held jewelry. And where would all these bags go? There was no room in the suitcase. It was a fucking mystery how she hauled all this shit here. Maybe I should go down to the lobby and buy her a bigger suitcase?

It had taken me way longer than I expected to pack up all her stuff and check her out of the room. By the time I was finally done, I'd broken out into a sweat. It was strangely intimate touching all of her stuff, but hell, she could be my wife. There was nothing more intimate than that.

I looked like a hobo as I hauled her suitcase and all the extra bags of crap back to my room. She was still sleeping in bed when I got back to the room.

I grabbed the bag of food and drinks I'd bought for her and sat on the edge of the bed near her. "Lacey, how are you feeling?"

She let out a long rumbling groan, so at least I knew she was alive.

"That good, huh? You can stay here tonight. I checked you out of your room and your assistant is going to text your new flight details. I've got to leave soon to catch my flight."

She moaned again, but it was a lot shorter this time.

"I'd like you to eat and drink a little before I leave. It'll make you feel better."

Her head turned on the pillow to face me, but her eyes remained closed. "No, I can't. I don't want to vomit again."

"You threw up? You're going to get dehydrated if you don't drink. I brought you a sports drink so you can get some electrolytes. Sit up and take a sip."

It took some convincing, but I was able to get her to drink a few sips and eat two crackers before she collapsed back on the pillow.

I was worried about her. Her hands were still shaking, and she said her head still hurt. I had to leave soon if I was going to make my flight and be home in time to tuck Kody into bed.

My head and stomach were both feeling better, but I was exhausted. Traveling right now would suck. Before I could talk myself out of it, I went out into the hall and called my parents. They were happy to watch Kody for another night. Then I canceled my flight. Before I headed back into the room, I opened up the pictures of Lacey and me. They made me uncomfortable, but I couldn't stop looking at them. I sent them all to myself in an email in case she ever demanded that I delete them. I needed to keep them, and I didn't want to think about why.

When I got back in the room, I left my T-shirt and basketball shorts on and climbed into the bed. It was a king-sized bed, so I could nap without bothering Lacey. Like a gentleman, I kept my distance.

She tossed and turned in her sleep a few times, but within minutes I had passed out myself.

The room was dark when I woke up. The clock said 10:26 p.m. I sat up and rubbed my eyes. Damn, I'd needed that sleep. I got up to use the bathroom and when I returned, Lacey was awake. She'd turned on the bedside lamp and was sitting up in bed.

When I asked, she said she felt better, and she definitely looked better. She drank some ginger ale and crackers and then disappeared into the bathroom with her suitcase and toiletries while I ordered us some room service.

Our meal arrived by the time she'd finished showering. She came out of the bathroom, wrapped in the white bathrobe, looking much better.

"I thought you had to catch a flight home?" She asked between spoonfuls of chicken noodle soup.

I was busy devouring the chicken dinner I'd ordered. "I decided to stay the night and leave in the morning. I wasn't sure you were going to pull through with all that moaning and groaning you were doing."

She sagged against her chair. "I'm sorry. God, I wasn't sure I was going to pull through, either. I think I'm done drinking. At least for a very long time."

Disbelief tinged my reply. "Everyone says that."

Her muted laugh proved she didn't quite believe it, either. "I'm really embarrassed you saw me like that."

"Drunk? Or hungover?"

"Yep. Both." She was studying her soup like it was the most fascinating thing.

I'd never seen her before when she wasn't absolutely put together, and I knew she must be feeling vulnerable. I wanted to let her off the hook. "You're an adorable drunkard."

Her cheeks flushed. "Now that you know I'm not going to aspirate on my own vomit, you should go out. You don't have to babysit me. Go gamble or hit the town. I don't want you to feel like you're stuck here with me."

Did she want me to leave? There was the gigantic elephant in the room from what happened last night that made our interactions slightly awkward, but I wasn't going to let her shoo me away. "I had enough excitement last night. And I'm going to get up early and drive home. So I rather take it easy tonight."

"You're driving? Can I go with you?"

I liked the idea of having her company for the four-plus hour drive. "I want to leave by 7 o'clock. Are you good with that?"

"Yeah. That's fine."

"Okay." I agreed. "We'll grab breakfast and then hit the road."

"Do you miss Kody?" Her voice was soft and understanding.

"Yeah." I pushed my empty plate aside. "I told him I was going to be home to tuck him into bed tonight. I'm sure he's fine, but I don't like to go back on my word."

"You're a good dad." The compliment was sincere and the accompanying smile friendly, yet it took my breath away. It lit up the room like a ray of sunshine on a cloudy day.

Her praise meant a lot to me. Why? I don't fucking know. I grunted out a thanks and began cleaning up my meal.

Neither of us was tired after our dinner, so we decided to watch a movie. It was a political thriller, which seemed like a safe, neutral pick until a steamy sex scene filled the TV screen. Under normal circumstances, I would have acted on my horny impulses with any other attractive woman, but things were decidedly awkward between us.

After the movie, she retreated to the bathroom to get ready for bed. She was still wearing the robe when she exited and by the time I'd brushed my teeth and washed my face, she was in bed and under the covers.

This was a bit awkward. "Do you mind if I sleep in the bed? I'll keep my clothes on and stay on my side."

Lacey scoffed. "I think we're beyond pretending that it's more scandalous to share a bed while sleeping than whatever else we've recently gotten up to."

At least she was joking about it.

She turned her back to me and closed her eyes. Faintly disappointed, I pulled off my shirt, turned off the light, and climbed into the king-sized bed.

There was plenty of room between us. I shouldn't have napped earlier, because I wasn't tired and sleep wasn't going to come easily. I stayed awake for a long time.

When I woke up, she was curled up in my arms. Jesus, I could get used to this. She was warm and soft; her head resting on my chest, our legs entwined. She was not going to be happy when she awoke, but I wasn't about to move. I'd bask in this heaven for as long as I could. Unfortunately, a certain part of my body was enjoying it too much. My cock was hard as steel, and my thoughts were taking a decidedly x-rated turn.

Her hand, which was resting on my chest, tightened as she let out a little shriek of alarm. She tried to pull away, but I didn't let her go.

My voice was rough with sleep. "I can't help it if you snuggled up to me."

Her body stiffened. "I did not! You obviously came over to my side of the bed."

I lifted my head to look. "Uh, we're clearly on my side of the bed, gorgeous."

"You probably pulled me over here!"

"Uh-huh." Wow, I really enjoyed ruffling her feathers. "How are you feeling this morning?"

"Much better. But, I'm starving."

I didn't want to let her go, but the longer we laid like this, the harder it would be to get my dick to calm down. "Okay, let's get you some food and then head out."

She sighed like she didn't want to get up either, but then she untangled from me and rolled out of bed. She was wearing a pink tank top with matching sleep shorts that showed off her body to perfection. Her hair was tousled and her face clean of all makeup, but she'd never looked more beautiful. Fuck, Lacey, what were you doing to me?

When we were ready to leave the room, I had to help wrangle her many loose bags, but she never commented on my terrible packing. We never found her other high-heeled shoe, so she left the one behind like Cinderella. We ate at a breakfast buffet, and I was happy when she ate a decent amount. It was obvious she was feeling much better.

We sat in companionable silence for most of the ride home with the music playing on low.

We were closing in on the outskirts of Los Angeles when she turned to me. "Should we talk about it?"

My fingers nervously tapped on the steering wheel of the rental car. "We're friends. We don't have to make a big deal about this, right?"

She let out a little huff of air. "It's kind of a big deal. Marriage. At least it is to me."

I sat silent for a minute. "Do you think we did?"

She bit her lip. "I'm not sure."

"There's no way anyone would marry us when we were so damn drunk. There's got to be some rule about that. We were plastered, Lace."

She shrugged her shoulders. "I just searched it on the internet. It takes about ten calendar days for a Nevada marriage certificate to be filed. I guess we'll know then."

I kept sneaking glances at her, trying to gauge her mood. "If we did do something crazy, don't panic. We'll just get it annulled and it'll be like it never happened. For now, let's just keep calm."

She was avoiding my gaze, staring out the side window. "I'll have my lawyers look into it."

When we got to her building, I pulled up to the curb at the front entrance and helped her remove her bags.

She looked upset.

I held out my arms. "C'mere, beautiful."

She stepped into my arms without hesitating.

I held her close, inhaling her scent. "Everything's going to be okay."

"Promise?"

"I promise." I pulled back and then kissed her forehead.

She gathered her bags and then headed into the building. She turned back as she opened the door. "Thank you for taking care of me."

"You're welcome."

"See ya later, Sebastian."

I winked. "See ya, Lacey."

Chapter 12

Lacey

I KNEW WHEN PENN, the Director of A&R at Castle Music, entered my office that the news was either going to be fantastic or terrible. He never made the trip to my office unless I'd explicitly set up a meeting here. A casual pop-in? Never.

The news was terrible. Castle Music had been courting an up-and-coming band, The Seditionists. Their manager had given Penn a courtesy call to let us know they'd be signing with a different label. Penn tried to counteroffer, but they firmly rebuffed it.

It was a huge loss for Castle. The Seditionists had immense talent and the right look to go along with it. It was a killer combination. I'd had a feeling about these guys — under the right management, they'd be huge — and my track record in picking bands was impeccable.

So I'd authorized Penn to roll out the red carpet. These days, I left all the wooing to his department, but maybe I should have gotten personally involved with this one when it was too big to lose.

Dammit. As soon as Penn left, I slammed my fists down on my desk in frustration. Who the hell had pilfered them right out from under our noses? I could probably find out in less than five minutes, but I didn't like to expose weakness to anyone. I'd wait for the news to be released to the public. It wasn't like I could change anything at this point.

Penn's news was just another dollop of shit-icing on the cake that was this week. I'd only taken a few days off work to go to Las Vegas and I came back to pure bedlam. Suddenly, it felt like everyone in the company urgently needed to meet with me while I was still trying to catch up on all the e-mails and meetings I'd missed. Then an ex-employee sued one of my managers, along with the company, for sexual harassment. I spent hours conferring with lawyers, so the matter could be handled delicately.

It came at me all at once while I was still grappling with whatever the hell had happened in Vegas. Yesterday, I'd managed to consult with a lawyer about that debacle. Nothing he told me eased my anxiety about any of it. The situation was sticky. A quick and easy annulment wasn't as sure of a thing as I'd assumed. Divorce took time, and publicity was an issue.

None of that mattered until I could determine if we actually got married. The lawyer advised me to wait for the marriage certificate to be filed because news could leak if he made inquiries and piqued someone's interest. I wasn't sure if a quickie Vegas wedding between me and Sebastian Archer would be newsworthy, but I'd rather not test it.

So, I had to sit back and wait, something I was decidedly not good at. Yesterday, Bash texted me just to check in on how I was doing. I knew I should fill him in on what the lawyer told me, but I was still emotionally reeling from everything.

After I received his text, I went to the ladies' room and discovered that I'd started my period. My reaction was shocking and out of nowhere. I broke down crying.

Of course, I'd been thinking about Vegas all week. One of my worries was that we might have had unprotected sex, and I'd been off birth control for months. In my mind, there had been a chance that I could be pregnant.

The terror that the possibility first brought had quickly and without my consent morphed into something else. My biological clock was ticking. Morph. I wanted a baby. Morph. Bash was a great father to Kody. Morph. I kind of liked Bash. Morph. Morph.

Before I knew it, I desperately wanted to be pregnant with Bash's baby. I actively fantasized about it for a few days.

Getting my period was a crushing blow. And it freaked me out that I was so upset about it. I was a complete head case.

Luckily, I only had a few more hours of work to get through before I could escape for the weekend and hopefully pull myself together. With the stressful week piling up, the bad news about The Seditionists, getting my period, and worrying about Vegas, I decided to spend the night at home. I didn't feel like being social. I'd order some food, eat in, enjoy a long soak in the tub, and just forget about everything for one night.

My admin, Nisha, stepped into my office holding a padded mailing envelope marked 'priority shipping'. "This came for you."

"Thank you, Nisha." I took the package from her and waited for her to retreat before ripping it open.

A jewel case slid onto my desk. I still got sent a surprising number of demo tapes from aspiring musicians. Usually, I had Nisha pass them along to an intern in A&R, even though I was pretty sure no one ever listened to them.

I flipped it over and froze.

My heart started racing. It wasn't a CD. It was a DVD with a picture of a white chapel on the front with the words 'Amore Mio Wedding Chapel' at the top. Across the bottom, it read 'Sebastian and Lacey' in a fancy scripted font.

Oh, my God. It was our wedding video.

I was married to Sebastian.

I quickly stuffed the jewel case back into the envelope and then sat stunned for several minutes. My mind was working frantically, but I wasn't quite sure how freaked out I was — atomic-level or just moderately panicked.

There was no way I was going to be able to work with this little time bomb ticking away on my desk. I ordered a car to pick me up at work and then began tidying up my office before I left for the weekend.

When my car arrived, I told Nisha to leave work early and start her weekend, and then I scurried out, clutching the incriminating envelope under my arm.

I was home before five o'clock, sitting on the couch and staring at the picture of the Amore Mio Wedding Chapel. I still hadn't gotten the courage to pop the disc into a DVD player. My stomach churned with nervous energy. I didn't think I could watch this alone, but no one else knew about my crazy weekend in Vegas. Normally, I'd confide in Kaylie, but that was definitely out of the question under the circumstances.

I picked up my phone and winced. It was a Friday night. He was probably heading out to party.

Me: Are you going out tonight?

Thankfully, he answered right away.

> **Bash:** No, hanging out with Kody.
> **Me:** Can I stop by?
> **Bash:** Stop by? Where are you?
> **Me:** Home.
> **Bash:** Sure, you can come by. It'll probably take you 45 minutes, though. I'm not close.
> **Me:** I know where you live.
> **Bash:** Do you want to come for dinner?
> **Me:** If you have enough. I don't need anything fancy.
> **Bash:** Chicken nuggets ok?
> **Bash:** Just kidding.
> **Bash:** Get over here.
> **Me:** See you soon.

I stuffed the DVD into my purse, grabbed my car keys, and was walking to the elevator before I could talk myself out of going.

My Mercedes was in its parking space just where I'd left it three weeks ago. I didn't drive my car all that often, using it mostly when I wanted to escape the city. Somewhere I'd heard that you should start your car at least once a week, but between Vegas and being busy, I hadn't driven it for almost a month. I breathed a sigh of relief when it started without a hitch and began the drive to Bash's house out in the suburbs.

It wasn't for too long in the stop-and-go L.A. traffic before I realized I was still wearing my 4-inch stilettos from work. I'd been so flustered by the DVD that I never changed out of my work clothes when I got home. Not about to turn around, I slipped the shoe off my right foot and drove the rest of the way barefoot.

I pulled up Bash's driveway and parked, and then I jumped out of the car right away before I could change my mind. I was nervous about seeing him again.

He answered the door wearing a fitted black T-shirt and gray sweatpants. How he made simple cotton loungewear look so hot, I'd never know.

"Hi." I stood on his porch awkwardly.

He stepped to the side and waved me in. "C'mon in. Kody is just finishing his dinner."

He led me into the kitchen where Kody was standing on top of the table, grinning ear to ear.

"Kody! How many times do I have to tell you?" Sebastian swept him off the table and then set him back in his seat. "No standing on the table. You could fall and get hurt."

Kody ignored his dad and waved his hand at me.

"Hi, Kody." I smiled at him. He was so cute and a little miniature version of Bash. There was no mistaking the resemblance between father and son.

"Kody, do you remember my friend Lacey?" Bash asked him.

Kody nodded. "Hi, Yacey. Do you want some nuggets?"

Sebastian stepped in before I had to answer. "Lacey is going to eat dinner with me, little man. Why don't you finish up so you can play before bedtime?"

"Okay, Dad."

His plate was almost empty, but I saw a few grapes, some broccoli spears, and a blob of sweet potato still remaining.

Bash leaned against the counter. "So, this is a nice surprise."

I swallowed nervously. "I wanted to talk to you."

His eyes flicked over to Kody. "Yeah. Let me get Kody finished up with dinner first. I've got some steak to throw on the grill for us."

My eyes widened. "You didn't have to do that. I wasn't expecting anything."

"No big deal." He brushed it off. "And I know you're a carnivore; you had steak in Vegas."

He'd noticed what I was eating, even though we weren't sitting near each other that night. Did it mean anything? Did I want it to?

We made small talk until Kody finished eating, then he set Kody up in the family room to play. He unrolled a kids' play rug that had a city street design on it and opened up a large bin full of play cars.

Kody grabbed a car in each hand. "Yacey, do you want to play cars with me?"

He looked so eager; I didn't want to disappoint him. "I forgot to change into my play clothes, Kody, so I can't sit on the floor. But I can watch you play."

I was wearing a navy power suit. Not the stodgy, buttoned-up woman's suit that was boxy and baggy. I only wore tailored suits with feminine details and sleek silhouettes that hugged and accented my curves. They showed a nice glimpse of cleavage, and the skirt always ended well above the knee. There was no doubt that my suits were a sexy statement, but they weren't the type of outfits that would impress a rockstar who had scantily dressed young women throwing themselves at him daily.

Bash looked me up and down. "If your work clothes are this hot, I'd love to see you in your play clothes."

Heat flushed over my skin. Wow! Was he flirting with me? Just wait until he found out that we were married. That'd put a damper on his flirtations.

I sat down to watch Kody play while Bash went to the kitchen to make dinner. He called out to me from across the open space, "Would you like a glass of wine?"

"God, no."

He chuckled. "Too soon?"

"Way too soon. I gave up alcohol. Remember?" I glanced over my shoulder. "But a glass of water would be great."

I sipped my water while I watched Kody creating traffic jams and car crashes on his mat. He was a little chatterbox while he played, narrating the action and showing me all his favorite cars. He told me about his dad's favorites and how his dad liked to drive them around the carpet, so I got the impression that Sebastian played this game with Kody all the time.

Watching Kody play while Sebastian made dinner should be the equivalent of watching paint dry. Such banal domesticity shouldn't warm my insides with quiet contentment. I shouldn't want to cuddle under a throw blanket and set up camp in Bash's family room.

Kody had been playing happily for quite a while when Bash finally came into the room. "Let's clean up your cars, Kody. It's bath time."

Kody started tossing his cars into the bin, and Bash knelt down beside him to help. It was impressive how Kody cleaned up without arguing.

Bash turned and gave me an apologetic smile. "The steaks need to rest, so I'm just going to give him a quick bath. He can play in the playroom while we eat dinner. Is that okay?"

"Of course." I understood that he had to stick to Kody's schedule. I shouldn't have shown up here with little warning. Sometimes I forgot that he wasn't out partying every night anymore; he had a kid to take care of. "I'm sorry. I feel like I'm disrupting you guys."

"No. It's not a problem. I'll be down in 15 minutes. Make yourself comfortable."

I kicked off my shoes and sat back on the couch while Bash gave Kody his bath. I thought about how Sebastian would react when he found out we were married. My mind drifted and wandered and soon he was back downstairs.

"Kody's so well-behaved. You've done a great job with him."

He waved me into the kitchen. "He has his moments, but for the most part, yeah, he's a great kid."

I stood by the kitchen island as he filled our plates with food.

"Filet mignon?"

He glanced up at me with a sly smile. "With garlic and herb butter. One of my specialties."

"Wow. That's impressive." I'd never cooked a steak in my life, so maybe I was easily impressed.

He shrugged. "I had to learn. I make dinner almost every night when I'm home. It was much easier when everything Kody ate came out of a little jar. Now I have to prepare stuff. Luckily, he's not a picky eater."

We brought our plates to the kitchen table and began eating. It was delicious.

"Is Kody okay by himself?"

"He's fine for short periods of time. I'll go check on him after we finish eating. Now that we have some privacy, what did you want to talk about?"

I might as well get this over with. "I met with a lawyer to consult about our ... situation."

I explained to him how the lawyer told me that a judge can only grant annulments for very strict legal reasons such as fraud, incest, or being underaged. We could argue that our 'mental capacity was unsound' because we were under the influence of alcohol, but we would actually have to prove that in court.

I put down my fork. "Even if we could prove that we were extremely drunk, the lawyer thought our chances were probably 50/50 that the judge would grant it."

"What's the harm in trying?"

"We'd be doing all of this in an open court, Bash. Declaring ourselves mentally unsound before a judge. Court records are public. I don't want that floating around out in public about myself." I pushed some food around my plate, suddenly nervous to bring up the most important aspect. "And what about you? What if you ever have another custody issue come up? What if being declared 'mentally unsound' could be used against you?"

He stopped eating. "Oh, fuck. I'm sorry, but there's no way I can chance it." He shook his head. "Christ, I never even thought about that."

As soon as the lawyer told me, I knew Bash wasn't going to go for that. I didn't blame him, but that meant we'd be married for the next six months.

"I understand." I took a sip of water. "We can go the divorce route. We can file for an uncontested divorce. It will take six months from the date of filing to go through. Official records of our marriage and divorce will exist, but I'm not sure how anyone would ever find out."

"That sounds like the better way to go." He began eating his dinner again. "That's assuming we actually got married."

I scrunched up my nose. "I'm pretty sure we did."

♫♫♪♪

Sebastian came back downstairs from tucking Kody into bed.

I was standing awkwardly in his family room, holding the DVD.

"It's so cute when he calls me Yacey."

"He has trouble saying his Ls. I talked to the pediatrician about it. She said it was quite common for kids his age and that he'd grow out of it by kindergarten."

"It's great that you're so on the ball with everything. You're a great dad. Kody is lucky."

Bash was looking at me funny and I realized that maybe I was gushing a little too much. We weren't used to being so friendly with each other.

He walked over to me and held out his hand for the DVD. "Well, wifey, are you ready to watch?"

I knew he was joking, but calling me wifey was doing things to me. There was a fluttering in my stomach that I was going to just chalk up to nerves. It had to be.

"No, I'm not ready. I'm so nervous. What if I made a fool of myself? I'm sure I did. I was so drunk."

"We both were." He had to pry the DVD from my hands because I was reluctant to let it go. He grimaced for a moment when he spotted the picture of the chapel. "If it's terrible, we'll burn it. But only after the divorce, in case we need it for evidence or something."

"I'm not sure I want to see it. Why don't we just burn it now?"

He pulled me close and then wrapped his arms around me. "I bet this is going to be hysterical. We were probably hamming it up the whole time. I hope Elvis married us. That would be pretty epic."

I was enjoying his arms around me way too much. I stepped back. "Only you would think that was cool."

His eyes lit up. "Should I make some popcorn?"

He was making me feel better. "Yeah, good idea."

Five minutes later, the popcorn was popped, and the DVD was inserted into his Xbox console. He sat down on the couch with the bowl of popcorn and patted the cushion next to him. "C'mon, wifey. Let's do this."

I walked over to the couch and plopped down beside him. "Are you going to call me 'wifey' for the next six months?"

He turned to me and smiled. "Yep."

I smacked his shoulder playfully. "Ok. Let's watch it."

It started off with 'Sebastian and Lacey's Wedding' being written out letter by letter before swirling and zipping off the screen using some cheesy effects. Then there was a short clip of footage taken from outside, showing the chapel before the camera zoomed in on a sign that read 'Amore Mio Wedding Chapel'.

I grabbed some popcorn from the bowl and began to munch. On the TV screen, I was walking down the aisle to the traditional Wedding March. God, I would never choose that for my real wedding. I wasn't skipping or stumbling; I looked quite serious, clutching the same wedding bouquet I'd left in Sebastian's hotel room. As I walked by the camera, the focus shifted to Bash, waiting at the end of the aisle. He was grinning like a fool.

I grabbed more popcorn and snorted. "We look so stupid."

On screen, Bash took my hand as I approached. "You are so beautiful."

A smile lit up my face. "Thank you, Sebastian."

His eyes were locked on mine. "Will you be my wife forever? I need you, Lacey."

Holy shit! This was so uncomfortable. Bash was shifting restlessly on the couch next to me. So far, none of this was a hysterical slapstick comedy. It was utterly embarrassing.

For some reason, I tossed the flower bouquet over my shoulder. "Let's do this! We're getting married! And then we can go make a baby!"

I choked on a popcorn kernel. A wave of mortification flooded me. I sunk a few inches lower on the couch, wanting to disappear into the cushions. Forever.

"Fuck," Bash muttered next to me.

Back on the screen, Bash was nodding his agreement. "A little brother or sister for Kody."

"Yes!" I clapped my hands happily.

Bash pulled me close to his body. His hand wrapped around the nape of my neck and tangled in my hair. "Do you love me?"

"Truth serum?" My gaze was locked on him.

"Truth serum."

"I love you," I said solemnly.

Please, make this stop. Please! For the love of God!

We started kissing. With tongue. The officiant had to pull us apart. It wasn't Elvis. It was a very short woman in a black dress. "Hold on, you two. Hold on and we'll begin."

She repositioned us and then spoke in a very theatric voice. "Today we are gathered to celebrate the love that Sebastian and Lacey have for each other and to recognize and witness their decision to journey forward as marriage partners. Your love has brought us here today. May it grow deeper and sweeter with each passing year."

We joined our hands together and interlocked fingers. Bash smiled sweetly at me.

The officiant turned to Bash and asked, "Sebastian, do you take Lacey to be your wedded wife? To have and to hold from this day forward, for richer or poorer, in sickness and health, to love and to cherish, for as long as you both shall live?

He nodded. "I do."

We were staring at each other on the video like two love-sick puppies.

The officiant asked me the same question and my voice rang out clearly, "I do."

"Now, you have each written some vows you'd like to express to each other. Lacey?" The officiant indicated that I should proceed.

I was starting to sweat. We wrote vows? While we were plastered? I was praying for a freak electrical storm to knock out the power so this nightmare would end.

In the video, I unfolded a piece of paper and began reading:

> Sebastian,
> I give you my hand and my heart,
> and pledge my love, devotion, faith,
> and honor as I join my life to yours.
> I promise to always be spontaneous
> and to cherish each moment,
> to be willing to try new things,
> to dream with you, to laugh together,
> to be your biggest fan,
> and to encourage you to chase your dreams.
> And I promise to be your accomplice
> in all kinds of mischief till the end of time.

How the hell had I come up with all of that? There must have been samples that we could choose from. It was the only explanation.

Bash took my hand and squeezed it. "Aw, wifey, that was really sweet."

I pulled my hand away. "Don't you dare make fun of me—"

I stopped because Bash was on the screen reading his own vows from a piece of paper.

> I choose you,
> Lacey Rae Davenport,
> to be my partner for life
> and my one true love.
> I promise you my deepest love,
> my fullest devotion, my tenderest care
> through the pressures of the present
> and the uncertainties of the future.
> I promise to be faithful to you.
> I promise to love you,
> to commit to you
> and support you.
> I pledge to respect your
> unique talents and abilities,
> and to lend you strength for all of
> your dreams.
> And most importantly,
> I promise to always keep you
> deeply and thoroughly satisfied.

He said the last part with a cocky smirk on his face. I launched myself into his arms. We were going in for another kiss when the officiant wormed her way between us again. "Hold on!"

She turned us to face the camera and then announced, "And now, it gives me great pleasure to say:

By the power vested in me by the State of Nevada, I now pronounce you husband and wife. You may—"

Bash and I were already going at it like horny teenagers.

"—kiss your bride!"

The screen faded to black as we were wrestling tongues and pawing at each other.

I sat motionless. I was too stunned to move. Absolutely gobstruck by the vows. The kissing. The lovey-dovey.

Bash was just as quiet, sitting next to me.

I'd expected to see two sloppy drunks getting hitched. Instead, it was this mushy, romantic lovefest.

I thought about making a run for the door. And then what? I'd live my life pretending it never happened. It was an option. An option that was looking pretty good right now.

"What the fuck?" Shock imbued his voice.

I refused to look at him. Nope.

"I don't even know what to say. That was..."

I threw out a few guesses to help him along. "Insane? Crazy? Fucked up? Shocking? Embarrassing? Awkward as fuck? Am I getting close yet?"

"Yeah." His chin dropped to his chest.

"Let's burn it."

"After the divorce. For now, I'll keep it under lock and key."

My head whipped around so I could pin him with my fiercest stare. "Don't ever let anyone see that."

A little huff of air escaped from his lips. "Believe me, I won't."

I jumped up off the couch. "I have to go. Let's never discuss this video again."

Bash stood up. "Sure, wifey."

Chapter 13

Bash

"I SHOULD HAVE BROUGHT some glow-in-the-dark condoms."

Noah was grinning; I could see his white teeth eerily glowing a few feet from me. The girl on his lap squealed and then whispered something in his ear.

We were at a club that was hosting a rave. The walls were glowing with psychedelic patterns and the patrons had come prepared with fluorescent clothing, neon face and body paint, glow-in-the-dark jewelry and nail polish, and tons of glowsticks.

I was wearing all black, so I was almost invisible except for some specks of phosphorescent lint on my shirt and for several smeared patches of neon pink paint that had rubbed off Carrie's face onto various parts of me.

Long ago, I'd ditched the glowing drink special and switched to beer. I had to hold on to it or else it, too, disappeared into the darkness.

Carrie was friends with the girl that was currently writhing on top of Noah. That was all that I knew about her. The music was too loud to do any talking. People were either dancing, drinking, or groping each other in the dark. I was probably the only one in the entire place not rolling on MDMA. A little molly would probably help me relax, but I didn't trust the capsule that Noah had pressed into my hand. I had real responsibilities now and even if the drugs were legit, I didn't want to chance a molly comedown when I was taking care of Kody tomorrow.

Noah was back in L.A. with his band, Burnt Crimson, preparing to record their second album. I'd jumped at the chance to go out with him when he texted. I hadn't been out in weeks. If I'd known his drummer, Dean Coswell, was coming out, I would have passed. While Noah was generally good-natured and fun to party with, his bandmate was a supreme asshole. Not a grumpy, brooding asshole, but a rude and abrasive prick with a giant ego and loud mouth who would slide a shiv in your side for simply looking at him the wrong way. I'd been around his type long enough in this business; I didn't need to endure it in my free time.

Apparently, Carrie wasn't getting enough attention from me because she swiveled on the couch and was now pawing at Dean, even though he was already occupied with another female.

I thought about texting Sid to make sure Kody was okay, but a glance at my phone showed it was after midnight. Sid had texted me hours ago to let me know that Kody had gone to bed with no trouble. He hadn't stayed overnight with Sid and Kaylie in almost a year, since well before she had the twins.

I knew Sid missed hanging out with him. A pang of guilt stabbed me in the gut. Sid had bonded with Kody when he was an infant — the time I should have been bonding with him. Thank God my best friend was a hell of a lot smarter than me.

Carrie turned back to me, almost jostling my phone out of my hand. She began rubbing up against me and trying to aim her tongue down my throat. I turned my head in time, so instead, she was stabbing at my jaw and neck with wet pokes of her tongue. I had to palm her face with my hand to get her to stop.

Undeterred, her hand slithered down to my crotch while she pressed up against me. I'd seen junkyard dogs who humped with more discrimination. For a brief second, I wondered if I should let her give me a blowjob. I hadn't had action, outside of my hand, for over a month. Ever since I'd gotten fucking married.

A few weeks ago, I'd gone out with Knox and Ryder. I'd met a gorgeous woman — a fashion model — and after my friends took off, we decided to head back to her place. Sometime during the cab ride, while we were kissing, I realized that I couldn't do it. I asked the driver to pull over, threw some tip money at him, and then jumped out of the cab, all the while apologizing to the bewildered girl.

Tonight wouldn't be any better. I'd been determined to have fun and get over my dry spell, but the downside of not being on drugs was to see everything around you with clear eyes. Carrie would hump anything or anyone in sight, and it disgusted me. I didn't want her to touch me. My hand would be much more appealing.

The random bursts of pulsating strobe lights were maddening. Carrie's clawing hands were worse. I stood up, leaving her an upended heap on the cushions, needing to get out of there.

I'd go back to Sid and Kaylie's place; it was only a ten-minute ride away. That way, I could wake up and have breakfast with Kody and visit for a bit with my nephews.

Noah turned his head to the side when I tapped his shoulder. I told him I was taking off. He either didn't hear me or didn't care and turned his attention back to the girl on top of him. I texted him the same message on the way out in case he wondered later and then I ordered a cab.

I pushed open the exit door and breathed in the cold night air. Silence buzzed in my ears after leaving behind the loud techno music. I was equally happy to leave behind the frantic strobe lighting, but this area of town was sketchy, so I hoped the cab would show up quickly.

The night had been disappointing. I was beginning to think that something was wrong with me. Had I lost my mojo? No, that wasn't it. I still attracted beautiful women; I just didn't want them. The fuck?

Having Kody had slowed down my man-whorish ways a lot, but I'd still always wanted to have sex even if it wasn't always practical. This new, troubling problem — actively turning down sex with attractive and willing women — all started with that stupid marriage fiasco in Las Vegas. It had been some kind of drunken caper that had gone wrong.

Something about being married, even if it wasn't real, was blocking me. It wasn't fair. Lacey was probably out having sex all the time. We'd never promised to be faithful to each other. Except in those vows. Those fucking vows.

Jesus Christ, I'd secretly watched that wedding video more times than I wanted to admit. At first, I needed to see it without Lacey being there, so I could process it all and maybe make sense of what I saw.

Watching it over and over didn't clear up anything for me. What I saw was troubling. Uncomfortable. I'd always had a little crush on Lacey whether I'd admitted it to myself before. When I met her, she was full of life and loved to party, kind of like the female version of myself. There was no doubt how sexy she was, and then Lacey, Sid, and I had that amazing threesome. My harmless crush was strangled by jealousy when she hooked up with Sidney after that. I began to avoid her. Somehow I knew that she was trouble for me.

And then, Vegas. I'd been too drunk to shield myself. Who knows how or why we ended up married, but I suspected it was probably some joke we concocted while plastered. I watched that video where she told me she loved me and made a comment about making babies. I'd studied my responses and it sure as shit looked like I was really in love with her. It hadn't been a joke to me and I didn't know what to do with that.

Now, I was acting like the marriage was real. I couldn't hook up with anyone; I was keeping my vows. It was ridiculous. I had to end this nonsense. She may have thought it was all fun and games, but this joke of a marriage was affecting my life. The more I thought about it, the angrier I became. How could she pull this stunt and just walk away? None of this sat well with me.

My anger was really brewing by the time the cab pulled up to the curb. I hopped in and slammed the door shut. Without thinking twice, I leaned forward and gave the driver Lacey's address.

I cooled my jets in the lobby of her apartment building while the doorman called Lacey. I hadn't really thought this through; she was probably still out.

The doorman hung up the phone and then approached me. "If you'll follow me to the elevator, sir, I'll key you in."

He ushered me inside an elevator and before I could ask him any questions, the door slid shut. Great, I didn't even know her apartment number; I'd have to text her. The elevator started ascending, even though I didn't see any indication of what floor it'd be stopping on.

I was too busy trying to figure out what I was going to tell Lacey my reason for being there was that I didn't even notice when the elevator stopped on the 35th floor, the very top floor, until the doors slid open.

She lived in a penthouse. Currently, the lighting was dimmed, but a quick glance around revealed the opulence. The place was open and airy with 12-foot high coffered ceilings and a wall of glass that looked out over downtown. White and modern furniture and tons of fresh flowers brightened the space. I remembered how my polyamorous blind date hated flowers. Clearly, Lacey didn't share that attribute.

"Where are you coming from?"

I glanced to the left where her voice had sounded from. She was in the kitchen, pulling something out of a large refrigerator.

"I was out with Noah Radner. He's the guitarist for Burnt Crimson."

She walked over to where I was standing and handed me a bottle of water. "I know who he is."

My jaw clenched. Of course, she did. She knew every musician in this town and then some. Noah was a complete womanizer. I wondered if he'd fucked Lacey and the thought pissed me off.

She walked into the living room and I followed like a puppy dog. She didn't bother turning on any more lights, but she did pick up a remote control and turned on the fireplace.

I was staring at her ass and I only ripped my eyes away just in time before she caught me. She was wearing a pajama set, a black silk camisole that had spaghetti straps with matching shorts. Sexy lace decorated the neckline of the top and the hem of the shorts. She'd been showing more skin in what turned out to be her wedding dress in Vegas than in these pajamas, but I could see her nipples pebbling beneath the silk and my mouth went dry. Fuck, she was so hot. I never saw her with no makeup on and her hair not perfectly styled. She was so fucking gorgeous.

She broke the silence. "You smell like cheap perfume."

What could I say to that? Carrie had been rubbing up against me all night.

Her eyes narrowed as she looked me over. "What is that pink all over you?"

Why did I feel so guilty? "There was some girl with face paint on. It was a blacklight thing."

"Are you drunk?" her voice was biting. "You hooked up with some girl, and what? She turned you down, so you came here? Or, you decided to come here for a second round?"

Damn, she sounded just like a nagging wife, and it ticked me off. "Actually, I turned her down. Just like I have all the other damn girls for the past month. Because I'm fucking married."

She laughed like she didn't believe a word I said and it got me even angrier.

"It's not funny. I need to speed up this divorce because apparently, I can't break my wedding vows. Some of us have morals."

"Oh, give me a break," she scoffed. "Bash, I give you my permission. You can break the wedding vows all you want. Is that what you need?"

Fuck. My chest rose and fell with rapid breaths. "What I need is a goddamn divorce!"

I immediately regretted saying it when hurt flashed in her eyes, but it was quickly covered up.

She turned her back to me and faced the gas flames of the fireplace. "We can't speed up the divorce. There's a mandatory 6-month waiting period."

I put down the water bottle on a side table. "I can't wait six months. It's driving me crazy." I stalked closer to her and ran a hand through my hair. "I can't stop thinking about Vegas. We're married, Lace!"

She wasn't responding, and I was about to start pulling at my hair. "I can't think about anything else. We made vows and I can't get over it. I haven't been able to fuck anyone. I tried. I can't even kiss anyone without getting disgusted."

She turned to face me. We were standing so close now, I could feel the air crackling between us.

Her question was softly spoken. "What do you want from me, Bash?"

"I want to fuck my wife."

Chapter 14

Lacey

"I WANT TO FUCK my wife."

The air between us sparked hot and heavy, making it impossible to draw a full breath.

I swallowed as a rush of desire swept through me. "That's not a good idea."

He stood so close to me, I could feel the heat coming off him. Why did he have to look so incredibly sexy right now? I desperately wanted to give in, but the smell of cheap perfume and the pink splotches on his clothes reminded me of how dumb that idea was.

Looking into my eyes, he reached out and put his palm on my cheek. "We're married, Lacey. There's nothing wrong with enjoying each other."

Quivers of longing ricocheted down my spine. I'd thought he was drunk when he showed up, but now I wasn't sure. It was almost 1 a.m. and he'd shown up out of the blue for a booty call. I didn't really believe his adult tantrum about keeping his vows and not being able to have sex. That seemed unlikely for someone like him.

He'd always been a man whore. I'd never minded in the past, but I was a different person now, looking for different things. I was 32 years old — past meaningless hookups and more into exploring longer-term relationships. I needed to send him home.

Trying to hold on to my sanity, I let out a soft breath. "That would just complicate things." I remembered the video of our wedding — how my stomach churned while watching it. It had dredged up weird emotions I couldn't even pin down. Or even worse, I thought about when I cried when I got my period because I wasn't pregnant with his baby. Fooling around with Bash was certainly not an emotionally healthy choice for me.

His thumb swiped slowly across my bottom lip. "Things are already complicated, wifey."

My eyes fluttered closed. It shocked me how much I wanted him. A desperate need pulsed between my thighs and my nipples tightened into two aching buds. Every nerve ending in my body was tingling with anticipation.

He dragged my lower lip down with his thumb and I couldn't keep the tip of my tongue from darting out to taste it.

Oh, God. I hadn't been with another man since the dominant/submissive relationship I had at the Scarlett Club. My dom had given me so many orgasms, but never with his cock. I hadn't had that type of intimacy with a man since Theo, and I missed it. And Bash was a good lover. We were actually married. Why should I turn this down? Would it be so bad to give in?

My eyes opened, and I moaned softly. He was watching me with his gorgeous green eyes that had darkened with arousal. He wanted me. I had no doubt that sex with Bash would be mind-blowing, just not so wonderful for my heart. I tried one more time to resist.

"Bash, this is not—"

He reached down to take my hands and planted them firmly on his chest. Then he pressed closer to me.

Desire crashed through me, heating my blood. His chest was rock solid beneath my hands and I knew, at that moment, that I was going to give in to my lust.

"Kiss me." It was a gruff command. There was absolutely no chance I wouldn't obey.

I leaned up on my toes and placed my lips against his. As soon as I made contact with his mouth, he took over. One hand slid behind my head, angling it perfectly to fit our mouths together, and the other wrapped around my waist like an iron band, pulling and then trapping me against him.

He'd told me to kiss him, but his mouth was the one mastering mine. His tongue was thrusting deep; his lips were demanding. He took, and took, and took everything I could give. Just one kiss had me drunk on his taste and wild with need. I moaned beneath his lips as my hips mindlessly pressed into his hardness.

After an intoxicating few minutes, he dragged his lips from mine while his fingers wrapped around my hair and gave a firm tug to expose my neck. He teased the delicate column of my neck with his lips and teeth and then sucked a bit of skin right at my fluttering pulse point. A sweet shiver ran down my spine as his lips traveled up to the sensitive spot just behind my ear.

"I'm going to fuck you so hard, you'll be screaming my name." His words were a dark, silky seduction that sent fire scorching through my veins.

"Yes." I was putty in his hands. He could do anything he wanted. I was already lost.

A deep growl of satisfaction rumbled from his chest. He turned my body, pinning my back to the front of his muscled frame. At the same time, his warm hand slipped under my camisole, his fingers splaying against my stomach. I felt so small compared to him, especially when I wasn't in high heels. He towered over me, engulfing me in his presence.

He nuzzled my neck with his lips while he slid his hand up to palm my breast. His thumb circled my stiff and aching nipple, over and over, sending a shockwave of sensation tearing through my body. I moaned when he gave it a sharp pinch and then he switched to teasing my other nipple with the same sweet torture.

My head fell back against his chest. I couldn't escape the overwhelming sensations even if I wanted to; he was holding me so tight. I never wanted this glorious seduction to end.

I gasped when his other hand slipped beneath my silky shorts and cupped my mound in a shockingly possessive manner. A raspy growl of approval had my knees turning to rubber. "Tell me this sweet pussy is mine."

I moaned but didn't answer.

He pulled on my nipple. "Who's pussy is it, wifey?"

"It's yours."

"Take me to your bedroom," he demanded.

I grabbed his hand and led him to my room as fast as my trembling legs would allow me. He was pushing all my buttons. We hadn't even gotten our clothes off yet, and I was drenched and panting with need.

He stopped me when we got to the edge of my bed. "Tell me what you want."

My gaze locked onto his. The intensity in his eyes was enough to melt my insides. "I want your cock inside me."

A predatory grin crossed his lips. "You're going to get it, don't worry."

Bash was vibrating with so much sexual energy I almost needed to step back.

He dropped my hand. "Take my shirt off."

I took a shaky breath. He was so controlling — the way he ordered me around. I absolutely loved it. I hated when a man was passive in bed. Or quiet. Bash was neither passive nor quiet. Those filthy, possessive words he uttered had me wetter than I'd been for a man in a long time.

I wasted no time sliding the shirt up his toned body and pulling it off. His body was made for sin, and I couldn't wait to worship it. My hands smoothed over his skin, exploring the ridges of his six-pack abs and dipping just below the waistband of his jeans.

"Take them off me, Lacey," he rasped.

Yes. I was very eager to see him; I had his jeans unbuttoned and unzipped within seconds. Dragging his briefs down with his pants, I quickly had him stepping out of his clothes and completely naked. I knelt in front of him, eye level with his cock. Arousal hit like a stormy wave crashing over me. I licked my lips, desperately wanting a taste, but I waited.

Bash groaned. "You have my head spinning, wifey. You can suck my dick, then I'm gonna fuck you good."

I parted my lips and, without a moment's hesitation, he pushed right into my mouth, thrusting a few times slowly in and out. When I was ready, I braced my hands against his thighs and lifted my eyes up to him. He anchored my head with his palm and then pushed his dick all the way to the back of my throat.

He retreated when my throat caught and squeezed reflexively against him, but I wouldn't let him escape too far. I slid my mouth back over his cock, alternating between sucking him hard or swirling my tongue along the underside of his shaft and giving extra attention to the head.

I didn't necessarily love giving head, but this was one of the rare exceptions. My fingers slid between my legs, trying to relieve the aching throb there, while my other hand worked in tandem with my mouth to pleasure him.

He shook his head. "That pussy is mine. I'll take care of it."

I hummed my disapproval around his cock, but stopped touching myself. Instead, I redoubled my efforts to make him come until my eyes were watering.

He looked so incredibly hot. He was biting his lip and making appreciative grunts with each thrust between my lips. I could tell he was about to come by the sexy noises he was making, but then he pulled out of my mouth.

"Those lips are going to kill me, Lacey."

He reached down with a hand to help me stand up. I was disappointed that he didn't come in my mouth, but I knew that he was probably saving that beautiful cock for something else I'd enjoy just as much.

His finger traced a path along my collarbone and then slid the spaghetti strap of my camisole off my shoulder. "I want you so bad it hurts."

I stood in front of him, shaking with need, but remained silent.

He tipped my chin up with a finger until I was staring into those mesmerizing green eyes. "You're so fucking beautiful. I want to lick every inch of your skin."

"Mmm... Yes, please."

His hands skimmed down my sides until he found the bottom of my silk camisole top. He dragged the fabric up over my swollen, tender breasts, muttering 'fuck' when they bounced as they popped free. He wasted no time pouncing on one with his mouth, lashing a nipple with his tongue, and tweaking the other with his fingers. My hands slid over his shoulders, anchoring me, so I didn't fall into a heap at his feet as he tortured my aching nipples.

He pulled away from my breast and a low, primal noise rumbled from his throat. In less than a minute, he'd whisked off my pajama shorts and walked me backward until I was falling onto the bed. Like a caveman, he pulled me by the ankles until I was settled at the edge, just where he wanted me.

I held my breath as he pushed open my thighs and waited for the bliss that was sure to come. After a few seconds of nothing, I opened my eyes. He was staring at my pussy. When he didn't make a move, I started to close my legs. That quickly snapped him out of his pussy-induced daze. He forced his shoulders between my legs and then the bliss really did begin.

He flattened his tongue and then lapped at my pussy in long, greedy strokes. When his thumb swirled in my moisture and then began rhythmically gliding over my clit, I fisted the bedsheets at my side and hung on for dear life.

His tongue fluttered over my clit, even as his thumb kept up its relentless torture. Fingers slid into my pussy and relentlessly rubbed against the sweetest part of me.

I could no longer keep up with what was happening to me because the pleasure was ramping up to near-unbearable levels. My hips were chasing his every move, rocking and bucking against his mouth until he pinned me down with his forearm so that he could wholly dismantle me by firmly sucking on my swollen clit.

A strangled groan tore from my lips. "Oh God, please. Don't stop."

The coil of pressure built as he played my body perfectly. His fingers stroked my walls in a steady rhythmic pattern and then, just as I was about to rush headlong over the edge, he'd stop moving his fingers inside me and focus his tongue on pleasuring my clit. The back and forth kept me on the edge for several delirious minutes until I finally exploded.

The rush of pleasure was fierce. My body coiled and spiraled, higher and higher, until my orgasm ripped through me with jolting force. I screamed out his name as my hands fisted in his hair. My pussy clenched in pulsing waves around his fingers, which were still buried deep inside me.

He pulled his fingers out, popped them into his mouth, and sucked them clean. "Fuck, you taste so good."

He stalked up my body like a predator and hovered over me. His lips met mine in a kiss that was long and sweet. I could feel his hard cock so close to my pussy, which was still trembling with aftershocks.

He laid a territorial hand on my breast and gave it a squeeze. "I'm going to take you from behind and fuck you harder and deeper than you've ever been fucked before. Turn over on your stomach."

A tiny shudder skittered down my body. My toes actually curled with anticipation. Bash pulled back and grabbed his jeans off the floor. He was searching for a condom.

I flipped over onto my stomach while I waited. The way he'd just worked my body with his tongue and fingers was magical. I'd never been with someone with such unchecked talent. He was a 9th-level black belt oral pleasure provider. A freaking grand master of cunnilingus.

The only other time that had come close was…

I flashed back to the night of the threesome. It was the first time I'd received oral sex from Bash and it was fantastic. If what I was about to experience was anything like what I'd felt that night, I couldn't wait to feel his cock inside me.

A weight sunk onto the bed. Bash was crawling up my body. He stopped at my ass cheek, nipped with his teeth, but then climbed directly over me, propping himself on his forearms.

I tipped my ass up. "Get inside me."

He took both my hands in his and then slid them up until they extended fully over my head. His breath was warm on my ear. "Patience, wifey."

I wiggled my ass. "Sebastian, please."

His full length pressed against my body. He took my hands and locked them in place with one of his, and then his other hand was skimming over my back and slipping between my thighs with a territorial sweep of the hand.

He sucked on the sensitive skin where my neck met my shoulder and I hoped it'd leave a mark. I squirmed impatiently and more of his weight settled on me.

If there was one thing I loved during sex, it was being restrained, and Bash had effectively trapped me underneath his body. He held my hands in an iron grip; his legs were entangled in mine, and the weight of his body pressed into me. His warm skin crushed against mine, rendering me helpless, and I just melted.

I whimpered with need. Desire curled in my stomach, and the pulsing ache tightened between my legs to nearly unendurable. I twitched when I felt his dick sliding around in my wetness. I spread my legs, and he pushed in slowly until finally he was fully seated.

He continued kissing me — on my back, my shoulder, my neck — as he thrust into me very slowly and deliberately. It felt so unbelievably good, and yet it wasn't enough. He shifted positions above me and I missed the feel of his weight on me, but then he slipped a hand under my hips and with his fingers slowly circled my clit in time with every thrust of his cock. It was heavenly. I wanted it to last forever.

Until he sped up. Then I was burying my face in the mattress, trying to stifle the crazy noises bursting from my mouth as I spiraled upwards at the speed of light. I was about to ignite.

"Scream for me, Lacey." He grunted out and pumped into me harder.

It hit me like a bolt of lightning. Zings of pure electric energy pulsed through every neuron and every nerve-ending in my body, and then I detonated into a writhing mass of bliss.

Even as the orgasm was wreaking havoc on all my senses, Bash was pulling my hips up and kneeling behind me so he could pound into me with more force. I did scream then.

It was four or five more thrusts before he tensed up and then was grunting with his own release.

I was so blissed out; I laughed a little bit. "That was so, so good."

Bash pulled out of me and I collapsed back onto the mattress. "Come back here." I wanted to feel wrapped up in him again.

"Let me take care of this first." He climbed off the bed and headed to the bathroom.

It was a good thing he remembered the condom. He had me so worked up; I would have gone bareback with him if he'd asked.

When he came back and climbed into bed beside me, I didn't move a muscle. I was in a dreamy, euphoric state. "Mmm. Come over here. I want to feel you on top of me again."

"On top of you?" He seemed confused.

"Mmm."

He scooched over and then gingerly climbed on top of me. He was resting on his forearms, not giving me all of his weight, but the full-body skin contact felt amazing.

"Like this?" he asked.

My eyes closed. "Yeah, just like this."

I was fully relaxed. I was warm, cozy, and safe. Fully sated.

"Fuck, Lacey. I'm getting hard again. Give me a few minutes. This time I want you to ride my cock so I can watch you come."

"Mmm. Sounds wonderful."

Chapter 15

Bash

I WOKE UP AS hard as a rock with a smile plastered on my face. Lacey was tucked in my arms; her killer body nestled closely next to mine. Waking up in bed with a woman usually set off a chain of panic-induced thoughts that usually ended with me making a plan for a quick escape. Instead, I was wondering how long I could stay.

Kody usually woke up early — he was probably awake by now — but he was in good hands with Kaylie and Sid. I could spend a few more hours here without raising any eyebrows. After the exhilaration of drowning myself in Lacey's body last night, I wanted to do it again and again. As much as she'd let me.

I had no idea how she'd feel this morning. Would she regret what we did? We didn't talk much after we had sex. I'd been gearing up for round two when she fell asleep. For a fleeting moment, I'd thought about leaving and staying at Sid's place, but then realized I was exactly where I wanted to be. I don't know if it was our fucked up marriage, my finally admitting to myself my attraction to her, or the fucking mind-blowing sex we'd had, but I didn't want to leave her side. I wanted to worship her body until this crazy infatuation ran its course.

Fuck, she was so hot. I pulled the sheets that were covering us down very slowly so that her breasts were exposed. Like a horny pervert, I checked them out. She was sleeping on her side, with her chest smashed against mine, so they looked extra fucking luscious. Suddenly, I had a vision of sliding my dick through the tight crack of her cleavage, and that in turn reminded me of how impressively she'd worked me with that mouth of hers, taking me to the back of her throat until I was seeing stars. She'd been hungry for me and that was arousing as fuck. I needed to cover up her tits because my already hard cock was now throbbing mercilessly.

She stiffened in my arms and her breathing hitched, but then she relaxed. "Sebastian," she mumbled sleepily.

Fuck, that one word — my name — sounded like gold coming from her lips. Every time she said it, it gave me a potent high like the quick hit of a drug. She'd called me Sebastian a few times during sex, and the resulting buzz in my veins almost had me coming.

I hoped like hell that she didn't regret last night. She hadn't pulled out of my arms yet, so maybe that was a good sign.

"Morning, wifey." I liked calling her that as much as I liked her calling me Sebastian. I had no fucking idea why.

Her eyes were still closed, but she smiled. "Why do you keep calling me that?"

"Because it's true. You are my wife. And I get a kick out of reminding you."

She groaned and then rolled away from me. She was getting out of bed, and I didn't like it.

"Where are you going?"

She looked at me over her shoulder. "To the bathroom."

"Fine," I grumbled. "But then get your sexy ass back over here."

I guessed there was about a 50/50 chance that she'd come back to bed. When she came back into the room, I didn't try to disguise that I was eye-fucking her glorious, naked body. She was way hotter than any skinny-ass model because she had delicious curves in all the right places. She climbed back into bed and snuggled right up to me.

My fingers ran lightly up and down her arm. "I have a proposal for you."

"You're a little too late." She laughed. "We're already married."

"Not that kind of proposal." My hand ran down her smooth skin. Fuck, I wanted her so badly. "I propose that while we're still married, until the divorce, that we keep having sex."

Her hand, which had been testing my biceps — which I may or may not have been flexing — stopped moving. "Bash, there's a reason we're getting a divorce and divorcing couples don't usually have sex."

"Why are we getting a divorce?" I didn't mean to sound obtuse, but her flippant answer kind of hurt me.

"Because we didn't mean to get married! We were both out of our minds, drunk on absinthe."

I had to dial it back a bit. She was getting upset. "Okay, true. But we are married right now and we just had sex. And it was enjoyable. Way fucking better than enjoyable. Lace, we're like dynamite together in the sack. Is it just me?"

She sighed. "No, I enjoyed it, too. Obviously. It was amazing. But, we're friends. We can't keep having sex."

"We're more than friends. We're married." Yes, I was hung up on that.

She pulled out of my arms and took the covers with her. "You keep saying that like it means something. I don't even remember marrying you. That video we watched of our wedding was like two other people saying those things. Plus, we're divorcing. So don't throw around 'we're married' like that should make me have sex with you. Like I'm obligated by marital duty."

I groaned. Somehow, I was fucking this up. "That's not what I mean. Lacey, I'm saying it does mean something. I don't know what, but we got married. And for whatever reason, I take the vows seriously. Even if we don't have sex again, I won't be with other women until we're divorced. I can't. And yes, we are friends. Friends who just fucked, and it was damn good, Lacey. Tell me you didn't think it was amazing. Why wouldn't we do it again?"

She fell back against her pillow. "You mean like a friends-with-benefits situation?"

"Yeah." I guess. If that's all she'd give me.

She bit her bottom lip, contemplating it for so long that I got nervous. "And we wouldn't tell any of our friends? We'd tell no one? It'd have to be a secret."

My eyes narrowed. "Why not?"

"I'm serious, Bash." She rubbed at her face with her hand. "No one can know we're having sex."

"Okay. I promise, Lacey, I won't tell anyone."

She stared at me for a long moment. "I'll only do it on one condition."

I was almost scared to ask. "What?"

A flash of nervousness crossed her face. "I want you to be my Dom."

I didn't know what I was expecting her to say, but it was not that. It took a few seconds for my brain to even figure out what she meant. I still wasn't entirely sure. "Uh, I don't know. I have an idea of what you mean, but I know nothing about that kind of stuff. You're talking latex and whips? That kind of thing?"

Her cheeks pinked. "I want to experiment. In bed. I want you to take care of all my fantasies. As my Dom."

I had to tread carefully here. "I'd love to experiment in bed with you, Lace. I'd do whatever you wanted. But a dom? I don't know how to do that."

She was picking at the sheets, not able to meet my eyes. "You are very dominant in bed. The things you do..."

My brows knitted. "That's just being a guy."

She looked up at me. "No, not every guy is. You're naturally dominant. For my whole life, I've ended up dominating most men in bed and you know what? I don't like it. It doesn't turn me on. I give any order and they follow it. In my professional life, too. All day, I make decisions. I make demands. I command. And they follow it. You hold me down and fuck me hard. It feels so good. Like you wouldn't let me up. You just take what you want."

I ran a hand through my hair. "Jesus Christ, you make it sound like rape."

"No, you would have stopped if that's what I wanted. There's a difference. If you were my Dom, there would be safe words, and it's all worked out beforehand. The likes and dislikes. The limits. And I'd only want you to be my Dom in the bedroom. During scenes. Playtime." The more she talked, the more confident she sounded. "It's a kink I have, and I'd like to explore it with you. Only if you were comfortable with it, of course. We'd take it slow and figure it out together. I trust you, Sebastian. We've known each other for a long time; I know what a good guy you are. And obviously, you're attractive and skilled in bed."

I wasn't sure what the fuck I was getting into, but I knew I'd do it for her. "So, we'd have sex again? Actual sex? Or are we talking only whips and chains?"

Her hair was all mussed up and her face was glowing. As she was growing excited about the topic, the sheet was slipping down her body and showing off her gorgeous tits again. I'd never seen her more beautiful.

"Playtime doesn't have to always involve sex, but apparently, I like sensual BDSM. So yeah, I enjoy the sex parts of it. If you ordered me to mop the floors or clean toilets, I'd tell you to fuck off. But slap some restraints on me and give me some sexy commands, and I'm your little whore."

A drop of unease teased my mind. I was jealous. It sounded like she'd done this before. I had to know. "You've done this before? With someone else?"

"I had a Da—uh, dom, I mean, for a while, who was very experienced. He was introducing me to the lifestyle, and the experience taught me so many things that I didn't even know about myself."

I didn't know him, but I already hated this guy. And what was that swirling, churning mass of anxiety in the pit of my stomach? Oh yeah, it was jealousy. I was half-jealous and half-pissed that she'd been with some guy that was 'teaching' her things when he was probably just getting his rocks off at her expense. But even I wasn't dumb enough to voice those thoughts. I bottled them up.

"So, what happened to him?"

She was gazing out the huge glass windows that made up one wall of her bedroom, her eyes unfocused. "I broke it off when I realized he wasn't right for me."

There was obviously more to the story, but hearing her say she was the one who ended things gave me a small jolt of satisfaction. I was such a prick sometimes.

She broke out of her trance and turned to me. "But I want to keep exploring this submissive kink I've discovered." A smile lit up her face. "We can be friends with kinky benefits."

I lifted a brow. "And do these kinky benefits include normal sex, too?"

"Would you consider what we did last night as normal sex?" she asked.

"Yes."

She nodded. "Yes, then we'll have normal sex, too. I loved everything about last night."

"And the other stuff? How do I do that?"

"We can start slow and figure it out together. The way you talk to me during sex and the commanding way you take over — it makes me wet just thinking about it."

She slipped out of bed and headed across the room. Fuck, she'd just told me she was getting wet, and then she was going to scamper away? My cock was begging to give her some 'normal' sex.

She came back to bed holding a cardboard box. "This is my toy box. I like to use these during scenes."

Holy fuck. It was packed to the top with sex toys, gadgets, bondage gear, a paddle...

"Maybe we can do a scene once a week?" She tapped a finger on her lip. "We'll talk it all through before we do anything, don't worry. We'll discuss safe words and aftercare and both of our likes and dislikes. If we communicate honestly with each other, we'll be fine. Safe, sane, and consensual is the motto."

I wasn't going to say that I wasn't a little intimidated. This was Lacey, a take-charge, hot-as-fuck woman. Would I be able to give her what she wanted? Was I good enough for her? Could I satisfy her?

I didn't know. But fuck yeah, I wanted to try. "I'm down for this, wifey, but I have a condition, too."

She hesitated for a second. "Okay. What is it?"

I crossed my arms over my chest. "While we're doing this friends-with-kinky-benefits thing, no other men. No sex, no kissing, no kinky stuff. You're just with me and I'll take care of all your needs."

She paused for a second. "Okay. And what about you?"

I smirked. "I already told you that I won't be with any other women while we're still married. We're exclusive moving forward."

"That's fine. But I'll warn you now — I am very needy."

The smile that crept over my face was huge. "I plan on keeping you very satisfied, Lacey."

A heated blush heightened the color of her cheeks. She was so gorgeous.

My dick was like steel. I was about to pounce on her. "Maybe we should practice 'normal' sex first?"

"What did you have in mind?" She smiled shyly.

I began to crawl towards her. "How about I eat your pussy first, then I'll let you ride my cock, and then we shower and see what happens next?"

"Is that all?"

She shrieked when I did pounce on her. "You only had two orgasms last night. That's not enough for very needy girls."

"So true."

Chapter 16

Lacey

I hadn't seen Sebastian Archer in over a week. Holy Shit! The pit of my stomach tangled with nerves just thinking about him. Was I really about to do this? With him? My freaking husband! Talk about life throwing you curveballs. Everybody expected curveballs once in a while, but this particular life pitch was something next level.

This was the first time our schedules allowed us to meet up. I usually worked 50 to 60 hours per week and though Ghost Parker was on hiatus after its last mini-tour, Bash was always busy taking care of Kody. He was a full-time dad and never shirked his responsibility. I admired that in him, even if it made it harder for us to get together for the kinky playtime he'd agreed to explore with me.

Tonight, Kody was spending the night at his grandparent's house. Bash was coming to my apartment, where I had him all to myself for the evening. I was assuming he'd stay over like he did last week; I'd bought some breakfast food just in case.

Although I wasn't sure this was the greatest idea, that tiny niggle of doubt was drowned out by near-breathless anticipation and delirious excitement.

I'd been fantasizing about this night all week. Sometimes I was sure that I must have exaggerated how good the sex had been between us in my head. Sebastian had made me orgasm so hard that I'd shifted into another dimension — a blissful, intoxicating state of pure sexual satisfaction.

Maybe I'd finally found that nirvana I'd been chasing? I hadn't even needed all the kinky bells and whistles to get there. Or should I say whips and chains, as Bash had put it? I couldn't even imagine how thrilling sex with Bash would be with all the kinky extras thrown in. Hopefully, I was about to find out.

Every chance we got this week, Bash and I had been discussing it, mostly over video calls after Kody had gone to bed. He lightheartedly complained that I was overthinking the whole thing, but he'd been listening to everything I said. I'd given him my kinky toybox so that he could familiarize himself with everything in it. I didn't expect him to be Daddy Dom proficient with everything right away, but he told me he had been watching videos — there really was a video about everything on the internet — and learning all that he could this entire week.

Some of our video chats had gotten a bit steamy. It was bound to happen considering the topic we were discussing, and the sexy sessions helped tide me over until I could get the real thing.

Now that the day was here, anticipation had me restlessly squirming and burning hot on the inside. I couldn't sit still, waiting for him to arrive. Should I go change my outfit again? I'd gone for casual — so as not to look too damn eager — but maybe sexy was the way to go? I did have some skimpy lingerie on under my rather plain clothes. Yes, that would be just fine. Bash was right; I was overthinking this.

The doorman finally called, and I knew Bash was on his way up. If this was going to be a regular thing, I'd need to arrange access for him. When I heard the soft whir of the elevator, I headed over to the vestibule to meet him.

The elevator doors opened, and I locked eyes with Sebastian. My stomach flipped once or twice and then the butterflies set in. Those beautiful eyes could make me do anything. He smiled lazily, like he knew exactly how devastating his smile was to the female sex. He usually kept his dark hair fairly short, but it was getting long enough that it was starting to curl up at the ends. I wanted to run my hands through it, preferably while his head was buried deep between my thighs.

He stepped off the elevator, holding the box of toys. He was wearing a black thermal shirt that was perfectly snug, a pair of dark wash jeans, and a pair of worn black boots. He looked like his ordinary self, absolutely delectable.

I swallowed down my nerves. "I hope you didn't let Clayton get a peek into that box. You could have closed it up."

He glanced at the box and smiled. "Who's Clayton?"

"The doorman."

"Oh, he got an eyeful." Bash smirked. "I told him I was returning some things you left at my house."

"You did not!" I feigned outrage.

He put down the box and then opened his arms for a hug.

My racing heartbeat calmed when I stepped into his arms. God, I could get used to this.

"I missed you," he whispered into my ear.

I squeezed him tighter, breathing in the fresh, woodsy scent I'd remembered from Vegas. It was warm and musky, a masculine blend of sandalwood and vanilla with hints of orange and tobacco that evoked strength and virility. I pulled out of his arms before I got caught huffing him like a teenager with an uncapped magic marker.

His scent must have gotten me high because the stuff that came out of my mouth next was ridiculous. "You look nice. Well, you always look nice, so I guess you look normal. But that's... nice." Shoot me now.

His lips twitched with a smile. "Were you expecting me to wear leather chaps?" He jammed his hands into his front pockets, growing more serious. "I have a pretty good idea of all the things you're interested in trying after our discussions. And I'm down to try all of that with you. But it's going to be you and me, Lacey. I'm not going to dress up in some whacky domination get-up. That's not me. But you, wifey, can dress up in whatever you like. I won't stop you from wearing kinky outfits if that's what you like. The tinier the better."

Jeez. I almost had to fan myself. I would love to see him in leather chaps. "What if I want to role-play? Would you wear a sexy cop uniform for me?"

His smile had my insides twisting. "I think I could manage that once in a while. But most of the time, it's just going to be the real me. Will that work?"

"Of course," I agreed. "I want it to be you. No one else."

"Good. So, how do we start this thing? I've read a lot of stuff, but I'm not sure how to go about this."

I grinned. "Well, you're in control here. Just let me know when you're ready, I guess. Would you like something to drink? A glass of wine?"

"Sure." He followed me into the kitchen, bringing the box of toys with him.

I started browsing through the under-the-counter wine fridge. "What's your favorite wine?"

He placed the box on the island. "Um, I don't know. I usually only drink wine when I'm out to dinner with my parents."

I pulled out a bottle. "Okay, then I won't waste a super-expensive bottle on you. This is a nice one."

I handed him the bottle and a wine opener while I pulled down a couple of glasses from the cabinet. He wasn't a complete novice because he made quick work of opening the bottle and then filled our glasses with decent technique.

We moved into the living room and sat on the couch a few feet apart. He'd hauled the box of sex toys with us and set it on the coffee table. It sat there like an enormous elephant in the room, reminding me of what was to come.

"So, how is Kody doing?"

Bash gave me a quick rundown of Kody's week, talking about his preschool class, his new friend, and a few funny stories about the silly mischief he's been up to like giving his stuffed dog a bath in the toilet bowl and writing his name with marker on the wall.

The entire time he talked, his knee bounced up and down. When he had half a glass of wine left, he tipped it back and finished it off. My guess was that he was more impatient than nervous. Unlike myself. This was exactly what I wanted, but I was nervous as hell. What if this night turned out to be an unmitigated disaster of friendship-ruining bad sex mixed with unerotic kink?

I pointed to his glass. "Do you want some more?"

"No." His answer was curt.

Leaning forward, I swirled the wine around in my glass. "I'm a bit nervous about this. I may have built this up in my head too much."

He glanced at me sharply. "You don't want to do it anymore?"

"I do. Very much. I'm just nervous." I swallowed. "Do you? Still?"

"Fuck yeah." He didn't hesitate. "I'm nervous, too. Not about doing it, but that I'll fuck it up and you won't enjoy it."

His admission helped me relax. "We've got the safe words. If it starts going in a direction I don't like, I'll say 'yellow'."

He put his empty glass on the coffee table. "Okay. And if you say 'red', I'll stop, of course."

I dragged in a deep breath. "And let's not freak out if I use the safe words. We'll probably need them a lot until we figure each other out."

"Okay."

I put my wineglass on the coffee table and curled my legs up under me. "I'm considering this a learning experience, so my expectations are pretty low for tonight. Let's just have some fun. There are no expectations of doing anything mind-blowing. We both agreed to start off slow with the kink stuff, so no pressure." I set out to reassure him, but mostly I was just reassuring myself.

"Okay, then let's have some fun." His voice slid over me like a dark promise, causing a shiver of anticipation to roll down my spine.

"Come here." He patted his lap.

My heart skipped a beat. Suddenly, I was feeling strangely shy — like a 15-year-old virgin. I stood up on shaky legs and closed the few steps of the distance between us, all the while my mind was going a mile a minute. Did he want me to sit sideways on his lap? Facing him? Or in front of him, between his legs? Or lay across his lap with my ass on display? I had no damn clue.

I turned around and then gingerly sat my ass on the end of his legs near his knees so that I sat primly away from his body, facing forward. It was probably the most awkward and unsexy lap-sitting I'd ever experienced. Maybe because this whole thing was so weird.

In my head, I was busy cataloging all the reasons why it was so weird

— reasons I'd studiously ignored the entire week while I replayed the fantastic sex we'd had over and over and fantasized about him fulfilling my every kinky desire. Let's see, there were so many reasons:

1. It was Bash.

2. We'd been friends for so long.

3. Years ago, we were in a threesome together with his best friend, Sid.

4. Sid was now married to my best friend, Kaylie.

5. Kaylie was Bash's little sister.

6. Bash and I were married, but getting divorced.

7. There was a box of sex toys on my coffee table.

Bash interrupted my runaway mental list. He moved my hair to the side and kissed my shoulder and neck. "Mmm. You smell so good."

This was nice. I closed my eyes.

He put his hands on my hips and nudged me backward on his lap until I was snug against him. Hmm. Even nicer.

His hands slid up to the top of my shoulders, and he gently massaged my muscles. "You seem tense."

Willing myself to relax, I let my body melt into his and rested my head on his shoulder. "I'm just excited."

He rubbed my shoulders for a few more minutes until I was almost content to spend the entire night doing nothing else, but then he said in a low and rough voice, "Take off your shirt."

I sat forward and pulled off my turquoise shirt and then leaned back against his chest again. While Bash was kissing up my neck again, leaving a fiery trail as he worked his way to my ear, I glanced at my breasts. The bra I'd chosen was perfect for this. It was a black uplifting open-cup bra, with a thicker band of support underneath to keep my full breasts lifted, but leaving most of my breasts and nipples exposed. My girls looked almost indecent, spilling over the barely there material.

A breath of hot air tickled my ear. "Oh, fuck."

Luckily, he couldn't see the little smile of triumph on my face at his reaction. He must have finally caught a peek at my breasts. Without pause, he licked his fingers and then went straight to my nipples, plumping them up. At the first touch, I arched lightly into his hands but then settled back against him and closed my eyes, relishing his attention on them.

After a minute of play, my nipples were two stiff, aching peaks. When his hands slid away and gently stroked over my belly, a surge of need fluttered in my pussy. I felt goosebumps break out on my flesh when his fingertips trailed lightly over my ribcage and then between my breasts before he traced the outline of the areola on each breast with the soft tip of his finger.

The ache that was pooling in my belly began to settle lower between my thighs. Both of his hands cupped my breasts and then began massaging them. In between the gentle tugs and squeezes, a finger would circle my nipple, teasingly close, without ever touching it.

Just when I thought that I couldn't take anymore, his fingers plucked at my intentionally neglected nipples. He wet his fingers and then focused relentlessly on them, flicking them with his thumb, rubbing, pinching, and sometimes twisting. Slow strokes became increasingly faster, soft pinching became firmer and light twists became stronger until I was squirming in his lap.

My breaths were coming out in shaky puffs of air and I was occasionally making a humming sound without meaning to. Could I orgasm from nipple stimulation alone? The agony of need between my legs made me think it might be possible.

When I was sure that I was one pinch or tweak away from exploding, he'd stop. Instead, his fingers would track the insides edges of my bra or go back to tracing my areolas. He wouldn't give me long to regroup before he went back to mercilessly arousing my nipples until the pressure grew again. Each pinch sent a rush of sensation throughout my body. He was edging me with nipple play.

"Your tits are gorgeous."

God, I liked this so much. In my imaginings, I thought he'd just tell me to strip, restrain me, and then fuck me right away. I liked this softer side of him; I'd never seen it before. This side of him was even more dangerous to me than the dominating side.

I'd never had so much attention paid to my breasts for so long, and Bash was incredibly good at it. It was hard to sit still. He put a hand on my hip to still my wiggling ass. Mindlessly, I pressed back into him and felt his hard length pushing against me. Oh, God. I wanted it.

I didn't even realize that I'd reached behind and pushed my hand against the front of his jeans.

He hissed. "Christ, Lacey. Don't touch my dick or I'm going to put it inside you. I'm not used to all this foreplay."

I removed my hand but groaned with frustration. "That's what I want. Your cock."

He grunted. "Sit on your hands."

"Yes, sir." I slid my hands under my thighs.

"Actually, stand up and take those pants off."

I stood up and kept my back to him while I took off my pants. I made quite a show of it, bending over and wiggling my hips sensually as I lowered my pants and whisked off my socks. My black thong matched my bra. The back of it wasn't that exciting, only two straps coming out of the tiny triangle above the cleft between my ass cheeks, but the front was a pretty patterned see-through mesh adorned with cute little bows. I stood still, tingling with anticipation as I imagined his eyes on me.

"Turn around, Lacey."

I turned around and watched his green eyes devour me, diffusing a heated sexual energy into the air.

His voice was gruff. "You're a fantasy come true, Lace. You look so fucking sexy."

My body instantly responded. A flush crept over my skin. Guys in bars handed out compliments like candy. I was used to hearing them, but Bash actually sounded like he meant it.

He leaned forward and took my hand, pulling me over to him. This time, I sat on his lap facing him with my knees straddling his legs.

Intensity swirled around us. I desperately wanted to kiss him. Touch him. Rip off all his clothes so I could see him. But he was in charge, so I waited for his command.

His hands were resting on my hips. "Slide your panties aside. Let me see your pussy."

"Yes, Sir." I sounded breathy.

I hooked a pinky into the side of my panties and dragged them aside, exposing my pussy, but when I looked up, he wasn't looking at it.

He was watching me with a quizzical look on his face. "Are you calling me sir?"

"Yes, Sir?" I hesitated. "Do you want to be called something else?"

He cocked an eyebrow. "Yeah, how about my name?"

I shook my head slowly. How could I explain this? "No, it needs to be different. It's only for when we do this and it needs to be something that indicates your authority. It helps me get into the right head space to be submissive."

He ran a hand through his hair. It was the first time he seemed uncomfortable about doing this.

"I know it seems weird at first. You don't like Sir? It's a common one. I don't think Master really fits with our dynamic. We could do Dom, King, or... Daddy."

I hesitated before I said Daddy. Please don't pick Daddy. I wanted to keep what we were doing completely separate from my experience at Scarlett. The last thing I wanted was to stir up any old memories while I was playing with Bash.

His eyebrow creased. "You can't just call me Bash? Bash sounds kind of menacing and dominating, doesn't it?"

My lip jutted out in a pout. "No, that's what everyone calls you. It has to be special. Just for you and me."

He leaned in and kissed me sweetly on the lips. "How about Sebastian? No one calls me that anymore. You've called me that a few times and I liked it."

"Sebastian." A lick of desire tightened my stomach. "Yes."

His smug smile told me he was pleased with my response.

"And what are you going to call me? You can't call me Lacey."

He threw his head back and groaned. "Sugar tits? Juicy?"

I laughed. "If you want. Or there're the usuals: babe, baby, kitty, bunny, pet, doll, princess, or you could go with my little fucktoy."

His hands pulled my body forward until he could suck my breast into his mouth. He worked my sensitive nipple with his tongue for a few seconds and then popped off. "While my little fucktoy has a nice ring to it, I think I'll keep that in my back pocket for only occasional use." He licked my nipple with his tongue, sending a bolt of desire straight to my pussy. "I think I'm going to go with wifey. Every good wifey obeys their husband. Isn't that right, wifey?"

"Yes, Sebastian."

"Now slide your panties aside so I can see my wifey's pussy."

His words alone sent a rush of arousal burning through my veins. I slid my panties aside again. This time Bash was looking his fill. He licked his lips with his half-lidded eyes, gazing at my glistening sex.

"Would you like to fuck my mouth, Sebastian?"

Chapter 17

Bash

Yes, I wanted to fuck her mouth, but I hadn't even dug into her box of sex toys yet. This past week, I'd spent a lot of time trying to figure out how to satisfy her submissive side the way she needed. I'd read about BDSM in general, impact play, and aftercare — all things Lacey had mentioned when we talked this week. I'd made sure I knew how her restraints worked and I watched videos on how to use the flogger, crop, and paddle safely and even practiced technique.

All the damn internet research I'd done flew right out the window the moment she offered to suck my cock. So far, I hadn't satisfied her. She'd had no orgasms. Was she thinking this was the lamest submissive experience ever? Fuck, maybe if I let her take the edge off my throbbing dick, I could concentrate on doing this dom stuff better.

"Take my cock out, wifey," I relented.

There was a gleam in her eye as she popped open the button on my

HOW TO MARRY A ROCKSTAR 177

pants and then slowly unzipped them. She started rubbing my cock through my underwear, but it wasn't enough.

I tapped her thigh. "Get up."

She slid off my lap and then pulled my pants and underwear down past my knees before she dropped to her knees in front of me.

I sat back against the couch cushions, getting comfortable, and spread my legs so she could kneel between them.

I slid my fingers through her hair and then grabbed her by the nape, guiding her head forward. "Make it good, wifey." God, I was such a dick.

Being on tour, I got my dick sucked a lot — at least daily, usually more often. I'd lost the excitement I'd used to feel about getting sucked off. It'd gotten old. Hell, I got my cock sucked while I was talking to other people and barely noticed. Yeah, it felt good, but it hardly ever made me come anymore. It'd just become another form of backstage currency.

There was something wild about having Lacey's mouth on me. She rubbed the crown of my dick along her lower lip, all the while watching me with those expressive eyes that were glazed over with desire. Pure lust shot through me with an intensity I'd never felt before, turning the blood in my veins to fire.

She took the base of my cock in a firm grip and glanced at me hungrily. I could see pre-cum leaking out of my tip, and I held my breath as I watched her tasting it with her wet tongue and smearing it all around the head of my cock and then down my shaft.

Then she really began working me with her hands in tandem with her mouth. Her lips were sucking, her tongue was swirling and licking, her fist was pumping and squeezing my shaft, and her other hand was fondling my balls. Even the gentle graze of her teeth ratcheted up the throbbing pressure that was building quickly.

She peeked up at me with those big eyes and moaned against my cock. Fuck, she was a goddess. She was sexy, playful, and intelligent. How did I get so lucky that she wanted to play these games with me?

I didn't understand her craving to be submissive. She wanted to let go sexually and just take orders, which was so different from her personality. She could have men lined up to lick her boots and begging to service her every need if that's what she wanted.

Instead, she wanted to be submissive to me. And I had this overwhelming urge to make sure I could meet and exceed all her needs.

Could I be that guy she craved? I was used to getting whatever I wanted from groupies. I'd always known that I was an extremely selfish lover. It went hand in hand with the rock star lifestyle. Some of the groupies and girls I'd had sex with were more adventurous in bed than others, but usually, I just had them do what I wanted and that was that. Sex was quick and to the point. That's all I needed from them — a quick physical release.

There was no talking. No spending the night. No spending time getting to know them. No foreplay.

Until ten minutes ago, I hadn't spent that much time playing with a woman's tits since high school. That was back when sex was still exciting. Now it was a quick blowjob before I had to get on stage or a race to the finish before I had to get back on the bus. I'd fucked women on nasty couches in dressing rooms, dark corners of nightclubs, filthy restrooms, the tiny tour bus bunks, and on the good nights in hotel rooms before I passed out.

Sex was just a means to an end, with one in a string of many nameless and faceless women. It had taken Lacey waking me up to realize I'd gotten numb to the act. When I thought about it, it was like watching professional porn with the endless fucking and realizing that none of the pornstars ever quite looked like they were really enjoying it. It looked like a lot of acting. How long had I been just going through the motions?

That's what I'd been doing — having wild sex that looked good from the outside. This entire week, while I'd been researching this dominant stuff so I could give Lacey what she wanted, I'd been feeling slightly uneasy. I couldn't quite put my finger on those disquieting feelings, but I knew what it was now. I felt inadequate.

Maybe I wasn't skilled enough to please a woman like Lacey. I was rusty. My last girlfriend was almost ten years ago. Since then, I hadn't been with the same woman more than once only a few times. I didn't know what my sex partners liked in bed because it didn't matter to me.

It mattered to me now, and it lent a whole new feeling to sex. Sex was bigger. More exciting. It made me feel more alive than I had in years. All because of Lacey.

It was inconvenient to have a major epiphany while my cock was in her mouth. The woman was going to kill me. Her mouth was magic, and I felt every lurid detail as she swallowed my cock over and over. White-hot desire rocked me and it was absolute agony to sit still and not rut like an animal.

It was time to take care of my girl — my wife — but first, I was about to come and there was no holding back from it. I gritted my teeth and sucked in a breath. Lacey looked up at me and then started working even faster. Fuuuck.

I firmly grasped behind her neck to get her attention, so that I could stand up. When I was standing, I held her head still with both hands and slowly thrust my dick in and out of her mouth. We were making eye contact the entire time, and it felt so damn intense. The tightening in my balls slammed into me and took my breath away.

I didn't want to come yet, but I was so worked up already and her mouth felt like heaven. I was pumping into her mouth like a savage now, and when she palmed my balls, I knew I was a goner.

"Take my cum, wifey," I gritted out.

I exploded. Wave after wave of orgasmic pleasure ripped through my body, and Lacey milked each one with her mouth and swallowed it all down.

I pulled up my pants and collapsed onto the couch before my knees gave out. That had been a fantastic release and my body felt weak in the afterglow.

"You deserve a reward for that."

She looked so happy her eyes were sparkling. Now, how was I going to keep that look on her face?

"Take your panties off and lay across my lap, wifey."

Within seconds, I was looking down at her bare ass. I slowly rubbed my hands over the round globes. They were perfection with enough meat to jiggle nicely. Her skin was soft and silky smooth, without a single blemish on it. My hands slid up her smooth back. I only saw two beauty marks on her skin: one on the back of her left thigh, a little above her knee, and a cute spot near her right shoulder blade. Otherwise, her skin was so perfect it looked airbrushed.

I massaged her ass cheeks and the top of her thighs, warming up her skin. From our conversations, she wasn't into too much pain from impact play; it was more that she got aroused from a sexy slap and tickle and that's exactly what I planned to give her.

I started with a few test slaps, more playful than stinging. When I rubbed away the slaps, she sighed contentedly. After a minute of gentle kneading, I gave her two stinging slaps, one on each cheek. This time, when my fingers trailed softly over the skin to soothe the sting, she was moaning and pressing her mound into my leg. She really did get off on spanking.

Her hands were resting on the couch up by her head. I gently grabbed each one and placed them behind her back, where I could trap both her wrists in my left hand. She made such a pretty picture as I looked down at her laying across me. Holding her wrists securely in place, I pinked up her ass cheeks with a few more slaps. Her writhing and sexy moaning were getting me hard again. I slipped my hand between her legs and ran a finger along her slit. She was soaked.

I nudged her legs open wider and then spent a minute very lightly playing with her clit. I switched over to rubbing her clit with my thumb while I sunk a finger inside her. From this position, it was very easy to reach her G-spot. I alternated between pressing the bullseye and sliding my finger back and forth over it. If there was one thing I was good at, it was sustaining a rhythm. Between my relentless attention to her clit and G-spot, I had her yelling out to God and panting my name in no time.

I didn't want her to come just yet, so I pulled out and gave her ass a few more taps. They didn't have to be as hard because she was already pretty worked up. This time, I gave her a good finger fucking. I slid my finger in and out quickly, making sure to press against the G-spot with every stroke. It didn't take me long to find out how much she enjoyed it because she came on my finger within a minute. Lying across my lap, ass in the air, and face pressed into the cushions, she looked gorgeous.

I let her wrists go and rubbed the top of her thighs while her inner muscles still fluttered with aftershocks around my finger.

When her breathing got steadier, I pulled my finger out. "Turn over so I can see you."

She slowly turned over while I licked my finger clean. My dick was straining against my pants. After watching her come undone like that, I wanted inside of her.

I lifted her left leg and put it over the back of the sofa so I had an unobstructed view of her pussy. The smell of her musk was like an aphrodisiac. My hand pressed possessively over her mound. "Who's pussy is this?"

"It's yours, Sebastian."

Fuck. I couldn't help the self-satisfied smirk that crossed my lips. "Damn right, it is. And I'm going to take care of that pussy."

The way she was looking at me right now was going to kill me. There was something shining in her eyes that made me feel like a fucking king. Adoration? Awe? Infatuation? Tenderness? Enthrallment? I couldn't really put my finger on it; it was probably just post-orgasm bliss and I shouldn't read too much into it.

"You didn't use any safe words." I wanted to check that the force of the spanking was okay with her.

"No. Who would want to stop any of that?"

My fingers traced over her stomach. "You want some more?"

"Yes." She didn't hesitate.

I didn't want to overdo anything, especially since this was our first time, but I really wanted to try out the flogger. I leaned down to give her a quick kiss, but when her arms wrapped around my neck, I stayed there and enjoyed her soft lips and wicked tongue. Her legs were still open wide, and I was right between them. Only the soft cotton of my briefs stopped my dick from sliding right into her.

I pulled away. "Get up and go stand in front of the window."

Her body shuddered slightly. She stood and walked over to the floor-to-ceiling windows with the phenomenal view across downtown Los Angeles. The lights were on in her penthouse, so only a pattern of lights from nearby skyscrapers could be seen dotting the blackness of the night outside.

I stood up and pulled the flogger out of the box. I stalked over to Lacey, fully aware that my dick was sticking out of the top of my briefs because I hadn't bothered to button or zip my jeans. My naughty girl was looking, and she was even wetting her lips with her tongue.

"Turn around," I commanded. "Hands on the glass, spread out."

I moved up close behind her to help position her the way I wanted. I spread her hands out wide and then spread her legs about shoulder-width apart.

My hand pressed against her back, urging her forward. "I want your nipples to touch the glass. Only your nipples and your hands, nothing else."

I slid her hair to one side and kissed her shoulder while my other hand slid down her back and around the curve of her ass. Then I lifted the flogger and began running the tails all over her creamy skin — over her shoulder, down her side, up her calf. Her breathing started to increase, and she was twitching slightly at the touch. Using the handle, I rubbed between her legs until she was gasping.

When I felt she was ready, I backed up a bit. I gave my seeping cock two pumps before I began. The first few whacks were gentle, but I increasingly added pressure. Single strokes became double. I painted a figure-8 motion across both of her ass cheeks for several minutes before switching to her upper thighs, making sure the tails didn't wrap around her skin.

I had to concentrate hard and stay diligent to not zone out because orchestrating this rhythmic motion was like heaven to me. It would be easy to get lost in it. I carefully listened to her breathing, her whimpers, and her moans and kept watch for any other clues her body signaled.

There was no disguising just how much she liked it. The surprising thing was how much I liked it, too. She was having trouble keeping her position against the glass, so I decided it might be a good time to end our session, especially on such a high note. I set down the flogger and then crowded up against her, putting my arm around her middle and pulling her back against me.

She collapsed into my arms. We both groaned when I slid my hand down her stomach and dipped my fingers inside her warm, slick pussy. She was absolutely creamy.

Fuck, it felt like my cock was going to drill a hole into her back, but this didn't seem like the right time. She seemed pretty spaced out. I lifted her up into my arms and carried her past the kitchen and down the hall that led to her bedroom.

At the end of the hall, I found the right room, a sophisticated girly room of pink and gold, and then settled her on the bed. I quickly shucked off my jeans and briefs and climbed in next to her.

I gathered her up in my arms. "Lacey, are you okay?"

"I'm fantastic."

I pushed a lock of hair behind her ear. "Are you sure? You seem kind of out of it."

She turned to look at me. "Do I? I feel really dreamy. Relaxed. That was so amazing, Sebastian."

I was stroking her hair and running my fingertips all over that silky skin. "Did you like that, wifey? Was there anything you didn't like?"

"Mmm." She closed her eyes and wiggled closer to me. "I liked it all. So, so good."

"Nothing ... hurt too much? Even the flogger?" I prodded.

Her eyes opened. "It stung a bit, but it was perfect. You could probably go even harder, but that definitely did the trick. I loved it."

"What did you like the best? What could I do better?"

She thought for a moment. "I liked when you trapped my wrists behind my back and then teased my pussy until I had a fabulous freaking orgasm. I told you that you were naturally dominant. Next time, you can use restraints on me. That would be even hotter." Her hand slid across my chest and teased my nipple for a moment. It was excruciating because I was still aching for her. "Is this inquisition over yet?"

I chuckled. "When I get to know what you like better, then we can just ... you know, do this, without the twenty questions."

"Do this?" she asked.

I remembered all my research. "Aftercare. Why do they call it that? It reminds me of daycare and little kids."

"Does 'doing this' include kissing?"

"Fuck, yeah." I captured her mouth and gave her a sweet kiss that quickly grew heated.

She broke away and frowned. "Was the flogging part boring for you?"

I bit back a laugh. "You do know what I do for a living, right? I would drum all fucking day if I could. I think what we did was actually better than drumming. There's a similarity except I'm doing it on a luscious naked body. It would only be better if I could make you come from doing that."

She bit her bottom lip. "If you add a vibrator to what you were doing, I'd definitely come. I was so close, even without it."

"Good to know."

"And being in front of the window,"—she let out a breathy moan—"that ratcheted it up. It was so sexy."

I was curious about her exhibitionist streak. She had mentioned it to me, which is why I'd placed her in front of the glass, even though the chances of someone seeing her were close to zero.

"You like being on display?"

"I ... do." She didn't sound too sure of what she was saying.

"Do you want other people to watch you having sex? Or for them to participate?"

A jolt of unease sliced through my gut. I remembered the threesome we'd had with Sid. I felt sure it wasn't her only threesome experience. What if she wanted to do that again? What if she wanted a relationship like Ghost had with Remi and Grey?

She laughed a little self-consciously. "In theory, I'd love to have sex on stage with a huge audience watching. But I think that's one of those fantasies that you don't really want to come true. It's just sexy to think about."

"What about sex with other people? Like threesomes?"

She stiffened in my arms. "I guess it depends. With another woman? No. Another man? Maybe if he just watched but didn't participate. Why? Do you?"

I released the breath I didn't even know I was holding. "No. I don't like to share."

A burst of laughter escaped her throat. "What? You're like the king of threesomes. What did you guys call it? The sandwich maneuver or something?"

"Let me amend my answer. I don't like to share *you*. No, wifey. Didn't we make some vows? I prefer just you and me."

I didn't give her time to answer before I grabbed her breast and sucked it into my mouth. I didn't want to think too deeply about what I'd just confessed. Yeah, I wanted to be monogamous with her. I wanted to explore this thing between us. The kink thing and a relationship beyond that.

I was insane. What the hell was I thinking? I was jumping ahead of myself. What was there not to like about Lacey? She was amazing. I needed to just enjoy the sex while I had it. She may be happy with me for the moment, but she certainly wasn't looking for a long-term commitment.

"Don't freak out if I tell you this. You're my dom. I think you can take it." She sat up and looked into my eyes. "I feel so close to you right now. Connected. With the sex and the cuddling and the talking about it after, it's just a different dynamic than I'm used to. I really like it. I trust you. You took such good care of me. Thank you, Sebastian."

Fuck, I rubbed at my chest. There was a heavy feeling in it. What the fuck?

I pecked at her lips and then averted my gaze. "I like it too, wifey."

She slid her hand down my stomach and palmed my hard dick. "Do you usually cuddle with women after sex?"

"Not really."

She stroked my shaft. "I'm not that experienced with cuddling either."

I stilled her hand with my own. "Is fucking a part of aftercare?"

She pressed her tits against my chest. "If I have any say so, it is."

"Fuck," I groaned. "I love aftercare."

I released her hand, and we spent the next few hours having non-kinky sex. It was as close to heaven as I'd ever gotten.

Chapter 18

Lacey

"D^{AD?}"

Something was pulling me from the most peaceful sleep.

"Dad?" The sweet voice was louder this time. More insistent.

My hand slipped down warm, bare skin and I remembered that I was in Bash's bed. It never got old waking up in his arms. Especially when they were such spectacular arms. I sighed contentedly and luxuriated in all of his naked, muscular body pressed up against mine.

"Dad!" This time, the voice was clearly frustrated. Kody was calling—

Oh shit! Kody was awake.

"Oh, my God! Bash, wake up." In a panic, I started violently shaking his shoulders. "Kody's awake. He's calling for you. What time is it? I must have overslept."

Bash woke slowly, his hand automatically moving to my breast. "Why are you—"

"Bash, he's awake. He's—"

"Dad? I'm hungry." Kody called out again, but it sounded like he was heading downstairs.

I scrambled out of the bed and reached for my phone. Shit, it was 7:52. I was usually out the door by 7:00, before Kody woke up. I found my overnight bag and began pulling clothes from it.

Bash had slid out of bed and was getting dressed, although not as frantically. "I'll go down and make him some breakfast. You don't have to rush out of here. Why don't you take a shower?"

I couldn't find my bra in my haste, so I just tossed on a T-shirt from my bag. "How am I going to get out of here without him seeing me? Can you distract him while I sneak out?"

Bash held up a finger. "Hold on." He walked over to the bedroom door and opened it. "Kody?" he yelled. "I'll be down in a minute to make you breakfast. Sorry, bud. I overslept."

I was busy sliding on some panties when Bash walked over to me and stilled my frantic motions. "Relax. It's fine. Why don't you shower and get dressed ... properly?"

He looked down at my shirt with a lifted brow and I realized I had put it on backward.

"I'm so sorry. I don't know why my alarm didn't go off. I thought I set it last night."

Even with his hands innocently resting on my shoulders, I still felt a tingle of awareness. "Lacey, it's not a big deal. In fact, I hate when you have to leave so early. Kody and I don't have any plans today. Why don't you stay and we can all hang out? Unless you have something going on?"

He wanted me to hang out with them? "I thought you didn't want

Kody to know about me?"

He chuckled. "Well, I don't want him to know that I'm sleeping with you. But we can hang out. We'll just pretend you showed up today."

Of course, I wanted to spend time with Bash and Kody, but was that a good idea? Our friends-with-kinky-benefits arrangement was just a month old and already I was starting to have fantasies about our relationship being real. Hanging out with him and his son like a real girlfriend would just confuse things.

"Wouldn't that just confuse things? Him! Confuse him, I mean." Whoops, that had slipped out.

Bash didn't seem to notice my slip of the tongue. "Nah. He'd just think of you the same way he does of Josie. Come to think of it, there is a bit of resemblance between you two."

"The nanny granny?" I smacked his arm. "Gee, thanks a lot."

"Well, you both drive me crazy. In very different ways, however." He pulled me into his body and began nibbling on my neck. He spoke in between kissing and nipping my sensitive skin. "Please say you'll stay and hang out. I'll make it worth your while tonight. I promise, wifey. And then you can sneak out bright and early Sunday morning."

Spending the entire day with Bash. And another night? It was a dumb idea, but I couldn't bring myself to say no. "Fine, I'll stay. I'll go shower now. But I'm not leaving this room until you come back and tell me the coast is clear."

His happy smile made my stomach flutter. He kissed my forehead. "Good. I'll feed Kody and make some coffee. I'll break you out of here as soon as I can."

After I showered and got ready for the day, I made Bash's bed and then searched the internet for ideas for some fun activities to do with toddlers. I needed to get outdoors. Even though it was the week before

Thanksgiving, it was unseasonably warm, with temperatures expected to reach nearly 80 degrees.

It was another ten minutes or so before Bash came back. He snuck me downstairs and into the kitchen with Kody none the wiser.

I sat on a stool at the kitchen island sipping my coffee while Bash cleaned up breakfast. "I have a few ideas that we can do with Kody today. Unless you don't want to go out?"

He tossed the sponge into the sink. "I'd love to get him out and running around. It's a nice day today. What did you have in mind?"

I listed off a few of the ideas I'd seen online. "Well, we could bring a picnic lunch to the park, or go to the Santa Monica pier — there's an aquarium there — or do the Warner Brothers studio tour, or we could go to the beach."

"I think he's too young for the studio tour. The other stuff would be fun. He really loves the beach."

Spending a day at the beach with them would be perfect. "I love the beach, too."

He rubbed at the morning scruff on his face. "Have you ever been to the beach with a kid, though? It's not very relaxing."

"Who needs relaxing? Has he ever flown a kite before?"

Bash came around the island and wrapped his arms around me. His lips started teasing my neck. He knew that absolutely melted me. "I don't have a kite, but I can imagine you running down the beach trying to get the kite up in the air. You're wearing this tiny red bikini that's not very supportive—"

Laughing, I smacked at his arm and shoved him away. "Behave! Kody might come in. And I hate to ruin your fantasy, but I don't have a bikini with me."

He looked me up and down. "You still look hot in your T-shirt and leggings. Maybe you could ditch the bra while you're running along the beach with this non-existent kite?"

"You're ridiculous." I shook my head, but my pinched-lip, pretend scolding face quickly morphed into a smile. "We'll stop at the store and buy a kite and we can pick up some food, too."

He stepped back and looked at me. "You really want to spend the day at the beach with us? Flying kites?"

"I can't wait."

He leaned in and gave me a quick kiss. "Give me 15 minutes to get some stuff together for Kody and then we'll head out."

While I waited, I tossed my damp hair up into a messy bun. Like I had every Friday for the past month, I'd come over last night with just a change of clothes for the morning. I'd planned to be out the door before Kody ever woke up, so I didn't have much choice in what I could wear on our outing. Unfortunately, it was pretty boring and not at all sexy.

I was playing on my phone when Kody came barreling into the kitchen. "Yacey! Dad said we're going to the beach!"

"Hi, Kody!" He was wearing tropical board shorts with a matching rash guard. He looked absolutely adorable. "Have you ever flown a kite before? We're going to try to fly one at the beach."

His eyes lit up. "A kite! Cool!" He started doing a funny dance, turning in a circle and wiggling his behind.

Bash came into the kitchen a few minutes later with his hands full. "Buddy, did you get your sand toys?"

As Bash set down a backpack, a blue nylon bag, a beach blanket, and a cooler, Kody raced out in search of his toys.

Bash stood up and my brain short-circuited. Holy Jesus. It should be criminal for a man to look so sinfully hot. He wore a gray tank top that did nothing to conceal the muscles rippling beneath and highlighted his drummer's arms and the sleeve of tattoos down his right arm. I almost had to fan myself as my eyes took in his swim trunks. They weren't the popular baggy trunks that fell to the knee. Bash's trunks were solid black with white contrast stitching and the cut was shorter and more form-fitting. He looked like a fantasy. Like a model. Not those beanpole, androgynous fashion models, but a fitness model with tons of bronze skin and rippling muscles.

"Put your eyeballs back in your head, wifey." The asshole was smirking.

"Please..." I rolled my tongue back up off the floor and into my mouth and tried to play it off. "I was just wondering how you stayed so tan at this time of year."

He glanced down at his body and shrugged. "I'm in the backyard with Kody a lot."

I kept sneaking peeks while he filled up the cooler with ice, and then bottles of water and some juice boxes for Kody. He gathered up some snacks, filling ziplock baggies with goldfish, grapes, or pretzels.

Kody came back carrying a mesh bag filled with plastic buckets and various sand molds. "I've got my toys. I'm ready, Dad!"

Bash finished packing and then put a black baseball cap on his head and slid on a pair of sporty wraparound sunglasses with blue mirrored lenses. I nearly swooned.

I motioned up and down his body with my hand. "You go out in public looking like that?"

He smiled. "We'll be fine. No one recognizes the drummer."

I wasn't worried about people recognizing him; I was more worried about women spontaneously ovulating around him, but I kept that to myself.

Bash dropped me off at the supermarket while he and Kody went to a nearby sporting goods store to find a kite. I had some subs made at the deli and then picked up some snacks — chips, cheese and crackers, some cut-up fruit, and a six-pack of cucumber mint vodka cans because it was deliciously refreshing and hello — no sugar, no carbs.

The boys were waiting for me when I wheeled my cart into the parking lot. Bash was covering Kody from head to toe with sunscreen.

"Did you find a kite?"

Kody held up two fingers. "We got two!"

"Two?" I questioned.

Bash nodded. "We got a kite that does tricks. I'm not sure if I'll be able to keep it up,"—he cocked an eyebrow, daring me to say something—"so we bought a no-frills one, too, just in case the other one is too tricky."

"It's good to be prepared." I began loading the grocery bags into the back of Bash's large SUV. I placed the subs, drinks, and the items I wanted to keep cold in the cooler.

Kody chatted about everything on the drive to the beach. At one point, Bash grabbed my hand and interlocked our fingers before resting it on the console between us. I was filled with warmth. There was no other place on the planet I'd rather be at that moment. I had to be careful that my heart-eyes weren't showing. He'd probably pull over, kick me out of the car, and speed away if he knew the crazy thoughts that were running through my head.

It was quite an undertaking hauling all the stuff down to the beach and setting up. The blue nylon bag turned out to be a beach tent that Bash was setting up. I spread out the blanket and began organizing all our stuff. Kody dumped out his toys and began playing in the sand.

As soon as Bash finished and sat on the blanket next to me, Kody piped up in his sweet voice. "I have to pee."

"Aww, bud. It's a hike back up to the restroom. We better go now."

Kody scrunched up his face. "Can't I just pee in the ocean?"

"Don't talk about peeing in the ocean in front of ladies. They don't know about that. It's a man-secret."

Kody glanced at me. "Ladies don't pee in the ocean?"

I listened to their conversation, trying not to crack up.

"Nope," Bash answered. "They hold it for as long as they can and then they hike all the way to the bathrooms and wait in a really long line. It takes forever. That's why they spend most of the day going to the bathroom."

Kody nodded like sage advice was being imparted to him. "You can pee in the ocean, but not in the bathtub. Right, Dad?"

Bash gave Kody a fist bump. "That's right, son."

I hid my laugh with a cough.

"Dad, do the fish pee in the ocean?"

Bash rubbed his jaw. "I guess they do."

"And sharks, too?"

"Yep."

Kody hopped around the blanket, kicking some sand up. "Everybody pees in the ocean except for ladies."

"Yep. All right, Kody, we better find the bathroom before you have an accident."

♫♪♩♩

Our beach day was picture-perfect. And when I say picture-perfect, I meant it literally. I was covertly trying to take a few pictures of Bash, especially when he pulled his shirt off and was running around with the kite. Luckily, the beach wasn't crowded at all. There was plenty of space to fly the kites.

I did take some videos when he was wrestling with the 'trick' kite.

He could get the kite up, but it zigged around making turns and loops so aggressively, there was no way for Kody to help, even though he squealed and clapped with every maneuver. When he got the regular kite up in the air, he let Kody hold the plastic handle until he eventually lost interest.

There was enough sustained wind up high so that we could tie the kite string to the tent pole and it remained aloft, hovering high above us. Bash hauled at least a hundred buckets of water up to our area and helped Kody make a sand castle. I made some cool shapes with his molds and helped him with decorating his masterpiece by collecting some shells, seaweed, bits of driftwood, and interesting pebbles from the beach. I hadn't had that much fun playing at the beach since I was a little girl.

Especially fun was ogling a near-naked Bash. When he plopped down on the blanket next to me after another bucket run to the ocean, I leaned into him and snapped a picture of us.

He laughed and then put his arm around me, pulling me close. "Take another one; I wasn't ready."

I took a few seconds to make sure we were both in the frame and snapped another. Without warning, Kody flew between us and climbed into my lap to get into the picture. I laughed. "Are you photobombing us, Kody?"

He smiled really big while I snapped another picture with the three of us. When I looked to make sure I got a good shot, I knew that it would be my favorite picture. Kody was a mini-me of his father. They looked so adorable together. And I looked happy. Because I was.

"You got Lacey all full of sand, bud." Bash was hauling Kody off my lap.

"That's okay." I high-fived Kody. "We got the perfect picture. That's what counts."

HOW TO MARRY A ROCKSTAR 197

We ate our lunch, enjoyed our snacks and a couple of drinks, expanded our sandcastle, and I had a go at flying the crazy kite with Bash's help. It was an idyllic day that I didn't want to end.

On the way home, we ate at a hamburger place for dinner, and then to top off the day, we stopped at a roadside ice cream parlor for dessert.

Bash carried a haggard Kody into the house when we got home. "Can you just grab the leftover food? I'll unpack the rest of the stuff later."

I collected the food we didn't finish and followed him into the house. Kody's head was resting on Bash's shoulder.

Bash leaned over and kissed me sweetly on the lips. I glanced over at Kody, but it looked like he was sleeping.

He whispered close to my ear, "A bath for Kody. Then a bath for you. I'll be back down soon."

I busied myself putting away the food and straightening up the kitchen while he was gone. He came back downstairs twenty minutes later with damp hair and fresh clothing. "He's fast asleep. I didn't even get the chance to read him a story before he passed out."

"It was a long day for a kid."

"It was the best day." Bash smiled. He pulled a couple of wine glasses out of a cabinet and then opened a bottle of wine.

He was freshly showered, and I was still sweaty and sandy from the beach. "Did you shower already? That's not fair."

He poured us each a glass and then took my hand. "I promised you a bath. Let's go take care of that."

We brought the wine upstairs to his bedroom. He led me into the bathroom and I sighed dreamily. While he was busy, he managed to fill the tub with a bubble bath and light a bunch of candles. It was so romantic.

I pulled my bun loose from its tie. "I have to rinse off in the shower first. I'm full of sand. And I hope you plan on joining me in that gigantic thing."

Ten minutes later, I was settled between his legs in the tub, sipping on my wine, in pure heaven.

Bash was very gently playing with my nipples, but he killed the mood when I felt his warm breath on my ear. "No peeing in the bathtub, wifey. It's a rule."

"Oh my God!" I started cracking up. I laughed so hard that I spilled some wine into the water with us, which only made me laugh harder.

When I finally settled down, Bash put a hand possessively on my stomach. "Come to Thanksgiving with me."

"At your parents?" I shook my head. "Uh, no. That would be too obvious."

He sighed with frustration. "You're best friends with Kaylie. My mother will just assume she invited you."

"And what will Kaylie assume?"

He growled. "I want to see you. Can you come over here after dinner and spend the night?"

I pushed a group of bubbles around in the water. "It might be late. I'm having dinner with my dad and his girlfriend at some fancy place downtown."

"Don't worry, I'll wait up for you." He nuzzled my neck and then sat back, stroking my skin languidly.

When the water cooled, we decided to get out. I was slightly disappointed that he'd had me naked in his arms and he'd barely touched me. After I wrapped myself in a white towel, I went into his bedroom and sat on the bed. I didn't have any clean clothes with me, not even pajamas. I'd never needed them.

Bash came out of the bathroom with the towel wrapped carelessly around his waist. "Did you have fun today?"

I collapsed back onto the bed. "Mmm. That was the best day. I can't get any more satisfied than that."

"I think you can." He went straight to his closet and pulled out the box of sex toys. "What does my girl want?"

I got warm tingles. He'd called me his girl. It was different from wifey. Was I imagining these romantic stirrings between us? Was it just wishful thinking?

I surprised myself by saying, "I don't think I'm up for anything intense. How about we skip the kink part?"

He put the box on the bed next to me. "We'll each pick one thing from the box. What do you want?"

I sat up and stared into the box. What should I pick? The cuffs were my first thought. Definitely not the paddle or flogger. Not tonight. Nipple clamps — no, I wasn't sure how much I really liked them. Gag? He'd never used that on me before, but I wasn't quite in the mood. I pulled out the blindfold and handed it to him.

"Good choice." His eyes gleamed. Then he dug into the box. "I choose the vibrator."

A surge of need slammed through me. The air between us felt charged as his gaze wandered hungrily over my body. His eyes locked onto mine, sending a pulse of aching desire shuddering through every nerve.

I dropped my towel.

Chapter 19

Bash

That was fucking intense. From behind, I wrapped my arms around her naked body and kissed her shoulder.

I didn't expect it. Secretly, I'd gone into it thinking it would be pretty corny. And I was really terrible at first. Everything I said felt stilted. Fake. I thought Lacey would break out laughing at any moment.

Earlier in the week, she'd told me she wanted to try a police officer/criminal role-playing scenario. We outlined the types of things I could do to discipline her and to discover the secret code. I had no idea what the secret code was for, but it was my job to get it.

It seemed even sillier when she'd handed me a cop's hat and asked me to wear it with nothing else but black boxer briefs. Then, I'd hid in my dark bathroom spying out into my equally dark bedroom waiting for my prey.

She tiptoed into my darkened room, letting a tiny sliver of light enter through the cracked door, and started rifling through the dresser drawers.

I sprung into action and wrestled her to the bed while she tried to fight me off. Actually, it was more like I'd been feeling her up, trying to figure out what the hell she was wearing while trying not to laugh.

I almost stopped trying to get her handcuffed when she put up more of a struggle than I expected. I paused, wondering if she was going to use the safe word, but she was a good actress. Or, she was really into the role. It took me so long to secure the cuffs in the dark while she was squirming that I was sweating by the time I finished. I had to force her hands into them. She didn't give up easily.

When I flipped on the light switch, my mouth dropped open. She was dressed in a black one-piece body suit with a plunging neckline. The material was some kind of faux leather that was smooth and extremely shiny. It was skin-tight — in fact; it looked painted on, showing off her hourglass figure to perfection. She was also wearing a simple black eye mask. The whole get-up made her look a bit like Cat Woman. A very sexy burglar that I was about to have my way with.

We had decided that the scene would end when she gave up the secret code. I actually ended it before she gave up the code because I'd already used the crop, the paddle, and the flogger on her. I'd 'forced' her to give me a blowjob, which was one of the things she specifically wanted to happen. On top of that, I'd also fucked her doggy-style while pulling her hair back and then gave her two more orgasms, one with my tongue and fingers and one with a vibrator.

She just didn't want to stop. When I found myself sliding deeper and deeper into the role, I knew I had to end it. I always loved the sex aspect of our play, but this time I'd gotten off on the power dynamic.

I gave her another sip of water and then smoothed the hair out of her eyes. "You okay, wifey?"

"Mmm. Sebastian, that was amazing. A hundred times better than I imagined."

"Everything was okay? Everything I did?" I asked.

"Yes." She pushed her ass back against me. "When you spanked my pussy with the crop through the body suit? That felt so good. That definitely has to happen again."

I chuckled. "Anything you didn't like?"

"Well, I like how you yanked my body suit down to my hips and ripped it off my legs. It was so forceful, but there was a zipper down the back. I think you stretched out the material, but it was hot."

I swept my hand up and down her arm. Her skin was so smooth; I could never stop touching it. "Sorry, I had no idea how that thing came off. I didn't see a zipper."

"It's kind of hidden."

Not only could I not stop touching her, but I couldn't stop thinking about her. I'd become obsessed with her. All week long while we were apart, I thought about her. I couldn't wait for the weekend when I could see her. Sunday mornings, when she snuck away, I was pitifully sad.

She was in my arms right this moment, but it was Saturday night. We'd fall asleep together, but then she'd be gone early in the morning. I was getting melancholy just thinking about it. I was already missing her, and she was right here in my arms. It was fucked up.

Christmas was in two weeks and I wanted to be with her. I wanted to wake up with her on Christmas morning and have her by my side when Kody opened his presents. My parents and Kaylie and Sid were coming over early Christmas morning, so she said she wouldn't come.

I was starting to forget why we were keeping things secret from our friends and family. What if we just told everyone that we were dating? We practically were. We saw each other every weekend, and we even brought Kody out on outings together. Kody loved spending time with her as much as I did; he always asked about her.

She was the perfect woman. I knew I was developing feelings for her, but what did she feel about me? Was I just the guy fulfilling her kinky fantasies? That was what she'd told me when we started this friends-with-kinky-benefits agreement. Could she ever see more in me?

What did I have to offer a girl like her? She had a high-powered career. She was smart and adventurous while I was a single dad who lived in the suburbs. I couldn't go out partying every night because I had responsibilities to my son. I couldn't jet off on a whim to some luxury resort. I couldn't even take her out to a fancy restaurant without a shit load of preparation.

Lacey was so out of my league. I'd never felt this way before. The feelings I had were strange and unsettling. I didn't know what to do. The only thing I was sure of was that I wanted to be around her as much as I could. As much as she'd let me. And yet, I still couldn't figure out a way to spend time with her at Christmas. Fuck, this was frustrating.

She stilled my hand, which had been absentmindedly plucking at her nipple. "Sebastian, I want to try something."

Christ, wasn't she exhausted? But I was half-hard just from lying next to her, so I was certainly game. "I'm almost afraid to ask. What is it?"

"It's called cock warming."

A hundred ideas shot through my head at once. It seemed that my cock would be involved with whatever it was, so that sounded like a good thing, but the 'warming' part made me think of dripping candle wax. I wasn't sure how I felt about hot wax dripping on my dick. "What exactly are we talking about?"

"It's very simple. You put your cock inside me and then we both relax. No moving, no thrusting. It's not for sex, just for intimacy and relaxation."

What the hell? That was even a thing? Honestly, it sounded kind of weird. "So, I just stick it in. And then what? I don't get it."

She snickered. "Then you just relax. We can talk or take a nap. It'll feel good."

"And you like this?" What kind of asshole was she with before that just stuck his dick inside her? I wanted to punch his face in.

"Yes. You can spoon me or lie on top of me. Just make sure you have a condom on since you'll be inside me."

I rolled over to grab a condom from the nightstand. All this unsexy talk of cock warming hadn't done the job to get me hard. I had to pump my cock while I looked at a naked and very rumpled Lacey lounging in my bed. She was resting on her side with the luscious curve of her ass on full display. That would do it.

A few more pumps and I was ready to slide the condom on. "On your stomach, wifey."

She made a little mewling sound, and I knew I'd made the right choice. For whatever reason, she loved to feel the weight of my body pressing into her. I didn't mind, but I didn't want to crush her. I always held some of my weight off of her, so I knew I was in for an arm workout. If I could drum for hours, I knew I could cage her under my body while she warmed my cock.

I used some lube because I had no idea how receptive her body would be to this. This was uncharted territory for me. I slid my dick in slowly, taking my time until I was fully sheathed by her and then rested my body on top of hers.

"Mmm. Sebastian. Yes." She used her flirty sex voice, which made my dick twitch in reaction.

HOW TO MARRY A ROCKSTAR

I took a deep breath. It felt phenomenal being inside her. It was a nice tight love squeeze. My cock grew harder.

I gritted my teeth. This was just unnatural. Sure, it felt good. Too damn good. My cock wanted to go. The urge to thrust was almost unbearable.

She made a decadent sound of feminine pleasure that almost sounded like a purr. That sound went straight to my cock, shooting a bolt of lust straight to my aching balls.

I didn't pull out any but ground myself against her. It wasn't enough.

"Sebastian, don't move."

Like hell, I was going to lie there and be tortured. I pumped into her, one quick hard thrust.

She moaned with appreciation, but then she scolded me. "Don't move. You're supposed to be relaxing. Just enjoy the feeling of being connected."

I slid my hand under her shoulder and hooked her right leg with mine before I rolled us both together until we were on our sides and I was spooning her. My dick was still begging to be let loose.

"Just relax," she muttered.

I grabbed her top leg and pulled it up and over my thigh so that her pussy was easily accessible. "Who's the one giving the orders here, wifey?"

"Don't talk to me like that. You're getting me excited." She clamped down on my dick with her inner muscles.

Fuck. Was she just messing with me? This couldn't be a real thing? Could it?

I wet my finger in my mouth and then zeroed in on her clit. I started very gently stroking it back and forth.

She tried to close her legs, but I had her locked in place with my own.

"Shhh. Just relax. This is called a clit massage. It has nothing to do with sex, just relaxation and intimacy."

"Sebastian!" Her mock outrage was ruined when she groaned with desire. I knew if she really wanted me to stop, she'd use our safe words.

I desperately wanted to pump my cock into her, but I held back. Instead, I switched to circling all around and over her clit with two fingers and was rewarded by her ass pressing back into me. Her fluttering breaths and little gasps let me know just how excited she was getting.

"Don't move, wifey. Just enjoy this relaxing clit massage while you warm my cock."

She hissed in response, and I almost laughed out loud. I wet my finger again and began rubbing right where we were joined together. I knew that was always a hot spot for her. Now she was actively squirming. My work was almost done.

My left arm was pretty much trapped, but I discovered I could just reach her nipple with my fingertips. The fingers on my other hand slid back to her clit, and I worked her nipple to the same rhythm that I worked her clit.

It took another five minutes of 'clit massage' until I had her riding my cock cowgirl style while I laid back and enjoyed every fucking second of it — from her bouncing tits to watching my cock get swallowed up by her, to the way her head lolled back as she called out my name.

I could get used to this cock warming thing.

Chapter 20

Lacey

I MUST BE GETTING old. I'd been at the Staples Center for two hours already, watching endless sound checks and now the final lighting check. It'd be another hour until the doors opened and then another hour and a half until the show actually started. Then, probably at least two more hours before Ghost Parker performed. I was already exhausted.

Ghost Parker was headlining this year's Christmas concert, so they'd be the last out of five bands to hit the stage. The boys wouldn't be earning the big bucks for this show compared to their normal tour shows, but knowing this business inside and out, I knew that the hype and exposure weren't something money could buy. This opportunity was phenomenal. It was probably an even bigger deal for the second band on tonight, Castle Music's own up-and-coming band that I'd personally helped get their start.

"Let's go backstage and see if we can meet any of the hot guys in the bands." Arianna gripped my arm, grinning like an overeager puppy dog. We were watching the activity from the floor seating directly in front of the stage, among the thousands of currently empty seats.

I didn't really feel like fending off the advances of the horny musicians who were most likely looking for a little pre-show action, but I'd promised Ryder that I'd keep an eye on his stepsister. She reminded me a lot of myself when I was 22 years old; it was like seeing a glimpse of the younger me. The girl was on a mission to hook up with a rock star and I just wanted to make sure she didn't do it on my watch. Once the show was over and she was Talia's and Ryder's responsibility, all bets were off. Along with her clothes, probably, but that wasn't my problem.

I wanted to take her by the shoulders, give her a little shake, and then a life lecture, but she wouldn't listen. I wouldn't have listened to the older me either when I was her age. She probably thought I was a big prude, and that thought had me laughing hysterically in my head.

"Sure, let's go see what's going on." I led her backstage. The VIP lounge wouldn't open until the doors opened, so we might as well go backstage. The rest of the crew — Kaylie, Talia, Grey, Remi, and Summer — wouldn't be showing up until closer to when the concert started. After the show, there'd be no hanging around and partying as per the facility agreement, so we were all going out to party together.

I'd attended a lot of Ghost Parker concerts over the years, but this was the first one where I was secretly married to the drummer. It felt different.

Bash and I decided that we'd maintain a distance as we hung out together after the show until we outlasted everyone. They were all married or had kids to worry about. Kaylie's tits would start leaking, so she'd run off to her babies after a couple of hours. Ghost would have both of his sex partners there, so he wouldn't stay out all night. Knox and Ryder wouldn't be much better with their girls.

I was acutely aware that I was the only outsider partying with them, and I wondered if it was really obvious. Even though I'd hung out with the band for years, I was suddenly self-conscious. I vowed to just keep my distance from Bash and try to act normal until everyone left the after-party.

I led Arianna through the winding labyrinth backstage until I found the chaos. It looked like all five bands were gathered among a crush of VIPs, radio contest winners, and media. I saw Ghost Parker's PR rep wrangling the guys for interviews and their manager, Donovan, schmoozing the crowd. The Castle Music guys noticed me immediately and tried to act more professional because the big boss was in the room. As if I hadn't been there, done that. I wasn't there to bust balls, but I guess they didn't know that.

Arianna quickly latched on to one of the band's lead singers, a hottie with lots of piercings and tattoos. I hovered around to chaperone; I wasn't going to let her leave the room with this guy.

Soon, Ghost Parker was involved in a long meet and greet for ticket winners and other VIPs of the local radio station. I'd been backstage at many rock concerts for both work and pleasure and I usually enjoyed the scene. Bash was naturally flirty. He made each girl or guy he met feel special. He was acting no different from the other guys in the band who were all taken, but it still irked me a bit to watch him fawn all over the fans.

The meet and greet took over 45 minutes. I spent most of that time using every skill I possessed to keep Ariana in line. I was the most subtle cockblock on the planet, succeeding to get each guy to give up eventually and try greener pastures. Arianna was having so much fun flirting, she didn't even notice my devious ways.

The meet and greet had just ended, but I was still trailing after Arianna with a drink in my hand. I knew the moment Bash's gaze narrowed in on me. The hair on the back of my neck rose, and a frisson of desire licked down my spine. He made his way over to me and lightly touched his hand to my hip, but then hastily removed it.

"Hey," he grumbled in his deep baritone.

"You ready for tonight?" I hoped he knew I wasn't talking about the concert.

His mesmerizing eyes darkened. "I'm ready."

Apparently, he knew exactly what I was talking about. I couldn't help but grin.

I was about to make a suggestive comment when we were interrupted by Ghost Parker's PR rep, Trudy.

Trudy placed her hand on his biceps, squeezing it to get his attention. "Bash..."

His eyes lingered on me, but he finally pulled them away and looked at Trudy. "What's up?"

Trudy pulled a young girl who was cowering behind her out and placed her in front of him. "This is Felicity."

Bash nodded and said hello, but then his eyes were back on me.

I took in the other girl. She was young, maybe 20 years old at most. She had that wholesome, girl next door look down pat, barely there makeup, shiny plumped-up lips, long wavy hair down her back, and non-slutty clothes that bared her flat midriff yet still looked innocent enough. She was even batting her eyelashes innocently at Bash.

Trudy pulled on his biceps again. "Felicity is the contest winner. She won the date with you. I'll bring her backstage after the show. I got a driver for you and made reservations at a restaurant at L.A. Live. The driver will have all the details."

Bash frowned at Trudy. "I've got plans already. Reschedule."

"Not going to happen." Trudy crossed her arms over her chest, not giving an inch. "This is for charity Bash."

His jaw clenched. "How come this is the first time I'm hearing about it?"

She shot him a warning glance. "I don't know. Did you read the email I sent you?"

The little doe-eyed girl with the perky tits and flawless skin didn't look too bothered by the conversation. Bash looked around the room and then bellowed out, "Donovan, get over here."

Donovan was standing less than ten feet away with his arm draped around another barely legal girl, this one in full-groupie attire.

Trudy's hands were on her hips when Donovan approached. "He's giving me trouble about the contest."

Donovan chuckled as he looked over at the winner, Felicity. He patted Bash on the arm and kept his voice down, but I could hear every word. "You're lucky she's so hot. Let her take some pics for her social media. It'll be great publicity. Give her a night to remember, if you know what I mean. A few times. It's for charity." Then he actually winked, clapped Bash on the back twice, and wandered away.

Trudy gave Bash a death glare and then retreated, leaving Felicity bouncing on her toes with excitement. "I can't wait for you to perform tonight, Bash. I'm a really big fan."

Disappointed, I turned to leave, but Bash caught my arm to stop me. He was pleading with his eyes for me to understand. "I won't go. I'll make Trudy reschedule."

Keeping my expression neutral, I said. "I have to go meet up with Kaylie and the others. They just got here. They're in the VIP lounge."

His hand dropped to his side. "I'll make the date real quick. An hour tops, I swear. Then I'll meet you guys out. I won't be long. I'll get it over with and then I'm all yours."

Not trusting myself to say anything, I nodded and then turned around. Before I left, I heard Felicity asking him in that sweet-as-pie voice for a picture of the two of them together.

Scanning the room for Arianna, I walked away. I found her making out with some big dude who I didn't remember being in any of the bands. I could see why Ryder wanted someone to keep an eye on her. She didn't seem to care who she ended up with.

It took some time to extract Arianna, but then we made our way out. I had to weave through all the young girls who were flashing tits and ass cheeks. I sighed. When did I start hating on young women?

I guess I was just feeling insecure. Maybe a bit older and wiser. It was frustrating to see all these young, fertile girls — just like I was — wasting their time chasing rock stars, thinking they had all the time in the world. Or maybe my biological clock was ticking so loudly it was driving me insane.

I could rattle off fertility facts like a freaking specialist. Women were most fertile in their 20s. Welp, that was long gone. At age 32, fertility started to decline. I guess I was in the declining phase. By age 35 — right around the corner for me — that decline sped up. At age 35, your odds of conceiving after 3 months of trying were just 12%, and it went downhill from there. While the odds nosedived, the risk of miscarriage, genetic abnormalities, or pregnancy complications began to rise.

So, maybe I was just jealous watching these young girls rubbing all over these rock stars. They still had lots of time while I felt like my window was closing fast. I'd always been a pragmatist. I needed to find a husband, so I could start the family I wanted.

Instead, I was chasing after a rock star, just like these clueless girls. These past few months, I may have stuck with only one rock star that rocked my world, but time was still ticking. In less than three months, we'd be divorced and our kinky sex agreement would be over. Bash would be free to go back to his lifestyle. Our marriage would be chalked up to a bad decision that would never be mentioned again and we'd both move on. I needed to prepare myself and stop fantasizing about anything different.

We got to the VIP lounge, and I was more than happy to pass Arianna off to Talia to babysit. I had a few drinks and chatted with Remi and Grey, who were getting a lot of attention in the lounge, even though there were other celebrities present.

There were too many invited band guests for us to watch from the stage wings, where it was complete chaos. There were so many bands playing, the sets were really short, and the crews were running around everywhere that we had to keep out of the way. We had pretty good floor seats for the show, which suited my bitter mood just fine.

I was tired, cranky, and pissed at Bash even if he didn't do anything wrong. Really, I was angry at the situation, or maybe myself for getting caught up in it. I was pretending to have a good time watching the show, but that only made me more exhausted.

The other bands were mostly a blur. Ghost Parker was on last. Their set was only about 35 minutes long. Toward the end, Candace Collins surprised the crowd by joining them onstage. Ghost channeled a little Elvis Presley when he did a duet with her, singing Blue Christmas. Then they ended the show with the crowd favorite, *Okay Babe*.

Instead of looking for Bash after the show, I hopped into one of the cars with Kaylie, Sid, Summer, and Knox and went with them to the after-party at some club.

I tried not to dampen anyone's enthusiasm, but I was bummed. Bash was out on a date with some fan. We were supposed to be hanging out together tonight; the plan was to go back to my penthouse after the show since we were already downtown. Kody was staying overnight with Bash's parents, so I'd been excited for a completely free night with Bash, with no worries about Kody waking up.

We'd been at the club for almost two hours and Bash still hadn't shown up. I was miserable hanging out with all these couples who were so in love.

What the hell was I doing with Bash, anyway? Playing some kind of sick game of house with him. But we were together only on the weekends and I always traveled to his house, except for rare occasions like tonight. Not only was I getting inconveniently attached to Bash, but to his adorable son, too.

This charity win-a-date that he had tonight had ruined my entire night. It had swept me up in a jealous tailspin of need and insecurity. It was a warning of things to come. I needed to put some distance between us for my own sanity. Starting tonight.

As predicted, Kaylie didn't last long. After she and Sidney said their goodbyes, I decided to leave, too. I kissed everyone goodbye and if they were surprised I was leaving, they didn't show it. I'd almost made it to the exit when Ghost stopped me.

"Why are you taking off so early?"

Ghost was king of the disappearing act, so I didn't know why he cared if I did.

"It's been a long day."

Now that we were out of the VIP section, he was getting noticed by the other club patrons.

"Keep me company while Grey and Remi are dancing."

He was disarming up close when all his attention was focused on me. "I wouldn't be good company tonight."

He leaned against the wall. "I noticed you weren't yourself tonight. Do you want to talk about it?"

"No." My lips twitched. Ghost was trying to get me to talk to him about feelings? He really had changed.

He rubbed his chin. "Is it about Bash?"

God, he was so perceptive. "It's more about me."

He looked like he was digging around for something to say, but I stopped him before he strained his brain too much.

"Thank you, but you don't need to worry about me. I'm a big girl. I'm heading home and you should get back to the VIP area before you get swarmed."

Ghost glanced around and frowned. Half the city probably knew he was here now. "Yeah. Do you want me to tell Bash anything when he shows up?"

I didn't have the energy to figure out what he was getting at. "No. There's nothing meaningful between Bash and me. Just a few insignificant fucks."

I left Ghost looking strangely stricken by my words. Why the fuck did he care? Why did I care? Why did I feel so out of control? Like I wanted to burn the world down?

I took a cab back to my building, but instead of going inside, I went to the small hole-in-the-wall bar down the block. I nursed a few drinks at the bar until closing time.

When I got to my penthouse, I wasn't surprised to see Bash there. I could tell by his damp hair that he showered. That girl had probably draped herself all over him and he wanted to wash off the smell.

"You showered again?"

He frowned. "Nothing happened with that girl. I told you I would only be with you. Why did you leave so early?"

"I wasn't in the mood."

He ran his hand through his hair and sighed. "I'm sorry, Lacey. That date was an obligation. I didn't even know about it and I didn't want to be there. I wanted to be with you."

Yes, I believed him and I knew I was being unreasonable, but I couldn't pull it back. I felt like if I didn't act like a stellar bitch to him right then, I'd be crying. I couldn't explain it even to myself.

He hugged me, but I remained stiff until he let go. Like I'd said to Ghost, like that famous break-up line, this was more about me than Bash. In our case, we had nothing to break up except a marriage and that was already in the works. I just needed to keep my emotional distance and maybe that included giving up the sex, too. The Dom/sub thing had really screwed with my head and made me feel more attached.

I really needed to find a vanilla lover. A man who could be a good father. Someone who was strong, stable, and kind. Just like that woman at the fertility clinic had told me. It kind of made sense now. I needed to find a father for my baby, not a lover for me.

We ended up in bed with Bash spooning me. He held on to me tight, but he was so exhausted after the long day that he fell asleep quickly. When I was sure that he was sound asleep, that's when the tears silently fell.

Chapter 21

Bash

I WAS LOSING LACEY, and I didn't know why. After the disastrous Christmas concert, she'd been avoiding me. She always had her excuses for why she couldn't hang out, but I wasn't an idiot. Was it all because of that stupid charity date contest? There was absolutely no comparison between that girl and Lacey and she wasn't the jealous type, anyway. I tried to tell her that, to talk with her the next morning, but she'd acted like she couldn't care less, so I didn't push it.

But now, suddenly, she was busy all the time. She didn't have time to take my calls at night and then she told me she had plans to go out this Friday night, which was our night together.

I didn't know what to make of it and I couldn't ask anyone for relationship advice without giving away our secret — a secret that I couldn't even remember why we'd thought it necessary in the first place. Who gave a fuck if Kaylie knew I was fucking her best friend?

Or if anyone else knew. I didn't get it anymore. It was driving me crazy. I debated asking Josie, but after the dates she'd set me up on, I was pretty sure any advice she had on relationships would be shit.

I'd wanted to see her on Christmas day after my family left, but she claimed she needed to be at her father's house. She came over the next day with a present for Kody.

Kody was ecstatic to see her. He gave her a tour of all his presents from Santa: the new cars and car carrying case, workbench and play tools, the water guns, pool floats, dinosaurs, books, play kitchen, and Lincoln Logs set. For Christmas, she gave him a wooden toy garage that had a working elevator and three levels with ramps and moving gates, a carwash, and a helicopter pad. Kody loved it and they spent a few hours together playing with it.

Then she left before I could give her the gifts I'd gotten for her. I had wanted to spend some time alone with her, but she'd used Kody as a shield to keep her distance.

When she agreed to come over tonight after Kody was asleep, I was more relieved than anything else. I wanted to give her the Christmas gifts I picked out for her and hopefully show her with the presents what I was feeling. Then, I would tell her that I wanted to move our relationship beyond the friends-with-benefits crap we were calling it. I wanted to have a real relationship with her where everyone knew. We didn't have to reveal our marriage to the world, but hiding that we were together was not what I wanted.

I really didn't have a clue how she felt anymore, so my anxiety was high. I was crushed when she took off after playing with Kody. She was freezing me out, but I didn't know why. Hopefully, tonight I'd fix all of it.

It was after 9 p.m. when she got to my place. She seemed a little edgy, so I settled her in front of the fireplace with a mug of hot chocolate.

I gestured to the wrapped gifts that I'd put under the tree. "You left the other day without opening your Christmas presents."

Her mouth dropped open in surprise. "You got me gifts? But I didn't get you anything."

I smiled to ease her worry. I hadn't been expecting anything. "You got Kody that toy garage, and he loves it. It turned out to be a gift for me, too. He spends hours occupied with it, so it gives me breathing room."

"I'm glad he likes it. It looked entertaining for a kid when I was shopping." She took a sip of her hot chocolate.

I bent down to retrieve one of the four packages. Fuck, I was anxious. Did I overdo it with the gifts? Was it not enough? Too much? Would she hate them? These definitely weren't friends-with-benefits kinds of gifts. I had no clue how she'd react.

She tore into the green elf wrapping paper and pulled out the pink and gold girly picture frame that had a photo of us in it. I'd picked out one of the pictures from our Vegas wedding, not one of the photos that looked like I was about to throw her down and fuck her, but the one where I was cupping her face and kissing her sweetly. The picture was beautiful. We were both closing our eyes, lost in the moment. I'd edited the photo a bit — sharpened the contrast, zoomed in, and centered it until it was perfect.

Several emotions flitted over her face. "Wow. Our wedding day. It looks so romantic, too bad I can't remember it. Thank you, I love it, but I'll have to hide it, so no one sees it."

Not if I had anything to say about it. I was determined to get her to agree to tell our friends about us. I grabbed the next gift and decided to prep her for it. "This is the naughty gift."

"Oh!" Her eyes lit up. "Gimmee." She made grabby hands and then ripped through the paper to get to the rectangular box. She pulled off the lid to reveal the silver chains nestled on the cotton bed. "A necklace?"

"Not just any necklace. A very sexy necklace. This part goes around your neck." I picked up the necklace and pointed out the thicker chain that ended in an open-circle pendant. Then I fingered the two delicate chains that attached to each side of the pendant and ended in soft, silicone rings that were adjustable. "And these two rings cinch around your nipples as tight or loose as you want. Then these chains will drape in a cascade from your breasts to the pendant. It looked sexy as fuck on the mannequin. I can't wait to see it on you."

That last remark got a chuckle from her. "Should I model it now?"

I reached under the tree for the next gift. "Not yet. You've got two more presents."

I handed her the small rectangular metal tin with the snowmen design on it. It was supposedly a gift card holder. It was a little weird, but the lady at the store suggested it and it worked for what I'd had in mind.

She shook it, but it didn't make any noise. "Not mints."

"Nope."

She opened the lid and pulled out the piece of paper. It was a homemade coupon for a weekend getaway.

She read it aloud. "To redeem on any weekend of your choice for two nights at a luxury treehouse hideaway. Amenities include stunning views, chirping birds, and sleeping under the stars among the lush greenery. The treehouse is well-appointed with all the modern conveniences. Pamper yourself with everything you'd expect at a luxury hotel room and then some. Get ready to unplug and relax on your quiet, magical getaway."

I'd copied the description from the website. The wording was a little cheesy, but the photos of the place looked amazing. "What do you think?"

"What about Kody? I know you don't like leaving him overnight with your parents."

I didn't, and I tried not to do it too often. I'd spent too many nights without him when I was on tour as it was, but I wanted her to know that she was important to me, too.

"It's only for a couple of nights and I want to go away somewhere with you. Just the two of us."

She tucked her foot under her leg. "And you're going to be able to just pick up and go? What if you have band stuff?"

I wasn't about to let anything get in the way. "Just tell me the dates you want to go and I'll make it happen."

Her face was an unreadable mask. "Isn't it a little cold to stay in a treehouse cabin in the winter?"

"They're heated," I clarified. "These aren't rustic little shacks. But if you want to wait until spring, when it warms up a bit, that would be fine."

She was studying me with a quizzical look on her face. I wasn't sure what she was thinking about, but she held it back. "Okay. It sounds really nice."

That wasn't exactly the enthusiastic response I'd been hoping for. It made me even more apprehensive about the next present.

She was going to think it was too extravagant. Or that I spent too much money, but spending $1,200 on her was nothing. I loved the necklace that I bought her. It was beautiful and as soon as I saw it, I knew that I had to get it for her.

"You got your naughty present; this is your nice one." I handed her the last box.

The box contained a pendant made of a hand-faceted blue topaz that was surrounded by sparkling diamonds and hung from an 18k gold chain. I had never heard of the Italian designer and I didn't know much about jewelry, but the piece was gorgeous and the stone matched the stunning blue of her eyes.

"Bash," she gasped. "This is too much."

"It's not. I thought of you as soon as I saw it. Let me help you put it on."

She lifted her hair, and I clasped it around her neck. I stepped back to admire it. "It's perfect."

There was a hint of uncertainty in her eyes, but then she hugged me. "Thank you for the gifts. I loved them all."

We held each other for an extended moment and I savored each second. Maybe I'd been imagining a distance growing between us. Everything felt right now that I had her in my arms.

Chapter 22

Lacey

Was I so easily influenced that a few gifts would sway me? Apparently, yes.

The last few days, when I'd taken a step back to get my head on straight, I realized that I couldn't do this friends-with-benefits arrangement anymore. Just like with my Daddy Dom from Scarlett, I felt myself getting too close. With Bash, those feelings were amplified a thousand-fold. Yeah, I'd loved the submissive aspect of my relationship with my Dom, but I didn't know him outside of our sessions at all. I was getting to know Bash very well, and I loved everything about him. It wasn't just about the sex. I even wondered if I was falling in love with him.

Then he went and bought me those thoughtful gifts. The sexy body jewelry I could have chalked off to general male horniness. I could have dismissed the expensive necklace, too. He could afford to toss around money without putting a dent in his pocket, so merely spending money didn't have to mean much, but it looked like he'd put effort into buying me something that I would like. The necklace was just my style, and I loved it. The framed photo and the weekend trip were harder to ignore. Those gestures took thought and effort and seemed very romantic. The last thing I needed was to start to get weird delusions in my head about how he felt about me.

Somehow, in our days apart, a crazy thought had popped into my head and set down roots. I was enthralled with it — daydreaming about it while I was supposed to be working and laying awake in the dead of the night just obsessing over it. As much as it captured my imagination, it also terrified me to my core.

I wanted Bash to be my Baby Daddy. It was an idea that had sprung into my head and wouldn't be exorcised no matter how much figurative holy water I threw at it.

I mean, we were already married, why not have a baby? I didn't even have to tell anyone he was the father if that's what he preferred. It was most likely a touchy subject with him with all he went through with Kody. Did he even want another kid? He was a great father, and he'd probably want to be involved. Could my heart survive if a child kept us close, but he moved on to relationships with other women?

Would he even want to have a kid with me? We'd be forced to be in each other's lives forever. And maybe he thought I was too slutty to be a good mom. He knew how promiscuous I used to be. I'd had a threesome with him and we were doing all this kinky shit together because I got off on it. I knew that my sexuality had nothing to do with being a great mother, but did he?

All these thoughts had gone round and round in my head non-stop ever since I thought it up. It was super complicated. A million times more complicated than our friends-with-benefits arrangement, and

I was already getting my emotions incredibly mixed up dealing with that.

Now, I was standing in his arms, scared as hell because I was thinking about testing the waters. I wanted to send up a trial balloon to see how he'd think about it without completely blurting out the insane idea, but I was tongue-tied. I knew he cared about me, but how much of that was tied into the sex for him?

We finally separated. I looked down at my chest and fingered my new necklace. "How about I show you just how much I like my new presents?"

His smile took my breath away. "Oh yeah? How are you going to do that, wifey?"

I walked my finger up his chest. "I'll do whatever you want me to for the night. Just tell me and I'll do it. Whatever you desire. I'll be your sex slave."

He caught my finger in his hand and held it. "What if I just want to hold you? Or maybe do the classic missionary position? With the lights out?"

"If vanilla's your flavor, there's no shame in it, but I'm sure you can get more creative," I teased. "I know, we can role-play. You be the sexy rock star — not really a stretch for you — and I'll be your adoring groupie. You can show me how you treat your groupies."

He tensed up, and his jaw hardened. "I don't want to be with groupies. That's far from my fantasy," he forced out through gritted teeth. "I'd rather just have sex with you. Instead, how about I see how many orgasms I can give you?"

God, I'd fucked that up. I had meant to be playful, but he'd gone cold at the suggestion and it probably sounded a whole lot like passive-aggressive resentment.

"I have a better idea." Desperate, I was trying to figure out how to undo what I'd said. "First, have a seat on the couch."

What better to make him forget my gaffe than to get naked? I'd do a little striptease for him. There was no music, no mood lighting, I wasn't wearing stripper heels, and my outer clothing wasn't very sexy. I was wearing skinny jeans with a fuzzy sweater and fuzzy socks, but underneath was some cute stuff, so I'd work with those. As long as you projected confidence, men didn't care.

When he was seated, I turned my back to him and then slowly lifted up my sweater, wiggling my hips a bit. I pulled it over my head and then looked over my shoulder at him before I threw it his way.

Taking my skinny jeans off was going to be a lot harder while remaining sultry. I almost needed to sit on the floor to pull them off, especially from the ankles, and that was not sexy at all. Wiggling them down past my hips, I then struggled with them in the most seductive manner possible until I got them off. I almost toppled twice and I may have mumbled a curse a few times.

When I turned back around, Bash's hand was partially covering his mouth and rubbing his chin. I'm pretty sure he was trying not to laugh, but he had that sparkle of mischief back in his eye — the one I'd doused earlier with my careless words. My amateur striptease was working.

I was down to my bra and panties, so I turned around to face him, satisfied when his jaw dropped. I was wearing a harness bra and barely there panties; they both consisted of more straps than fabric.

Hoping it looked sexy, I shimmied my boobs a bit before I unhooked the bra and then tossed it aside. The last to go was the panties. I teased the waistband string up and down my hip several times before I whisked them off.

Now that I was naked, I didn't know what to do, so I stalked over to the couch and straddled Bash's lap.

He planted his hands on my hips. "So far, I like your idea."

"Wait till you see what's next."

His eyes darted over to the staircase. He looked concerned. "We should take this upstairs."

Shit, I forgot about Kody. What if he came down? "Yes, take me to bed, Sebastian."

He teased at my entrance with the tip of his thumb and the look he gave me was so heated that lust ignited inside of me like a raging inferno. "Your wish is my command."

He took my arms and placed them around his neck. He was ridiculously strong to be able to stand up with me still in his lap. I wrapped my legs around his hips and he wedged a forearm under my ass for support.

He stopped to gather up my clothes – he pulled my sweater and panties from the couch and then kind of used his foot to gather my balled-up jeans that were half under the Christmas tree — all without letting me go. Then he carried me up the stairs and to his bedroom.

He placed me gently on the bed. "I'm going to peek in on Kody. I'll be right back.

By the time I was finished using the bathroom, he was back.

I sat down on the edge of the bed. "You're way overdressed, Sebastian. It's time for you to strip."

"Yes, ma'am. " He reached behind his head and pulled off his shirt, showing off his rippling muscles in the process.

I placed my hand on my hip and frowned. "Don't call me ma'am. Ever. I'm wifey to you."

He smiled. "Okay, wifey."

"Let's go." I pointed to his pants. "Get nakey."

He didn't hesitate. He pulled down his pants and boxer briefs all at once and then took a few seconds to slip off his socks. While he hadn't put on a striptease show as I'd attempted, he somehow managed to be much more graceful than I'd been.

I gestured toward the bed. "Lay down on the bed."

He lifted a brow but then complied. "You're bossy tonight."

I went to his closet and pulled out the box of sex toys. Tonight, I wanted to take control, but what the hell was I going to do to him that would drive him wild?

My eyes landed on the flogger. I'd never used one before, but it didn't seem that difficult. Maybe to tease him a bit, but somehow I didn't think that would make him crazy with lust the way it did to me. Instead, I grabbed the bottle of lube and then the blindfold and cuffs and headed to the bed.

"Put this on." I tossed him the blindfold.

He paused for a moment and then put the black satin mask over his eyes, slipping the stretchy elastic band over his head.

I knelt next to him on the bed, taking in his impressive body while I poured some lube into my hands and worked it around my palm. I stroked his cock a few times, using a firm grip. His cock was already hard, but it seemed to get even bigger the more I worked it. Every so often, I made sure to give his balls and upper thighs some attention, too. I was really enjoying giving him a sensual massage.

I slid my hand over his entire length. "Whose cock is this?"

"It's your cock, wifey." A faint trace of a smile flirted with his lips. He was amused.

Even more than I wanted that cock to impale me, I wanted to tease him until he was begging for mercy. I straddled his hips, planning to slide my pussy on top of his rock-hard length when his hands landed on my hips to help me move. I grabbed them and he let me pin them above his head. My breasts grazed his chest as I leaned forward.

"Kiss me," he demanded.

Without thinking, I followed his command. My lips were already touching his when I realized what I was doing and pulled back. "You don't give the orders here. Do it again and I'll have to gag you."

He growled, and a muscle clenched in his jaw, but he didn't say anything.

I needed to wrest back control and take my pleasure. Keeping his hands trapped over his head with mine, I moved up his body until I was straddling his face and then lowered my pussy onto his mouth. "Make me come."

It took a little while since he was only using his tongue, but I wasn't shy about taking what I needed to get there. I rode him hard. Black stars speckled my vision as I bucked and thrashed without restraint, my orgasm slamming into me with a fierce intensity. I wanted to collapse into a puddle of ecstasy as my thighs quivered, but I was probably smothering him with my pussy. Gasping for breath, I rolled off his face.

I slid back down to straddle his stomach. Reaching behind me, I grabbed his cock and fisted his length, planning to tease him a bit while I caught my breath.

His chest rumbled below me. "If that cock is yours, why don't you use it? Give it a kiss, or better yet, sit on it."

Frowning, I bit my lip. "I'll do what I want with it."

I was planning to, but now I felt like whatever I did, I'd be following his orders again. He was undermining me, and I was worried that he wasn't enjoying this as much as our usual sex. Secretly, I wished that he was the one dominating me. I couldn't deny that it drove me crazy, as nothing else did.

Stalling, I stroked him a few times while I played with my clit to hold on to my post-orgasm arousal. He thrust up against my hand, and I got tired of delaying what we both wanted. Sliding back, I positioned myself over the head of his cock before sinking down onto him.

I pumped my hips up and down his cock a few times. I was so bad at this. Neither of us was enjoying this lackluster sex, but I felt backed into a corner. I had to finish what I'd started.

"Yellow," he blurted out.

I stopped and asked warily. "You don't like this?"

"I don't like being blindfolded. I want to see you." He blew out a frustrated breath. "And I want to touch you. I don't enjoy laying here like a lump."

"I don't prefer this either. It's not driving me wild with insane need," I confessed.

My words unleashed the beast. Within seconds, he'd flipped our positions and straddled me as I lay face down on the bed. My pulse began rioting as my blood filled with fire and lightning. He pulled my hips up while he pushed my upper back and face down into the mattress. A firm tug on my hair had me positioned right where he wanted me. I couldn't deny how his dominance whipped up a wild storm of white-hot lust in me that was centered right between my legs.

He'd always dominated me with sexy words, commands, and through his sheer physical strength, but this rough play was new and it made my heart sing like nothing before. He held me down and lined up his cock at my entrance.

Pressing his chest against my back, he growled into my ear. "Do you want this, wifey?"

"Yes," I choked out.

He gave my ass a firm slap. "Tell me. Tell me if this is okay."

Like a good dom, he was checking in with me and I knew more than anything that I wanted it. "Green."

He plunged into me. He didn't hold back; it was rough and controlling. I whimpered with an answering need. Desire sizzled hot and heavy as he pistoned into me.

And then I remembered.

"Red!"

He'd pushed into me full hilt but immediately paused at my outburst. He stopped for a few seconds. My heart was pounding out of control.

"Lacey? Did I hurt you?" He pulled out of me and turned me over, brushing the hair off my face. Concern filled his eyes. "Fuck, talk to me, baby."

I was panting. My head was spinning. I wanted him to keep going like I'd never wanted anything else in the world.

"Condom," I stuttered out. "You forgot the condom."

"Okay, right." He blew out a breath of relief. "Lacey, I haven't been with anyone since before Vegas. I'm clean. But I'll go get checked and show you the results, just to ease your mind."

He rolled off the bed and began searching through the nightstand. "I lost my mind and forgot the condom, but it felt so good. You can trust me. After I get the results back, we can ditch the condoms. I don't want anything between us."

I had to tell him. "We have to keep using condoms. I'm not on birth control."

His head whipped in my direction. "What? Why?"

"I've been on the pill for almost fifteen years. I wanted to give my body a break from the hormones." There was some truth to that, but it wasn't the exact truth.

"You're not on anything?" He sounded disbelieving.

I shook my head.

He threw up his hands and asked almost accusingly, "This whole time? Why didn't you tell me before?"

"We always used a condom. I made sure." I was getting defensive and more than a bit annoyed.

His jaw clenched. "Condoms can fail."

I turned away from him and wrapped my arms around my body.

He sat down on the edge of the bed. "I just don't want you to be in a position that you don't want to be in. That's all."

Meaning he didn't want me to get knocked up. Message received. "I'm not on birth control. If you don't like it, you don't have to fuck me anymore."

"Jesus, Lacey!" His hand tunneled through his hair. "I'm just trying to be an adult about this."

Fuck, this stung. So much for asking him to be my Baby Daddy. How fucking stupid was that idea?

He grasped my chin and forced me to face him. "I'm sorry. I didn't mean to get upset. I was just surprised. We'll talk more about this tomorrow, okay?"

"Okay." I nodded, but the damage was done.

He put the condom on and we had sex. Between him suddenly treating me like a porcelain doll and his reaction to the birth control thing, I lost my enthusiasm.

The sex was nice, but he wasn't rough anymore. It wasn't animalistic like before. Sure, I'd had an orgasm five minutes ago when I rode his face, but this time was the first time we'd ever made love and I faked it. I wasn't in the mood while that conversation kept replaying in my head. I had years of experience faking it with mediocre lovers, so I quite convincingly faked an orgasm so he would finish.

While he was taking care of the condom, I pretended to fall asleep. I was becoming quite the faker.

The next morning, I woke up to an empty bed. I couldn't tell if I was losing him or pushing him away and I felt panicky at the thought. What a mess I was.

Before I could get out of bed and hop into the shower, Bash came into the room. He was up and dressed for the day.

"Morning, sleepyhead." He came over to my side of the bed and kissed me on the forehead. "I'm going to drop Kody off at my parents' house. I'll be back in 30 minutes. Stay in bed if you don't want to get up yet."

"What time is it?" I mumbled into the pillow.

"It's 9:30. Do you want me to pick up anything while I'm out?"

"No." He knew I didn't eat breakfast.

"All right. There's coffee downstairs. I'll be back." He kissed me again and then left.

It was time to figure out what I was going to do to fix this giant mess, starting with myself.

Chapter 23

Bash

I'D HAD TO LEAVE the bed this morning before I got drawn into fucking her again. Her warm, naked body made me lose my mind.

Communication was more important than fucking, though. We needed to have a real talk. First, I had to make sure Kody was taken care of, so I arranged to drop him off at my parents' house. I couldn't afford any distractions.

Today, I was determined to talk to her about our relationship. I had no real experience with relationships, but I needed to know what she was thinking and I wanted to tell her how I felt. Communication was the key to moving forward. I wanted to get everything out in the open.

The argument about birth control was definitely a miscommunication between us that wouldn't have happened if we had talked to each other honestly from the start. We were great at talking through the kink stuff, but not the emotional stuff and I was too dumb to understand why she'd pushed me away the past few days, but I was determined to find out. I couldn't fix something if I didn't know what it was.

When I got home from dropping off Kody, I heard the shower running. The sex last night wasn't that great. I had already been wary from when she was freezing me out and then her joke about how I treated groupies twisted my gut. Then, she got upset about the birth control argument. It had put a damper on our mood.

When we did talk, I wanted to make damn sure it was fresh in her mind how sexually compatible and how amazing we were together. It wasn't being manipulative; I was just putting my best foot forward with a little sexual persuasion. I was pretty sure she considered my abilities to be my best asset, so I was going to use them. Besides, I hadn't showered yet today, so it made sense in my twisted mind.

I raced upstairs, stripped off my clothes, and joined her in the shower. Neither of us said a word. We just attacked each other. This time, the sex was steamy and satisfying.

We locked lips and tangled tongues for a long, romantic kiss before I broke away. I quickly washed my hair and body. "I'll leave you to finish up before you lose all the hot water."

After I toweled off, I wandered into my closet to get a fresh pair of briefs and then quickly stepped into them when I heard the shower water turn off.

I wanted to bring a coffee up to her, so I headed downstairs without bothering to get dressed. Kody wasn't home, and this would give Lacey another chance to ogle my body. I needed all the ammunition I could get for this talk and I wasn't above fighting dirty to get what I wanted.

I was in the kitchen, adding the special sugar she used to her coffee when I heard the front door open. Not really alarmed, more like curious, I walked out of the kitchen toward the door to see what was up.

Sid and Kaylie stood just inside the door.

"Eew!" Kaylie averted her eyes. "Where are your clothes? Gross."

Sid chuckled and raised his eyebrows.

"This is my house. I can be naked in it if I want."

She pushed past me and walked into the family room, staring at my Christmas tree. "You didn't answer your phone. Didn't you hear us banging on the door? I had to use my key."

I shot Sid a look of annoyance and then rubbed my chest. "What are you doing here?"

"We came to take Kody to the park with the twins."

I looked around. "Where are Brady and Emerson?"

She spun around but kept her eyes on my face. "They're in their car seats. They're both sound asleep."

Just then, Lacey called down from upstairs. "Hurry up, Sebastian, I've got a surprise for you."

At the same time Kaylie made a sour face, Sid chuckled and said, "Sebastian?" He snickered. "Dude."

"You brought a bimbo here? In front of Kody?" Kaylie shrieked.

"She's not a bimbo." And then I added, "Kody's at mom and dad's."

Her eyes narrowed. "She's not a bimbo?" She bent down and then picked up Lacey's discarded bra by the tips of her fingers as if it was contaminated.

The bra was more a collection of straps that did nothing to cover, only to highlight. Lacey had looked like a sex goddess in it. I couldn't think about that now though, or I'd get hard. I thought I'd picked up all her clothes last night so Kody wouldn't stumble upon them, but apparently not.

Sid whistled, and that earned him a smack on the chest from Kaylie.

Kay dropped the bra like it'd burnt her fingers. "If she talks like a bimbo and dresses like a bimbo..."

I glared at her. "Sid, get your wife out of here."

Sid was smiling with amusement. "C'mon, babe. Let's give him some privacy."

Kaylie crossed her arms like she wasn't budging.

I blew out an exasperated breath. "Why did you come here?"

She scoffed. "I thought you'd be lonely. That you'd want some company."

Sid turned to her and said, "I told you he wasn't lonely."

I was ushering them back to the front door when Kaylie screeched like a shrew. She was looking over my shoulder in horror.

I turned around and there was Lacey, looking like she was about to faint, naked as a jaybird except for the nipple jewelry. I was right; it did look fantastic on her.

"Fuck!" I quickly moved to step in front of her, blocking the view.

"Oh, my God." Lacey bumped against my back, trying to hide.

Kaylie's voice rose an octave. "What is happening here?"

Even Sid looked shocked. "C'mon, Kaylie. We've gotta go."

Kaylie ignored him. "Why are you naked? And what is on your tits?"

"I think we know why they're naked, babe," Sid deadpanned. "But I'd like to know what's on her tits, too. That's a good question. I only got a quick peek—"

Thank God that Kaylie smacked him in the stomach or I'd have to do something to shut him up.

I pointed to the door. "Will you two just leave? Don't you have kids to take care of?"

"Sid, go check on them." Kaylie put her hands on her hips. "And

I'm not leaving until I found out what the hell is going on here."

Sid, the coward, shrugged and then went out the door to do as she asked.

I turned my angry gaze on my sister. "This is none of your business, Kay. But if you're going to be a giant pain in my ass, at least you could turn around so that we can go upstairs and get dressed."

She sighed dramatically but then turned around. I quickly ushered Lacey up the stairs and into my room. I shut the door and turned to her. She was scrambling to pull clothes out of her bag.

"Lacey, take a deep breath and stop panicking. This isn't how I'd want them to find out, but I don't care that they know. What we do privately is none of their business."

She pulled on a pair of panties and then stepped into some leggings. Then she looked down at her chest. "You were taking so long, so I just came down to surprise you. They saw me naked. And wearing ... this!"

I looked at her chest in the nipple jewelry and goddamn if I wasn't getting hard in the middle of this disaster. I had no control over it; she looked so beautiful. "You look like a fantasy come true. They only caught a glimpse. They're probably thinking that I'm lucky as fuck."

She tugged at the chains. "Help me get this off."

"As long as you wear it later. I didn't really get a good chance to admire it." I gently pulled at the adjustable cinch to loosen the nipple rings.

She shifted from foot to foot. "Oh, damn. That feels good."

My cock twitched. "Fuck," I muttered as I felt a throb of pure need pulse in my groin.

We got the necklace off and then we both finished getting dressed.

Lacey looked up at me. "Do I really have to go down there?"

"No," I answered. "I'll kick them both out if you want."

She sighed. "Let's get it over with."

HOW TO MARRY A ROCKSTAR

Kaylie and Sid were sitting at the kitchen island when we went back downstairs. I popped Lacey's coffee mug into the microwave oven to warm it up and then gave it to her. I figured she could use it.

"So?" Kaylie slapped her hand on the marble counter.

"So, what?" I asked.

She threw up her hands in disgust. "I can't believe this, Bash. Lacey is my best friend."

I choked back my anger. "You've got a lot of nerve throwing the best friend thing around. Look who you're married to."

Sid put his hand on Kaylie's arm, trying to calm her down, and Lacey just stood back, watching the scene unfold.

"I guess that's fair," Kaylie admitted. Her eyes were blazing. "But I don't really care about you. I care about her. She doesn't deserve to be used and thrown away by you. She's a really great person."

"Fuck! I know she's a great person. I'm—" I was going to say married to her, but I caught myself at the last second. "—dating her."

Sid looked startled by the revelation. Kaylie gasped.

But, Lacey, she tore my heart out. "We're hardly dating. We're just fucking." She said it so calmly, authoritatively.

It hurt. Worse than a punch to the gut. It felt like an invisible hand squeezed my heart so hard that I wasn't sure I'd be able to take another breath.

"We're dating," I repeated, but not with any confidence.

Lacey scowled. "We're friends-with-benefits, Bash. With an actual deadline when this is over."

Sid winced. He'd known me forever. He could probably see the devastation all over my face.

Kaylie scowled. "Friends-with-benefits? Why didn't you tell me, Lacey? We tell each other everything. You told me all about Theo."

Kaylie was talking to Lacey, and it gave me a chance to try to force air into my lungs. I rubbed at my chest with the heel of my palm as my stomach churned with bile. I had no idea how Lacey was answering Kaylie. I was in shock. There was only one time in my life when I'd felt this devastated, and that was when I thought I might lose custody of Kody. My soul felt broken and battered.

Sid stepped around the island and put a hand on my shoulder to get my attention. The girls were still talking. He kept his voice low. "I'm going to get her out of here, brother. Call me later if you need to talk."

I just nodded.

Sid finally got Kaylie to leave, insisting that the twins were going to wake up at any moment.

Lacey finished her coffee and then put the mug in the dishwasher. "I'm going to go, too. I think we could both use some time to think. I'll call you later."

In less than five minutes, she'd gathered up her stuff and was gone.

The whole, long day stretched out in front of me. I was alone with my despair and dark thoughts, and the coffee I'd had this morning was churning in my stomach like I'd chugged a vat of acid. A sharp pain clawed at my chest and I wondered if this was heartbreak.

Chapter 24

Lacey

After a night spent tossing and turning in bed, I woke up to intense period cramps. A quick trip to the bathroom confirmed that I'd gotten my period a few days early. Yay, just in time for New Year's Eve celebrations.

I had the perverse desire to call up Sebastian and say, 'Congratulations. You don't have to worry! None of your swimmers slipped past the latex.'

I had no idea where I stood with him. Sidney and Kaylie knew about us now — at least that we'd hooked up — and I assumed that meant that word would eventually spread among our friends. As long as Bash didn't mention anything about my kinky proclivities or that we were actually married, I guess I was okay with that. I didn't have much choice.

Yesterday had been a rollercoaster of emotions. Highs and lows that kept on coming one after the other. The highs had been incredible. I touched the pendant that was hanging from my neck. There were the thoughtful Christmas presents he'd bought me. The amazing shower sex. And the looks that he gave me sometimes, which were so tender and filled with not just lust, but adoration, that it made me stop and wonder.

But then, there were the lows. The offhand comments that hurt each other. The worst low was Bash's negative reaction to the big revelation that I wasn't on birth control. His response completely obliterated the abso-fucking-lutely insane idea that I'd had for him to father a child with me. Good Lord, I could only blame the PMS for that one.

Of course, I couldn't forget the total embarrassment of getting caught naked with Bash by Kaylie and Sid. There were already enough weird currents running between the four of us — adding nakedness to the mix couldn't be good. To top it all off, Bash blurted out that we were dating to try to explain it all away. It made me snap with irritation. His pretending to be more committed to me so he wouldn't look bad just highlighted how dumb I was to fall for him. My brain just couldn't take it anymore.

I blamed PMS. If anyone else blamed my emotions and reactions on my period, I would likely go berserk. But, yeah, in my own head, I could secretly blame it on PMS. What other excuse could I make?

Now I worried about what kind of damage control I'd have to employ with Kaylie. Not only was I boinking my best friend's brother behind her back, but she knew all about my baby craze. That was one of the reasons she let me butt into her life with the twins so much. I loved being around them. I was their unofficial auntie. If Kaylie happened to put my baby obsession together with her brother, things might get uncomfortable when she grilled me. She would grill me, that

I knew. I'd have to play our friends-with-benefits off as a giant lark — just fun-time Lacey getting her rocks off.

But it was far more than that. The baby scheme with Bash I could chalk off to temporary insanity. It was so cringe-worthy that it was better to take that idea to the grave. Regardless of my bad idea, I had feelings for Bash. They ran deeper than I'd originally suspected.

Now that I knew him, I wanted to be dating him. I'd been pissed by his remark to Kaylie and Sid about us dating, but maybe he really did believe that? When I thought about it, it wasn't too far off the mark. We took Kody out almost every weekend. We went to dinner occasionally and certainly spent a lot of our free time with each other. Maybe that's what he considered dating, but we'd never labeled it that. I'd been calling it friends-with-benefits. My assumption was that he was using our accidental marriage as an excuse to have fun until the divorce went through.

What if I was wrong?

If he didn't want any more kids, could I date him? Could I give up my dreams of having a family to be with Bash? I was certain I could love Kody like a mother, and maybe that would be enough. Why the hell did my mind wander down these ridiculous paths? I may be married to Bash, but we were certainly not on the same wavelength as far as marriage and lifelong commitments went.

The ring of my cell phone thankfully cut my run-away thoughts short. It was probably Kaylie calling, but I hoped it was Bash. We needed to talk. When I glanced at the screen, it turned out to be my mother. It was unusual for her to call, so I answered.

"Lacey, darling, how are you?" I could hear her exhaling a long puff of cigarette smoke as she spoke.

"Hello, Audrey. Where are you these days?" I didn't even bother trying to keep up with my mother's schedule. She never stayed in one place for too long.

"Barbados. I'm getting married, darling."

I sat down on my bed. "Who's the lucky victim?"

My mother laughed off the insult. "His name is Henri Delacroix. We've only known each other for four months, but what the hell? Why should we wait? We're getting married on New Year's Eve. Isn't that so romantic?"

"Congratulations," I muttered half-heartedly. I could just picture Henri now: at least ten years older than my mother with a full head of gray hair and a fat bank account. This would be husband #4 — each successive husband had gotten older, grayer, and richer than the last.

"Thank you, darling. I knew you'd be happy for me. I took care of all the arrangements. Your flight leaves tomorrow. Oh, and I have the perfect dress for you. As long as you didn't gain any weight since I last saw you?"

I massaged my temple; I felt a migraine coming on. "You can't expect me to come last minute? I have New Year's plans!"

She puffed on her cigarette. "You're my maid of honor, dear. Of course, you have to come."

"You're wedding is in two days. You couldn't tell me sooner? I've got a job, responsibilities, plans..."

"Surely your father will give you the time off from your job? Darling, you know I'd move heaven and earth to be with you if you were getting married and Henri would love to meet you."

I'm sure he would. My mother's lovers were always intrigued by the younger version of their trophy girlfriend. I was surprised Mother was letting me meet him before the ring was on her finger. Maybe that's why I'd just found out at the last minute.

I stood up and began pacing back and forth. "Are you sure you want to do this, Mother? Maybe you should get to know him better before jumping into another marriage."

She blew out a long breath. "Some of us don't have to dot every i and cross every t before we get married. With your meticulous nature, you'll never get married, darling. How old are you now? 29? And you're still single!"

I grimaced and bit my tongue. I ignored the fact that she got my age wrong because I knew how hard it was for her to admit that she had a daughter who was over 30. The barb about marriage would have stung more, except for the laughable fact that I actually was married. Knowing her, she would've approved of my quickie Vegas wedding. If she knew who I was married to, she'd probably be downright jealous. I knew she still enjoyed young lovers, even while she was married. I made a mental note to keep her away from Bash.

"Fine, I'll be there." It was easier to give in to her demands than to suffer the petty consequences.

"I'll have Ada send you the travel details."

"Who's Ada?" Did I even care?

"She's my personal assistant."

I snickered. My mother hadn't worked a day in her life. "What does she assist you doing?"

She ignored the jab. "Will you be coming alone? Or is there a man in your life?"

Even if Bash could jet off to Barbados at a moment's notice, I wouldn't bring him around my mother. Who knew if 'ole Henri could still get it up? Maybe my mother was looking for a new young stud to try out.

I thought about Bash and my stomach sank. I'd finally given in and agreed to go to a New Year's Eve party with him. The party was being held at Tyler Matthew's house. He was the lead singer of the band, Cold Fusion, and was currently a popular judge on a reality

TV show. The party would be filled with interesting people and I was weirdly excited to go now that our secret hook-up status had been outed among our close circle of friends. What would the reaction be?

Now, I'd have to tell Bash I couldn't go. He'd be upset. My hand reached up and stroked the blue stone of the pendant Bash had bought for me. I cherished the gift already. I didn't ever want to take it off.

"Darling?" my mother prompted.

"I'll be alone. Send me the arrangements. I need to rearrange my schedule to make this work. So, I've got to go, Mother. I'll see you tomorrow."

"Ciao, darl—"

I hung up the phone before she could even finish.

♪♫♩♪♪

The building was fairly empty. A lot of people took the week between Christmas and New Year's off, but I knew I'd find my father in his office as usual. He'd always worked harder than anyone I knew.

I waved to Gretchen and went straight into his opulent office. Dad was sitting behind his desk, but rose and came over to greet me with a hug when he saw me.

"Lacey, I didn't think you'd be in today."

Dad was still very handsome with his salt and pepper hair, his penetrating blue eyes that missed nothing, and his trim physique. My father was Audrey's second husband. After she had me, which she'd confessed was an 'oopsie', she made a valiant effort and stuck around until I was six years old. Dad never remarried. He had focused on raising me, though I knew he dated women on occasion. It was probably tough for him with all his money. There were lots of women, just like my mother, who targeted men like him. Audrey had probably made him cynical for life about women and turned him off of marriage.

Dad gestured me toward the couch and sat next to me. "What brings you here to see your old man?"

I twisted a lock of hair around my finger. "Audrey is getting married. She called this morning to request my presence in Barbados for the happy nuptials which are on New Year's Eve. Isn't that nifty? I'm leaving tomorrow morning."

Dad chuckled. "I don't know who I feel worse for, you or the poor chap she's marrying."

"Me, of course!" I fake pouted. "I'm going to miss a fabulous New Year's Eve party at Tyler Matthew's house."

"Who is she marrying?" Dad looked mildly curious, but not upset in any way. "Do I know him?"

I used my snootiest voice to exaggerate the pronunciation of his name. "On-Ree." I rolled my eyes. "Henri Delacroix. I think I'll call him Hank ... or better yet, Hankie. That should piss him off."

Dad patted my hand. "That should do it." He chuckled. "I've never had to worry about you, Lacey. You're such a strong woman. I hope I can take some of the credit for that."

"Thanks, Dad." I smiled.

Dad had always believed in me. He made me start at the very bottom of his company and work my way up, but it had been the best gift he could have ever given me.

Now that I'd worked my way up the ladder, I was above all the hands-on work with the music talent, above the scouting and the wooing, above the star-making. I missed it. Would my dad's position fulfill me? There was no other place left to go. Luckily, I didn't think he'd be retiring any time soon because I didn't think it would be enough.

If being at the very top wasn't enough, what the hell did I want? I wanted a family, but I also needed to work. The charity with Kaylie was fulfilling. Maybe I should expand to other charities? Would that be enough? Would anything ever be enough for me, or was I just like my mother? She was always going through men looking for someone more handsome with more money and power. She was never satisfied.

I knew I shunned commitment in my early adult life because of my mother, but now I craved it. Was it to prove my mother wrong? Was I running to the idea of having a baby to prove that I was better than her? That I was worth more than being abandoned by her? And how did my complicated feelings for Bash fit into all of that? I needed a damn therapist to sort it all out.

Chapter 25

Bash

It was a new year, and Ghost Parker was in a bit of a pause right now. No tours were scheduled. There was no deadline for our next album. We had nothing to promote, so there were no interviews or late-night show gigs to perform. A few one-off shows were booked, and we'd be appearing in about ten shows this summer with a big touring music festival. Beyond that, the calendar was blissfully empty.

Even Donovan hadn't been breathing down our backs. He was busy with another project that was sucking up all his energy. He'd signed a new band that he was sure was the next best thing. We didn't care because that meant he wasn't pestering us daily or trying to book us gigs we didn't need.

We owed BVR one more album on our current contract. They wanted to keep us, so for once in our careers, we were in the driver's seat. They were giving us some space and, as a band with all our young families; it was needed. They knew if they kept pushing, we wouldn't sign with them, so the parameters of our next album and tour were largely up to us. And, if BVR kept us happy, why wouldn't we stay with them?

It was hard to know what would happen. Ghost was itching to break free and create a different type of music. Knox wanted to stay with BVR and milk Ghost Parker for everything it could give us. Ryder didn't comment too much about it, so it was hard to tell what he was thinking. Sid and I would most likely go with the flow.

If Ghost went solo, we could continue without him. Ryder could front the band. Knox could too. I had no idea what our new music would sound like without Ghost's creative input, but we'd always have a huge fan base, even if we just relied on old material.

For now, messing around and playing music with my friends under no pressure from the outside was pretty close to ideal. Sure, the spotlight drifted off us a bit, but that was okay. Our crew was all touring with other bands right now, but they'd come back to us when we were ready, as long as we were still a hot item.

Besides drumming in my free time, I was fooling around with music production behind the scenes. Ever since we'd produced *Okay Babe* with Vance Beaufort, I'd been interested in the production aspect. I had a great ear for music and working with Beaufort, a freaking legend, had confirmed that for me. Over the years, I'd bought some of my own equipment to play with and I was mulling over the idea of building a recording studio in my pool house.

Right now, Ghost Parker was practicing in our rehearsal space. We were mainly playing around with a new song Ghost was working on. I could tell that it'd never be material that our band would use, but we had the time and freedom to experiment, so I didn't mind.

I changed up the beat a bit and Sid automatically followed me on bass. We were always in sync. Ryder added a flourish on guitar and then Knox followed up with his own wicked skills, trying to outdo Ryder.

Ghost stood up abruptly, looking at his phone. He signaled for us to stop. "I've got to take this. Gimme five."

He left the room and then Ryder and Knox put down their guitars and grabbed a drink from the refrigerator. They were joking about something across the room.

I put down my sticks and wiped the sweat from my brow with my sleeve.

Sid put down his bass and then stepped around an amp to stand next to me. "Lacey back yet?"

Lacey had gone to her mother's wedding in Barbados. She'd missed the New Year's Eve party that should have been amazing but felt kind of empty without her there. Sid had decided to spend his night quietly at home with his family. It was the first time I'd spent a New Year's without him. I'd had tons of friends there, including my other bandmates, so it wasn't like I didn't have a good time. But I'd been missing her.

"She's back, but I haven't seen her."

I saw the pity in his eyes. "Are things okay with you two?"

I huffed out a breath. "Things are a little awkward after you and Kay barged in on us and saw her naked."

Sid didn't even have the decency to look even a little bit sorry. "What the hell is going on between you two? For real — not some bullshit. You said you were dating her."

I groaned. I'd told him to drop it the last time he'd asked, but I knew he wouldn't leave it alone forever. "I thought I was dating her, but apparently we were just hooking up on the regular."

Sid crushed his lips together. "Friends-with-benefits, she called it.

And you want more?"

I gave him a look to let him know he was treading on thin ice. "I don't know what I want. She's been hot and cold with me. Fucking impossible to figure out."

"That's women." He nodded his head sagely like he was an expert. "Do you want me to get Kaylie to find out what's going on?"

"What? No! This isn't middle school." I grabbed a hand towel from the top of the stool next to me and wiped my face. "I'm going to see her tonight. She's got plans for us — detailed plans — for after Kody falls asleep. I don't know, brother. Things are complicated."

Sid crossed his arms and scowled. "So, she's just using you for sex? Is she seeing anyone else?"

I looked over to make sure Knox and Ryder weren't listening. "No. At least, I don't think so."

She did go to Barbados for a week. And I hardly ever got to see her. But we'd agreed to be exclusive. She was just busy with work and I had Kody.

Seeing her for half the weekend just wasn't enough anymore. I wanted to see her every day. Jesus. She was in my every thought. Hell, she was in my every breath.

Sid was like a brother to me. He'd always had my back. I pushed out the words that felt bottled up inside me. "Something that always bothered me. You had sex with her after our threesome."

"I thought you were okay with that?" A hint of guilt flashed in his eyes.

"I was." Uncomfortable, I ran a hand through my hair. "I am, but it bothered me a little bit. Maybe I was good back then, but now I don't fucking know. I'm not mad. It's just, I think about it sometimes. And then you walked in and saw her naked at my house and it made me remember that you've had sex with her, too."

"Fuck." Sid looked miserable. "I don't feel anything for Lacey. I love Kaylie. I'm just not interested in other women. There's really no room. It's only Kay."

Fuck, I shouldn't have said anything. "I know. It's weird. I'm sorry I brought it up."

"No, let me tell you, bro. So that you understand. That night, when we were all together, it felt good. It was probably the best time we'd had with another woman." He scrubbed a hand down his face. "I feel guilty even talking about it now, but it was way before I even thought there ever was a possibility to be with Kaylie."

I really didn't want to hear this. I was going to stop him, but he waved me off.

"Then that night we saw her at that club. I wanted to see if I could feel that again. To capture that magic. I was feeling down about myself, I guess. The sex was good. I mean, it felt good. It was great, but there was no connection. It felt meaningless. Kind of hollow. I don't think she felt any spark, either. Dude, if you've ever felt the difference, you'd know. Sex with Kaylie is way different. There's this—"

I punched his arm to shut him up. "Ugh. I don't want to hear about you and Kaylie."

"Sorry." He grinned unrepentantly at me. "I was actually shocked that there was no romantic connection between us, but I was happy that we remained friends after. I've gotten to know her even better since then and she's a really great girl."

Lacey was amazing; he didn't have to tell me that.

He raised his brows. "I do want to hear about what the hell she was wearing — that jewelry. She was smoking hot. I'd like to see my wife with that get up on. Especially while she's still breastfeeding."

"Fuck, Sid! You are killing me. That's my sister you're talking about. And my girl—" I was going to say girlfriend, but I stopped myself.

"And Lacey. I thought you weren't interested in other women like that?"

He smirked. "I'm not interested in her, but I have eyes in my head, dude."

I shook my head. "How is everything after, you know, marriage and babies? It must change."

"Well, I'm not spending Saturday mornings fucking her brains out." He gave me a sly glance. "Because of the boys, but you know how kids are. They expand your love. It's amazing. I'm the luckiest man in the whole goddamn world and sometimes I wonder, why me? How did I get so lucky?"

Good thing our conversation was put to an end when Knox and Ryder strolled over. It was getting too sappy.

"What are we gossiping about, girls?" Ryder asked.

Sid chuckled. "Bash's love life."

Knox raised a brow. "Oh, do tell, mate. Anything interesting?"

That night, when Lacey came over, I fucked the hell out of her. I used every secret bit of knowledge about her body and everything in my sex arsenal to make sure she was more than satisfied. If I held on to her a little too tightly or clung to her like a needy freak, she didn't mention it.

In fact, at her suggestion, we'd even tried cock warming again. It failed in spectacular fashion but ended in orgasms all-around and a few laughs, so not a bad way to end the night.

Then we spent the next day with Kody and she seemed happy to be spending time with us. Kody was delighted with the big-boy bike she gave him for his birthday and she listened to him tell her all about his birthday party at the trampoline park.

She didn't offer to tell me much about her mother's wedding and I didn't push. She stayed until Sunday morning when she left bright and early before Kody woke up. I asked her to stay for the day, but she declined, saying that she didn't want to confuse Kody.

Kody was probably far less confused than I was. She'd come back from Barbados and we'd resumed our friends-with-kink-benefits like nothing had changed between us. Maybe I was the only one who was changing?

We did our scenes, and she got her kinks satisfied. I just loved spending time with her now. I was supremely happy when I was with her, but I was not happy with our relationship status. Was I just being used like a kinky sex toy? She never mentioned the weekend getaway Christmas gift that I'd been so excited about, but she was wearing the necklace I'd bought her and I clung to that.

We were still seeing each other, even if she didn't call it dating, and I was determined more than ever to show her that we could be more than great sex.

Chapter 26

Lacey

"I'm not sure most friends, even those without benefits, would agree to this, Lacey."

We were stopped at a red light in a busy intersection just outside of Hollywood; Bash was behind the wheel.

I shot him a worried look. "What do you mean?"

"Your cousin's husband's 30th birthday party? Dragging me to a pub crawl with a bunch of people I don't know. What about your cousin? Did you tell her you were bringing me? Does she know we're just friends with kinky benefits?"

He was just teasing me. He'd actually been pretty excited when I asked him to go, although he tried to play it off. Sometime in the past three weeks, Sebastian and I agreed that we were quasi-dating. It was pretty useless for me to cling to the friends-with-benefits label, especially when I wanted more.

"She knows you're coming." I watched the traffic as we started moving again.

"This feels awfully like a date, wifey. Are you sure you're okay with that? What if your cousin thinks I'm your boyfriend?" He gasped in fake horror.

"I told her we were banging each other every weekend like clockwork." I slid a glance over at this profile. "She's happy for me. What did she say? Hmm. She said you had a really nice body, and you were well-endowed. That's a direct quote."

Bash scrunched his eyebrows adorably. "Well, duh. But, how does she ... Is she a big fan of Ghost Parker or something? Those fan websites can be freaky with the stuff they post."

I suppressed a laugh. Bash was in for a big surprise when he saw my cousin. Years ago, she'd had such a crush on him that she begged me to take her to every party I knew Ghost Parker was attending. Until that one time, when she spent the night with Bash and then woke up the next morning to find an infant in front of his door. That infant was Kody, and that was the end of the budding romance between them, even if the romance was only ever budding in my cousin's mind.

Sadie was now married to her goth prince — a khaki shorts-wearing computer nerd. She was a different woman. She even wore colors besides black every once in a while now. I wasn't sure if Bash would even recognize her.

I looked at the temperature display on the navigation screen between us and groaned. "It's 54 now. It dropped another degree. I'm going to freeze. I say we ditch the party when we get to the first pub. We'll just stay behind, and they'll never notice. I don't want to be walking around outside all night."

I'd forgone any sense of fashion to wear my heaviest pair of jeans, a black base layer shirt that was made for skiing — because Sadie told me we would be getting matching T-shirts to wear so I couldn't wear anything bulky, and my Chunky B platform sneakers. I'd brought along my puffer jacket, a beanie, and a pair of gloves as well, just in case. Inside the bars, I'd probably overheat, but I hated being cold.

Bash turned onto the famous Sunset Boulevard. We were getting close to where we'd meet up. "I think you'll survive 54 degrees. It's actually pretty nice out for the end of January. We can always sneak a cab instead of walking between bars."

After we parked in the parking garage Sadie suggested we use, we set out to meet up with the group. We saw them from afar as we approached. They looked like a group just escaped from a Star Trek convention; maybe it was the matching mustard-yellow T-shirts that they all wore. It wasn't until we got closer that I could read the glow-in-the-dark neon green lettering printed on the back: The Nerd Herd.

Bash suddenly looked nervous. He was giving me the side eye, but I kept a poker face.

Sadie squealed when she saw us approaching the group. She broke off and ran towards us in her ugly mustard, nerdy T-shirt. "Lacey! You made it. And Bash! Long time no see, huh?"

It took a few seconds for Bash's brain to catch up to what he was seeing. "Sadie? What are you doing here?"

Watching the emotions flit rapid-fire across Bash's face was fun: confusion, dawning recognition, denial, anxiety, suspicion, and finally an uneasy acceptance of the situation.

"Well, it is my husband's birthday party, and I did all the planning, so I invited myself," she deadpanned.

He looked back and forth between us. "This is your cousin? Sadie? Wait, you two are cousins?"

We looked nothing alike. I was the champagne blonde, blue-eyed, sun-kissed California girl, and she was the dark-haired, heavy makeup with pale skin goth girl. She still wore black lipstick and heavy makeup, but she'd toned down the rest of the look ever since she got married.

"She didn't tell you?" Sadie snickered and then locked her arm with Bash's, leading him toward the group. "Marius, that's my husband — can't wait to meet you. I told him all about you. Well, not everything." She gave me an exaggerated wink. "Marius is a lot like Sheldon from The Big Bang Theory, but even hotter."

Bash was clearly uncomfortable, but I thought I'd let him stew for a bit before rescuing him.

Marius broke away from his friends and gave me a hug and a kiss on the cheek when he saw me. "Lacey, I'm so glad you could make it."

Sadie pulled Bash up in front of us. "Marius, this is Lacey's special friend, Bash."

Marius clapped his back heartily. "Hey, Bash. Thanks for coming. Come meet The Nerd Herd."

Marius had nerd tendencies, but he was very gregarious and a genuinely kind person. He brought out the absolute best in my cousin. His friends ran the gamut from low-level nerds, like Ross Geller on Friends, to complete nerds like Napolean Dynamite.

We were introduced to all of Marius's friends, mostly people from his job, but some high school friends, his old college roommate, and his brother who was a beanpole version of Marius with glasses. They all had weird nicknames like Chewie, Bug, and Decaf. Even the girls had nicknames like Coco, Peach, and Leeloo, and I noticed that Sadie was called Raven by the group.

Sadie handed us our Nerd Herd T-shirts and soon Bash and I matched the group. As twilight fell, a monstrosity of a vehicle pulled up to the curb in front of us; it looked like a bar on wheels and it was captained by a woman wearing a purple wig and an eye patch.

A boisterous cheer went up from the nerds who'd all been stealthily doing shots on the sidewalk.

Bash had been doing a shot with Bug, but he came over to eye the crazy contraption with me. "What the fuck is that thing?"

It kind of looked like an open-air trolley car. A long bar top ran down the length of the vehicle on each side. Where the bar stools would be were six bike seats on each side hooked up to actual pedals at each station. A wide bench seat made up the back. The roof was blazing with flashing LED party lights and the speakers were cranking out *Let's Get It Started* by the Black Eyed Peas.

While we waited for the last three people in our group to show up, Chewie made sure everyone had a red solo cup filled with the 'special' Hawaiian Punch, and someone loaded up the party bike with coolers and snacks.

We clambered aboard when the last three people arrived. I sat on the far side of the party bike between Bash and a guy they called Qwerty. It took some effort to build up enough inertia to get the pedal-powered contraption moving at a steady clip. I was barely putting any effort into pedaling, and I wondered just how many other cheaters we had on board.

There were individual cup holders at each seat, so everyone had plenty of booze available at all times. The herd was waving to people walking on the sidewalks as we barely passed them, doing about 5 mph and blasting out *Uptown Funk* from the speakers. It was a little embarrassing at first until I realized that most of the people we passed were waving back and generally reacting positively to the nerds. Bash and I were definitely the quietest ones in the group. I think we were both just trying to acclimate to the situation.

I finished my first drink and Qwerty scrambled to fill me up. He'd been talking my ear off. Bash was talking with the girl next to him,

Coco, I think, but I could tell he was keeping tabs on me, too.

We stayed at the first bar for about half an hour before the nerds wanted to get back to the bike. We had plenty of alcohol on board, so they figured why spend too much money at the bars? I thought they just liked riding around the city on the bike, getting attention wherever we went.

The group was getting drunker by the minute. I could tell when everyone screamed out the words to *I've got Friends in Low Places*.

At this point, there was a lively conversation about kinetic energy calculations, calorie burning, and E=mc2. Bash was looking like he'd just landed on another planet.

I stopped pedaling and leaned toward him. "I know a secret about you. In fact, I know something about you that you don't even know."

"Oh really? And what is that?" He looked me up and down and then smiled lazily at me.

For a moment, I wondered if I looked absurd. I was wearing my knit beanie, fur-lined gloves, and the ugly yellow T-shirt, but I was buzzed enough to not really care.

"I'm not sure I've had enough truth serum yet to tell you," I teased.

His hand rested low on my back. "I have other ways of making you talk, and I think you should slow it down, Lacey. Whatever is in those drinks is strong."

I didn't have time to reply because the party bike was pulling up to the second bar. By the time I made it out of the restroom, Bash was holding a glass of water for me. The small neighborhood bar was packed with people. We wedged ourselves into a corner and watched the activity.

I was tipsy and wanted some attention. I cozied up to Bash, wrapping my arms around his neck. "Kiss me and I'll tell you the secret."

He locked lips with me and I was in heaven. I didn't care that we were in the middle of a crush of bodies. I would happily ditch the bicycle bar and head home with Bash to finish our night with a bang, but I hardly ever saw Sadie anymore.

It took me a few seconds to regroup after his kiss left me dazed. "Mmm. That was nice. I owe you the secret. So, one night Sadie and I got drunk, and she confessed something to me."

Bash blinked a few times. "I don't want to hear any of Sadie's secrets."

"Well, this one has to do with you." I poked his chest with my finger. "She told me that even though she told you otherwise, you never had sex with her."

He cringed. "What?"

I pulled him down so I could speak right into his ear. "It was the night before Kody showed up at your door? She had a big crush on you back then. That night, she followed you into your room, but you were very drunk. You stripped down and passed out right away. You didn't even know she was there. She was drunk, too. She just climbed into bed with you and then let you think you had sex with her in the morning."

He looked stunned and maybe a little irritated about being lied to. "So, I never slept with Satan ... uh, I mean, Sadie?"

I shook my head. "No, and by the time the baby shower happened, she was over her crush. Isn't that funny? I've known for years that you didn't sleep with my cousin."

"That's kind of disturbing. Why would she say that? I don't get it." He rubbed the back of his neck.

"She thought she might have a better shot with you if you already thought you slept together. That it might lead to more, but then Kody showed up, and she lost interest." I shrugged like that was a good enough explanation.

"That doesn't even make sense. It's just weird."

"Well, she's weird." I laughed. "We're riding around Hollywood on a 16-person bicycle with a herd of nerds, thanks to her."

We couldn't discuss it any further because the group was heading out back to the party bike. This time, *Ice Ice Baby* was booming from the speakers as we pulled away from the curb.

Qwerty was pretty drunk. He was talking too loudly, almost yelling, as he flirted with me. "So, yeah, I built my own custom software to track my cryptocurrency portfolio. Did I mention how big my portfolio is? Larger than the average guys."

I hoped Bash wasn't listening to this. "That's very interesting."

"You know," he leaned his elbow on the bar and smiled at me, "my IQ is 148. With my brains and your beauty, we could make a superior baby."

Oh Jeez. I took a big gulp of the spiked juice. "You know, Qwerty, I'm actually smarter than I am beautiful. I got my MBA at The Booth School of Business at the University of Chicago. I graduated summa cum laude."

His eyes lit up. "Did you know a woman's pleasure buttons are mostly in her brain? I could stimulate your brain cells and you wouldn't even need all that ... brawn over there."

I'd never been hit on by a nerd in such a manner, so I didn't have a comeback ready on the tip of my tongue.

It didn't matter because *Sweet Caroline* began playing and the entire group started swaying and fist pumping to the song. Qwerty had completely forgotten me.

For the rest of the night, I avoided Qwerty and made more of an effort to spend time with Bash, Sadie, and Marius. After two more bars, most of the group was plastered. Bash was driving us back to my place, so he hadn't had much to drink all night.

We pulled up next to my Mercedes in the parking garage of my building.

Bash tucked a stray piece of my hair, which was crazy from wearing a hat all night, behind my ear. "How are you doing, nerdy girl?"

I giggled. "That was so insane but fun. Those nerds were quite the partiers."

"They really were. How drunk are you right now?" he asked.

Earlier in the night, I'd been feeling tipsy, but then I began moderating my drinking. "I'm not too bad; I'm glad you slowed me down and made me drink water. I'm definitely up for some action."

He raised an eyebrow. "Hmm. You want me to stimulate your pleasure buttons?"

I scrunched my nose. "What?"

He pinned me with an intense stare. One heated look from him and my panties melted. "The ones in your brain. I guess you don't want me to touch the other ones anymore. With my brawn and all."

The odd conversation with Qwerty came back to me. I guess Bash had been listening after all. Reaching over, I squeezed his biceps. "I love all your brawn," I purred. "And button-pushing."

"You don't think I'm too dumb for you?"

His words broke through my lust-induced daze, and I realized by the somber expression on his face that he was serious.

"What? Of course not!" I scrambled to reassure him, but I couldn't help but think his question somehow went deeper.

Chapter 27

Bash

"LET'S JUST MOVE THOSE giant purses and sit down. Saving seats should be against the rules," Josie complained.

Every seat that appeared to be empty had purses or coats or even phones sitting on them.

"Don't touch anyone's stuff," I hissed. "How early did these people get here?" We were right on time but appeared to be the last to enter the small gymnasium.

I walked down the center aisle between the rows of folding chairs, scanning for empty seats.

"Let's just stand in the back," Josie grumbled. "I won't be able to see anything from back here if we're sitting down, anyway."

We were attending Kody's preschool performance. The three, four, and five-year-olds were performing some skits and singing some songs. Kody was pig #2 in The Three Little Pigs and he'd been practicing his line for the past few weeks: 'No, not by the hair on my chinny chin chin.' Based on his practice sessions, I gave him about a 50% chance he'd get it right.

We moved to the back of the room and leaned against the back wall to wait. It didn't look like the performance was going to begin anytime soon. Parents were milling about, and there was no sign of the kids.

Josie dug through her purse and pulled out a mint. "Alice said you were a big prude."

"Okay." I didn't care. "And Alice, is who exactly?" Oh damn, I took the bait.

Josie smiled victoriously. "Angelique's grandmother. She thought you might be gay."

"Angelique?" I laughed with disbelief. "The woman with a van-load of kids who fucked some greasy-haired stoner for a bucket of arcade tokens? That one?"

"Don't get all huffy on me. I set her straight." She patted my arm. "I told her you weren't a prude. That you were wetting the willy quite regularly. You were just selective. Then, she accused me of calling her granddaughter a skank. We're not talking at the moment."

I shook my head but didn't say anything. It was better not to fan the flames.

"You haven't been going out much? You never ask me to babysit anymore," she prodded.

I folded my arms across my chest. "I've got my parents and Kaylie to help. And you're always busy with Kay's kids."

"The twins are adorable. They're crawling all over the place now. Double trouble, those two."

"I can imagine." One of Kody was more than enough at a time.

Josie turned her all-seeing eyes on me. "You've been seeing someone."

"No," I denied calmly.

"Yes, you have. You've released some of that tension."

Oh, God. Please tell me that's not what she meant. "What gave you that idea? Or should I say, who? Was it Kaylie?"

Josie scoffed. "Kaylie is up to her neck in diapers and breastfeeding. She wouldn't know if you were knocking boots with her best friend right under her nose."

Did Josie know something? My face remained neutral even as I wondered if Kody had mentioned Lacey and any of our outings to Josie.

"Speaking of Kaylie's best friend," she glanced over at me before resuming her scan of the crowd of parents beginning to collect their seats, "Lacey is so good with the twins. And with Kaylie. She visits Kay, brings her coffee, takes her out — they work on that charity thingee at the coffee shop, and they go out for girl time. It gets Kaylie out of the apartment so she can recharge."

I knew they were best friends, but I didn't realize they still saw each other so much. They didn't live too far away from each other, so I guess it was easy for her to visit Kaylie during the week. I'd asked Lacey to attend Kody's performance today, but she said she had an important meeting at work. I tried not to be jealous that I only got to see her on weekends when Kaylie apparently saw her all the time, but it wasn't working.

Josie continued, "She really is a good friend. I had my doubts about that one early on. I thought she was either dumb as a box of rocks or a first-class bitch. It's usually one or the other with girls that look like that."

I shifted back and forth on my feet, wanting the one-sided conversation to end.

"She looks like a modern Marilyn Monroe. Did you know that

Marilyn Monroe was about a size 4? She had that curvy figure, but she wasn't plus-sized. She was a size 12, I think, but in today's sizes, she'd be a size 4. Lots of people think she was much bigger."

"Uh-huh."

"Anyhow, I haven't seen her around much lately."

My brow creased. "Isn't she dead?"

"I'm talking about Lacey. Keep up, drummer boy." She checked her watch, impatient for the show to start. "She won't be able to stay away from those boys for too long, so I'm sure I'll run into her soon."

"Yeah, probably," I agreed.

"Kody seems to like her."

So he had been talking about her. "Yeah, they get along."

"You know, Lacey really wants kids of her own."

"She does?" I'm not sure why that was so surprising, considering how great she was with Kody. She never complained about him coming out with us. She never demanded my time over Kody.

"Of course. She goes gaga over babies. Haven't you ever noticed? She'll be an amazing mother."

A teacher came to the microphone and began speaking. Thank God, because that was a weird conversation. Josie always had a hidden motive, and this time she was singing Lacey's praises for some reason. I scratched at my jaw. I'd never thought of Lacey as a mother before, but I decided that Josie was right. She'd be amazing at it.

♫♪♩♪♩

It was the weekend after Kody's preschool presentation. Lacey hadn't arrived until late last night, so we hadn't done much talking. She had led me straight to the bedroom, which was fine by me. I loved how we couldn't seem to get enough of each other.

After I finished getting Kody dressed and fed, Lacey appeared out of nowhere, showered and ready for the day, as if she'd just arrived. She'd been adamant about keeping her overnight visits a secret from Kody. I was no longer sure it would be such a bad thing for him to know, especially since we were dating and exclusive, but maybe I was just being selfish. I guess it depended on how long I thought our relationship might last. It was something I didn't like to dwell on because I had my doubts. Just how serious was Lacey about us? I didn't know.

Kody spotted her, ran into her arms, and gave her a hug. He began telling her all about his week, including his theatric debut as Pig #2.

Lacey had always been good with Kody, even when he first was born. She helped Kaylie organize his baby shower, and she never shied away from him when he was a baby. Of course, I knew how well they got along together now, but after Josie had made those comments, I was watching her in a different light. Did she really want kids of her own? Her career meant everything to her; I'd never seen her as the maternal type before.

"What are we gonna do today, Yacey?" Kody asked.

It was a beautiful February day, sunny and warm, but not hot. It was the perfect day to get outside and enjoy the sunshine.

"I don't know, Kody. I haven't talked to your dad about where we should go yet." She gave me a conspiratorial wink. "But I'd love to get some ice cream later. After lunch, of course."

"Ice cream, yay!" He jumped up and down. "Can I show you how I'm riding my bike? I've been practicing."

She stood up from her crouched position. "Sure! I'd love to see that."

I gave Kody a high-five. "Go grab your helmet, little man, and we'll meet you in the garage."

Her palm smacked her forehead. "I forgot the helmet! Oh my God, I should have bought him one."

I pulled her in for a hug because she looked genuinely upset. "No worries. We went out, and he picked one out the next day. It's a mohawk helmet. Wait until you see it. He looks like a total badass four-year-old."

She leaned in for a kiss. "Good thing I didn't pick it out then. I would have picked something totally uncool."

We spent most of the morning in front of the house with Kody showing off his bike riding with training wheel skills to impress Lacey. They chatted together the whole time. Lacey even told Kody about the 16-person bicycle we rode and when he didn't quite believe it, she pulled out a photo we took in front of the contraption.

After Kody's interest in bike riding started to wane, we decided to go to the Santa Monica Pier for lunch. After eating, we walked around, watched some street performers, played some arcade games, and then finally got some ice cream.

The three of us were walking down the pier, licking our ice cream cones, and stopping every once in a while because, evidently, Kody had a hard time walking and eating at the same time. It had been the perfect day from when I woke up with her in my arms, to playing with Kody, to hanging out on the pier and eating ice cream. And, in a few hours, I'd have Lacey all to myself when Kody went to bed.

When the metaphorical black cloud showed up, it was noticeable. I saw the guy long before Lacey did; I think it was a parent thing. You always had one eye on your kid, one eye on the people surrounding you, and one eye out for any potential obstacles or dangers for a 4-year-old. It was crazy that parents needed at least three eyes when out in public.

We had stopped about 15 feet away from this guy and I felt him staring. My sense of heightened alertness mellowed a bit when I realized he was gazing appreciatively at Lacey. I was a man, and I recognized the look. It bothered me slightly, but she was a very attractive woman and it wasn't the first time I'd caught guys checking her out.

Then, he started to approach us. At first, I thought he must be soliciting something. He didn't look like a panhandler, but maybe he was handing out brochures for some cause.

I grabbed Kody's hand to keep him near me, but then I discovered that he actually knew Lacey. He greeted her with a big smile. "Fancy meeting you here."

He looked like he'd just rolled in off the beach. He was taller than me by a couple of inches, had hair to his shoulders — which was all wet and straggly, had at least two days' worth of scruff on his face, and obviously spent a lot of time at the gym. His shirt was completely unbuttoned, showing off his deep tan and stupid muscles. He had a bunch of leather bracelets wrapped around his wrists and a bandana around his neck. I instantly hated him.

Lacey was completely thrown by his appearance. "Hi," was all she replied.

He turned to me and I could feel him assessing me, judging how much competition I was. He stuck out his hand. "Liam Wright."

I reluctantly shook it. "Bash." I purposefully didn't give him my last name. "And how do you know Lacey?"

Lacey jumped into the conversation before he could answer. "We're old acquaintances. It was nice to see you, Liam."

"Lacey,"—he looked at her pointedly—"can I talk to you for a minute?"

Her eyes darted around the pier. She clearly felt trapped. "We were just leaving."

I stepped closer to her, but the asshole shuffled forward and practically blocked me. If Kody wasn't with us, I'd probably have bumped him on purpose.

"Just give me a few minutes, Baby Girl."

She winced, and her eyes darted to mine. I wondered if she could see the jealous rage that just exploded inside my body like a pile of dynamite tossed onto a campfire.

She debated which would be faster — to keep arguing with him or to give in. Giving in won.

She rested her hand on my chest soothingly. "I'm going to go talk to Liam for a minute. I'll be right back."

They headed down the pier together about ten feet away. Halfway there, she turned back to glance at me, looking guilty as fuck, and I wondered who the fuck this guy was.

Lacey's back was turned to me, so I couldn't hear what she was saying or see her face. Kody was happily licking his cone in an ice cream trance, so I turned my attention to the pair of them.

His hand was on her elbow in a proprietary grip. He seemed very possessive of her. He just gave off that vibe. I was not happy. If Kody wasn't with me, I'd step in and interrupt them.

Baby Girl.

Did he call her baby girl?

Fuck.

He was someone she had a past with. Who obviously knew her well. And who still had feelings for her. Maybe it wasn't all in the past?

They'd fucked, I was sure of it.

She came back alone a few minutes later. She was out of sorts. Her face was flushed. She looked uncomfortable. And guilty. Like she'd been caught.

"Sorry about that." She leaned down to Kody. "Wow, you almost finished that whole cone already."

She was just going to pretend nothing had just happened?

"Who is he?"

"He's just an old friend." She wouldn't meet my eyes. "Someone I used to know."

Chapter 28

Lacey

WHAT WERE THE ODDS of running into Liam Wright aka my Daddy Dom on the Santa Monica Pier? I would think they were infinitesimally low. Yet, it happened.

I once ran into someone I knew in New Orleans. Not in a bar and not during Mardis Gras, but in a rinky-dink souvenir shop way off Bourbon Street on a random day in May. One time, when I was on a train in Switzerland, I bumped into a high school classmate. The old saying 'It's a small world' always amazed me when it proved true.

So, less than 20 miles from where I'd met Liam, at a popular area attraction on a beautiful February day, it was probably not so crazy to bump into him. But fate was not always on the serendipitous side. If there were two worlds I did not want to collide, it was Daddy Dom's and Bash's.

Until that moment on the pier, Liam and I didn't even know each other's real names. Everything about him was in the past for me. I didn't even think about him anymore.

I saw the look on Bash's face and I knew he had questions about Liam, but he meant nothing to me. That's how I rationalized not telling Bash who he was. How the hell could I explain it?

How would Bash understand the things I did with Liam? The kinky stuff? If Bash had done those things with some other woman, I'd have issues. Severe jealousy issues. Insecurities. Maybe even resentment. And I didn't want him to feel any of that because I knew Liam didn't matter to me.

What Liam gave me was purely physical. He helped me delve into parts of my sexuality that I'd only dabbled with before, but he always held back pieces of himself. What he shared with me, he also shared freely with others. Liam and I lacked any true intimacy, and that was something that I not only craved but absolutely required.

I'd found that intimacy with Bash. Our relationship was no longer just about physical closeness. He not only fulfilled my sexual needs, but he far exceeded them. Even more important was our emotional connection, a connection that Liam could never achieve. There was a big difference between the two. I knew it inherently when I broke things off with Liam and I fully understood it when my relationship with Bash grew deeper and deeper. There really was no comparison.

Liam wanted to see me again; he claimed to have missed me, but I'd shut him down hard. I had no interest and told him that. When he mentioned that I could contact him on the Scarlett app, I deleted it on the car ride back to Bash's house from the pier.

There was no need for Bash to be suspicious. Running into an ex wasn't a crime. It probably wouldn't even have blipped his radar if Liam hadn't called me baby girl. My stomach twisted, remembering the look on Bash's face. If hearing that had upset him so much, I couldn't imagine how he'd feel learning about all the rest.

I pulled into Bash's neighborhood. It was Friday night, the start of our weekend together. Earlier in the week, Bash called and said he got a babysitter for Wednesday night. He wanted to come downtown to my place and take me out to a nice dinner. It was the first time he'd even suggested we get together during the week.

I would love to have gone, but it turned out I was already busy that night with a work commitment that I couldn't back out of gracefully. I was disappointed, but I think Bash was even more so.

This weekend, I planned to take his mind off it. He wouldn't be wondering about Liam or disappointed by the canceled dinner date by the time I was through with him. Maybe we could even pick out a weekend to spend together using the treehouse getaway he'd bought me for Christmas.

In the background, there was the weird tick-tock of our divorce looming and I wondered if that was going to change things between us. Lately, I'd been thinking that it wouldn't. Why would an arbitrary date when our divorce was finalized make us give up this relationship we'd built? I knew that he felt we were more than friends with benefits; he'd even said it. We were beyond that. I hoped we were heading toward a more permanent commitment.

I pulled into his driveway and texted him that I'd arrived so he could open the door for me since Kody would already be in bed. The kid was such a good sleeper; he'd only gotten out of bed once when I'd stayed over and that was because he felt sick. Bash spent the night taking care of him and Kody never knew I was there.

Bash greeted me at the door with a soft kiss. It was still early, so we decided to watch a movie. He got us some drinks while I searched for a movie.

By the time he returned with a beer for himself and wine for me,

I'd gone through the currently trending movies and had been digging deep into the library in search of some hidden gems.

"Have you ever seen *Almost Famous*?"

He tilted his head. "I don't think so."

I patted the cushion next to me for him to sit down. "You have to see it. It's a rock and roll classic."

Since I'd already seen it before, I didn't have to pay too much attention to the movie. Instead, I had other pursuits in mind. I pretended to watch the movie, but my true goal was trying to get frisky with Bash without giving it away. I wanted to get him so worked up with lust that when the movie ended, he would pounce on me.

Starting my plan slowly, I just reminded him that I was there every few minutes. I leaned my head on his shoulder, pressed my thigh up against his, and casually touched his arm every so often.

When I leaned forward to grab my wineglass off the coffee table to take a sip, I rested my other hand on his thigh and left it there when I leaned back. A few minutes later, as I wiggled in my seat to get more comfortable, my hand 'accidentally' brushed against his cock.

He grabbed my misbehaving hand and interlocked our fingers, holding it trapped against his thigh. My move had been a bit obvious, but I didn't think he'd caught on to my game yet.

I turned toward him, snuggling into him even more, resulting in my lips being close to his jaw and my right hand resting on his chest. He let go of my other hand so that he could put his arm around me. Perfect.

After waiting a few minutes, I tilted my head so I could brush my lips against the hollow of his neck and give him a sweet, lingering kiss. He turned his head to look at me, but I just snuggled against him, sliding my hand from his chest down to his flat belly.

When he didn't return to watching the movie, my lips brushed against his ear as I whispered, "This is a good part. Pay attention."

I didn't know if it actually was a good part, but I wanted to keep teasing him and it felt like he was a few seconds away from giving up the movie, flipping me on my back, and ravishing me.

He turned back to the movie. Less than a minute later, my hand slipped under the hem of his T-shirt and rested against the warm skin of his abdomen. Bash shifted next to me. So this is what it must feel like to be a teenage boy feeling up his date. I had to swallow down a laugh.

Needing to step up my game, I grabbed a throw pillow and put it on his lap. I laid my head on it and made sure that the hand under the pillow was tucked up tight against the juncture of his thighs. I could feel the heat coming off him and I was pretty sure that his cock was hard.

His fingers began playing with my hair and lightly touching my face. I closed my eyes to savor the moment. Who was seducing who? I was getting sidetracked from my mission.

I squeezed his thigh lightly to remind him where my hand was located. A few minutes later, my hand was wandering higher, innocently sliding over his cock as I adjusted my position.

"Lacey..."

I thought I was busted playing my juvenile games.

"Take off your clothes," he growled.

I bit my lip. "Why?"

"Because you're horny as fuck," he bit out. "And I'm going to take care of my girl."

My heart exploded. Did he just call me his girl? I scrambled to sit up. "What about Kody?"

He grabbed a throw blanket off the back of the couch. "You can get under this."

I yanked off my shirt and then stood up so I could quickly tackle my pants. I didn't know if my mission had failed or succeeded, but I didn't care.

When I was naked, I settled under the blanket, my head resting on a pillow, and turned to watch TV with my bottom resting across his lap so he had easy access.

For the rest of the movie, Bash's right hand played between my legs while I pretended to watch the movie. His left hand grazed up and down my body and stopped often to play with my breasts. Mercilessly, he kept me on edge, slowing down when I moaned or when my hips thrust into his hand. His eyes never strayed from the TV screen, even when he paused to lick my juices off his fingers. His payback for my little game was spectacular.

Before the credits stopped rolling, his shoulders were pushing between my legs and his mouth was on me. It was a full-blown assault from his mouth, his lips, his tongue, and his fingers that he had me seeing stars. After so much buildup, it only took me a few minutes to orgasm, splintering into a billion pieces.

My limbs still felt rubbery when he wrapped me in the blanket and carried me up the stairs to bed. We used no toys — no blindfolds or cuffs, no flogger or paddles. There were no props, no sexy lingerie, and no role-playing. It was just the two of us touching and worshipping each other. I wore the delicate topaz necklace he'd bought me and nothing else.

We took our time, kissing and touching. We didn't speak much; we didn't need to. Bash looked into my eyes while he fucked me at a slow and sensual pace. That didn't mean that my body wasn't combusting like a star going supernova. Our passion was toe-curling in its sheer intensity. I felt it deep in my soul.

Lying in his arms, basking in a post-orgasmic glow, I came to the realization that I'd finally found my nirvana. I'd been searching for this nebulous and elusive state of mind, and in the end, I didn't get it through letting go and submitting. I didn't get it on the other end of a riding crop or by playing kinky games.

I found it in Sebastian's arms, where I felt safe and secure. Cared for. Intimately connected, body and soul.

It hit me like a ton of bricks.

I loved him.

I loved him! That was the bottom line. I'd never felt that way about any other person in the world, at least not romantically. Hadn't ever come close.

I loved Sebastian, and I didn't want anyone else. He was the one. I wanted to stay with him forever. I wanted to live with him and Kody. Hell, I'd move to the suburbs and commute daily, if I had to. I wanted to get married for real and wake up in his arms every day. I wanted to plan with him. Entwine our futures. Create a beautiful family with him where we could share our love.

As soon as I realized it, it became clear as day. It all gelled into place as soon as my mind admitted it. My future was with Sebastian. He was my other half. It was never about the kinky stuff. That was just the icing on the cake. We were soul mates and I must have felt that connection in that long-ago threesome. It had been Bash all along.

I wiggled closer to him because I was absolutely overflowing with love for him. It was hard to contain.

Sebastian sighed with parted lips. "Again? You're insatiable, wifey. Give me a few minutes."

Chapter 29

Bash

I LOVED SATURDAY MORNINGS. I got up early with Kody and fed him breakfast. Then I'd get him set up playing with his toys in the playroom while I 'took a shower'. He usually lasted at least an hour, so that was when I snuck back into bed with Lacey.

This morning, I was happy to crawl back into bed with her until she woke up, but she had other plans. She play-wrestled with me until she had me pinned down, and then she had her way with me. She definitely got off on being submissive in the bedroom, but on occasion, she loved to take over. The only thing I could do this morning was lie back and enjoy the ride.

After we showered, I snuck her downstairs so that she could appear to have just arrived for the day. We were sitting on the couch enjoying a cup of coffee and debating where we could take Kody for the day when my phone rang. It was Sid.

I answered and put the phone to my ear. "Hey, man. What's up?"

"Two babies at the ass-crack of dawn. Brady's napping now, but Emerson won't go down. I think he's teething again."

I stretched my legs out in front of me. "That's exhilarating. Is that why you called?"

"Fuck off or I'm going to go lick your sister's tit."

My face soured. "Goddammit, Sidney," I growled.

He chuckled with triumph. "Ghost called a band meeting tonight. Dinner at his place and then we're hanging out."

"What?" I was confused. "Why does he want us to meet? We're not even doing anything right now. Unless we're adding a tour or something? Do you know what it's for?"

"Don't know. But if it's a tour, Kaylie's not going to be happy. The twins are a handful right now. Plus, I'm trying to knock her up again, so if she gets pregnant—"

I cut him off. "Fuck, Sid. Enough talking about my sister."

I heard Emerson crying in the background. "Kay said you could bring Kody over here for the night. She'll watch him while we go. She said your parents were away?"

Fuck, I didn't want to go. I'd have to leave by 4 o'clock to drop off Kody and get to Ghost's apartment in time for dinner. I'd miss a lot of time with Lacey, including spending the night with her. And then she'd be gone for the week.

Unfortunately, I didn't think I'd be able to get out of it. I tried to think quickly to figure out how I could still spend the night with her. "It sounds like Kaylie already has her hands full. I don't want to add Kody to that. I'll just get a sitter and then go for dinner and the meeting and then come back home."

"Whatever, man. Just make sure you get your ass there. Ghost said it's just going to be the five of us, so I'm not sure what's up."

I sighed. "Yeah. I'll see."

"I've gotta run and help with Emerson. I'll catch you later."

"Later." I hung up.

Lacey was messing around on her phone, but she looked up. "You're meeting with the band?"

"Yeah." I tossed my phone on the table in front of me. "Some important meeting, even though we're not doing shit as a band right now. Why the fuck on a Saturday night?"

"You need to get a babysitter for Kody?" She asked.

I nodded. There was only one babysitter I trusted besides my family or Josie and if she wasn't free, I'd have to bring Kody to Kay's.

"I can watch him," she said tentatively.

'No' was on the tip of my tongue, but that would mean she'd be here waiting for me when I got home. I'd get to at least spend the night with her. It was selfish, but I was a greedy bastard when it came to her. "You don't have to do that. I'm sure it's not exactly how you envisioned spending a Saturday night."

"I don't mind. Just let me know what his usual routine is. I can order pizza for dinner or whatever he likes. It'll be fun."

Kody would like that and I'd like knowing she was waiting for me. "Okay, on one condition."

She cocked an eyebrow at me, letting me know I wasn't in the position to be making conditions. "What?"

A slow smile crept over my face. "That you stay here tomorrow and spend the day with me. No running off early."

She didn't hesitate. "Deal."

♫♪♩♪♪

My stomach grumbled when I walked into Ghost's apartment. I smelled the food before I saw the spread. Sid, Knox, and Ghost were already sitting at the round table that sat about six feet from the kitchen island that was laden with food.

I headed straight for the food. "You guys started eating? Where's Ryder?"

"We wanted to dig in while it was still hot. Ryder's on his way. Beer's in the fridge." Ghost replied between mouthfuls.

There was a huge spread of a variety of Thai food. Grabbing a plate, I began piling food on it: Thai BBQ, fried rice, papaya salad, pork stir fry, spring rolls, Thai curry with chicken, Pad Thai, and cashew chicken. I grabbed some soup and utensils and carried my overloaded plate to the table before I pulled a Singha Beer out of his refrigerator.

I went back to the table and sat down next to Sid. After I shoveled in a few bites of food, I addressed the table. "So, what the hell is going on and why am I always the last to know?"

Sid elbowed me. "I don't know shit either.

"We have to wait till Ryder gets here." Ghost leaned back in his chair.

Sid grumbled in frustration. "For fuck's sake, at least tell me if it's a good thing or a bad thing. And if we're going back on tour."

Knox glanced over at Ghost. "It's definitely good. And it has nothing to do with the tour."

Sid seemed satisfied. "Okay, I can wait then." He went back to eating.

I frowned. "You know too, Knox? And why isn't Donovan here?"

Just then, Ryder walked through the door. "Looks like I'm late. I hope you fuckers saved me some food."

We chowed on the fried bananas and mango sticky rice for dessert while we waited for Ryder to catch up. When we were all finally finished eating, Ghost herded us all into the living room.

Sid and I settled into the brown leather couch with Ryder perching on the arm of the couch next to me. Knox sunk into an oversized ottoman coffee table. Ghost walked over to his home bar setup.

He pulled out a bottle of alcohol. "For this fine occasion, I selected a beverage to celebrate. This is the best 12 Year Old single malt around, according to the guy taking my money."

He held out a bottle of Macallan.

Scotch? My gaze slid over to Knox. I suddenly had a feeling I knew what we were celebrating.

Ryder laughed. "Oh fuck. You finally grew a pair of balls and did it?"

Ghost started putting ice cubes in some rocks glasses with a tong. "Hold on, we need to get our drinks first."

Knox shook his head. "You heathens don't know how to drink a good scotch. You drink it neat, with a wee bit of water to reduce the bitterness if you must. No ice. And those glasses are sub-par. You need a tulip-shaped whisky glass to enjoy the aromas."

Ghost stopped putting ice in the glasses. "I don't have that shit. Rocks glasses, it'll have to do."

He poured some amber liquid into each glass, handing Knox one of the neat glasses.

Knox held up a hand to stop us all from tasting. "First, give the glass a shoogle. Then, nose the whisky." He dipped his nose into the glass and inhaled. "Try to think about what you're smelling. I smell a sherried note, some dried fruit. Something like caramel."

We all copied. I didn't smell anything special; it smelt like whisky to me.

Knox swirled the liquid around in his glass. "Now take a taste."

I took a sip and waited for the flavors to explode on my tongue. I grimaced. "It tastes like raisins. Did you get this bottle from Josie?"

Sid chuckled next to me. "It kind of does have a hint of raisins to it."

"Fuck. I can't drink this. I hate those little black demons. Even the hint of them is too much." I dumped the rest of my drink into Sid's glass and then stalked over to the bar to make a new drink.

Ghost walked over to stand next to Knox, throwing an arm around his shoulder. "So, tell everyone the good news."

"I finally convinced Summer to marry my arse." Knox was grinning ear to ear.

A collective cheer went up and then we were all congratulating him with slaps to the back and manly hugs.

Ryder sat back down. "Did Summer start planning already? Give us the details. When and where?"

Knox shifted from foot to foot like a little kid about to detonate if he didn't let out a big secret. "The wedding is going to be in Kentucky. And we can't dither too long, because I put a wee bairn in her."

Sid screwed up his face. "Haven't you been putting that in her all along?"

Knox's brow wrinkled with confusion. "Huh?"

I was back at the bar mixing up a drink with what Ghost had available but listening to Sid. I added a splash of more vodka to my glass. "A baby, you dumbass. Summer's pregnant."

Understanding dawned on Sid's face and then we all were back to congratulating Knox all over again. I could see how damn excited he was to be a father. He radiated pure happiness. He deserved all the good coming his way, but I couldn't help but feel a little envious that I'd never gotten to experience that kind of excited anticipation with Kody.

Music started spilling out of the high-end speaker system. It didn't take long for the other guys to start getting plastered, but I knew I was driving back home tonight, so I took it easy.

After a few hours, I slipped away from the guys and stepped outside the sliding doors to enjoy the crisp night air on the balcony. I leaned over the railing, peering at the dark outlines of the tall buildings against the night sky and the city lights twinkling in the distance. I heard the doors slide open behind me and someone step out onto the balcony with me.

It was probably Sid, wondering what the fuck I was doing out here in the cold. I turned and was surprised to see Ghost. "Hey, man."

He was vibrating with energy. "What are you doing out here?"

I turned away from him to gaze out over the city. "Just getting some fresh air."

"Sure you're not hiding?" He joined me at the railing.

"From what?"

"The happiness in there?" Ghost rubbed contemplatively at his chin. "You're the last single guy in our band, and I'm the last one without a kid. We're the odd ones out. But maybe both of those things will change in the future."

My mouth fell open in shock. "You guys thinking about having a kid?"

"Who knows?" He smiled faintly. "I'm thinking about selling this place. I'm never here anymore. I'm always with Remi and Grey. That's where I need to be. Not here."

"You trust them both?" I chanced a quick glance at his face, hoping I wasn't pissing him off. "After everything that happened?"

"I do. And I've never been happier." He turned to face me until I couldn't hide from his scrutiny. "How about you? What's going on with Lacey?"

I let out an exasperated sigh. "Fuck. How do you know?"

His eyes were crinkled with amusement. "Sidney may have mentioned something, but I have eyes."

"It started in Vegas. Probably because you put the idea into my head," I accused him half-heartedly.

"You've been together since Vegas?" He seemed surprised.

"It started with a friends-with-benefits kind of thing because she has a kinky side. I was feeding her fantasies. Who the fuck knows what she wants now?" I shrugged like it didn't matter too much to me.

"Maybe you should ask her?"

"That was the plan, but I thought I'd hook her a bit more first. I'm not sure how well it's working."

His intense eyes bored into me. "You need to tell her how you feel. Tell her that you love her before she starts looking elsewhere for what she needs."

I turned my back on the city and leaned back against the railing. "Did you know that she has her MBA from the University of Chicago? She graduated at the top of her class, too. Man, she's super smart. She practically runs Castle Music right now. She's smarter than the five of us combined. I'm just a dumb drummer."

He frowned. "You went to college."

"Community college doesn't compare to the University of Chicago. It's not even in the same ballpark." I gazed at my feet, scuffing my shoe against the concrete.

"Why are you putting yourself down? She sees something in you that she likes."

"I'm just the guy that fulfills her kinky side." I thought about that guy on the pier who'd called her baby girl. "Do you know a guy named Liam Wright? I think he's an ex-boyfriend."

"I don't know." He tilted his head as if thinking hard. "She was with that Theo guy for a while. Never heard of a Liam."

I jammed my hands into my pockets. "She's back at my house right now babysitting Kody. I'm going to take off soon so I can spend some time with her."

"I hear you, man. Just remember to be honest with her. Don't let your fears get in the way of opening up and being vulnerable with her. If you can do that, then you have a real chance of making it work with her."

Ghost clapped me on the back as he walked past me towards the door.

Chapter 30

Lacey

I WAS DISAPPOINTED THAT Bash had to go downtown to meet his band and was more than a little curious as to what it was all about, but I didn't mind watching Kody. The fact that Bash trusted me with his son brought a grin of happiness to my face. I enjoyed spending time with Kody and our deal meant that I'd be spending all day Sunday with them both.

It was cold and windy outside, so Kody and I played indoors. He took me to his playroom, where he showed me all of his favorite toys. We ended up playing cars and a game of catch until the pizza arrived.

While we ate our slices of cheese pizza, Kody helped me pick out flavors of cupcakes that I was getting delivered for dessert. I had to steer him away from ones that I didn't think he'd enjoy, like the coffee cupcake which looked delicious in the photo. In the end, we ordered several each of double chocolate, chocolate and peanut butter, s'mores, and a black forest cupcake for me.

We played hide and seek while we waited for the cupcakes to be delivered. The rules were that there was no hiding upstairs, so it was pretty easy to spot Kody. Plus, he couldn't keep quiet for too long.

It was close to 6:30 when the doorbell rang. Kody was hiding under the kitchen table, so I raised my voice so that he could hear me. "That must be our cupcakes! Come out of your hiding spot so we can eat."

When I answered the door, a lean man in a blue baseball cap and a gray polo shirt with the words 'Home Tight' embroidered on it was standing on the porch. He was looking down at a clipboard and not carrying any food order bag that I could see.

"Can I help you?"

He looked up and smiled. "Hello, ma'am. I'm with Home Tight Security and we're in the neighborhood installing a security system for one of your neighbors. Their home was recently broken into when they were away on vacation. And I can tell you that they were not the first people to be robbed in this area. Have you heard about the recent break-ins?"

"No." I glanced over my shoulder to make sure Kody couldn't hear any part of the conversation. I didn't want him to get scared.

He clicked the pen open and closed a few times and then scribbled something quickly on his clipboard. "They were likely targeted because they didn't have any deterrents to petty thieves like cameras or a home security system. As we've been in the neighborhood working, we've noticed several houses, like yours, that didn't have security systems."

I didn't want to get into the fact that I didn't live there, that I was just the babysitter. "Thank you for letting us know." I began closing the door.

He wasn't discouraged. "I don't know if you have any children, but I'm sure you want them to be safe at home. Since we're already working in the neighborhood, we can offer you a discounted package if you sign with us tonight."

Nope, I was done. I couldn't stand the high-pressure sales pitch, but it was probably a good idea to think about a security system since Bash had Kody to worry about. "Which family did you say you're installing a system for right now?"

He shifted. "I don't want to give out their personal information, but I'm sure if you look in the local police blotter, you'll find the information about where the burglary took place."

He couldn't tell me? What if I wanted to use them as a reference? It wasn't my business, anyway. I'd relay the information to Bash and he could decide if it was worth pursuing.

"No, I'm sorry, but I'm not interested at the moment. Do you have a business card you can leave for me?"

The man pulled a card out of his pocket and handed it to me just when the most heart-stopping and utterly horrifying shriek pierced the air and terrified me to my core.

Kody!

I fought against the rising tide of blind panic as I raced toward the sound. I'd never been so scared in my life. His cry was primal. Something was horribly, horribly wrong.

My heart was pounding so fast I thought it might burst inside my chest. I tried to force a breath past the fear that had crawled up my throat and made it too tight to breathe.

Dread engulfed me when I saw Kody lying on the ground beside the kitchen table, writhing in pain. His skin was deathly pale and his eyes were wide and unfocused with fear and pain. The wrenching sobs mixed with shrieks of distress that were coming from his mouth sounded animalistic in his agony.

My own fear had rendered my brain nearly incapacitated. I had to mentally jump-start it. Kody needed me; I would not let him down.

I dropped to my knees beside him, my mind frantically racing. Did he fall off the table? Did he bang his head? Concussion? Spine injury? Brain hemorrhage? Ruptured spleen? My brain scrambled in all directions at once, none of them good. I was scared to move him — scared to even touch him. What if I made it worse?

My hands were trembling and my voice wobbled unnaturally. "Kody, I'm here. It's going to be okay. Where are you hurt?"

I couldn't even tell if my words got through to him. As my stomach churned with nausea, I desperately tried to recall any first aid knowledge that I had. I didn't have any formal training; I only knew the basics. As a teen I never babysat, so I'd never taken any courses.

My whole body shook with panic. I never should have taken responsibility for Kody without knowing basic first aid that even most teenagers knew. I shut down the panic that seized me in a vice-like grip.

Assess the situation.

I didn't see any blood. Should I turn his head and check for blood or a bump? Wasn't it important not to move someone if there was a possible spinal injury? The uncertainty of what to do paralyzed me. What if his brain was bleeding right now, and I was wasting time that he didn't have?

I pulled out my phone and dialed 911.

Waiting for the ambulance to arrive while I answered questions from the 911 operator was the longest wait of my life. I tried to hide my fear from Kody and speak to him soothingly, but he ignored everything outside of his pain and that had me dizzy with worry. I must have sweated while I waited, but now that sweat had turned cold, and I was shivering with full body shakes.

When I heard them arrive, I scrambled to the door. Raw panic laced my voice as I answered it. "Hurry! He's in here." I didn't want to leave him alone, even for a second.

The emergency responders quickly and efficiently took over, leaving me hovering in the periphery after answering only a few questions, trying to interpret their jumble of words to piece together an understanding of Kody's injuries.

With shaky hands, I pulled out my phone to call Bash. I wiped the tears from my eyes and swallowed while I waited for the call to connect.

It went straight to voicemail. One of the ambulance crew approached and was talking to me. I shook my head to clear it, but I couldn't clear it of the sight in front of me: Kody in a cervical collar and strapped to a backboard.

"Will you be riding in the ambulance, miss? We're ready to head out now."

I turned to him. "Yes. Is he going to be okay?"

"We immobilized him to be on the safe side. His right arm is broken, so we splinted it. They'll run tests at the hospital to make sure there isn't a concussion and check for further injuries." His voice seemed like it was coming from far away.

The man rested his giant palm on my shoulder. "Does he have a favorite stuffed animal or a blanket that you can bring? That might help comfort him."

The other men began lifting Kody onto a stretcher.

"Yes, I'll go get it."

My body felt almost numb, but my heart was still racing. I willed my feet to hurry as I went into Kody's room, searching for the stuffed dog I'd seen several times early in the morning when I was here. I found the fluffy dog with the floppy ears resting on his bed.

The man was waiting for me by the front door. He led me into the back of the ambulance and showed me where I could sit. The ambulance raced out of the driveway and headed for the hospital.

Kody wasn't wailing uncontrollably anymore, but he was still whimpering. I knew how scared he was when I saw terror reflected in his eyes.

"Kody, I'm right here with you," I said, trying to comfort him. "I'm here, baby."

He looked at me, but it was like he was looking at a stranger. His lips quivered. "I want Daddy. Daddy! I want Daddy."

He was crying for his father, over and over, and my heart felt like it was going to break. I showed him his stuffed dog and let it rest so that it was touching his face where it might give him some comfort.

I kept trying to reassure him. "You're going to be okay, Kody. I'll be with you until your dad gets here."

He needed Bash. I reached for my phone, but my pockets were empty. It took me a few seconds to realize that in my haste to get out the door, I'd left my phone behind.

I was a completely irresponsible fuck up.

Everything was a blur when we got to the hospital. Admittance became a swirl of answering questions, explaining that I wasn't Kody's mother, and trying to contact Bash. Without my phone, I didn't know anyone's phone numbers except for my admin's. I called her and gave her the hospital information and asked her to contact Kaylie. I knew Nisha had Kaylie's contact information because she set up a lot of our Cyber Angels' meetings for us. Nisha promised that she'd hunt down Bash, whatever it took, and I didn't doubt her, but she had no way of calling me back and letting me know.

So, I just had to sit and wait. They allowed me to stay in the curtained exam room in the ER with Kody. The doctors and nurses all talked to me like I was his mother, and I didn't say anything because I didn't want to be kicked out.

After a round of visits from different specialists, the doctors were able to remove the cervical collar and deduced that his head injury was not severe enough for a CT scan and just needed monitoring. We were still waiting to get an x-ray of his arm. Everyone was very reassuring and my sheer panic began to abate. He was going to be okay.

Kody was no longer crying, but he was just staring off into space, his jaw slack. I tried to talk to him, telling him that the doctors were going to fix him up, but he ignored me. My gut twisted with guilt as I hovered over him. This was my fault. If I had been watching him better, this wouldn't have happened.

A man in blue scrubs finally came to bring Kody to get an X-ray. They allowed me to go with him and wait outside while they performed it. Twenty minutes later, we were back in the ER exam room.

I was brushing a lock of hair back from Kody's face, trying to soothe him, when a nurse pulled the curtain open. Bash stormed in, looking as frantic and worried as I felt.

He rushed to Kody's side and Kody started crying. "I'm here, little man."

I turned away from the scene because I was two seconds from breaking down myself.

The nurse looked at me. "Miss, his father is here now. You'll need to return to the waiting room."

Bash spun around, anger etched across his face. "What the fuck happened?"

"I'm not sure," I stuttered. "I think he fell off the table."

His nose flared. "What do you mean, you're not sure?" He stabbed a pointed finger at me. "Fuck, Lacey, you were supposed to be watching him."

Tears spilled down my cheeks, but Bash didn't see because he'd already dismissed me. He was busy cradling his son.

The nurse, who'd been much friendlier before, gave me the stink eye. "I'll escort you back to the waiting room."

In the waiting room, I sunk into an uncomfortable chair. I had no phone and no money. I could call Nisha and get a ride home, but I didn't want to leave Bash and Kody.

I sat in a daze for what seemed like hours but was only 80 minutes according to the clock when Sid walked into the waiting room.

He crossed the room to me. "Lacey, are you okay?"

I started balling. Was it his concern for me when I wasn't the one who deserved it? Was it guilt for not watching Kody properly? Or was it just the release of a ton of stress?

He wrapped me in his arms and hugged me for a few minutes while I cried.

"How's Kody doing?"

I wiped my eyes on my sleeve. "He has a broken arm and they're observing him for signs of concussion, but he seems okay besides that. It was so scary. They had him in a cervical collar and strapped to a backboard. He was so scared. I was so scared! I freaked out, Sid. I didn't know what to do. I didn't want to move him."

Sid rubbed my arms. "You called the ambulance. They're the professionals. You did the right thing."

He looked around. "Where's your stuff? Your phone? I was texting."

"It's at Bash's house. I was so panicked to get into the ambulance that I forgot it. Then I couldn't get in touch with Bash..."

Sid pulled out his phone and began texting. "Let me talk to Bash and see what's going on. First, I'll see what he needs, and then I can take you home."

Slumping back into my chair, I shook my head. "I don't want to go.

I'll stay here."

"If you need to be with someone, I can take you to Kaylie. You look like hell. You can stay over at our place tonight."

I shook my head. "Thanks, Sid, but I don't want to leave them."

"You need a coffee? Or some food?" He sat down next to me.

"No, I don't think it would sit well in my stomach."

Sid was busy on his phone while we waited. It was another 45 minutes until Bash came into the waiting room. His hair was sticking up like he'd been pulling at it.

Sid and I both stood up, but it was clear that Bash was avoiding me.

He addressed Sid. "He needs surgery. They're going to have to put screws in his elbow or some shit. They can't do it tonight because he's eaten, so they are going to schedule it for first thing in the morning. Tonight, they'll set the bone and then discharge him."

"Shit," Sid blew out a breath. "Poor kid. Whatever you need, let me know. If you need me here tomorrow—"

"Thanks, man. My parents are coming tomorrow, but I might need you. I'll go crazy just sitting here waiting."

I was wringing my hands, feeling like an outsider. Bash wouldn't even look my way.

"Bash, I'm so sorry—" I stepped forward, lifting my hands up to hug him, but he stepped away from me.

The expression on his face was ugly, a mixture of revulsion and contempt. "Just go home, Lacey. We don't need your help."

Chapter 31

Bash

EVERYTHING WAS SLOWLY GETTING back to normal. The horrible day of the surgery was three long days ago. My parents helped me settle Kody back at home and stayed over a few nights. They were gone and Kody had already milked his injury for all the balloons and ice cream that my friends and family could give. It was just the two of us again, except that Kody was bored and frustrated with the limitations that his cast imposed. Tomorrow I would get him back to preschool and hopefully, that would help him feel less cranky.

Over the past three days, I'd seen or talked to most of my good friends, but for one glaring exception. Lacey. Still upset with her, I'd told her not to come over because I needed some time to get Kody situated. I'd barely spoken to her, just enough to update her on his progress.

I wanted to talk to her, but I was still so pissed off. And I felt guilty that I'd left Lacey in charge to babysit, especially since my reasons were so selfish. I wanted to come back home and have sex with her. Fuck, it was so stupid. I should have dropped him off at Kaylie's and stayed there overnight instead of wanting to get back to her so badly. Then Kody wouldn't have gone through all this trauma.

I was mostly feeling guilty and angry at myself, but Lacey had let me down, just like I'd let down Kody. I trusted her to keep him safe, and she failed. It felt like a betrayal.

My cell phone was in my hand, my finger hovering over Lacey's name when the doorbell rang.

A quick glance out the window let me know it was Mrs. Travis, the lady who lived across the street and walked her black labrador through the neighborhood twice a day. She was holding a plate wrapped in aluminum foil.

I opened the door. "Hello, Mrs. Travis."

"Hi, Bash." She smiled weakly. "I didn't want to bother you while you had all the activity going on, but it looked quieter over here today. I wanted to see if Kody was okay. I saw him being loaded into the ambulance and I was so worried."

"He had surgery on his arm, but he's doing just fine now."

"Oh, I wasn't sure what happened..." Her voice trailed off.

She was a nice woman, so I didn't mind her prying. "He climbed up on the table and fell off. He broke his arm and there was some worry about spinal injury or a concussion, but luckily it was just the broken arm."

"Oh, thank God! I saw the neck brace when they wheeled him out. It was scary." She frowned.

I opened the door wider. "Why don't you come in and say hello to him? I'm sure he'd be happy to see you. Then you can see how well he's doing."

Kody would be more excited to see her if she'd brought Oreo over with her. He loved that dog.

Mrs. Travis stepped inside and I closed the door behind her. I called for Kody and he came out of his playroom. "Mrs. Travis stopped by to see how you were doing."

"Hi, Kody. I heard you broke your arm, so I decided to bake you some brownies to help you feel better."

I took the plate from her hands. "Thank you, Mrs. Travis. That was very kind of you. I'm sure that will cheer him up. What do you say, Kody?"

Kody raised his fist in the air. "I love brownies!"

I pinned him with a dad look. "And what else do you say?"

He giggled. "Thank you, Mrs. Travis."

It was nice to see him smiling and laughing again. If it took a plate full of sugar and cavities to do it, so be it.

Mrs. Travis beamed. "You're welcome, Kody. I'm so glad you're feeling better and you'll get that cast off your arm in no time."

Kody glanced at his cast and frowned, but then he looked at me. "I'm gonna go play cars, Dad."

He was running back to the playroom before I could respond.

Mrs. Travis put her hand on my arm. "Thank goodness he's okay. I've been laying awake at night wondering what happened to that poor boy. I'm relieved to see he's doing so well."

Squeezing her hand briefly, I started leading her to the door. "I'm sorry that you were so worried. You should have stopped by earlier."

She shrugged it off. "I didn't want to intrude. Mr. Travis already yells at me for being too nosey. I was already keeping an eye out when I saw that man hanging around the neighborhood. Your babysitter was talking to him, so I figured he must be okay. But when the ambulance came, well, I was really worried. I wanted to rush right over here, but

Mr. Travis stopped me."

"Wait..." I pulled my hand back from the doorknob. "Lacey? She was talking to a man? The day Kody got hurt?"

Mrs. Travis looked guilty. "I noticed him because he parked down the street. In front of the Miller's house. He sat there in his car for a long time, so I decided to keep my eye on him. You've heard about the recent break-ins in the neighborhood?"

I shook my head.

"Well, two houses were broken into when the owners were away. That beautiful craftsman-style house on the corner of Pine and Jackson. And one behind me on Adams. There was also a car break-in. Mr. Gradola said that someone stole all the change out of his car, but I suspect he's getting a little senile. He probably emptied it out himself and forgot."

I waited patiently for her to finish. "But what about the guy you saw talking to Lacey?"

"Is she the blonde lady that was here? Kody's babysitter?" she asked.

"Yes," I confirmed. "What happened?"

"Well, the guy got out of his car and walked straight up to your door. I thought it was strange that he was parked down the street." She paused for a moment, waiting for me to comment, but when I didn't, she continued. "He was just talking to the blonde lady. Then my phone rang, so I went into the kitchen to answer it. It was my sister, and I got distracted talking to her. The next thing I know, there's an ambulance in front of your house. It was frightening because I didn't know if the man was somehow involved in whatever happened, but his car was gone. Then I saw Kody being wheeled out on the stretcher."

My stomach was twisting up in knots. Lacey had been talking to a man when Kody got hurt? Why hadn't she mentioned that?

I tried to keep my tone casual, even though a warning signal was blaring in my head. "Can you tell me what this man looked like?"

"I made sure to get a good look at him in case he was up to no good. When he was walking up the street heading this way — before he put his baseball cap on — I got a pretty good look at him."

I shifted on my feet and nodded for her to continue.

She rattled off a description so quickly it sounded rehearsed. "He was young and strong-looking like he went to the gym and worked out a lot. Probably around your age, but maybe a tad taller than you. He had light brown hair with some lighter streaks in it, but it was on the long side, kind of unkempt looking. He looked like he spent a lot of time outdoors and he was wearing jeans and a gray, short-sleeved shirt. Do you think I should make a report to the police about him?"

As she described the guy, right away, I thought of that guy from the pier, Liam. Her description matched him right down to the longish hair.

"He didn't have anything to do with Kody's accident, Mrs. Travis. But it's nice to know you're keeping an eye on the neighborhood," I reassured her as I opened the door.

"Well, all right. Bring Kody over to play with Oreo soon." She waved over her shoulder as she headed down the steps of the porch.

"Goodbye. And thanks for the brownies." I shut the door and leaned back against it.

My thoughts were turning darker by the second. Did someone come to visit Lacey after I left that night? Why didn't she mention it? Maybe it was because it was that guy, Liam. Maybe she was sneaking around with him. It seemed preposterous. He'd shown up at the pier while we were out together, but why would he come to my house? I thought about how Mrs. Travis said he'd parked down the road and not in front of the house. Just like she'd said, it was suspicious behavior.

Chapter 32

Lacey

Running a hand down my black silk blouse, I fought the urge to run back into my bedroom and change. I'd already changed outfits a million times and messed with my hair and makeup until I thought I'd scream. I checked my appearance one last time in the mirror. Everything looked fine. The blouse was gorgeous, and I'd paired it with jeans to keep the entire outfit looking casual.

Bash was coming to my apartment and instead of that filling me with excitement and anticipation, I was filled with anxiety and dread. I hadn't seen him and had barely spoken to him since Kody's accident. He was shutting me out.

I knew he was dealing with a lot. Between Kody's surgery and then taking care of him, he had a lot on his plate. When I'd dumped all my fears on Kaylie, she told me to give him some space.

Still, I was worried about us. Not just Bash and me, but Kody, too.

I was worried that Kody was upset with me. I recalled in detail that dull vacant stare when he looked at me in the hospital. Intellectually, I knew he was scared and hurt and wanted his dad, but that look chilled me. What if he blamed me?

Kaylie told me that Kody was slowly getting back to his normal, cheerful self. I guess I just wanted to see him so I could reassure myself that he was okay and that we were still friends. Then, I felt guilty and selfish worrying about my own feelings when Kody was the one that went through everything.

This morning, I got the dreaded text from Bash. We need to talk. Those words seemed so ominous. I'd wanted to talk to him for days, so I should be ecstatic that he was ready, but I was getting bad vibes.

I knew I fucked up with Kody. My heart wrenched as I thought about how much I had hurt him. Somehow, I had to make things right again. I spent a lot of time scouring the internet for fun activities that the three of us could do together, even with Kody's broken arm. I needed to be in their lives again and for everything to be normal.

Bash told me that his parents were watching Kody at his house. He was coming into the city to see me, but he didn't want to leave Kody for too long, so he wasn't staying over.

That text, after the 'we need to talk' text, had me even more anxious. Why didn't he ask me to come over to his house? Was he trying to keep me away from Kody?

I wiped my sweaty palms on my jeans when I heard the elevator. I walked toward the foyer with trepidation.

The elevator door slid open, and he stepped out. My insides clenched with how handsome he looked. His hair was uncharacteristically long for him, curling up at the ends slightly and he had the perfect amount of 5 o'clock shadow. He was wearing a casual, plaid button-down shirt with the sleeves rolled up and a pair of perfectly broken-in jeans.

He looked so good, and I'd missed him so much that, before I could stop myself, I hugged him. He remained stiff in my arms. One arm hung limp at his side and the other awkwardly pressed against my back for a second. I held in a gasp of surprise and stepped back, laughing nervously.

I quickly turned so he wouldn't see my eyes well up with tears. "Do you want a glass of wine?"

"No. A glass of water would be good." He followed me into the kitchen.

I busied myself pouring a glass of water for him and a glass of wine for myself. I had a feeling I was going to need it. "How is Kody doing?"

"Fine."

"Did he get my get-well presents?" I'd gotten him a teddy bear with a cast on his arm, some balloons, a bag of M&Ms, and a 5-pack of toy cars for his impressive collection.

"He did."

I took a sip of my wine. I was so freaking nervous and Bash wasn't helping with the curt answers. "Is he ... mad at me?"

"He hasn't mentioned you."

I flinched as if I'd just been slapped. Emotionally, it felt like I had been. Everything was all wrong. I had to fix this. "I was so scared that he'd been hurt really bad. Do you think I overreacted by calling 911? I'll pay for the cost—"

"Shit, Lacey. This isn't about the fucking cost." Anger laced his words.

Five feet of marble on the kitchen island separated us, so I circled around to stand next to him. "I'm sorry. I panicked when I saw him lying on the ground in so much pain. I wasn't sure what to do." I pleaded with my eyes for him to understand. "But, I enrolled in some first aid courses. A basic first aid and CPR course and another one that's tailored specifically to first aid for babies and children. I realize I should already know all this stuff, but I don't."

Bash looked at me calmly. "How did he get up on the table with you watching him?"

I unclenched my hands, which had balled into fists at my side. Thinking back to the moment of terror that had taken over me, I felt my heart rate accelerating. "I don't know. We were playing hide and seek and he was hiding under the table. I knew he was there, but I pretended I couldn't find him. The next thing I knew, he was screaming. It was awful. I could tell something was wrong."

I still heard that hair-splitting scream in my mind over and over. It would haunt me forever.

I could see the muscle working in Bash's jaw. He was grinding his teeth. "Lacey, I trusted you with my son. Now he's got a broken arm and a few screws holding his elbow together for the next six weeks. As bad as that is, I'm lucky he only broke his arm. What if he broke his neck? Or ended up with a spine or brain injury?"

Those scenarios had been running rampant in my head for days. "I would never forgive myself if that happened. Bash, I'm so sorry. I only turned away for a moment. I feel absolutely awful that he got hurt."

He pinned me with a frosty glare. "Maybe you weren't watching him that well. Maybe taking care of a four-year-old kid isn't exciting enough for you?"

Everything inside me froze right down to my very cells. What he said was horrible. Hurtful. Shocking. I stepped backward. "What are you saying?"

I closed my eyes, hoping he'd take it back. He was just angry and didn't mean it.

"Maybe you were bored, so you called your boyfriend, Liam, over to join you and you were too busy with him to keep an eye on Kody?"

His words were ugly, but the sneering look on his face was uglier.

A lump of anguish formed in my throat. "What are you talking about?"

He stepped closer to me, looming over me, intimidating me. "Did you invite a man over to my house while I was gone?"

I shook my head in denial. "No, that's crazy. I would never do that. Why are you doing this?"

He scoffed in disbelief. "I don't know, Lacey. How about you tell me?"

I couldn't believe what he was accusing me of. I took a deep breath to try to get my bearings. "You and I agreed to be exclusive. I haven't been seeing other men. Liam has absolutely nothing to do with what happened to Kody."

He ran a hand down his face in frustration. "Then who is he, Lace? Why won't you tell me?"

"Where is all of this coming from? I don't understand." My head was spinning. "I told you there haven't been any other men."

"I don't believe you," he spit out.

My eyes widened with shock. "What? I trusted you when you went on that date with the fan. If you don't trust me, Bash, then we don't have a real relationship."

He started pacing back and forth in my kitchen, running his hand through his hair. "You're fucking lying to me."

"No."

He wasn't even looking at me anymore as he continued ranting. "You're lying about Liam. You're lying about Theo. And you're lying about what happened to Kody."

Shock blasted through me. I couldn't believe what I was hearing. And I was starting to get pissed. "Theo!" I shouted. "What the fuck does he have to do with any of this?"

"I can't anymore." He stopped in his tracks and turned to me. "I have to protect my son."

I sagged against the kitchen island. My voice sounded like defeat. "You think I'm a threat to Kody? I would never hurt him."

He was speaking calmly now. It was unnerving. As if the argument was over and I had come up short. "I have to protect him physically ... and emotionally, too."

I swiped a hand over my eyes. Tears were threatening to fall. "From me?"

He shook his head bitterly. "I can't do this. Whatever the fuck this is. Kody is my first priority."

"What are you saying?" I whispered hoarsely.

"I guess your little kinky playtime is over." He turned and walked away toward the elevator.

I didn't follow him. I didn't run after him and beg him to stay. The elevator beeped, the doors slid open and then closed, and he was gone.

None of what had just happened made any sense. It actually took a while for my mind to catch up to the reality of what had just happened. But when it hit me, it hit hard. Bash and I were finished. I sunk to the floor in a heap of grief. It was as ugly as it was painful.

Chapter 33

Bash

I WAS HITTING THE cymbals too forcefully, adding way too much fill, rushing through the rhythms, and generally playing without focus. Drumming always felt therapeutic to me, but I usually saved the real therapy sessions for when I played solo, not in front of the guys.

They'd each shot me a few looks as we practiced, but no one had said anything. Lately, we'd been practicing together as a band about three times a week. We didn't have to, but we all enjoyed getting together and making music. Most of what we were doing was unstructured fooling around. We hardly played any of our own music; we'd done lots of jamming to our favorite bands and even messing around with some new material. The atmosphere was generally relaxed, and it made for some fun sessions together.

Drumming had become the only time when I could escape my thoughts. When I wasn't drumming, I was still mourning the loss of

Lacey in my life. That's the only way I could describe it. Mourning. Almost a month later, I still wasn't over her.

I was depressed as fuck. No matter how many times I told myself I was doing the right thing for myself and my son, I was miserable. I couldn't help but worry that I'd thrown away something so amazing without even fighting for it.

When Kody first showed up on Sid's and my doorstep, I walked away from the responsibility. It was a decision that I'd regret for the rest of my life. By far, it was the biggest mistake I'd ever made in a long list of blunders. I looked back and hated myself for being so weak. And Kody had turned out to be the best thing in my life.

Was I doing it again? Was I walking away from Lacey because she scared me so much? I was supposed to be the 'dominant' one in our power play games, but it was frightening how much power she held over me. Was I too damn afraid to embrace something that could be real love?

I'd brutally cut myself free from the hold she had over me, but I felt no freedom. This morning should have squelched any lingering sense of responsibility I felt toward her. It should have concluded our story. Period. I was now free to do whatever the fuck I wanted. Instead, that official envelope had sent me into a tailspin.

Our divorce was finalized.

My last tether to Lacey had been cut.

I launched into an aggressive beat down on my drum set, not realizing that at some point, the others stopped playing. I ended the manic solo with a jaw-jarring crash of cymbals.

Ghost looked at me contemplatively as the ringing sound vibrated in the air and called for a break. Knox went to the fridge and grabbed some beers to pass out. "Looks like we could all use one."

I wiped my face with a hand towel and then took a beer from Knox.

I guzzled half of it down, trying to calm my thoughts and cool off.

Ghost slapped Ryder on the shoulder. "How is Zoe doing?"

Zoe was Ryder and Talia's daughter. The last time I'd seen her, a few months ago, she was just learning to walk. She'd been determined to keep up with Kody, which was near impossible for anyone.

Ryder rubbed his face. "She's okay. Running around as if nothing happened. Somehow she learned that if she lets out a high-pitched, glass-shattering scream, we all come running. It's been fun."

I really looked at Ryder and noticed the dark circles under his red-rimmed eyes and his unusually pale skin. He looked tired. "What happened to Zoe?"

I saw a momentary flicker of fear in Ryder's eyes, but then he schooled his expression. "She was sliding down from the couch and banged her head against a plastic princess castle. It sliced open a nasty cut on her forehead. She had to get stitches. We were in the ER for hours, which was brutal with a baby."

"Fuck, poor kid," I sympathized.

"Head wounds bleed a lot. Just so you guys all know." Ryder laughed shakily. "It was like a crime scene."

I looked around the room. Everyone already knew what happened except for me. "Wait, is there some kind of group text that I'm not on? How come everyone knows about this except me?"

Ghost sat down on the couch and stretched out his long legs. "The girls all have a group chat. That's how I found out. Didn't Lacey tell you?"

My stomach jolted at the sound of her name. "No," I answered simply, and then stood up and walked around to the front of the drum set to distract myself.

Knox took the other spot on the couch, leaving me and Sid stuck with stools. "How's Kody doing? He must be getting the cast off soon?"

I grabbed one of the stools and dragged it closer to the guys. "He still has at least another two weeks with the cast on. I can't wait to give him a bath without worrying about getting that damn thing wet. Then he has to get the screws removed and probably wear a brace for a bit."

Knox scrunched up his nose. "Screws removed? I don't remember having to do that when I broke my arm."

I shrugged. "I guess it depends on the type of break."

Sid pointed his beer bottle at me and laughed. "Do you remember when you fell out of that tree and broke your collarbone?"

Kody's injury had brought that memory back to me. "Yeah, it had to be wrapped and my arm was in a sling. It felt like it took forever to heal. I couldn't drum or do anything. It was impossible to sleep comfortably at night."

Ghost tipped his head back and sighed. "Fuck, I broke my wrist when I was about five years old and then my elbow when I was eight.

"I broke my ankle playing basketball." Ryder put down his empty beer bottle. "And I can't even remember all the times I had to get stitches from doing dumb shit."

Knox rested his ankle over his knee. "Oh yeah. My poor mum. Between me and my brothers, we should have gotten a frequent customer discount at the hospital A&E."

Ryder laughed cynically. "Just think of what you have to look forward to with Brady and Emerson, Sid. Double the fun."

I didn't mean to speak, but I couldn't stop myself from blurting out, "Not if you're keeping an eye on them properly."

All the joking stopped, and the room got quiet.

Ghost was looking at me with his unnerving stare. "There's no way you can prevent a kid from ever getting hurt. Unless you bubble wrap them and never let them go anywhere or do anything."

Sid agreed. "Kids get hurt. It happens. You just have to teach them not to be so much of a dumbass that they do something really stupid."

I swallowed down the acid that had risen had the back of my throat. "Kody fell off the table."

Everyone was studying me now. Ryder punched my shoulder lightly. "You're not blaming yourself for that, are you? Kids climb shit all the time."

My knee began bouncing nervously. "I wasn't watching him."

Sid swiveled his head to look at me, his eyes wide with shock. "Lacey was watching him."

"Lacey?" Knox's brow furrowed in confusion. "You mean our Lacey?"

"There's no fucking 'our Lacey'. She's mine." I growled out the reply before I could bite my tongue.

The room grew deathly quiet again as four pairs of eyes landed on me. I jumped off my stool and began pacing. Shit, I was losing it.

Sid shook his head in disbelief. "Is that why you've been such a sad sack of shit these last few weeks? Did you fucking blame her, and she dumped your ass?"

"Wait, you guys were together?" Ryder looked just as confused as Knox.

"They were together all right," Sid confirmed. "I happened to catch the very naked evidence of that. And if I had to bet, I'd say that Bash was in love with her."

Knox threw up his hands. "Mate, what the fuck? What's going on?"

I glared at Sid with clenched teeth. He wasn't making this any better. "We had a thing for a bit, but we're not together anymore."

"Because of Kody's accident?" Ghost prodded.

I wanted to escape. This was the last thing I wanted to discuss with my friends. "Fuck, that was part of it, but we were never an actual couple. We were doing this friends-with-benefits thing while we were married—"

A collective shout of surprise went up from my friends. Ah, fuck. My big mouth.

Sid's bellow of surprise drowned out the others. "What the fuck! You two are fucking married?"

Even Ghost looked surprised. "Whoa! What do you mean by married?"

I rubbed my temples. "We got married in Vegas. That night after your birthday party. You fuckers all went home with your wives and girlfriends and left me all alone. Apparently, I got married to Lacey."

Ryder's eyes crinkled with amusement. "Only you, Bash. You pull babies and wives out of thin air."

"You've been married to her all this time? Wait, does Kaylie know about this?" Sid asked.

The cat was already out of the bag, so there was no point in keeping any more secrets from my friends. "I don't know. Lacey didn't want anyone to know. We were just going to quietly get a divorce, but then we decided to be friends with benefits until the divorce went through and things got complicated."

"You've been fucking her since Vegas? You are so gone, mate." Knox chuckled.

I wasn't quite sure what he meant. "It doesn't matter now because I got the divorce papers this morning. We're no longer married and we're no longer fucking."

"So, she's not going to give it up anymore now that you're divorced?" Ryder snickered.

"No. It's because I was an asshole. I blamed her for Kody's accident."

Ghost stood up. "Everything is making a lot more sense now."

He rubbed his hands together. "We've got to come up with a plan. Our boy is in love and he needs to win back his girl. Lacey won't make that easy, which is completely understandable since Bash, being a Neanderthal, has totally fucked this up. We can't leave it in his hands or he's doomed to failure. We'll have to brainstorm some good ideas, but first, we need more beer."

I watched him heading over to the fridge to get more beers, a protest on my lips. "I admit I may have overreacted about Kody's accident, but there are other issues. Fuck, I just don't think I'm capable of being in a real relationship."

The guys all looked around at each other while Ghost began handing out beers. "Have you had sex with anyone besides Lacey since Vegas?"

"No," I muttered.

He raised a brow. "How about in the last month since Kody's accident?"

Sid laughed and then answered for me, "Obviously not."

Ghost sat back down on the couch. "I'd call that a pretty real relationship. I can't remember you ever having sex with the same woman twice, let alone for half a year. That proves you're more than capable."

I took a long pull at my fresh beer. "I haven't had sex with anyone else, but sex with Lacey was never the problem. Outside of the bedroom, I've had a fuckton of trouble figuring her out. You guys make it look so easy. I'm not like that."

Ryder eyed me like I was crazy. "It's not fucking easy. Especially at first."

"Seriously, man?" Sid laughed. "It took me fucking years to figure it out. I mean, I knew I loved Kaylie since she was 15 and shoved her hand down my pants."

"Sidney, you fucker." I glared at him and he laughed. "Shut the fuck up."

Knox ignored us. "I went through a lot of deep, dark shit with Aila. You guys know most of it. It almost made me fuck things up with Summer. Thank God I pulled my head out of my arse before it was too late."

Ghost was the last to pile on his words of wisdom. "Yeah, I was the king of denial about my feelings, and then I believed the worst in someone who loved me. It's not easy, brother, but it's worth it. There's really only one question to answer and then the rest will fall into place. Do you love her?"

I stared them down, scared to admit the truth. "It's not that simple."

Sid shook his head in disgust. "It's obvious that you do."

Ghost agreed. "Yeah, man. I think so, too."

"Yep, there's no use fighting it, mate." The corners of Knox's mouth turned up in a teasing smile.

We all turned to Ryder and waited for him to weigh in. "Don't be a stubborn asshole."

I eyed them all warily as I drank my beer. Getting this outside my own damn head was actually refreshing. I knew my friends had my back, no matter what. And they all seemed to be in support of a relationship between Lacey and me. Ghost was right; I could use some damn help.

I was ready to admit to them what I'd already admitted to myself in the deep, dark hours of my long, sleepless nights.

"You assholes are fucking right. I love Lacey. Now, what the hell do I have to do to get her back?"

Chapter 34

Lacey

I'D LEFT THE OFFICE late because I got tied up on a phone call right before I was leaving for the day. Tired and cranky, the 15-minute trip felt like an hour. Just as I reached my building, I got a call from Nisha.

"I forgot to remind you before you left. You have a meeting with Kaylie for Cyber Angels tonight. I just talked to her; she's on her way over to your place right now."

"Tonight?" I huffed petulantly. "I don't remember setting that up. I thought it was next week?"

"No, sorry. It's tonight. Shall I call her and cancel?"

I waved to Clayton, the doorman, as I crossed the lobby to the elevator. "No, that's okay, since she's already on her way over. That would be rude. Ugh. I just wanted to relax. It's been a day."

"Sorry, boss."

"No worries, Nisha. Have a good night."

I hung up the phone and turned to Clayton before getting on the elevator. "Clayton, Kaylie Anderson is on her way over to see me. Send her up, please."

Clayton gave me a thumbs up. "Sure thing, Lacey."

When I got up to my apartment, I slipped off my heels and sat down for a moment. I wanted to strip out of my work clothes and take a long hot shower, but I didn't have time for that. I settled for changing into some soft yoga pants and an oversized sweatshirt.

When I came out of my bedroom, I heard the elevator, and then Kaylie was breezing in holding some brown shopping bags.

She headed straight for the kitchen. "I brought dinner. Salmon and chickpea salad."

"Thank God. I don't think I have the energy to rustle up anything to eat. Sorry, babe, I forgot about the meeting tonight."

"That's okay." She began pulling plates out of the cabinets. "I'm up to speed on all the reports from SRI and I've touched base with all our 'red' clients."

Kaylie was our client liaison. She'd been the victim of revenge porn, so she intimately understood many of the things our clients were going through.

She also kept up with the reports from SRI, the company we engaged that helped us scrub the internet using their expertise, resources, and some magic that I didn't understand to remove and mitigate any online information that damaged our clients and kept it from spreading.

Over the years, our clients had run the gamut of all types of people: teenage girls, older women, and even a surprising number of men. Their tormentors loved to extract maximum shame and humiliation from them by exposing their most private moments to their families, friends, coworkers, employers, teachers, and their communities. That's where Cyber Angels came in and shut it down and, in some cases, when the client was willing, spent the resources to go after the bad guys legally.

"Any clients we should be worried about?" I moved to her side to help her plate the food.

"No. Everything's looking okay. I'm setting up a new client with SRI tomorrow and vetting a few more people that reached out to me."

Now that we had a full understanding of what services our clients needed, we'd been slowly expanding our new client budget. I was in charge of securing the finances and our fundraising efforts. "I don't have anything new right now on the money side. Our spring fundraiser is moving along nicely."

Kaylie shrugged as she spooned food onto our plates. "Cyber Angels is running smoothly. That's all I need to know. I just wanted to get out of the apartment for a bit. Sid is driving me crazy. I just finished weaning the twins, and now Sid wants to knock me up again. The boys are still such a handful."

My hands froze over the plate. The topic was heading into murky waters for me. I wanted to be there as a friend for Kaylie, but she was hitting all sorts of emotional triggers right now.

She snuck a glance over at me and then asked almost too casually, "Have you been seeing anyone lately? Any hot new prospects?"

"No." I busied myself by grabbing some seltzer water from the refrigerator. I didn't even have to ask; I knew that's what Kaylie wanted to drink.

She sighed. "You've been avoiding the subject for a month now. Let's get it over with. It's time to rip off the bandaid."

"What's the point? It's over now. Besides, it would be awkward talking to you about your brother." I grabbed my plate of food and escaped to the table.

She followed behind me. "We're best friends! You literally picked me up off the sidewalk when I was at my lowest point and you helped me reconnect with Sidney when I was being stupid. The least I can do is listen to you. Besides, you had sex with my husband and my brother. In fact, I heard you were actually married to Bash. So, we're pretty much related."

Shit, she sounded so blasé about it, but was she still upset about me sleeping with Sid? "You promised you would never hold that against me. It happened so long ago."

She had a twinkle of amusement in her eye. "Let's just say I hope that incident has faded from his memory."

"I can hardly even remember what his dick looks like anymore. Except for that little—"

She threw her napkin at me. "Don't use the word little when talking about my husband's dick. There's nothing little about it."

A genuine burst of laughter escaped my lips, and it felt good. "I may have had sex with him, but I've never made love with him." I snickered.

Her nose wrinkled. "It's creepy the way you say it. Made love."

It was fun talking about sex with her. Two years ago, she would have fainted at the mere mention of the word. "At least he never made me squirt."

"Lacey! Oh my God!" Her gaping mouth snapped closed, and then she laughed. "How about Bash? Was my brother good in the sack?"

Our joking banter came to a halt. "You really want to hear about sex with Bash?"

She thought for a moment while she chewed her food. "Not particularly. You know what's funny? I feel like the four of us — me and you, and Sid and Bash — have come full circle. They're best friends. We're best friends. We've all seen each other naked. Except for Bash and I, because that's barf-able."

I chuckled. "Shit, I'd almost forgotten that you saw me with that nipple jewelry on. Thanks for reminding me of that trauma."

"We're even now." She swirled her fork in the air. "You saw my sex tape."

I scoffed. "It was hardly a sex tape. You make it sound like it was some hard-core pornography. I've seen racier stuff in a PG-13 movie."

After Kaylie had come to terms with her revenge porn situation, I'd had to sit down with her and show her all the amateur porn that was available for free on the internet. It was an eye-opening experience for her to see what people willingly put online for the whole world to see. It helped her put her own bout with internet infamy into a better perspective.

She set down her fork. "Don't try to distract me. We were talking about Bash. My husband told me that you two got married in Vegas. I'm a little hurt that you didn't tell me."

I guess Bash had spilled the beans on our wedding. "I'm sorry. We both agreed to keep it a secret and just quietly get a divorce. Then we started this friends-with-benefits thing that kind of got out of control. After a few months of that, we decided to try exclusively dating, and it was going really well until it completely blew up in my face."

"Now we're getting somewhere. There's one thing that I have to know. Are you interested in trying to work things out with him? Or have you washed your hands clean of the whole thing?"

My heart started hammering in my chest. "Work things out? Kaylie, he's had four weeks to talk to me. To apologize or make things right. He's done none of that. You realize that he dumped me, right?"

She shook her head in dismay. "God, he's so stupid. He's been a complete wreck ever since. He told the guys that he loves you, Lacey. If you tell me you're done with him, I'd understand and I'd back off right away. But, if you still have feelings for him..."

"I do have feelings for him. Most of the time, it involves me wanting to kick him in the nuts." I dropped my fork on my plate and sat back. "We had huge problems, Kaylie. He thinks I'm irresponsible and blames me for what happened to Kody. I take some responsibility for that, but he said some nasty things to me. The bottom line is he doesn't trust me. It doesn't seem like a great foundation for a relationship."

"He wants to talk to you, Lacey. Don't be angry with me, but I think it's a good idea." She spread out her hands in front of her. "You need to discuss what happened now that he's removed from all the scary emotions that Kody being hurt churned up."

I was wringing my hands together on my lap. Did I really want to churn all that up again? "I don't know if I could handle another rejection like that. I barely got over what he said to me last time. If I didn't have work, I would probably have crawled up into a hole somewhere and broken down."

"If you don't talk to him, I have a feeling he's going to do something drastic," she confided.

"What do you mean?"

She took a quick breath and blew it out. "Well, Bash confessed everything to all the guys in the band. They all know that you got married in Vegas."

I held up a hand to stop her. "Did they all have a good laugh? At my expense?"

"What? No. They smacked Bash upside his head for completely screwing it all up. And then they came up with a plan to win you back."

I groaned, but I couldn't deny that little spark of hope that lit when I heard that he wanted to win me back. "What kind of plan?"

"It was an incredibly dumb and elaborate plan. Those five geniuses decided Bash needed to perform a grand gesture, like in the movies. It included a hot-air balloon, a boom box, a flash mob, and a pair of handcuffs. I stopped him just in time. Trust me, you did not want any part of that train wreck."

"Why stop him? You should have let him grovel."

I was trying to act aloof, but she saw right through me. "Because that's not what you two need. You need to sit down and work out your issues. You need to lay it all out there. I know my brother. He loves you, Lacey. He's scared of those feelings, but not anymore. I think you should give him a chance. And I've seen you this past month. You two are meant to be together. He's grown up a lot in the last six months. Even more this past month. I'm not going to say anything else. He needs to be telling you this."

"He actually told you he loves me? Is it even possible?" I wanted to dismiss it, but hope foolishly bloomed inside me.

"It's easier to see from the outside. Yeah, I believe he does love you." She grabbed my hand with hers. "Is there any chance that you'll talk to him? I mean, really sit down and talk. No games. No friends-with-benefits nonsense. Just truth."

I drew in a deep breath and closed my eyes. "I barely got over what he said to me. He said some ugly, hurtful things. He nearly shattered me."

"I know." She squeezed my hand. "It wouldn't hurt so much if you didn't love him. It's worth the risk."

I nodded.

"He's waiting to talk to you."

Now, my heart was threatening to beat right out of my chest. "Right now?"

"Yep."

"But..." Was I ready for this?

She pulled out her phone. "Can I tell him to come up?"

Chapter 35

Bash

More than a month had passed since I walked away from Lacey. Doing it had hurt like hell, but I'd been so sure that I was doing the right thing. I smothered that immense pain because I told myself it was in Kody's best interest. Playing the martyr and using Kody's accident as the excuse to end our relationship fell apart pretty quickly. Besides being a shit thing to do, accusing Lacey of not watching Kody closely enough and blaming her for the accident never seemed reasonable.

What I had to figure out was why I did that. I painted her in a negative light, assuming she wasn't serious about Kody and me, that our relationship was based entirely on sex. I worried that she wasn't capable of being faithful or sustaining something deeper.

It was harder to realize I was subconsciously doing this and even harder to figure out why. For a guy who rarely thought past the surface,

I had a lot of deep, dark digging to do. I needed to strip away all the layers of protection I'd built up — layers that only served to insulate me from the truth.

My epiphany came when I was talking to Ghost. He was trying to give me advice while we were smoking a joint. Somehow, he went off track and started talking about Greyson and Remi. For a guy who never used to talk much, he certainly turned a page. Now, he was practically a relationship counselor.

I was half-zoned out and only partially listening to him. Something he said triggered a light-bulb moment. My criticisms of Lacey were classic projection. I cast her as the villain who wasn't capable of being in a relationship when it was me all along. I'd projected my fears and weaknesses about myself onto her.

Even blaming Lacey for not watching Kody closely enough was one of my own fears. How often had I caught Kody standing on top of that same table before I'd shooed him down? Kids got hurt. The parent's job was to set up guide rails, but not completely bubble-wrap their lives until an essential spark of life was smothered.

Instead of acknowledging my own shortcomings, I'd projected them onto Lacey and sabotaged our relationship. It took just about as much introspection as I possessed to figure this all out, but from there, it all fell into place for me.

The love I felt for her was undeniable. My awareness of it had been gradually growing over the last few months, but until now, I hadn't been able to accept it. There was no questioning it anymore.

Now, how the hell was I going to make her understand my life-changing epiphany, because when I thought about how I reacted from her perspective, I really came up short. It had taken me a month to figure it all out, and now I had one chance to explain it all to her. I was a simple man and not very good at expressing my emotions with words.

That's why my bandmate's plan seemed perfect. Was it kind of crazy? Yes. But I needed to do something big to show her just how serious I was about us. As a grand gesture, I felt it was pretty solid. I wasn't sure my bumbling words would cut it.

Kaylie was a woman, and she was Lacey's best friend. She'd cautioned me that the guys' plan to win her back was not going to work. She said I could romance Lacey all I wanted after I had an honest discussion with her.

When I got the all-clear from Kaylie, I headed up to Lacey's apartment. I hadn't seen or spoken to her in over a month and I missed her like crazy, but it felt like a brick was sitting in my stomach.

I was walking into the proverbial lion's den, armed only with the truth. Most of the truth was ugly: my weaknesses, my missteps, my inadequacies. Somehow, I had to convince her to overlook all of that and focus on the most important truth — that I loved her.

I didn't have a bouquet of roses in my hand. I didn't have diamond jewelry. There were no romantic trips to whisk her off to. No gimmicky gestures. I didn't buy out an entire restaurant for a romantic dinner. There were no giant flashcards to hold up to profess my love. No Jumbotron marriage proposal. And no yacht rental, as suggested by Sid.

It was just me, and I felt a little empty-handed. Kaylie better not be wrong or I'd kick her ass.

I stepped into her apartment. She wasn't there to greet me, so I wandered inside. She was sitting on a chair in front of the large windows, looking at her phone.

"Hey," I said softly. Seeing her again, after so long, had butterflies dancing in my stomach.

She looked up. "Hey."

The silence grew deafening, and I realized I needed to say something. "If you give me the rest of time, I'll show you every day how much I love you."

Her lips pinched together with disgust. "How long did it take you to Google that one?"

Ten seconds in and I'd blown it. "Fuck. I knew it! I should have gone with the first plan. Talking through my feelings was never going to work for me. I'm shit at it."

She rolled her eyes. "Bash, what are you doing?"

I took a few steps closer to her, so we weren't separated by miles. "It took me a while, but I figured out some shit. Not just that I love you — like I mean, I really love you — but I figured out a lot of my issues. My issues. I put them all on you because I was scared. Please forgive me, Lacey. I pushed you away when all I really wanted to do was wrap my arms around you and never let you go."

She blinked a few times. "Let me refresh your memory, Bash. You accused me of, let me see, being so bored when I was watching Kody that I invited another man to your house, presumably because we were fucking behind your back and I wasn't paying any attention to Kody, so I was to blame for his accident. Did I get that right? I'm unfit to be around children, selfish, irresponsible, a liar, and an unfaithful whore. Did that cover it? Or was there more?"

"Oh, God." I was such an asshole. "I didn't mean it like that. I was scared—"

Her cheeks burned red and her voice rose. "You thought the moment your back was turned that I snuck some guy into your house? With Kody there? Does that make any sense? Do you think so little of me?"

"No. It sounds really, really dumb."

She threw up her hands in disgust. "I don't even get it, Bash. Where the fuck did you get that idea? I haven't been with another man since Vegas. I never gave you any reasons to doubt me."

We needed to get this all out in the open, but it was going to be painful to admit how horrible I was. "It was my neighbor. She came over after the accident and told me she saw you talking to some suspicious-looking guy right before Kody's accident. He even parked down the street. When she described him — he sounded just like that Liam guy from the pier."

Her brow creased. "The security guy? I talked to him for about two minutes. Some guy rang the doorbell, trying to sell home security systems because there were some burglaries in the neighborhood. You thought that was Liam?"

Fuck. Fuck. Fuck. "No. Yes. I don't know. I was insecure about that guy, Liam. He seemed really familiar with you and you were pretty evasive about who he was. I don't know, Lacey. I was jealous! I've never felt that way before and then Mrs. Travis told me you were with some guy that you never mentioned after the accident."

She shook her head. "That just proves how little you trust me."

I took a seat near hers, my chair slightly turned in her direction. "Look, I don't blame you for Kody's accident. Before it ever happened, I caught him standing up on that table several times. Under my own supervision. And I understand that throwing the blame on you was a horrible thing to do. I used his accident as an excuse to throw everything away because I was so scared of what was happening between us. Even though I wanted it so badly, I was too scared to admit it to myself. I knew that you were too good for me. It was a weird protective mechanism."

She sighed softly. "That's a very convoluted explanation."

I rested my head in my hands. "I know. It makes much more sense in my head."

She shook her head bitterly. "I just don't get it. Everything was going so well. I thought you were happy with us?"

Glancing up, I looked her directly in the eyes. "I was insanely happy when we were together. And I don't mean just the sex, but when we spent time together. But I was insecure about our time apart. I wasn't sure why you were even with me. You've got it all together. I'm a suburban dad. Why would you bother with me — outside of the fantastic sex? What did I have to offer?"

"Bash, that's just insane—"

I wanted to get it all out there. "I fell in love with you, Lacey. That's something I've never felt before. And you kept reminding me it was just friends-with-benefits, but I wanted so much more. I tried to express my feelings for you, in my own shit way. I just didn't do a very good job of it. Talking about my emotions isn't exactly my best skill, as you can see."

Lacey stood up and walked over to the window, and peered out at the city.

I groaned softly. "My grand gesture is turning into a grand flop."

She turned to me with a half-smile. "I heard there was going to be a flash mob?"

"Kaylie told you?"

She turned her back to the window. "Vaguely."

I pulled out my phone. "Would that work? I'd have a flash mob out on the street in front of this building in five minutes flat if you told me that would give me another chance."

She shook her head, and we both lapsed into silence for a few minutes.

"We were both pretty terrible at communicating. I held back some things, too," she admitted.

"Like what?"

She crossed back to her chair and sat with her body facing me. "How I felt about us, what I wanted for the future, my past relationship with Liam."

"Is there any hope for us?" My gaze implored her to tell me that there was still a chance for us.

"I don't know," was her soft reply.

Desperation crept in, so I decided to lay it all on the line. "I love you, Lacey. I want to be with you. I'll do whatever you want if you give me another chance. We can take it slow. Start at square one. We can date. No sex if you're not ready. Last time we did it all wrong. We started off married, then we went to sex, and then to dating. This time we'll do it right. We can start dating and work our way up to sex and then maybe someday marriage and kids."

Her eyes widened, and her eyebrows rose, clearly surprised at my words. "That's what you want?"

"I want a future together. Exclusive partners, out in the open, so all our friends know we are together. I want to build honesty and trust. I want what I've wanted from the moment we got married. To be with you forever. By my side. When you're ready, I want you to live with me and Kody and be our family. And then to add on to that family. I don't want to do the weekend thing. I want you to move in with me. God, I want it all, Lacey."

We ended up talking the entire night. I meant what I said; I'd do whatever I needed to win her back. We talked, and we cried — I swear, it was mostly her tearing up — and we made promises.

The grand gesture was pretty low-key, but it worked. I got my girl back, and we were a hundred times stronger than before. Living life secure in each other's love was worth all the angst we had to go through to get there.

That's not to say that there weren't going to be plenty of flash mobs, yachts, diamonds, roses, and hopefully a jumbotron in her future. The giant flash cards were definitely way too cheesy.

Chapter 36

Lacey

Bash called the big bed perched on the top floor of the treehouse cabin, our nest. If he could keep me in the nest for the entire four days that we were here, he would. The circular room was surrounded by windows on all sides and was sparse in furniture and decor except for the bed. At night, we could see some stars peeking through the leafy canopy through the domed skylight.

In the morning, the birds woke before dawn and started their morning chorus. For a city girl, I was less than thrilled with the surprisingly loud wake-up call. Sitting on the deck during the day and listening to their song was peaceful. At 4 a.m., the chorus was deafening.

This morning, I'd eventually fallen back to sleep, but now nature was calling. Unfortunately, the bathroom was down a spiral staircase on the main floor. I delayed as long as I could before having to get up. Bash mumbled an objection to me leaving the nest, but he was exhausted, so he didn't put up much of a fight. We'd had so much sex in the last 48 hours, I was surprised either of us was still functioning.

It was the perfect morning to grab a cup of coffee and sit on the deck, so I started the coffeemaker before tending to my business. When that was completed, I fixed a coffee for Bash and myself and then headed out onto the wraparound deck.

Holes were cut into the flooring of the deck in three spots, where tree trunks passed right through. A hammock that was tied between two of the trees was gently flapping in the breeze.

The main treehouse structure was elevated from the ground, with the bedroom rising about 18 feet into the trees. From a distance, the treehouse looked like a mini castle — it was tall and skinny with an odd turret-like extension. The circular bedroom was tucked behind the structure and looked a bit like a UFO landing on top. It was an odd sight, but the inside was lavishly appointed. It was the perfect hideaway.

I sat back to enjoy the morning. The breeze had picked up some and some gray clouds were rolling in. The birds that I had cursed quite creatively in my head hours ago were silent.

As I knew he would, Bash joined me on the deck a few minutes later. He had thrown on a pair of sweatpants but didn't bother with a shirt. It was a treat for my eyes, but I shivered looking at him. Even in late spring, it was still chilly in the morning hours.

"Morning." He kissed the top of my head and then sunk into the outdoor loveseat beside me. "Looks like a storm is rolling in."

Just then, we heard a distant rumble of thunder. I grabbed my phone off the table. It felt like we were in the middle of nowhere, but in reality, we weren't too far off the beaten track. Civilization was close by. I opened my weather app. "Thunderstorm. Looks like it'll be raining in about 15 minutes."

Bash took a sip of his coffee. "Looks like we're going to have to skip that hike."

We'd promised each other that today we'd leave the nest and hike out to see the waterfall that was supposedly a 30-minute hike away. "Hmmm. I guess we're stuck inside."

A smile teased his lips. "What are we going to do?"

I waved my phone at him. "I could read that new time-traveling romance novel I've been meaning to get to."

Bash pushed his bottom lip out in a pout, but then quickly recovered his mischievous grin. "How about you download the audiobook, and we can listen to it while I tie you to the bed — naked and spread-eagled — and do all sorts of wicked things to you?"

A pulse of longing throbbed between my legs. I couldn't resist him. He knew exactly how to get me going. "Sweeten the pot a little, and it's a possibility."

He laughed. "You are so perfect. How soon can we be married again? I miss my wifey."

Bash hadn't called me wifey since our divorce and I missed it. "Uh, we just got divorced two months ago."

He gathered me in his arms and pulled me onto his lap. "But I want to be wifed up as soon as possible. Maybe I could put a baby in you today. What are we waiting for? Let's ditch the condoms. I think we just about went through the entire box, anyway."

I inhaled a shaky breath. The last two months had been incredible. We were dating and, more importantly, we were communicating. We'd gone straight back to having sex because I saw no need to deprive either of us of something so good, and I had unofficially moved into Bash's house with him. We weren't keeping any secrets anymore, to ourselves or to our friends and family.

A roll of thunder bounced along the clouds.

HOW TO MARRY A ROCKSTAR

"Let's elope." I said it out loud.

Bash looked stunned. "Right now?"

I bit my lip. "Maybe?"

He was staring at me like he was trying to read my mind. "You wouldn't miss all the bells and whistles like at Kaylie's wedding?"

I thought for a moment. In a way, I would miss some of it, but eloping seemed much more our style. We could always have a big party later. "No. I have a dream wedding gown, but I could do without all the rest. Including the hassle of planning it."

Bash looked off into the distance as a louder clap of thunder rumbled overhead. "How about this: you order your dream gown, or whatever you have to do, and let me know when you get it. Then, be prepared to elope to Vegas with me."

I brushed my lips against his. "That sounds like a very good plan."

A few fat drops of rain began to fall. I scrambled to get off his lap. The sky was about to open up. I was about to scurry inside when Bash wrapped his arms around my waist and stopped me.

I smacked his arm. "Hurry, Bash, we have to get inside or we're going to get drenched."

He tightened his hold on me. "I believe you just agreed to be my wife."

Lightning streaked through the sky and the rain began to fall harder.

"I did."

He pulled me tight against his body and weaved his hand into the hair at the nape of my neck. "I believe we have a book about time traveling to listen to."

The intensity in his eyes had my insides firing up. "We do. Did you bring the bondage rope?"

His eyes were smoldering now. "I did."

The sky opened up, and the rain turned into a heavy downpour.

I blinked against the water dripping off my eyelashes. "Bash, I'm getting wet."

"That's what I'm counting on, wifey."

His lips descended on mine for a kiss in the middle of the crazy storm that was lashing the trees and lighting up the sky all around us.

♫♫♪♪

It was a beautiful weekend in June when we decided to elope. We decided at the very last minute, so we dropped Kody off at Bash's parent's house, then hopped into my Mercedes to drive to Las Vegas. We stayed the night at The Venetian bringing back all the memories from our first wedding — not that I remembered the actual ceremony.

We ordered the same exact wedding package we'd ordered the first time. A limousine chauffeured us to the Las Vegas Marriage License Bureau and waited until we had the completed paperwork. Then, it took us to the Amore Mio Wedding Chapel, where I was allowed to get ready in a little dressing room while Bash waited outside.

I slipped into my dream wedding dress, a strapless white ball gown with a sweetheart neckline. The bodice was adorned with intricate beading and pearls, and the skirt had a beautiful tulle overlay that fell gracefully in delicate waves to the floor. The overall look was both classic and modern, timeless yet fashionable.

I peeked into the full-length mirror to see how I looked. I'd already had my hair and makeup done earlier at the hotel. The hairdresser had pulled the sides of my hair back in a twist and tucked them into a cluster of pink magnolia blossoms and left the rest of my hair hanging down my back in soft curls. I clipped the delicate chandelier earrings onto my ears and then stepped into my heels.

I grabbed the wedding bouquet that had been supplied by the venue, the one that was identical to the bouquet from my first wedding and took a deep breath. The bouquet was cheaper looking than the rest of my ensemble, but it held some nostalgia. Overall, I felt like a fairytale princess. I felt a pinch of regret that none of my friends or family would experience this day with me, but I pushed that aside. Brimming with excitement to be marrying Bash, I took a deep breath and stepped out of the room.

I gasped in surprise. Bash was waiting for me, wearing a tuxedo. He looked stunning. "A tuxedo! You look—"

He stopped me and reached for my hand. "You are so gorgeous. I was so impatient to get married, but it was absolutely worth the extra weeks of wait to see you in this gown."

He twirled me around slowly and whistled softly. "Damn, this ceremony better be quick. I don't know how long I can keep my hands off you."

"Judging from the video of our first wedding, it'll be over really quick," I responded dryly.

He tilted his head but didn't comment. "C'mon, let's go get this over with. Let's go find Elvis."

We took selfies while we waited for the couple before us to say their vows, and then suddenly it was our turn.

We walked up to the lectern in the room that looked like it came straight out of a VFW hall. Fake Elvis seemed drunk, but it was hard to tell with his giant sunglasses. He was wearing white bell-bottom pants with a matching blazer decked out with rhinestones. His oversized sideburns and pompadour were clearly a wig.

"Are we all ready, folks?" He asked in a surprising Australian accent.

I glanced at Bash and he simply nodded.

Elvis picked up his pen and then scratched out something on the paper resting on the lectern. "Sebastian and Lacey, is it?"

"Yeah, that's us."

"Let's go then, mates." He turned to address the dark-haired lady behind him. "All set, Priscilla?"

Priscilla rolled her eyes and then held up her cell phone. "Ready." I guess she was the videographer.

Elvis turned back to us and then cleared his throat. He waited for a few beats and then began, his voice much huskier and deeper, now with a southern drawl. "Welcome, everyone. It's time to rock and roll."

He stepped out from behind the lectern and spread out his arms. "Turn to face each other and hold hands."

Bash and I held hands while Priscilla circled around us, holding up the phone to record.

"Sebastian, are you ready to take Lacey to be your wife?"

Bash looked into my eyes. "I am."

Elvis fed Bash the lines and he repeated,

> "Lacey, Let Me Be Your Teddy Bear,
> With you, Any Place is Paradise,
> no more Suspicious Minds,
> You Belong to my Heart."

"Lacey, do you take Sebastian to be your husband?"

I squeezed Bash's hands. "I do."

Then it was my turn to repeat after him:

> "I promise to never step on your Blue Suede Shoes,

or leave you at the Heartbreak Hotel,
I Can't Help Falling in Love With You,
I promise to Love you Tender,
and never Return to Sender,
I'm just a hunk of Burning Love for you."

Well, that was cheesy, but I guess that's what you get from an Elvis impersonator.

Elvis did a weird leg shake. "Congratulations, you may kiss the bride!"

Bash pulled me in, but I turned away from his kiss. "Wait. We didn't say our special vows."

We both had memorized the vows we'd spoken at our first wedding, planning to use them at this ceremony.

Bash's brow creased. "It doesn't matter. What matters is that I know I love you and I'll remember this moment for the rest of my life."

"Yea-uh," Elvis agreed. He looked at his watch. "Time to kiss your bride."

I pulled back. "But you didn't even officially pronounce us man and wife."

Elvis burst out in fake laughter. "Sorry, honey. You must have gotten me All Shook Up. I pronounce you man and wife. Now, will you please kiss your bride? Time's a ticking."

Bash laid a scorching kiss on me and I soon forgot about the lackluster ceremony. We quickly signed some papers and were ushered out the door by Priscilla so the next couple could begin their ceremony.

We hopped into the waiting limo with Bash being extra careful not to wrinkle my dress.

He leaned back with a sparkle of amusement in his eyes. "Any regrets?"

Did I have any regrets? No, not of marrying Bash again. But, maybe we should have made a bigger deal about the wedding. We should have hired a real photographer. And a real videographer. And maybe it would have been nice for my friends and family to see me in this fabulous wedding dress. I knew our marriage meant a lot to Bash — even our first marriage meant something to him — but the wedding trappings obviously did not. But he was right. What was important was that we loved each other.

I looked down at my bare finger. "I wish we had thought to buy rings. It would be nice if we were wearing them right now."

He smacked his forehead. "Shit, that was stupid. We'll pick some out tomorrow. There's a nice jewelry store at the hotel."

He looked upset, so I tried to lighten the mood a bit by adding in a teasing manner, "Don't tell anyone, but I might regret the Elvis part. The little lady officiant from our first wedding was better — at least for the part that got recorded."

"Who knew Elvis was Australian? Come here, wifey. I need another kiss."

Bash leaned in to kiss me, but I was looking out the window. "Where are we going? We're heading away from the hotel."

"Oh, I forgot," Bash said offhandedly. "The deluxe package included a free luncheon. It's probably not the fanciest meal, but we might as well eat. I've worked up an appetite and we'll need our energy later for our wedding night."

The quality of any luncheon that was provided by the Amore Mio Wedding Chapel was suspect. "Let's just go back to the Venetian and eat there."

Bash looked at me like he was about to pounce on me. "If we go back to The Venetian, I'm going to drag you back to our room and strip you out of that gown and keep you there for days. Let's eat first.

Plus, I want to show off my new bride in her wedding gown. You look so incredible, Lacey."

"Okay." My wedding day was a bit underwhelming, but I was married to the man that I loved so desperately. My big news would have to wait. I had big, fat, exciting news, and I was bursting to tell him. I'd made it this far; I guess I could handle a mediocre lunch, and then maybe I'd be the one dragging him back to the hotel room. He looked absolutely delicious in that tuxedo. I had some plans for him and that tux was not going to come off until he'd delivered several orgasms.

We left The Strip and arrived at the restaurant somewhere in the Vegas suburbs, about twenty minutes later. I was surprised by how lovely it looked. Flowers overflowed giant cement containers near the entrance and the inside was tastefully and elegantly decorated.

I smiled with relief. "This place is beautiful. Maybe we'll get a nice meal after all?"

His hands cupped my cheeks, and he laid a gentle kiss on my lips. "I will see you soon, gorgeous."

"What?" Someone grabbed my elbow from behind and I spun around to confront them.

It was Kaylie.

Kaylie?

She was dressed in a beautiful gown of cerulean blue and holding a luscious, cascading bouquet of flowers.

"Kaylie? What are you doing here?"

"I'm here to help get you ready for your wedding. That's what a matron of honor is for. Let's go. We don't have much time, and your lipstick is a mess." She tugged on my hand.

Stunned, I turned back to Bash to find out what was going on. He was gone.

Kaylie led me back to the room where the bridal party was getting ready. I stepped into a sea of beautiful women wearing blue.

Talia handed me a glass of champagne. "Drink this. It looks like you could use it."

I took a very tiny sip, looking around the room with wide eyes. "How are you all here?"

The girls went to work getting me ready. After a whirlwind of activity, twenty minutes later, we were lined up outside the closed double doors waiting to start the procession.

The groomsmen arrived and found their partners. The ring bearer and flower girl were given last-minute instructions. My mother appeared at my side and gave me air kisses. I was too stunned to say much when she congratulated me warmly. Then her new husband, Henri, escorted her to her seat.

Sid gave Kaylie a kiss. "You look beautiful, Kay. It's time for me to go stand by Bash's side." He turned to me and gave me a wink before he headed inside.

The music changed, and then the procession began. First, Knox escorted Summer down the aisle. Then, Ryder and Talia, followed by Ghost and Remi. The last couple to walk down was my cousin, Sadie, escorted by Bash's brother, Brent.

As matron of honor, Kaylie had the honor of walking down the aisle solo. She checked me over one last time, gave me air kisses, and then handed over my gorgeous bouquet. Finally, it was time for the ring bearer, Kody, to walk little Zoe, Ryder and Talia's daughter, down the aisle, holding the pillow with the fake rings and the tiny basket of rose petals. With a bit of nudging from me, Kody took Zoe's hand, and they slowly proceeded down the aisle. It took a long time. They would take one step, then Kody would pull out a single rose petal from the basket and hand it to Zoe, who would toss it on the ground. I was peeking from behind the doors as they repeated this process all the way down the aisle. The processional song had to be played three times.

I stepped back and straightened out my dress.

"Lacey."

I spun around. "Dad!"

He looked amused. "Were you expecting someone else?"

My eyes began tearing up. "Mother's here, too."

"Of course she is." He smiled like it was no big deal. "I've already spoken with her. And I've met On-Ree, too. Poor chap."

I laughed. "Thank you for coming, Dad. Even if I didn't even know about all this."

He locked my arm in his. "You've got a wonderful man in Bash. He'll make a great husband. And he's one lucky bastard, that I know. Now, let's get this thing done before you start blubbering."

He knew me so well. The music changed, someone opened the doors from the inside, and I began my walk down the aisle and into a new life.

Most of the ceremony was a blur, but there was a professional videographer capturing everything, so I'd have another wedding video to remind me.

I repeated the vows that I'd made at our first wedding.

> Sebastian,
> I give you my hand and my heart,
> and pledge my love, devotion, faith,
> and honor as I join my life to yours.
> I promise to always be spontaneous
> and to cherish each moment,
> to be willing to try new things,
> to dream with you, to laugh together,
> to be your biggest fan,

> and to encourage you to chase your dreams.
> And I promise to be your accomplice
> in all kinds of mischief till the end of time.

I hadn't watched our old wedding video again, so hearing Sebastian repeating the words he'd told me that crazy night put a lump in my throat.

> I choose you,
> Lacey Rae Davenport,
> to be my partner for life
> and my one true love.
> I promise you my deepest love,
> my fullest devotion, my tenderest care
> through the pressures of the present
> and the uncertainties of the future.
> I promise to be faithful to you.
> I promise to love you,
> to commit to you
> and support you.
> I pledge to respect your unique talents and abilities,
> and to lend you strength for all of
> your dreams.
> And most importantly,
> I promise to always keep you
> deeply and thoroughly satisfied.

The words that had embarrassed me so deeply less than a year ago were perfect. Sidney pulled the wedding rings from his pocket and then we did the ring exchange. I couldn't stop glancing at that powerful symbol of our commitment on my finger. After the ceremonial kiss to seal the marriage, which wasn't as racy as our first, first kiss but definitely not chaste, Kody joined us and we walked back down the aisle as husband and wife.

The reception was fantastic. How could it not be with all of Ghost Parker in attendance? I never wanted it to end. One by one, the couples in the wedding party made fun entrances to the reception as they were announced. Bash and his mom did some crazy mother-son dance with choreographed moves to a medley of songs. My dad made a wonderful speech that had me tearing up again. Not to be outdone, the boys of Ghost Parker did a rehearsed dance routine together that had everyone cheering and laughing.

My surprise wedding was perfect. I knew at that moment that I was the luckiest woman alive.

Later that night, after we made sure our second marriage was thoroughly consummated, I knew it was time to let him in on my little secret. I rolled over to face him and took a deep breath.

"Bash, our wedding was amazing. I have no idea how you pulled it off, but it was the absolute best surprise of my life. But I think I have an even bigger one for you."

He was silent for a few moments, and then he kissed me. "Okay, I'm ready. Hit me."

"Kody's going to be a big brother."

Bash stared at me for a few seconds, his face a mix of surprise and joy. When he finally spoke, his voice was almost a whisper.

"You're pregnant?"

I nodded and his thumb swiped away a tear of joy that escaped the corner of my eye.

"Fuck, wifey," his voice trembled. "Are you serious?"

I laughed shakily. "Yes."

His eyes misted over with tears, and then he gathered me in his arms. I felt the warmth of his embrace as he held me tight.

"We're having a baby," he said, his voice filled with awe.

"We are," I confirmed, my heart overflowing with love.

Epilogue

Bash

SID AND I SAUNTERED into the practice space, laughing at a dumb joke, but instead of the guys riffing on their guitars, everyone was sitting around with glum expressions on their faces.

Ghost stood up. "Instead of practice today, I wanted to have a meeting."

I immediately sobered. I felt the ominous weight of change pressing down on me.

Sid and I exchanged troubled looks before we pulled the rickety chair and remaining stool up to the couch that Knox and Ryder were hogging.

No one looked happy, and I had the unsettling feeling that we were staring down the barrel at the end of Ghost Parker.

An ache exploded in my chest. It was the end of a really fucking good time. We'd had a tremendous run. We'd all grown since the five young men who'd come together and known next to nothing about the music business. We weren't the same guys who partied like it was our last night on earth and fucked anything that moved.

Against the odds, we'd made it big. None of us needed the money any longer. Individually, our needs and goals had changed. We all had our own families now, which were even more important than touring with the band. We each had to fulfill our own dreams and do what made us happy.

I understood it. Hell, Lacey was pregnant, and I'd been questioning how I could make it all work for myself. Still, it hurt. The reality of Ghost Parker breaking up felt like a body blow.

Ghost started off hesitantly, "We're obligated to do one more album for BVR. I'd like to start working on it. There's no rush from the label, but I'd like to get it out of the way. I'd like for all five of us to collaborate on it, from start to finish. I'm up for recording anything. All top 40 hits. We could get Sid to write some more bubble gum pop. Make some bank with the catchy tunes. Do a modified tour. Finish up our obligations and go on hiatus for a while."

Knox ran his hand through his hair. "You're talking about the end of Ghost Parker?"

I wasn't surprised. I knew that Ghost wanted to do something different with the music. I saw it coming. We all did. I was more surprised that I wasn't quite ready to let it go.

"Not the end." Ghost sat on his stool and his leg began bouncing. "A hiatus. A year. Maybe two where we could each explore some other projects."

Ryder picked at a ragged thread on his jeans. "We won't be signed again so easily if we drop out for two years."

The words started coming out of my mouth before I could stop them. "I'm thinking of starting a boutique label with music that I want to produce. It's been on my mind for a while. I'm going to build a studio in my pool house. It won't be as elaborate as Beaufort's, but it'd be enough for unknown talent just starting out. Maybe I could produce some of that weird shit that you're dying to write, Ghost?"

Ghost looked at me with surprise. "Fuck, Bash. You should do that."

Ryder looked around the room. "I could use a break. Maybe fool around a bit with a different band for a year or two. But I don't want to lose you guys."

The intensity in Ghost's eyes was crazy. "Ghost Parker will be forever. No matter what; it's the five of us."

I felt a lump of sadness forming in my throat. It was happening. We weren't ending today, but our days were numbered.

"The twins are wearing me down," Sid spoke up from next to me. "Kay and I are trying to get pregnant again and we're applying to be foster parents. It's a lot, man. Touring is going to be rough."

Knox tapped the side of the couch. "I'll keep playing no matter what, but it's time that I wifed up Summer. I want to take her to Scotland to meet my family before she's too far along to travel."

Ghost nodded as he studied each of us. "Let's vow to always stick together, no matter what life brings. Even if the band's not actively together for a few years, let's stay in each other's lives."

We all nodded our agreement and Ryder added, "I don't think the girls will let us drift apart."

It was true, our wives and girlfriends had all become great friends with us and to each other. We were a pretty tight group, so even if we drifted apart musically, it didn't have to mean the end of our friendship.

"Remi's pregnant."

Ghost dropped that bomb into the room, but he was the one that looked shell-shocked.

We all congratulated him, but I could see how shaken up he was about it.

Ghost stood up and picked up his guitar and began strumming some chords. "I'm fucking excited. But I'm freaking out. I'm not sure I'm father material. My dad was a piece of shit, so I didn't have a good role model. But Remi is going to be a great mom, and I've never seen Greyson so excited."

Sid stood up and walked over to Ghost. "Man, everyone is nervous as fuck when they find out they're going to be a father. It's a tiny little person that you're completely responsible for. But, shit, there were never two more unprepared people in the world to be a father to a child than Bash and me when Kody came along. If we could do it, trust me, you'll be fine. Especially with Remi and Grey helping."

Ghost closed his eyes. "I felt myself pulling away from them, thinking I'm not good enough, but they won't let me. Talking to my therapist about it helps."

I stood to add my support to Sidney. "I know your father was a fucking bastard, but you're nothing like him. You don't have one selfish bone in your body, Ghost. You can't even imagine right now the enormous amount of love you're going to have for that baby. You'll be a great dad and you'll have all of us standing behind you and supporting you."

Ghost put down his guitar and hugged me. Sid joined in and then suddenly, all five of us were in a huddle. Ghost, our leader, gave us an inspirational pep talk just like he'd done countless times before when we jogged out onto the stage in front of thousands of fans.

"Ghost Parker still has a lot of gas left in the tank. This isn't the end of us. Just a new chapter. Ride or die, brothers."

"Ride or die," we all confirmed.

HOW TO MARRY A ROCKSTAR

7 years later...

It turns out that Kody is not going to be a drummer like me. He's crazy smart in math and likes robots. His playtime went from playing with cars as a kid to constructing his own complex Lego models and then on to robotics sets. Currently, he was obsessed with computer coding. I didn't understand any of it.

Delilah is a little spitfire like Lacey and she was most definitely Daddy's little girl. It turned out that she may be our little drummer. Ever since she started crawling, she'd crawl over to me while I was drumming, demanding to sit on my lap. She would rest her tiny hands on my forearms while I played. I had to play slowly and modify my movements, but I loved spending time drumming with her. I got her a tambourine, and she'd march around the room playing it while I drummed. Now, at not quite seven years old, she excelled at drum lessons and I could see the passion in her eyes when she played. I wasn't sure how I would ever handle it if she chose to drum in a rock band like me, knowing the lifestyle that would bring with it, but I knew I could never stifle her passion. Luckily, I had a few more years to figure that all out.

Then there was Jack, our four-year-old whirlwind of energy. He kept us all on our toes with his strong will and his gift of persuasion, even at his young age. He'd make a skilled politician or lawyer someday.

My boutique record label, which I ran with Sid and Lacey, was doing well. A year after we were married, Lacey resigned from Castle

Music to help me secure my dream. Without her, it never would have happened. She was managing the business side and scouting the talent while Sid and I produced the music.

We'd recorded two albums for Ghost, which weren't commercial successes, but important artistic contributions to the music world. Ghost had a hardcore fanbase for his work and he was already exploring ideas for his next album. After years of back and forth with Candace Collins, Lacey finally reined her in. Our little label was able to help her reach her potential, and it resulted in our first commercial success with her album. It put us on the map and enabled us to give more unknown artists a chance. We weren't in it for the money. It was more important that we loved what we were doing.

Our house was overflowing with three active kids and a dog, our black and white beagle, Smoopy. I can't believe how much my life had changed and how much for the better. My heart had expanded so much, sometimes I was afraid it might burst. I loved my family fiercely. I often thought about knocking up my wifey again. She said she was getting too old to have kids, but there was a definite gleam in her eye when I suggested it.

My best friend, Sidney, and my sister, Kaylie, bought a house across the street from us. The cousins went to the same school and spent so much time together. They were cousins, but they loved and fought like siblings. Brady and Emerson were 8 years old and their daughter, Aria, was six. They had two foster kids, Luca and Owen. Luca was placed with them when he was 6 years old and a year later, they officially adopted him. They were still in the process of adopting Owen, who was now five years old. I knew Sid, and I was pretty sure that Owen wouldn't be the last foster kid to join their family.

Besides recording some new stuff, Ghost had participated in a few acting stints on a lark. The roles that Greyson had helped him land were minor, but he had a definite presence on the screen. Grey finally got killed off *Devious* and was trying to break into a movie career. It wasn't easy, but he'd landed some roles. Besides juggling three kids, Emma, 7, Colt, 5, and Maya, 4, Remi was the author of a best-selling book. It was her third political spy thriller and will have more than one politician clenching their ass cheeks as they read the 'fiction'. The three of them made juggling their family, their careers, and their unique relationship look easy.

Ryder was a success in his new band. He was the frontman and had his own huge following. To his chagrin, the most requested song they got at shows was for the cover of *Okay Babe*. He'll never get away from it. Talia had her own business as a personal shopper. I didn't know too much about it, but it was so successful that she had to hire people to help out. Zoe was almost 9 years old, and they had another daughter, Harper, who was six.

Some sad news for the Ghost Parker family was that Summer's mother passed away last year. Summer took it hard, so we all joined forces to help her get through it. Over the years, Knox jumped from band to band, always keeping busy. He helped collaborate on Ghost's albums, so for a while, four of the five of us were working together again. Knox's younger brother, Ian, moved to California a couple of years ago and we saw him often at gatherings.

The Ghost Parker family had exploded. What started out as five guys (or five manwhores making music, as Lacey liked to say) had grown to five guys with their six soul mates, 15 kids, 4 dogs, a few cats, a turtle, and even a weird chinchilla. We may not be sleeping a few feet away from each other's bunk anymore, but we were still as tight as ever. Ghost Parker wasn't going away anytime soon.

I ran back into the house to grab some more hamburgers and buns for the grill. Sadie's husband, Marius, was inside by himself, probably enjoying the air-conditioning and quiet.

"Hey, Bash." He looked a bit shell-shocked. "I don't know how you do it. Every time I come to one of these things, I go home and thank God that Sadie didn't want to have children. It's like a zoo out there."

I smiled. "You get used to it."

When I stepped back outside, it was pandemonium. Kids were running everywhere. Most of them were either shrieking, laughing, or shouting. Their parents were all keeping an eye on them, but there was no reining in the chaos. And I loved it. I wouldn't have it any other way.

I delivered the burger patties and buns to Sid, who was on grill duty, and then handed a cold beer to Lacey's dad. He was still the head of Castle Music, but he was remarried now and enjoyed spending as much time with his grandchildren as he could.

Lacey's mom was on her 5th husband. We didn't see her much, but she did manage to send cards and gifts for all of our birthdays. We recently saw her at Lacey's surprise 40th birthday party. Both mom and daughter had hated to be reminded of their age on that day, but we'd done the party up big and were looking forward to a slew of new 40th birthdays to celebrate. Lacey had vowed to get us all back.

I searched the crowd, looking for my wife. I finally spotted her chatting with Remi and Summer. She felt my gaze on her and looked up. Our eyes met across the wide expanse of our backyard. She said something to the girls who laughed and then she was heading my way with a secret smile on her lips.

"Come with me." She grabbed my hand and then led me back into our house and up the stairs to our bedroom.

My mind was already spinning with dirty thoughts. We didn't have a lot of time, but I was a fast worker. I pulled her into my arms and kissed her with an urgency that even surprised me. After all these years,

HOW TO MARRY A ROCKSTAR

she still got my motor racing. I was as hard as a rock in a few seconds.

She pulled her lips from mine, laughter dancing in her eyes. "Sebastian, there's an entire party going on in our backyard."

I grumbled a reply. "They won't even notice we're missing."

She patted my chest. "You're going to have to wait till later for that, but I can't wait any longer to tell you something. You know when I had to run out to the drugstore right before the party started?"

"Yeah." She hadn't even gotten back before the first guests started arriving. I figured it was an emergency run for girl supplies, so I didn't question it.

She pulled away from me and walked over to her nightstand. She opened the drawer and then took something out of it, hiding it behind her back. "Close your eyes and hold out your hand."

I shook my head but played along with her game. She placed something very light in my hand.

"Open your eyes."

I looked at the white plastic stick in my hands. I'd seen one of these before. It was a—

PREGNANT.

The digital word in the gray window was staring at me.

"Holy fuck!" I looked up at her, my mouth gaping open in shock.

"Surprise!" She tucked her hair behind her ear and laughed nervously.

The shock that had rooted me to the floor slowly wore off as happiness flooded in. I tossed the stick on the bed so I could pick her up and spin her around, all the while whooping like a madman.

I put her down and then placed my hands on her shoulders. "Are you okay with this, wifey?"

She wiped a tear from her eye. "I'm more than okay. I'm ecstatic, but a little nervous. Are you ready to do it all over again?"

"You mean the long nights, the interrupted sleep, the diaper disasters, not leaving the house without bags of baby supplies?" I asked.

"Ugh," she groaned. "It's going to be so hard."

I pulled her back into my arms. "It's going to be so amazing. I feel like I'm bursting. I want to run outside and announce it to everyone right now."

"Not yet, Sebastian. It's still really early."

I captured her lips with mine. "Okay, wifey. But tonight, we celebrate."

Ten minutes later, we were back at our party. Even though I only had a few beers for the rest of the night, I felt drunk. I was just in a state of pure happiness.

Donovan waved for me to come over. He was talking to the guys. Ever since Ghost Parker's last album and tour, he'd been working on getting us back together. He was married with two kids now, and he always reminded us that his kids needed a college fund.

He flashed something from his phone screen as I approached, but I wasn't paying much attention. "All the dates that we already announced sold out. I'm working on expanding the tour."

Shaking my head, I chuckled. I should have known that it wouldn't be the 'limited' and 'exclusive' reunion tour that he pitched us.

I looked around at each of my bandmates: Sidney, Ghost, Ryder, and Knox. "I'm so fucking stoked to be going on tour together again."

We huddled up.

Ghost looked at each of us. "Rehearsals start Monday. Be ready to shake off the rust. It sounds like our fans are ready for us, so let's give this our all. Ghost Parker is back."

It was the best motivational speech Ghost had ever given. And probably the only one that didn't include any curses. Maybe fatherhood had matured him.

Ryder threw in our chant. "Ride or die, brothers."

"Ride or die," we answered enthusiastically. Everyone was pumped up.

I already had so much to be thankful for and so much more to look forward to. My family was growing. Our reunion tour was sold out. Fuck, I was a lucky bastard.

This wasn't the end of Ghost Parker — it was a new beginning.

The End

Rock Me series

Before there was Ghost Parker...

Meet the hard-rocking boys of Cold Fusion: Alex, Tommy, Nick, and Tyler.

Rock Me series

Who doesn't love the tattooed bad boys of rock star romance? Get ready to toss your panties on stage — it's gonna get wild!

ROCK ME: WICKED

Lena never forgot...
Alex Lavigne would always be the one who got away. Now 10 years

later, Lena's dreams are haunted by x-rated fantasies starring the sexy hunk who has since become lead guitarist for the wildly popular band, Cold Fusion.

Alex's world is turned upside down...

When Lena reenters his life, she rocks his whole world. He'll do whatever it takes to hold onto her.

Together...

Their passions explode beyond their most wicked imaginings. But is that enough to overcome the many obstacles standing in their way?

Rock Me: Naughty

Allison has loved the band, Cold Fusion, since she was twelve years old. Her older brother is the bass guitarist, so the band has always treated her like a kid sister. The problem is that now that she's graduated college, Allie can't get within five feet of the band without embarrassing herself. Her body seems to betray her and give away her secret desires. And one of the band members especially fills her nights with naughty dreams and forbidden fantasies.

Allie is still a virgin and she's tired of it, but all the boys she's dated have left her cold. One night of uncontrolled passion changes all that when she is taught the art of carnal pleasures. But that one night her wild passions unleash a chain of events that can never be undone. Will her forbidden lust cause her to lose everything? Or will her new knowledge unlock the key to her heart's desire?

Rock Me: Crazy

Tommy doesn't do relationships.
Livvy doesn't do one-night stands.

By the time she finds out that he's a rock star with serious commitment issues, it's too late, she's fallen for him. But, how can an average girl snare a sexy rock star? By pretending she's not so average...

Tommy, drummer for the band Cold Fusion, is used to partying hard. Every night there's a new woman in his bed, and that's the way he likes it. From the moment they first meet, Livvy intrigues him; she's so different from all the other girls. Despite his reluctance for 'repeat sex', he is drawn in by her crazy antics.

Livvy knows she has to step up her game to keep the hunky playboy interested. When she turns the tables on him, Tommy can't seem to get enough. But can she keep up the crazy charade or will she find herself in way over her head?

Rock Me: Sexy

Forced into a job she didn't want...

When fate conspires, Katie must leave behind the prestigious world of documentary filmmaking and step into the fast-paced world of low-brow reality television. Reluctantly, she becomes the Executive Producer for Rock Star Diaries, a reality show following the band Cold Fusion on tour. From day one, she is intrigued and challenged by the sexy rock star, Tyler Matthews.

A chance to outshine the brightest spotlight...

Tyler Matthews, lead singer for the rock band Cold Fusion, loves being in the spotlight. He leads the life of a bad-boy rock star to perfection. He's got everything at his fingertips: power, fame, money, sex, drugs, and rock 'n roll. But sometimes the spotlight can burn too brightly, especially when a 'fake' reality show begins to unmask the superficiality of his life.

A passion that eclipses it all...

Katie is no fool; she knows that Tyler is trouble with a capital "T". The tattooed and cocky hunk goes through women faster than he goes through alcohol. Never in her wildest dreams, did she think she would fall hard for him.

Tyler's got it all. So why can't he get the sexy producer out of his mind? One taste has always been enough for him before...

Everything changes...

When lines blur and fiction becomes reality. Scandal, deceit, and sacrifice become the cruel price of fame. Can an unexpected love between the two most unlikely of people survive the cold harsh realities of life in the glittering spotlight?

Arabella Quinn Newsletter

Let's keep in touch!

Sign up for my newsletter and be the first to know about new releases, sales, giveaways, and other exciting news. As an added bonus, you'll receive a FREE ebook as my thank-you for signing up!

Arabella Quinn newsletter
subscribepage.io/ArabellaQuinn

Other Novels by Arabella Quinn

MY STEPBROTHER THE DOM

A sizzling stepbrother romance with a twist:

(Keep turning the pages for an excerpt from my bestselling novel that climbed to #5 on the Amazon store for ALL BOOKS!)

For years, I had the worst crush on my stepbrother, Cole Hunter. We used to ride bikes, skateboard, and go fishing together — now I couldn't even be in the same room as him without my pulse racing. One cocky half-grin from Cole would have my face blushing while my panties melted. It was insane — and completely humiliating.

It was a painful secret that I guarded fiercely. Cole was off-limits. *Forbidden*. If he knew how I felt, I would die of embarrassment.

I avoided Cole for years, until one wild night, when my best friend took me to a club. I thought I was going to see a grunge band, but it turned out to be a much kinkier kind of club. A club where anything goes, and well, things got a little crazy. Make that a lot crazy.

No one would ever know what I'd done, right?

Then I discovered who the man behind the mask really was...

IMPOSSIBLE (TO RESIST) BOSS

A sexy billionaire CEO. His headstrong secretary. And a computer file that exposes her most secret and dirty fantasies about him.

Lilliana

I hate my boss.

He's an inconsiderate and demanding tyrant. I hate his juvenile rules, his micro-managing ways, and his selfish and unapologetic manner. But most of all, I hate how insanely sexy he is — how all the women around him can't help but fawn all over him.

He's a wealthy, ego-driven maniac that has a new bimbo at his beck and call with the mere snap of his fingers. Despite these irrepressible naughty fantasies I keep having about him, I wouldn't stroke his ego for all the money in the world.

Jason Kaine

I may have found the one.

After years of fruitless searching, I've found the perfect secretary. She's scarily efficient, not afraid of hard work, detail-oriented, and best of all, she doesn't complain about my important rules. She's a dream come true.

So why can't I keep the image of her, deliciously naked and spread out invitingly across my desk, from invading my head? I didn't get to where I am today by being stupid. I've got plenty of willing women to choose from who understand my absolute no-strings policy.

Lilliana is strictly off-limits, but I see the way her eyes devour me. I see how her pulse pounds whenever I get near. I know she's ripe for the taking, but that would be disastrous for both of us. It might be the worst mistake ever, but something's bound to give.

Also By Arabella Quinn

BAD BOYS OF ROCK SERIES

How to Seduce a Rockstar

How to Tempt a Rockstar

How to Date a Rockstar

How to Catch a Rockstar

How to Marry a Rockstar

ROCK ME SERIES

Rock Me: Wicked

Rock Me: Naughty

Rock Me: Crazy

Rock Me: Sexy

ROMANCE NOVELS

My Stepbrother the Dom
Impossible (to Resist) Boss
Being Jane

THE WILDER BROTHERS SERIES

(small town romance)

Fake Marriage to a Baller
Luke – coming soon

About the Author

A*rabella* Q*uinn* *is a* New York Times *and* USA Today *bestselling author of contemporary romance.* When she's not busy writing, you can often find her clutching her Kindle and staying up way past her bedtime reading romance novels. Besides contemporary romance, she loves regency, gothic, and erotic romance — the steamier the better. She also loves thrillers, especially psychological thrillers. She saves reading horror for when her husband is away on business but doesn't recommend that. She averages about five hours of sleep per night and does not drink coffee. Also, not recommended!

A*rabella* Q*uinn* *newsletter*
subscribepage.io/ArabellaQuinn

Excerpt

My Stepbrother the Dom

Chapter 1

AVA

"So, have you seen your brother since you've been back home?"

"Cole?" I squirmed in my seat. I hated talking about Cole with Julie. She'd had a monumental crush on him ever since we were in the eighth grade and Cole was a junior in high school. Her crush hadn't diminished at all in the ensuing eight years.

Julie playfully smacked my arm. "Of course, Cole! Do you have any other hot brothers that I don't know about?"

I picked up my beer and took a quick sip, hoping Julie wouldn't see the blush that was heating my cheeks. "Nope. Last time I saw him was at graduation."

"Is he still as hot as ever?" Julie's eyes widened with excitement.

If my freakishly unnatural reaction to him was any indication, I'd say he was looking even hotter than ever, but to Julie, I casually shrugged my shoulders. "He seems the same to me."

Julie frowned and asked almost tentatively, "Does he have a girlfriend?"

Feigning disinterest, I took another sip of beer. "I don't know. I don't talk to him about that kind of stuff."

"What do you talk to him about? What is he doing now?"

I knew Julie's curiosity would never be sated when it came to Cole. She could talk about him all night. Frankly, I wasn't in the mood.

"I don't see him all that much anymore. Really, Jules. He's got his own life."

Julie picked at the label on her beer bottle. "But you two used to be so close. God, I was always so jealous of that."

I had been very close to Cole at one time. "We were just kids. People grow up. Life moves on."

Despite what I said to Julie, I missed Cole a lot. His mother had married my father when I was just eight years old. You'd expect there would have been a lot of bumps in the road when our families blended, but it had been surprisingly seamless. I still looked back in amazement at how well it had all worked out.

Dad dated Cole's mother for years before they married. Cole and I had become friends right from the start. I was a tomboy and suddenly I had someone to share adventures with. We spent hours exploring the woods near Cole's house. If we weren't kicking a soccer ball around the backyard, Cole was teaching me skateboarding tricks. On hot summer days, we splashed around in the above-ground pool at my house from practically sunup to sundown.

When Dad and Marissa announced their engagement, I was genuinely happy. I wanted Marissa to become my real mom and I wanted Cole to be my brother. It felt like I was getting the perfect family. I could barely remember my mother who died suddenly when I was three years old. Not being able to picture her face in my mind used to send me into a spiraling panic, until I had Marissa in my life. When Dad married Marissa, I felt secure again.

The adjustment was more difficult for Cole when our parents married. He had to leave his home and school and move in with us. He had to deal with a new father, who was much more of a disciplinarian than his sweet-natured mother.

Still, Cole and I got along wonderfully after the wedding. He was the perfect brother. Everything was great, that is until puberty hit and I realized, literally overnight, how amazingly attractive he was. That seemed to have ruined everything. Even though I had tried desperately to hide my feelings, nothing ever seemed the same between us.

Julie's elbow nudged me out of my daydream. "Earth to Ava."

"Sorry," I turned to Julie, "what were you saying?"

"I was saying..." Julie rolled her eyes in mock exasperation, "that you should invite Cole out for drinks so that you two could catch up. And of course, I'll be there, just in case Cole happens to notice me, for once."

Julie was gorgeous. She never had any problem attracting attention from men. The fact that Cole never seemed to pay any attention to her irritated her to no end. In a maddening ironic twist, his indifference made her infatuation for him grow even deeper.

I tried to hide my creeping annoyance. "Jules, I'm not going to play matchmaker for you and Cole again. Remember how it turned out the last time?"

Julie's shoulders slumped in defeat. She had spent days sullen and angry when the 'chance' encounter I had arranged between them didn't live up to her fantasies.

We left the bar early that night. No one we knew showed up at the bar and I had shattered Julie's good mood by bursting her 'Cole' bubble once again. To my relief, Julie decided she wanted to head home early.

That night, as I was lying in bed, my mind inevitably drifted to Cole. Right before I had graduated from college, he had moved out of the house. I had had my share of boyfriends in my four years of college, but Cole was always in the back of my mind - torturing me with what could never be.

Cole and I barely crossed paths in those four years - a few holidays here and there, and a few weeks in the summer. The summer after my sophomore year, I met one of his girlfriends. I knew that he must have had many girlfriends over the years, but I had always carefully shielded myself from that reality.

When his beautiful girlfriend was in our home- right in front of my face- there was no longer any way to deny it to myself. Seeing her with Cole felt like a sucker punch to the stomach. It made me sick. The truth was that Julie's crush on Cole looked like simple puppy love compared to what I felt for him.

Somehow, along the way, Cole must have figured out exactly how I felt about him. No matter how closely I tried to guard my feelings for him, I must have let something slip: a longing glance or a shiver of desire when he brushed by too close. And it must have disgusted him. He had kept his distance from me ever since. I couldn't blame him.

I was ashamed of my feelings for him. We weren't related by blood, but we had grown up together. We were as close as any brother and sister could be. When he pulled away from me, I was horrified. He had discovered my secret and it had repulsed him.

I vowed to keep my distance from him. I still had my pride. I had never acted on my feelings, so my utter disgrace was mostly self-imposed. Just knowing that he suspected was humiliating enough.

The other main reason I stayed away from him was because, despite it all, I still felt that way about him. My body still reacted like fireworks were exploding inside me every time he came near. No man could twist my insides with a single glance like Cole Hunter could. When Cole Hunter entered the room, there was a good chance that my panties were soaked.

I flipped around in my bed trying to work Cole out of my brain. Damn Julie for talking about him! I had been doing so well trying to forget about him. I sighed and slipped my fingers inside my panties. I needed to banish thoughts of Cole from my head or I'd never fall asleep. Instead, it was Cole's name that softly fell from my lips as I made myself come.

Chapter 2

COLE

You would think that a staff meeting at a sex club would be pretty exciting stuff. I did. Turned out I was wrong. It was fucking boring. Purchase orders, accounting, staff complaints, and marketing discussions made it just as boring as any corporate meeting.

I had been bartending at the 'Sanctuary' for over four months now because I had a little gambling issue that I needed to take care of quickly. I had learned my lesson the hard way. The 'interest' on my debt had skyrocketed unbelievably. If I didn't pay it down quicker, I'd soon be meeting up with some brass knuckles in a dark alley.

I'd done just about everything I could think of to raise cash quickly. It pissed me off, but I had to let go of my brand-new motorcycle at a huge loss. Still, it put some cash in the palms of the loan sharks and bought me some time.

I worked a full-time job with decent pay, but it wasn't enough, no matter how much I cut back my expenses. I briefly considered moving back in with my parents to save on the rent money, but what fucking 25-year-old man wants to live with his parents? Besides, Ava was back home. There was no way.

So, I took a second job at Sanctuary. I worked every hour I could pick up, practically living at the club on the weekend. The pay was better than the average bartending job and some of the customers tipped really well.

The owner, Betsy Kline, a plump grandmotherly figure, hired me on the spot. She had me take off my shirt at the interview. She examined my tattoos, pronounced my physique 'not too bad', and told me to work on my tan. Then she welcomed me to the Sanctuary.

My bartending uniform turned out to be a pair of jeans with biker boots and a tight black ribbon that I had to wear around my neck like a choker. I was working shirtless. It felt strange at first, but after all the things I had seen go down at the club since then, it was now no big deal. And, I think it helped with the tips.

The staff meeting sounded like it was finally wrapping up when Johnnie spoke up. "Don't schedule me with anyone but regulars this weekend, Betsy. I'm tired of spending my time babysitting desperate housewives."

Johnnie, who was known as Master Jay, was the most senior Dom in the club. He looked like an aging hippie, but when you saw him working, there was no doubt that he knew his craft.

Betsy pursed her lips. "Those desperate housewives pay the same kind of money that our regulars do. We cater to everyone in this club."

I knew the type Johnnie was talking about. Mostly, they were just a harmless bunch of ladies looking for something to spice up their dull lives. After experiencing a session with one of the Doms, usually they hung out with me at the bar for a couple of hours. The ones that I knew Johnnie despised were usually my best tippers.

Johnnie shook his head stubbornly. "Then get someone else to cater to them. I'm done. They're not interested in a real Dom/sub session; they're interested in some kinky sex from a movie star. They take one look at me, and their face sours. It's insulting. All the training in the world wouldn't make them good submissives."

A few of the other Doms mumbled and shook their heads in agreement.

Betsy addressed everyone in the room. "Look, this is a business. We build our clientele by word of mouth. Our reputation means everything here. We'll take every dollar they hand out to us, no matter who they are or how interested they really are. Those people are paying for an experience. Your job is to give them that experience and maybe educate them a little along the way."

Dave, another Dom, frowned. "I'm sorry, Betsy, but I'm with Johnnie on this. A lot of those women are looking for something else entirely. It's changing everything — the club, the atmosphere, everything. It's getting annoying."

Betsy's expression softened. "I know we've had a lot of lookie-loos coming in lately. It's because of that new movie. It'll die down, I'm sure. Just now, every curious housewife and bored sorority girl is coming out of the woodwork. And because of that movie, their expectations are a little ... different."

Johnnie snorted. "Different? They're not looking for a real Dom. They're looking for an actor. Some hot young stud to fool around with."

Several heads turned in my direction.

I shuffled uncomfortably in my seat. "Don't look at me. This has nothing to do with me."

Betsy looked thoughtful. "They do all seem to swarm around the bar quite a bit..."

She was joking, right? I laughed hesitantly. "Oh, no way. I don't know anything about that stuff. I'm just here to serve drinks."

"But you're just the type of guy they're looking for." Betsy was nodding to herself as she spoke. "You're young, built, sexy, the tattoos, the abs, Jesus — exactly what they're after."

I suddenly felt trapped with the whole room staring at me and nodding their heads in agreement. "I'm not about to have sex with a bunch of horny, sex-starved housewives."

Johnnie shook his head. "It's not about sex."

I felt my jaw clenching. "Whatever. I'm not into this stuff."

Betsy had a gleam in her eye. "Okay, everyone. The meeting is over. Let's get to work. Cole, hang around — I want to talk to you. Dave, you stick around too."

It only took a few minutes for the room to clear. I prepared myself for Betsy's assault. The woman was tenacious, but there was no way in hell I was going to become a Dom — even if it was a fake Dom.

Betsy didn't even talk to me. "Dave, how long would it take to train Cole to perform at Level 1?"

"Just Level 1?" Dave leaned back in his chair. "Easy. Wouldn't even take a week."

Betsy smiled triumphantly. "Terrific. Dave will be your mentor, Cole. Observe his sessions for the next week. I'll keep him on Level 1 clients—"

I interrupted her crazy idea before it went too far. "Whoa. Whoa. There's no way I'm gonna do this."

Betsy ignored me. "Dave, by the end of next weekend, I want you to start letting Cole interact with the clients - under your supervision. I think he's going to be a big hit with the ladies, so give him lots of space to get his own rhythm going."

I growled a warning, "Betsy—"

She held up her hand to stop me. "Cole, it's just Level 1 stuff. Just a little slap and tickle. Light bondage, blindfolds, feathers, maybe some role-playing. Just some tame playtime the ladies want to experience."

"No way. This isn't my thing—"

She didn't let me finish. "Don't turn me down until you hear about the increase in your salary. The huge increase."

Chapter 3

Three months later...
AVA

I looked around the mostly empty bar. "You know, we really need to find a new place to hang out. Nobody we know comes here anymore."

Julie scanned the room for the hundredth time looking as bored as I felt. Suddenly her eyes widened. "Hey! Guess who I ran into last night?"

"If you were here — nobody."

She smirked at my lame joke and then blurted out, "Jessica Holden."

I still pictured Jessica in pigtails and dressed in her cheerleading uniform. "She's still around town? I would have thought she would have ditched this place by now. She was always complaining about how boring it was."

Julie agreed. "I know, right? Anyway, she went to a club in the city last week and said it was the coolest place ever. She said I should try it out. It's called 'Sanctuary'."

"I've never heard of it."

Julie sat up straighter and her eyes got that sort of fervent look that I knew meant she really wanted to go. "It's semi-private. But she gave me the deets and we could totally get in!"

I had already had two cranberry kamikaze shots, so I was feeling pretty generous. "Sure, that sounds like fun."

Julie jumped out of her seat, her eyes sparkling. "I knew you were my bff for a reason. I'll drive since you're such a lightweight."

I was totally unprepared. "Wait ... what? Not tonight... I meant, like, you know, some other night—"

Julie put her hands on her hips. "Don't you dare back out on me now, Ava Cooper. You even said yourself this place was totally boring."

I looked at my watch. "But, it's like — almost eleven o'clock. By the time we get into the city, it'll be like-"

"It'll be exactly the time when everything starts hopping."

"Look at what I'm wearing!" I glanced at my favorite jeans and the black button-down satin blouse. "I'm not dressed to go clubbing."

Julie grinned — like she knew she had me cornered. "This isn't a 'mini-skirt and sky-high stilettos' kind of club. Your clothes won't matter. What you're wearing will be fine."

"Really? Is it like a grunge club?"

"It's just different. Jessica highly recommended it."

I wasn't as adventurous as Julie, but if Miss 'perfect' Jessica Holden had been there, I could certainly handle it. The alcohol swirling in my bloodstream and the fact that I didn't need to strap on some ridiculously high heels helped cement my decision. But, it wouldn't be me if I didn't lay some ground rules.

"I'll go with some stipulations. First, you can't ditch me."

Julie's mouth opened in mock outrage. "Of course, I won't."

I raised an eyebrow. "Second, you have to stay sober so you can drive us home."

She agreed. "Not as fun, but I really want to check this place out, so if that's what it takes..."

"Okay, and third, we leave when I say we leave. No matter what."

She downed the rest of her beer in one gulp and pushed aside the bottle. "Deal."

Less than an hour later, we were driving through the city. I watched out the window as the bright lights of the downtown dimmed and finally disappeared. We drove into a more industrial area. It was dark and somber looking.

I looked over at Julie. "Are you sure you're going the right way? This area doesn't look too safe."

Julie didn't seem concerned. "I'm just following the GPS. We should be there in a few minutes. Jessica said it was in the middle of nowhere."

I nervously chewed on my nails while Julie drove. Finally, we pulled into a parking lot behind a huge non-descript building.

My voice squeaked, "This is it? I didn't see anything. No signs. No lines of people waiting to get in—"

"Chill out, Ava. I told you this is a private club. Jessica said we're supposed to go knock on a black door back here. It must be that one." Julie pointed to the plain door at the back of the building.

I was starting to have serious second doubts. "I don't know, Jules. What kind of club is this anyway? Is this another male stripper club, like that Australian stripper show you made me go to?"

Julie got out of the car and headed for the door. "It's some kind of a sex club. Don't worry, you don't have to do anything. You can just hang out and watch if you want to."

I scrambled to catch up with her. "What? Julie, you didn't tell me this was a sex club! No way I'm going in there. I can't believe you!"

Julie huffed. "You're such a prude sometimes. C'mon, we're just going to check it out. Jessica told me all about it. Seriously, you don't have to do anything there that you don't want."

My voice was screeching in my panic, "I'm not going in there, Jules!"

Julie stopped and turned to me. "After I drive all the way out here, you're gonna chicken-shit out on me now?"

I felt bad that she had driven so far, but she should have told me sooner. I took a deep breath. "I'm stone-cold sober now, Jules. My buzz has totally worn off. And this place looks creepy. Please, let's just go home."

Julie turned and headed toward the door. "You don't have to go in. But, I'm gonna go check it out."

I stood staring at her stupidly as she walked to the door and knocked. I suddenly realized that she had the car keys; I couldn't even wait for her in the car. There was no way I was going to stand out in the dark lot all by myself.

The door opened and I ran to catch up with her.

A big beefy bouncer dressed in a three-piece suit ushered us inside. "Hello, ladies. Welcome to Sanctuary. Do you have a reservation?"

I was hoping we'd get turned back when Julie stammered nervously to the man that we didn't have a reservation.

Instead, the man just smiled. "Is this your first time here, then?"

Julie nodded.

"Just wait one moment while I get Sasha. She'll take care of you."

The man crossed the small entrance room and exited out a wooden door.

I grabbed Julie's arm. "Now's our chance. Let's just get out of here."

Julie shook off my arm. "Stop being a baby, Ava. Jessica said there's a beginner's introductory package that caters exactly to your individual needs."

"Oh my God, Jules. I don't have any needs. This is crazy! You're crazy! Just—"

I couldn't finish, because a petite woman, wearing a scandalously revealing outfit, walked into the room. "Hello, lovelies. My name is Sasha. Since it's your first time here, we'd like to go over a few things with you first. We'll have you ready for some fun in no time. Please, follow me."

Julie followed the woman. I wasn't sure what to do, so I miserably trailed after them. Sasha led us to a small room, which was bare except for a red upholstered couch and a TV mounted on the opposite wall.

"Please have a seat on the couch and I'll start your introductory video."

I was so far out of my depth that the video might as well have been in a foreign language for all that I got out of it. The video focused on proper club etiquette and safe words and always respecting other's boundaries. I found laughter bubbling up from the sheer absurdity of it all on several occasions.

When the video ended, Julie complained. "So far this is boring."

Just then, the door opened and Sasha motioned to me. "Come on. We'll do your interview first."

I stood and reluctantly looked back at Julie until I let Sasha lead me from the room. She led me further down the hall and into yet another room. This room was a cozy but cluttered office with a gray-haired older lady sitting behind the fancy wooden desk.

The lady waved me in. "C'mon in. Have a seat. I'm Betsy."

I sat down. "Hi."

"Can I see your driver's license, dear? Just need to double-check that you're of age."

I pulled my wallet from my purse and fished my driver's license out of the clear plastic sleeve that was holding it. "Um. This is an interview? Like, for a job?"

Betsy laughed heartily. "No. No. Since this is your first time here, we just need to understand what your expectations are — what you're hoping to experience tonight. And I want to find out if there are any things you definitely do not want to experience. We like our guests to be comfortable."

"Um, okay. That's good." I didn't even know what to say. I had no idea what I was doing there, let alone what my expectations were.

Betsy looked up from reading my driver's license. "So, Ava, what did you want to experience at Sanctuary tonight?"

I had no idea. "Well, I heard there was a beginner's package?"

Betsy nodded in agreement. "That would be perfect for you! The cost would be $100 for the hour, and then of course, you would be welcome to hang out in the common room or at the bar. It's a wonderful deal for a beginner like you. Would you like to pay with cash or credit?"

I reluctantly dug through my wallet for my credit card. One hundred bucks! I was going to absolutely kill Julie when this was over.

"Now, Ava, can you give me some guidance on what your personal comfort level is? Or, if it's easier, let me know if there is anything that you don't want to experience tonight. Don't worry, the beginner's package is very, uh ... mild on the BDSM scale."

BDSM? What the hell was I doing here? Shit! I tried to remember what BDSM entailed from that movie I had recently seen. "Yeah, okay. Um, I don't want to have sex with anyone."

"No, of course not." Betsy seemed nonplussed by my statement.

Here was the chance to set my boundaries. "I don't want to be naked. And no blindfolds."

Betsy was busy writing onto a notecard of sorts. "Anything else?"

"No whips or anything. Or restraints. I don't want to be tied up or restrained at all."

"Okaaaay. I've got it." Betsy put down her pen.

I thought of a few more. "Oh! No nipple clamps or anything — God no! And no anal stuff. That would freak me out."

"Okay ... starting off slowly is ... smart. Is that all?"

I thought for a moment. "Um, am I missing anything?"

Betsy shook her head. "No, dear. I think you've got it all covered here."

I chewed on my lip, worried that I might have missed something big.

Betsy patted my hand. "Remember that you can stop or slow down a scene at any time. Remember the safe words from the video?"

I nodded. "Yellow and red."

Betsy eyed me thoughtfully. "Sometimes my clients are a bit nervous. I find that a little bit of anonymity helps them feel more comfortable — freer to explore. Would you like to wear a mask tonight?"

I would wear a bag with eyeholes if I could. "Yeah. That might be helpful."

Betsy tapped her pen on the desk. "Ok. Good. So, can we call you Ava in the club, or would you like to go by a different name while you're here?"

I didn't even have to ponder my answer. "Oh, a different name, I think. Um ... April would be good."

"Perfect." Betsy picked up the phone on her desk and punched a button. "Sasha? Would you please escort April to the Red Room?"

She hung up the phone and then began digging through a drawer in her desk. "Here it is."

Betsy pulled out an elaborate mask. It reminded me of Mardi Gras festivals. The eyepiece part of the mask was gold colored and decorated with sequins. Bursting from the top of it was a plumage of peacock feathers. It was elegant and gaudy all at the same time.

"Is that the mask I'm supposed to wear?"

Betsy handed it to me. "Only if you feel comfortable wearing it."

I slipped the strap over my head and found it fit quite comfortably. It didn't go very well with my blouse and jeans, but it did feel like it concealed my identity fairly well.

The office door opened and Sasha poked her head inside. "April?"

I stood and it looked like Sasha did a surprised double-take when she saw me, but then she quickly composed the strange look on her face. "Follow me."

I took a deep breath and then followed Sasha out of the room and down the hallway once again. I was mesmerized by her practically bare ass swaying ahead of me. I almost bumped into her when she suddenly stopped at a door.

Sasha gestured for me to enter the small room. "Please kneel in the center of the room. Master Royce will be in shortly."

Chapter 4

AVA

I knelt awkwardly on the floor, feeling foolish. Master Royce? Once again, I thought about killing Julie for getting me into this. I wondered what she was doing that very second herself.

Five minutes later I was beginning to get annoyed. This is what I spent a hundred bucks on? Kneeling on a cement floor until my knees were bruised and my back aching?

By the time the door opened, I had grown so weary of kneeling that even my annoyance had faded, but when I glimpsed the giant man who entered the room, my mind immediately snapped to attention.

He looked like a gladiator. I couldn't help but gawk at him. He had on a gold metal helmet of sorts that covered the top half of his head and only left his mouth and jawline exposed. He had no clothes on except for a form-fitted pair of black shorts — they reminded me of biker shorts but a bit shorter, and a long red cape trimmed with gold.

Besides the costume, what made me think gladiator, was the man's body. He had a stunning physique. He was well over six feet tall, extremely toned, and incredibly strong looking. He didn't look like a roided-up bodybuilder; it was just that his muscles were very well defined.

His shoulders were broad. The left side of his chest was covered with tattoos. My eyes lowered down his body, checking out his six-pack abs, his trim waist, and the light trail of hair under his belly button that led to...

I swallowed nervously. Not only was he the sexiest male specimen I had ever laid eyes on, he was certainly the most intimidating-looking man on the planet. His piercing eyes, staring at me through the holes in his mask, didn't help. They seemed to be penetrating right through my own mask, straight into my soul.

Holy shit, I couldn't do this. I felt my whole body slumping under his scrutiny as if I was trying to disappear from his sight. I quickly looked away from that knowing gaze.

"Sit up straight." His commanding voice startled me, sending shivers down my spine. I complied immediately; there was no mistaking the authority in his voice.

My heart was beating furiously and I felt my body begin to tremble slightly. I was scared out of my mind. I bowed my head slightly and waited with trepidation for whatever was to happen.

My knees were hurting even worse in this unnatural position, but I kept my back ramrod straight. I dared to peek and see what Master Royce was doing, but he seemed to be just staring at a piece of paper that sat on the corner table near the door.

Finally, Master Royce approached me. He circled me slowly. The atmosphere was charged. I was so excruciatingly nervous that I began to visibly shake.

He spoke from behind me. "You watched the safety video, right?"

"Um ... yes."

Suddenly, he was inches from me, on my left side. He grabbed a handful of my hair in his fist and began tugging it downward. It forced me to look directly into his eyes. It didn't hurt at all, but it scared the crap out of me.

His eyes were flashing coldly. "When you address me, show me some respect. You may call me Sir."

Oh shit. I felt my lip tremble. "Oh, sorry. Sir."

He let go of my hair. "Tell me your safe words."

My voice was shaky, "Uh, yellow is slow down and red is stop ... I mean, Sir. Sorry, I forgot to say it. Sir."

He circled in front of me. "Stand up."

I stood up but barely felt the burning in my knees, because I realized as I stood before him, just how much bigger he was than me. I was in a room alone with this man — this stranger. In a freaking sex club! There was no way I could physically stop this man from doing anything he wanted to me. He was so much stronger. I began to feel dizzy.

"Take off your shirt."

My hands flew to my shirt and started unbuttoning it. Why was I following his orders? This wasn't happening. I was panting now, practically hyperventilating.

I just couldn't. "Yellow!"

Master Royce folded his arms in front of him. "I know your limits, April."

I felt my cheeks flaming. "I don't want to get naked."

"Are you wearing something under that shirt?"

I nodded miserably as my mind desperately tried to remember exactly what I was wearing underneath. Was it my usual everyday underwear: grannie panties and a no-longer crisp white utilitarian bra?

Master Royce didn't move a muscle. "You won't be naked then. Now follow my orders or you'll be disciplined. Do you understand?"

"Yes sir," I answered meekly but I was still frozen in place.

Master Royce sighed. He was clearly exasperated with me. "Take. Off. Your. Shirt."

I began unbuttoning my shirt again. The process was painful because my fingers no longer seemed to be functioning. I couldn't concentrate on the task because my brain was running ahead of me. What was going to happen next?

Reluctantly, I began sliding the silky shirt off my shoulders. Master Royce held out his hand and I gave him the shirt.

I almost giggled out loud with hysterical relief when I realized that I was wearing a black push-up bra — one of my nicer ones. I also recalled that earlier that evening, I had slipped on black panties cut in a bikini style to match. Not exactly the sexiest underwear in the world, but certainly better than the usual style that I wore — grandmotherly.

Thank God he wasn't looking at me. I noted with near panic that my nipples had hardened and were prominently poking through the thin fabric of the unpadded portion at the top of my bra. I wanted desperately to cover my chest with my arms. It must have been the cold air, there was no way any of this was turning me on. I was too deathly scared to get any pleasure out of this.

"Now, take off your pants." His voice brooked no disobedience.

I felt helpless to resist when he spoke like that. What had he said? That I'd be punished if I disobeyed? I shivered.

I began to unfasten the button on my jeans. "But, but .... Sir? This..."

"Are you wearing panties underneath those jeans?"

"Yes, but —"

Master Royce tapped his foot impatiently. "Then you won't be naked. I told you already, April, that I will respect your limits. But I won't tolerate any more disobedience from you."

Oh my God. I was taking off my pants for him. Why? Why didn't I just leave while I still had some semblance of my dignity intact? He couldn't keep me here against my will.

I awkwardly stepped out of my jeans and then placed them into his outstretched hand. I stood uncomfortably while he crossed the room and set my clothes aside.

"Stand up straight."

The push-up bra was already doing fine work with my breasts. When I stood up straight, it felt like I was obscenely sticking out my chest for his inspection.

Master Royce slowly started circling me, looking me up and down. The slight tremor in my muscles got worse. My legs started to wobble. I felt nauseous.

"Use your safe words if you need them." His voice sounded gentler.

I squeezed my eyes tightly shut. I was panting like I'd just run a marathon. I suddenly couldn't get enough oxygen into my lungs. When I felt something slightly tickle my collarbone, I nearly jumped out of my skin.

"Shit, April. Come here." Master Royce grabbed my hand and pulled me over to the couch against the back wall of the room.

He sat and pulled me down on the couch at the same time, managing to plant me squarely on his lap. I might have been half-naked and sitting on a half-naked man's lap, but I wasn't about to cuddle up with him. I sat up ramrod straight.

He began briskly rubbing my arms. "You're shaking like a leaf."

I couldn't think of a thing except for the fact that my ass was nestled up against his 'private area'. We fit together like two pieces of a puzzle with only the thin fabric of my panties and his weird stripper shorts separating me from his pure maleness. I could feel the heat coming off him and I actually had to resist the urge to wiggle my bottom against him. I was certifiably insane.

"Are you okay?" He sounded sincerely worried.

I took a deep breath. "I'm sorry, Sir. I was ... scared."

Master Royce sighed and ran a hand through his hair. "I would never hurt you, April. That's not what I want. At all."

I didn't move.

He grabbed a blanket from somewhere behind the couch and wrapped it around me. "I don't think you're looking for a Dom. Or this kind of experience, at all."

I shook my head, afraid to speak.

His fingers were gently running up and down my arms under the blanket. "Why did you come here tonight?"

I wondered if I should tell him the truth. I was suddenly too weary to put on any more pretenses. And, he was being so nice. In fact, my body had finally stopped shaking in fear. I felt safer. A familiar sense of comfort was seeping into my bones. His voice was soothing. He was no longer barking out brisk commands. He seemed genuinely concerned about my feelings.

I stifled a yawn and felt my stiff spine loosening a bit. "It was Julie's fault. I thought I was going to see a grunge band."

Did I just lean against his chest or had his arm pulled me closer to him? I wasn't sure, but I didn't have the energy to sit back up again. I closed my eyes and breathed in his earthy male scent. It was intoxicating.

"So, you're friend lied to get you here?" His arm was wrapped around me securely.

Without thinking, I snuggled closer to him. My thoughts were getting harder to formulate; I was so damned tired suddenly. "Well, she didn't exactly lie. It just turned into a big disaster. I should..."

I was drifting off to sleep...

My hand was drifting across his chest, exploring the hard planes of his muscles. I was in heaven in his arms.

Suddenly, I was standing before Master Royce. I unsnapped my bra and let it fall to the ground. Then I was peeling my panties off. I stood before him totally nude. He pulled me against his hard length.

Then I felt his hands on my body — one squeezing my ass, and one sliding down my stomach and then between my legs. When his fingers delved into my core, I was wet and ready for him. His rhythmic ministrations left me breathless. My clit was greedy with need and my pussy throbbing with desire. Every stroke of his fingers brought me closer. Any moment I would fall apart. I cried out in ecstasy at last when my orgasm violently exploded.

I jolted awake.

The dream.

Master Royce.

"Oh. God. Oh God. Oh God." I was cuddled in Master Royce's lap. I had fallen asleep.

Master Royce's voice sounded slightly strained. "Don't worry. You just fell asleep. No big deal."

No big deal? That dream? Was the orgasm just a dream or did it really happen? Did Master Royce know that I just had an orgasm while I slept in his lap? Holy shit! No big deal.

I tried to jump up and out of his lap, but he held me firmly in place. My panties were soaked and I'm sure he could feel their wetness against his thigh. "Hold on, April. Don't run away."

I had to get out of there. "Let me go. I just want to leave."

"Wait." He loosened his grip on my arms, but his steely thigh had my leg trapped in place. "I can get your money back for you."

I looked at him in surprise but shook my head. "No, this is all my fault. And I took up your time."

"Don't worry about that. I'll talk to Betsy."

I looked at him pleadingly. "No, please don't. That would just make this more embarrassing than it already is."

"Okay. I won't. But, don't be embarrassed." He kissed the top of my head and then let me go.

This time I made it off his lap. I shot over to my pile of clothes and began stuffing my legs into my pants. I couldn't get out of there fast enough.

"Goodbye, April." A few seconds later, Master Royce was gone. He walked out the door leaving me scrambling to get dressed.

A shuddering sigh wracked my body. I zippered and buttoned my jeans and then picked up my wrinkled blouse. My fingers stumbled on the buttons, but finally, I was dressed.

My Stepbrother the Dom

Printed in Great Britain
by Amazon